Games

Vera Cowie

G A M E S

DOUBLEDAY & COMPANY, INC.
GARDEN CITY, NEW YORK
1986

ISBN 0-385-19960 0
Library of Congress Catalog Card Number 85–10116
Copyright © 1986 by Vera Cowie
All Rights Reserved
Printed in the United States of America
First Edition

Library of Congress Cataloging in Publication Data

Cowie, Vera.
  Games.

  I. Title.
PR6053.0959G3   1986   823'.914

game. amusement, sport; scheme to defeat another; trick, cunning device; a contest played according to rules and decided by superior skill, strength or good fortune.

Oh, the games people play, now
Every night and every day, now
Never meanin' what they say, now
Never sayin' what they mean . . .

Games

game. amusement, sport . . .

THE PARTY had reached that pitch of cross-conversations, drunken laughter rising to a crescendo of noise which betokens shortage of space and overconsumption of alcohol. The hostess, nervous both for her still-precarious social position and her newly decorated and hideously expensive Eaton Square penthouse, was torn between pride in the fact that one hundred people had accepted invitations to her housewarming and terror that sooner or later one of them would knock over one of her so carefully chosen works of art, or flick careless ash on to her specially dyed silk carpet, or spill a glass of wine over the specially woven pure silk velvet of her upholstery. The noise was making her head ache, not to mention what it was all costing . . .

"Ah, Julia." Eagerly she seized the arm of the tall redhead who happened to be passing. "It is all going well, don't you think?" Her anxiety showed, like rust through peeling gilt.

"Very well," Julia assured her kindly.

"I've heard such complimentary things said about you."

[1]

"As long as you are happy," Julia murmured diplomatically. "You are—were—the client."

"Who still has to present her husband with the bill."

Julia smiled at the archness, knowing damned well that Leila Bainbridge was married to a newly made millionaire who didn't give a damn how his wife spent his money just so long as she left him free to spend his time as and how he wished, which was always with other women.

"I've given your name to several people," Leila was saying earnestly. "I do hope it results in many more commissions."

"I only work here, as they say," Julia told her ruefully. "But I am glad you are satisfied."

"Satisfied! My dear, I am absolutely thrilled. You are *so* talented."

"And you are very kind. Now I can leave happy."

"Oh, but you are not going yet, surely. I want to introduce you to some important people."

Julia notched up her smile. A commission was a commission was a commission. "In that case . . ."

"Now don't you go away. I'll just go and say goodbye to those people who are leaving first . . ."

WHICH WAS WHAT Brad Bradford was thinking of doing. He had arrived late, brought by the woman who was his current mistress—a fling that was in its dying fall—and he was bored, in the grip of that nerve-scratching, senses-tautening tension brought on by the old stifling sense of ennui which hit him every now and then. If something didn't happen soon he would break loose, plunge headfirst into one of those mindless, endless pools of reckless excess which always left him feeling worse than before. He was through with Angela; he had known that the moment he set eyes on her again. He would end it before he went back to Boston. He needed something, *somebody*, new. He needed a fresh challenge, greater heights to scale, different obstacles to overcome.

And then he saw her. Her face hit him like a blow. Where had *she* come from? Her impact coursed through him like a shot of adrenaline. What a stunner, he thought. Will you look at that face! He took a deep, tingling breath. God had just answered his prayers. He had not seen her before; she must have been in one of the penthouse's dozen other rooms, but better late than never. She was exactly what he needed right now.

Her face was strong-boned, its natural expression somewhat grave, and she had an air of impenetrable reserve, of show-me aloofness. Just the kind of challenge he relished. On the other hand, her smile was the kind of glow which warmed, hinting at all kinds of promise. Well worth his time and attention; exactly the kind he loved to topple. She should be good for a first-class game. She had all the attributes.

Apart from her glorious face she was simply and stunningly elegant in that timeless way of a woman who knew exactly what and who she was. Her dress was loose, of cream silk jersey, but cut in such a way as to cling where it touched, hinting at a body so lush as to be opulent, and she had legs that began at the armpits. From where he stood, some distance away, he could not determine the color of her eyes, only that they were large, deepset and smoky. And she had hair the color of the Concord woods in the fall. She held herself superbly: straight-backed, head perfectly balanced, moving with a natural dignity which laid cold hands on any attempt at familiarity. Mid-twenties, he judged, and what he classified as a glacial. Very sure of herself; all of her securely in her own possession and not inclined to share. Oh, yes, he thought, on a relishing thrill, a glacial, all right. One of those whose icecap overlay a volcano . . .

From that moment on his gaze never left her; wherever she moved he stalked her with his eyes, and though she never once glanced in his direction he knew, by the set of her shoulders, the slight rigidity of her head, that she was well aware of him and what he was doing. Never approaching her, he bided his time for the perfect opportunity. This one had to be handled with care.

Finally, his chance came. He saw her leave the group with whom she had been talking and move toward the French windows open to the terrace overlooking the square. A man stopped her, said something, but she shook her head firmly, left him looking after her as she slipped away from the hot and stuffy room, the smog of cigarette smoke, the babble of voices, and out into the freshness of the air. Stopping a passing waiter, Brad lifted two glasses from his tray and followed her. She was at the railing, her head lifted to the night, breathing deeply and pleasurably. The early April evening was springlike and sparkling, and as her lungs drew in the clean air her firm but soft breasts rose and fell under the thin stuff of her dress. Brad felt himself stir; oh, yes. This one was all woman, all right . . .

Atingle with anticipation and expectation, he stepped through the windows to join her.

"You look as if you could use one of these," he said, proffering her one of the glasses.

She did not take it; just regarded him with that air of hauteur—and from a very great distance.

[3]

"No strings," he urged, turning up the voltage of his smile.

She took the glass. "Thank you." It was cool; very cool. "You are very observant," she added. It was her drink: gin and tonic.

"I've been watching you all night."

"I know," she said calmly, offering him nothing.

"Do we make small talk or have a real conversation?" He was in no way put out.

Talk is the last thing on *your* mind, Julia thought. Everything about this man radiated sex. And all of it way over the top. He was too handsome, too self-assured, too—oh, everything, she thought irritably. The kind of man who rubbed her the wrong way. They thought they owned the world and had *droit de seigneur* to all the women in it. But she was acutely conscious of his eyes; could feel them like fingers. An odd color, she thought. Not blue, not green; like the sea when the sun fled across it, changing from moment to moment. There were little lines of wit and impudence at the corners of eyes and mouth, but the face was too handsome; too chiseled. For all the world like a male model advertising an aperitif, she thought scornfully.

"Would you prefer me to introduce myself formally?" With a start she realized he had moved closer while she had been listening to his voice. Not wholly American, but not English either. No intrusive *r*, for instance. Perhaps an English education . . . Now, he was so close she could feel him; like the heat of a four-bar electric fire.

"My name is Bradford—Brad, to my friends. I know who you are. I asked."

He was holding out a hand, but it was his eyes which held her. They seemed to widen, draw her into them. As she took his hand, unwillingly, felt his touch, her entire body seemed to burst into flame. She dropped it instantly; found she was struggling for breath. This is madness, she thought. What in God's name is wrong with me? He was enveloping her in the heat of his sensuality; she was conscious with microscopic intensity of the height, the physical brilliance, the vividness of his eyes, the warmth of his smile. She felt he was radiating a force field she could feel, even seemed to hear, shattering her defenses into thousands of tiny pieces.

This is ridiculous! she thought, shaken by the thick, fast stroke of her heart.

"You could at least give me the benefit of the doubt," he was encouraging sunnily.

About you I have no doubts, Julia thought, as she replied: "I would much rather you took no for an answer."

[4]

"Nine hundred and ninety-nine times out of a thousand it means yes."

"Don't look now, but that's number one thousand coming up."

"A malfunction, obviously."

He was—what was the word Americans used?—unfazed. Yes, that was it. His bold confidence fascinated even as his cockiness irritated.

"I do my own repairs," she answered cuttingly.

Another laugh. "You wouldn't be trying to cut me down to size." His eyes wandered over her in such a way as to make her body tingle. "What is yours, anyway? Five feet eight, a hundred and thirty pounds?"

Shocked, Julia realized he was dead right. Practice obviously made perfect.

"That gives me a five-inch advantage."

"And I'll bet you always take them!"

His laugh was exultant. She came right back at you every time! Not only a sharp tongue but a quick mind. Exactly the sort of challenge he needed right now. "We are wasting time," he said confidently.

"No. You are wasting yours."

Oh, lovely! Verbal dexterity in a woman made the preliminaries that much more fun. "I never waste anything," he assured her seriously. "In my book, waste is the eighth deadly sin."

"Oh, *you* wrote it!"

This time his laugh had the effect of placing her back to the wall. He was the most physically disturbing man she had ever met. She could feel him right down to toe and fingernails. Never in her life had she been so deeply conscious of any human being. It was as though he had ripped away bandages and laid hands on acutely sensitized skin.

"I can see we are going to get along beautifully." Pause. "It will be almost as beautiful as you are."

Nil response. "You don't like being told that you are beautiful?" Head tilted to one side. "No . . . I can see that must be a cliché by now. Sorry. I won't make that mistake again. I would hate you to think me just another boring male."

"I don't think of you at all," she assured him. "Now, would you let me past, please."

"And leave me without the opportunity to reply? Hardly."

"Watch me!"

"I've been doing that all evening. I was rather hoping we could take it on from there."

"I am not going anywhere with you," Julia said.

Over Brad's shoulder a voice called: "We are off to Annabel's, Brad. Coming?"

"I know a much nicer after-hours than that," Brad said hopefully.

"A before-hours too, no doubt. Would you please let me past."

"Only if you will let me take you on somewhere."

She set her glass down on the low brick wall. "I would not advise you to take me anywhere at all," she said. And before he could stop her she had pushed by him, giving him a quick drift of heady perfume—Chanel No. 19, he recognized—and disappeared into the throng.

Her one thought to escape, Julia headed for the bedroom where the coats had been put. Searching for hers, a brunette she knew slightly came in and said: "I saw you talking to Brad Bradford out there."

"Is that what it was?"

The brunette's laugh was chagrinned. "Came on strong, did he? Like always. But he is gorgeous, isn't he? You going to give him a tumble?"

"I never do when that is what they so obviously have in mind."

"Angela will be livid. She thinks she's got him all sewn up."

"That one is impervious to the needle," Julia said darkly.

"I don't get you." The brunette was frankly puzzled.

"Neither will he," said Julia.

But as she came out of the bedroom he was leaning against the wall, unmistakably waiting for her.

Julia's unfailingly strong sense of the ridiculous got the better of her.

"You have a lovely laugh," he said. "Goes with your voice." It was like those chocolates he always took back for his mother from Bendicks: a crisp outer shell which broke into bittersweetness; one was never enough.

Julia felt she was being backed into a corner; there was an implacability about his pursuit which disturbed her deeply.

Somebody passing called: "See you in Boston, Brad."

He turned his head, flashed a smile. "Yeah . . . sure . . ."

"Is that where you are from?" Julia asked, intrigued in spite of herself. "The home of the bean and the cod."

Another laugh. "True. But I haven't gotten around to speaking to God yet. I leave that to my mother."

Julia made one last try. "Look, I have my own car."

"Leave it; I'll arrange to have it delivered to your house."

She met the gleam in his eyes and felt her stomach plunge. Cheeky! she thought. He not only came on strong, he overwhelmed. His formidable confidence had collided with her own authority and clanged.

[6]

This one would take a great deal of containing; his whole attitude was that of one who had only to wait.

"My own car is right outside." He took her arm. The moment he touched her Julia was lost.

His car was a Bentley Continental tourer, the convertible, silver gray. "Matches your eyes," he said.

Julia shook her head, but on a laugh. "You are incorrigible."

She must have drunk too much, she decided as she got into the car. There were flies buzzing about in her head. Alcohol—or excitement? She could not be sure; she was only sure that this was not what she had intended; was angry with herself for allowing it. It was just not *like* her! Hitherto, she had always applied an instant cold compress to any man's fevered susceptibilities. It would not stay put on this one. It made her uneasy. She had decided long ago on a policy of noninvolvement; felt this man had called it into question; knew it had begun the moment she had felt his eyes. Some disenchanted evening? she thought.

It had been her brief and disastrous marriage which had disenchanted her. She had been married at nineteen, divorced at twenty-one after her husband had left her for another woman. Now, at twenty-six —twenty-seven in four months—she had remained scrupulously and stubbornly on her own ever since, carrying the failure of her marriage around with her like a shell, into which she retreated at the first sign of interest on the part of any man. This one, she thought uneasily, seemed likely to crush it. Talk about being armored in self-esteem! Yes, of the kind that came from a 100 percent success rate with women. She had no doubt she was number one thousand. Variety, she was sure, was the spice of this man's life. He probably picked women like flowers, threw them away when they wilted. Not for me, she thought firmly. Why look for trouble? And then something her husband had said as he was leaving her echoed in her mind: "You don't need me, Julia. You don't need anyone. You have yourself. The trouble is that you keep it under lock and key because you are terrified of burglars." Julia felt the old recrudescence of pain. Well, she thought self-justifyingly, I am just not the type to leave myself lying around for on-the-make Americans from Boston to pick up.

"Pleasant thoughts?" this one asked.

"No."

"Ouch! You are not supposed to say things like that this early in the game," he reproached, but with sparkling eyes.

"I never was fond of sports. Would you take me home, please."

"Where is home?"

"Kensington—Hornton Street."

"Oh, I know where that is."

Julia had the top floor of a house: large rooms and just across the road from the tube, a few stops away from Sloane Street, where she worked. As the car turned in to it, she had her hand ready on the door handle. "By that lamppost." As the car stopped she said, "Thank you for the lift."

"My pleasure. Now how about showing yours. I could go a cup of coffee."

He was like a weed, she thought exasperatedly. No sooner had she dug him up than he sprouted somewhere else. Except she was not going to give him the chance to plant himself in her bed.

"A cup of coffee you can have," she told him clearly.

He followed her up a flight of red-carpeted stairs to a door at the top of them, which she unlocked, and into a hall which ran at cross angles, across that and through another door into a large living room with a semibay of big windows overlooking the street. Switching on the lamps from a central point, Julia went across to draw the curtains: heavy cotton satin in a poppy-strewn print of scarlet and black on white. They echoed the upholstery of the sofa and matching easy chairs. The floor was solid wood-block, varnished ebony black; several silky Chinese rugs in the same colors were thrown here and there, and she had scarlet and white carnations massed in black lacquer bowls. Shucking his topcoat, Brad dropped into one of the easy chairs while Julia disappeared into what must be the kitchen.

"Black, no sugar," he called after her.

Tilting his head, he read the titles on the spines of the books which crammed the floor-to-ceiling shelves fitted into alcoves on either side of the fireplace. A lot of books on art and design; novels, biography, history—and Alistair Cooke's *America*. Well, well, he thought. No wonder she had known about the bean and the cod. There was a whole shelf of books on the United States. Oh, yes, this was going to be very interesting.

"That was quick!" he exclaimed, as she came back with a tray on which was a ceramic coffeepot, cups and saucers, cream, but no sugar.

"I always set the coffee to percolate before I go out; that way it's ready when I come in. I like a cup before bed."

"Me too!"

He took out cigarettes and lighter, placed them on the coffee table before accepting the cup she handed him; Spode, the willow pattern his mother loved. She declined a cigarette, picked up her own cup and

[8]

sat back on the chesterfield, long legs crossed, to regard him with a dead-sure composure which said: Do your damnedest. It still won't get you anywhere!

Excitement and anticipation revved inside him. He loved a challenge, and he had been feeling the onset of the old ennui badly. This one should be good for a championship game. He liked to win over the difficult ones, and this one would, he was positive, give him a run for his money.

He smiled across at her. "I like your silences," he complimented, showing he was not in the least disturbed by them, "and your coffee is good too."

He glanced contentedly around the comfortable room with its zinging yet soothing colors, pleased that she did not chatter nervously or overbrightly—a dead giveaway with the inexperienced. But then, a woman who looked as she did must have been dealing in men since she had donned her first pair of nylons.

But he also had the feeling that she went a long way down, and all he had done so far was dabble a toe in the water. Time to take the plunge. Stubbing out his cigarette, he set his cup and saucer on the table before crossing to the couch. Sitting down beside her he took her own cup and saucer to lay them by his own. Then he put his hands on her shoulders, turning her to face him. She made no protest; only regarded him from behind the smoke screen of her incredible eyes. Close to, her skin had the fine texture of a baby's, and the gray eyes had tiny black flecks in them. She smelled headily sensuous and the light from the white silk shades of the lamps highlighted the sheen of her mouth erotically. Bending his head, he put his own to it, lightly, but not tentatively. She did not draw away. Just let him.

"I've been wanting to do that all evening," he told her.

Her eyes told him nothing, but her mouth had been soft, succulent.

"I will take your silence as meaning I may do it again."

This time his kiss was in no way tentative, nor was the way he drew her fully into his arms, feeling the pressure of her breasts and the long length of thigh. This kiss was different.

The overture was over; they were into the first act. If I don't want this, Julia thought fleetingly, now is the time to say so. But her mood had swung; she now felt not so much an apathy as a resigned fatalism; any protest would be no more than wasted time. Besides, she had *known* this would happen, even if she had not been prepared to give the admission houseroom. And she found it hard to think anyway, because he was kissing her in a way that was unlike anything she had ever

[9]

experienced. He did not do it as a preliminary, as Derek had done, before getting down to the main event. He did it as a prelude, a foretaste of delights to come, and its effect on Julia was oddly paradoxical in that while it seemed to drug her senses it also awoke in her hibernating feelings and responses she had not realized were asleep. She was conscious that his mouth and tongue were producing in her a shivering response to the most concentrated of exquisite sensations. It seemed her mouth had become a highly sensitive antenna, capable of receiving—and sending, if his own response was anything to go by— the most subtle of feelings. The kisses deepened, became more impassioned, more unrestrained. Julia had the feeling she was being consumed; irresistibly pried loose from self-controlling fingers which lost their grip under this man's unrelenting, passionately tender assault.

The phone rang. Brad lifted his mouth fractionally, as though questioning her need to answer, but Julia seized the opportunity to come up for air.

It was Chris, her oldest and closest friend.

"How was the party?" she wanted to know.

"Oh, the usual . . ."

"Anybody worth while?" Chris always used such occasions as a manhunt.

"Too early to say."

As always, Chris heard the unsaid. "You've not got somebody there!"

"Well . . ."

"My God, Julia! Don't tell me I've interrupted something."

"Not really."

"Say no more. You in tomorrow night?"

"Yes."

"I'll be round; eightish, okay?"

"Fine."

"I can't wait!"

When she returned to him, it was not to join him on the couch, but to the chair he had vacated, where she poured herself more coffee. Damn that bloody phone. It was clear that as far as she was concerned, that was the end of *that.* Just as he had got her going nicely. Nicely! Jesus! he thought. That's the understatement of my life. There were fires down there such as had not warmed him for many a long time. He had been so right about her.

"Dinner, tomorrow night?" he asked.

"No."

Taken aback: "Saturday, then? We could even spend the day together—"

"I have things to do at weekends."

"Okay, dinner Saturday night, then."

He found his smile becoming fixed but hung on grimly, because it was the stabbing of the needle of challenge which hurt most. He had not felt this sense of hungry anticipation for so long. Thank God he had decided to go to that party.

Julia watched him watching her. Spoiled, she thought. Spoiled rotten. Not used to being told no. She shook herself mentally. Thank God for Chris. Saved by the telephone bell? Because she had definitely felt she was going under for the last time. What do you want with him? she asked herself coldly. A playboy womanizer who only wants a good time —at your expense. Well, argued her other self. Since when were you looking for Derek's replacement? Be thankful that all this one does want is fun and games.

She rose abruptly. "It's late, I have to work tomorrow."

He rose too but said implacably: "You haven't answered: dinner Saturday?"

It was to get rid of him that Julia said: "All right."

"I'll call for you at seven-thirty."

Damn! She had hoped to arrange to meet him and not turn up. "I can easily meet you," she suggested.

"I wouldn't dream of it," he assured her smoothly, making her think he knew very well what she was up to. That was when she resigned herself.

He did not kiss her again, which irrationally disappointed her. "Till Saturday, then," he said.

She closed the door on him.

"WELL?" DEMANDED CHRIS as she bounced through the door. "Who is he, what is he; most important, *why* is he? I can't stay long," she went on without pausing for breath. "Tony is coming at ten." Tony was her current—married as always—lover.

"He's an American, of all things," Julia answered, still sounding astonished. "His name is Bradford—Brad Bradford."

"Sounds like a film star."

"He looks like one."

"Which one?"

Julia thought. "Robert Redford—but six inches taller."

"Wow!" breathed Chris. "Do tell!"

"Nothing to tell." Julia went to pour them both a sherry.

"Oh, now, Julia! This is Chris! If he is up to your standard then he has to be something else!"

"Oh, he is—everything else!"

"Sounds like a handful," Chris sparkled.

"*Both* hands."

"And you all of a sudden a butterfingers?"

Julia avoided her friend's all too experienced and knowledgeable eyes.

"Heavens!" Chris marveled. "This is not the Julia we all love and fear."

"Now that I have had time to think, she's due to be fined for dereliction of duty."

"Oh, for God's sake . . . don't you ever give your brain a rest?"

"You know my opinions on the stupid—and wholly unnecessary—games men and women play."

"Only because you got badly beaten first one you played."

"A lesson well and truly learned."

"And don't we all know it! Still . . ." Chris eyed Julia thoughtfully. "I've never known you let them get as far as the actual laying on of hands."

Julia's flush revealed all.

"Just how far did he actually get?"

"He kissed me, that's all."

"All! Listen, I can tell within thirty seconds of meeting a man if I want to sleep with him or not."

"You are different."

"No! *You* are!" Eyeing her friend's flushed face. "How was it?" Chris asked.

Julia tried to shrug. "That's the trouble. It was—well—incredible."

"Ah . . ." Chris's carefully plucked eyebrows all but disappeared into her blond hair. "One of those."

"One of what?"

"A grandmaster. Normally, they should be worked up to; with you it will be like learning to hold your liquor on Krug *Grand Cuvée!*" Thoughtfully: "He sounds to me like a professional— No, I don't mean he does it for a living! I mean he does it to live! There's a hell of a difference." In the face of Julia's horror. "You mean you've never actually met one of them?"

"No, thank God!"

[12]

"No . . . you wouldn't, of course; they don't turn up in enclosed convents, and if you will live like a nun—"

"I live the way I prefer to live."

"Oh no you don't; you exist, which is a horse of an entirely different color!"

When Julia bridled: "Well, you did opt out of life after Derek, didn't you?"

"If you mean the kind of life *you* live—then yes, I did."

Chris was unperturbed. "Oh, I know my reputation: anything in pants so long as what's in them is male. But it is you we are talking about. You, Julia Carey, being pursued by a man with E for Excellence and Experience, and acting like it was beneath your dignity to notice."

"Because it would be stupid! He's an out-and-out womanizer. The one thing I don't need!"

"What the hell has that got to do with anything? Don't you *ever* do anything just for the fun of it?"

"Never!" Julia said. "It is not in my nature."

"You mean you won't allow it to be."

"Have I ever been the sort of woman who went in for sex per se?"

"I've never known you to go for it at all, and all because one man— the wrong man for you—turned you off it. Have some *fun*, Julia, for once. Take what this Brad is offering, and in the spirit in which it is being offered, only for God's sake don't get drunk on it. It is very potent."

Julia's expression said she was teetotal.

"Who better to learn from than a man who knows it all?" Chris asked enviously. On a sigh: "It's that face and body of yours. No man looking at you is going to believe you are not up to your armpits in admirers. Just because you dipped a toe in the water and it froze you is no reason to refuse to take the plunge ever again."

"Not for me," Julia repeated firmly. "I don't need it."

"What has that got to do with it?"

"Every instinct tells me I would regret it."

"Oh, we are in a mood! Shall I get you the knife or would you prefer the sleeping pills? Coward's way out again, is it? You and that almighty terror of being hurt. It is five years since Derek and by rights you should have developed calluses, but not you; your heart is still in its virginal state even if you aren't. Why are you so afraid, anyway?"

Julia was silent before replying flatly: "Because I don't think I have enough emotional resilience. It's just the way I am."

"Is it? Or the way you prefer to be?"

[13]

Chris, Julia thought vexedly, had a shrewd way of shoving the knife right where it was not wanted.

"I know you, Julia. I ought to, after all these years. I also know men. I've had more of them than hot dinners. I *love* sex; it is one of life's great pleasures, but you regard it as some sort of distasteful aberration! Go on, tart yourself up to the nines, wear something sensational, spray something that will blow his mind and then go out and play him at his own game. You've all the right equipment!"

Julia's expressionless face was eloquent. Chris sighed inwardly. She and Julia had been friends since school, but whereas Chris had many others, Julia did not make friends easily; her air of aloof disdain kept people at several arm's length. Chris had seen the permafrost deepen ever since Derek Allan, the only man with whom Julia had had a relationship that was not platonic. Which was how it had really been with Derek anyway.

THEY TOO HAD GROWN UP TOGETHER, known each other all their lives, drifted into marriage though Julia had insisted on keeping her job. On leaving art school, she had gotten herself a good job with a design firm in Leeds; Derek had been doing postgraduate work, studying for his Ph.D. It was essential, Julia said practically, that she keep on working. It was when her job turned out to be more important and more satisfying than her husband that the rot set in. Julia worked all the hours God sent, leaving Derek to return to an empty flat, no dinner ready, no woman waiting. And when he kicked they fought. And when they fought they slept apart. And they fought more and more frequently. Which had resulted in Derek finding himself another woman, eventually leaving Julia for her. "You are married to your job, Julia, not me," he had told her bitterly, "and I find ambition a very cold bedfellow."

"Just as I never found you a ball of fire!" Julia had thrown back. "With what I get from you is it any wonder I prefer to spend my time on more satisfying endeavours!"

Which was when he had slapped her, placing one last barb before walking out. "You are no woman, Julia. You only look like one."

What had amazed Chris was the way Julia had taken it. Like a mortal wound. Until Chris realized it was not Derek and the failure of her marriage which had savaged her; it was the fact that she had made a mistake.

Julia, Chris reflected, was practicality incarnate; ran her life like her job. Systematic, thoroughly capable, ruthlessly organized. She was a born manager and had complained to Chris about Derek's not appreciating this. "I worked, I scrimped, I saved, then he has the nerve to complain! Why else did I do it if it was not for him?"

"Was it?" Chris had asked. "You are sure it is not your pride he has hurt?"

But Julia had taken her mistake as a dreadful warning, and taken scrupulous care never to repeat it. She had left Yorkshire for London, got a job in a designer workshop where, once again, she proceeded to climb the ladder of success. She had talent and the application to show it off. She was now a senior designer, handling selected commissions on her own; she earned a high salary—and what did she do with it? Put it in the bank, Chris thought disgustedly. She must live on only half her income—if that! What was it about Julia that made her so proud of doing without? Look at the way she had not lifted a finger to stop the divorce. Pride, Chris thought now. Rampant, arrogant pride! Unless I can get her to swallow it she is going to be found dead clutching it. Really, she thought despairingly, she's got the face of an angel and the soul of a bookkeeper!

"Is it help, advice, you want?" she asked. "You know I'll give it gladly. I've been through it all—still am going through it."

"Tony?"

"Who else?"

Julia thought Tony was a lying, devious, selfish son of a bitch, but Chris had taken the big fall for him. He was always saying he was "going to leave his wife." But always—not yet. Lately, Julia had noticed Chris chafing at the bit.

"He's got to choose," she said now. "I'm sick and tired of hanging around." She saw the look which Julia banished as soon as she felt Chris's eyes. "I know . . . You think I'm every kind of a fool, don't you? You wouldn't hang around . . . But I want Tony. I need him . . . and if nagging and prodding are the only way I'll get him then nag and prod I will."

"I'd rather die!"

"I know. That's where we differ. You would rather be right—if alone. I'd rather be wrong and together." Taking her refill: "What is it about this one?" she asked.

"I think he's spoiled, I'm sure he's careless. Wants a good time and no consequences. He'll call the tune, I'll dance—and pay the piper. Then he'll throw *me* a coin before looking for the next dancer. He sees it all as some kind of a game; a sex Olympics in which nothing must come between him and his umpteenth medal as World Champion Cocksman!"

[15]

"So play him at his own game!"

"With my amateur standing! It would be purely defensive."

"The kind of game women have always played! Men are supposed to do the hunting, love; at least, they think they are. Let them keep their illusions if it pleases them. Just remember you don't have to do anything you don't *want* to do. Never get yourself into a situation you can't get out of."

"Always supposing I will be able to recognize it."

"You are a woman, aren't you?"

Am I? thought Julia, recalling Derek's comment. Was that why she had stopped being one?

"Just play him at his own game, as I said," Chris was saying. "Read up on the manual as you go along or ask me. I've bluffed my way out of many a tight situation. My best position is back to the wall."

HE BROUGHT IN fresh air and excitement on Saturday night. It had been raining, and his thick, brightly blond hair was aglitter with diamond drops. The sea-change eyes were brilliant and he smiled at Julia in such a way as to make her realize that never in her life had she *felt* a man the way she felt this one: with every nerve ending. He really was, she admitted to herself, disturbingly sexual. He made her feel all woman. His eyes flattered her. "You look like a million dollars."

"Then it is just as well you can afford me," Julia countered lightly, hoping desperately he was not about to bankrupt her.

He tweaked the pussycat bow which tied the neck of her black chiffon dress. "I like you in black; makes your hair take fire . . . But you're not in mourning for something—someone?" Julia felt a distinct frisson of shock, made herself meet the questions in his eyes. "You'll have nothing to mourn over with *me.*"

I hope not, Julia prayed as she said: "You did ask for the benefit of the doubt."

"*I* have none." There was a disagreeable twist to his mouth.

"You don't like doubts?"

"Not from my women, I don't!"

Which put her, she thought, exactly where he thought she belonged. Which was where she had no intention of staying, that being the case.

"You don't answer," he prodded, not liking the quality of her gaze. He hoped he had not turned her off; not the way she turned him on. In that black dress, those sheer nylons . . . He was already hard and ready; had been keyed to an intense pitch since meeting her, which

Angela, as a stopgap, had done nothing to relieve; she had only served to increase his desire.

"Was that a warning?" she asked finally, very cool.

"No. Just a hint as to what I'm like."

Her smile appeared. "I had rather hoped you were going to let me find out for myself."

Good humor restored: "Exactly what I have in mind." He picked up her coat, eager to be gone. "Nice," he approved. It was black velvet, with a collar of mink to match the cuffs. Above it, her hair glowed like flame.

HE TOOK HER to what she at first thought was a private house: a sumptuous dining room, furnished like a country seat; pictures on silk-hung walls, flowers everywhere, a big fire in a marble grate. The tables were at least six feet apart and there were more waiters than diners. The atmosphere was hushed, with that breathless awe which pertains in the face of a great deal of money.

One waiter addressed Brad by name; another brought a silver bucket in which a baby-wrapped bottle of champagne lay in a bed of ice; a third brought a silver bowl, also resting in ice, which was heaped high with gleaming gray pearls that Julia knew must be caviar, though she had never eaten it. A fourth shook out her heavy, double-damask napkin before reverently laying it over her knees with a flourish like El Córdobes citing a Miura bull.

"Dig in," Brad ordered, helping himself liberally before layering it on toast so thin the paper could have been read through it. Fish roe—even if it was that of the sturgeon—was not one of Julia's predilections, but she was willing to try anything—once. Its taste was an acquired one, she decided, but one she could acquire. The waiter poured champagne. Picking up his flute, Brad held it out: "To us," he said, "and our beginning."

Touching it with her own: "You do like them?"

"They are better than endings."

"You've had a lot of them?"

"My fair share. You?"

One too many, Julia thought, answering with a negligent and, she hoped, experienced shrug, knowing it would not do to tell him that. What he thought she was and what she really was had not so much as been introduced. She would have to be careful. Trouble was, he had penetrated her carefully protected consciousness to a depth which alarmed and upset her; had her already tilted off center.

"Let's not talk of endings," Brad said roughly, the little stitch which meant displeasure knitting his brows. "Tonight is *our* beginning."

Oh, yes? thought Julia. Of what?

The champagne was so chilled it numbed the palate before exploding along her veins.

"Good?" Brad asked her.

"Mmmmmm . . . delicious."

"Champagne and beautiful women should always be taken in conjunction."

"I thought that was a planetary aspect."

"Well, didn't fate bring us together? I almost didn't go to that party."

She did not ask why. That was another thing which intrigued. Her needling lack of curiosity.

"But I'm glad I did," he went on.

Nor did she reply with the expected: "So am I."

"Are you?" He forced it.

Her lids lowered, hiding her mysterious eyes. "I hope to be."

That was better. She did fence well.

THE MENU was astonishingly small.

"Everything a specialty and cooked to perfection while you wait. You don't come here to be seen, you come to eat. I can recommend the sweetbreads."

Something else Julia had never tried, but he had been right about the caviar so she backed his fancy once again. The waiter refilled their glasses.

"Drink up," commanded Brad.

"Wine makes me sleepy," Julia hedged.

"I'll soon wake you up."

As their eyes met, once again Julia felt him slide deeply within her. She was totally at a loss as to how to account for it; for his whole effect on her. Truth to tell, she had always thought such effect was greatly exaggerated romanticism; had tended to agree with—was it Voltaire or had it been La Rochefoucauld who had said that if love had not existed it would have been necessary to invent it. After all, hadn't she thought she'd found it once before, only to realize she had bought a paste facsimile? Steady on, Julia, she thought quickly. Love is not the name of this game. Sex is what he is after; has been from the beginning. His whole attitude has been: "I'm game, how about you?" Back to games again, she thought.

[18]

Once more she lowered her lids and her face took on the blankly flawless unreality of a statue. Except that he knew by now of the mind which worked ceaselessly behind it. As for her real self, that lay a long way down. He would have to dive, with this one. Trouble was, he had the feeling you could go so deep you'd get the bends coming out.

He watched her in pleasurable silence. She really was classy, he thought contentedly. Beautifully controlled; everything a smooth progression, from the way she moved to the way she handled a fork, a glass; took everything in her smooth, unfaltering stride—especially him. But then, with a face like that she must have been dealing in men at least half her life. He liked that. He had left ingenues behind with his adolescence. No; this one was *all* woman; sexy, mysterious, tantalizingly remote. Excitement licked him with a hungry flame. The anticipation of the hunt, as always, quickened his responses, heightened his awareness. He loved the chase; the reconnoitering, the plays, the forward passes; trouble was, often it was more exciting than the kill. But with this one, he was positive, both would turn out to be incredibly satisfying.

Hot plates were set before them. The sweetbreads were served. Picking up her fork, Julia sampled.

"Good?" Brad asked, watching her.

"Delicious!" She sounded surprised.

Gazing around the beautiful room: "What is this place?"

"You've not been here before?"

"No—not this one," she tacked on.

"It's a private dining club."

"You know it well, of course."

"I know a lot of things." He paused. "Except about you. Tell me about yourself. Like where you are from."

"I was born in Yorkshire. My parents died when I was small and I was brought up by an aunt. I was married once—briefly."

"Why are you no longer married?"

"It did not work."

"How long—since the divorce, I mean."

"Almost six years."

"How old are you?"

"Twenty-seven in four months."

"I'm thirty-one next time around."

That was all he said about himself, and she asked no questions of her own. It was as though, he thought, puzzled and not a little annoyed, that the less she knew the better she liked it. Did I say deep? he thought.

"And since your divorce, you've lived alone?"

She knew what was meant.

"Yes."

She had no intention—acting on Chris's advice—of telling him about the cloister she inhabited. He probably wouldn't believe her. Men didn't. It was her fatal beauty, she reflected ironically. They refused to believe she did not take full advantage of it. But this particular man . . . . It was instinct she relied on to guide her; telling her to keep her touch light, her wit sharp, her perception—and thank God she had plenty of that—at full scan. Her fastidiousness would keep until later—depending, of course, how far this went, what it turned into and how long it lasted. So when he asked, as she knew he would, "Why?," she countered with a cool shrug: "Why not?"

"Because it is not natural for a woman as beautiful and desirable as you."

"And just exactly what is 'natural'?" He could have shaved on the edge of her sarcasm.

"It's what is right. And it is not right that you should not have a man —men—somewhere in your life."

"You think I can't manage without one?"

"I'm damned sure you can, but that's not what I meant and you know it."

Julia regarded him with what she hoped was amusement. "It just so happens it suited me."

"You mean no man suited you."

He didn't believe it either! But his smile was approving. Chris was absolutely right! Talk about illusions . . .

"You have every right to be choosy," Brad assured her seriously. "A woman as beautiful as you can well afford it."

His smile was the smile of the man who has just been chosen.

Julia drained her glass, all of a sudden ablaze with confidence. " 'Come, fill the Cup,' " she quoted.

"And drain it so that it can be filled again."

And I'll bet you've lost count of the times you've done just that, Julia thought, watching the bubbles in her tall, narrow flute rise to the surface and explode.

Brad could feel his own tension unreeling; that taut sense of anticipation when it was the first time.

"Brandy with your coffee?" he asked.

"Why not?"

One Armagnac became two. They lingered long at the table, talking. He showed no signs of hurry. Everything he did was for her, his absorbtion in her total and insidiously flattering. Julia had noticed the stares he got from the other women in the room, but he noticed none of them. His attention was solely on her, making her feel as if she were, for him, the only woman in the world. She felt she was an object of adoration, and the way he was focusing himself on her increased her own awareness of self. And him.

She had been conscious of him as a physical being from the first meeting, but now she found her glance wandering over him, even as she wondered what his body was like under his clothes. As handsome as his face? She had noticed he had long legs, found herself, for the first time in her life, wondering about what he carried between them. She had to force her mind away from it, but his physicality was such that she found it difficult. His tomcat sensuality, his quizzical grin, his lazy, predatory confidence, all had her breathless and more than slightly panic-stricken.

All too soon the bill was presented. Brad signed it, while a waiter brought Julia's coat. Another presented, with a flourish, a long-stemmed rose from the centerpiece, his eyes openly lustful. Julia floated out into the street, where Brad took her hand, tucking it in his, smiling down into her eyes.

They strolled slowly through the highways and byways of Mayfair, browsing in the brightly lit shopwindows. Julia wondered if, when they came to a shadowy corner, Brad would kiss her, but he did not, which only served to increase her desire for him. She had left her qualms behind with her crusts. When other couples passed them, hand in hand, Julia felt like smiling at them; for once she was half of a pair. How often, walking briskly up Sloane Street after working late, had she passed strolling couples, pausing, as she and Brad were doing now, to gaze into shopwindows, the girl laying her head on the boy's shoulder. It made Julia feel eighteen again, and filled with hope.

They must have walked in a circle because they came back to the car, into which Brad put her as if she were priceless porcelain. They turned into Park Lane and then off it again, and within minutes were drawing up before a tall, narrow house with black-painted iron grillwork. Ushering her up spotless marble steps, Brad let himself in with a key. A marble hall, an elevator of the same grillwork but this time black and gold, which took them up three flights. She stepped out onto a white marble floor, two doors on either side of the landing. Brad opened the one on the right, stood back to let her precede him. Julia's outer self crossed the threshold confidently; her inner self constricted. Now! she thought.

He led her into a long, narrow room, luxuriously furnished. An Adam fireplace, a bright fire burning, casting rosy warmth on the apple-green silk of a superb French sofa. Brad switched on several lamps so that the room took on a seductive glow. Shrugging out of his topcoat he came for hers. "Want to freshen up?" he asked, and led her through a door into a small lobby where he opened another door, hidden in a wall hung with Chinese wallpaper, to reveal a small bath-room complete with handbasin. Gold taps in the shape of dolphins, thick towels in sugar-almond colors, an unwrapped tablet of Guerlain Fleur-des-Alpes soap, a lingering, expensive fragrance. Her feet sank into inches-thick buttermilk carpet.

She used the john, washed her hands, inspecting her face in the mirrored wall behind the shell-shaped basin. Her face revealed an outward self unchanged; a little windblown, perhaps, and with eyes like spotlights. She tidied herself, applied a little more lipstick and a fresh drift of Arpège. When she went back to join Brad he was in the act of uncorking yet another bottle of champagne. She sank down into one corner of the sofa, took the glass he handed her. She sipped with relish. She had drunk more champagne tonight than she ever had. Eaten her first caviar and sweetbreads. And in a little while would take her first lover. Wouldn't she?

Her trepidation, which had been awaiting its cue in the wings, now made its entrance. Had she not drunk to their beginning? If she did not wish to start anything now was the time to say so.

She forced her mind through the view-blocking press of her emotions in an attempt to look at it all—at him—objectively; to compare his attractions: his senses-arousing sensuality, his compelling physical at-traction for her, his charm, his good looks, his brook-no-failure per-sonality, his certainty that something had happened between them at first glance, his blatant but flattering pursuit, the sense of importance he gave her, against his drawbacks: the casualness of it all, his sex-is-the-name-of-my-game attitude, the nail-gnawing uncertainties of be-coming involved and/or embroiled in a game that was new to her, even if his motives were not. She found distaste warring with desire; found the thought of becoming another digit, another toy for a woman-spoiled, money-ruined playboy to play with filled her with dismay even while the memory of Chris's "Krug *Grand Cuvée*" egged her on. She longed for her friend's ability to jump first, ask questions afterward, even as she felt the prod of her words shoving her along the diving board. And at the back of it all, Derek's annihilating words about her only looking like a woman . . .

What *am* I doing here? she thought, bewitched, bothered and totally bewildered. Torn by curiosity and a desire to know and experience something Chris says I have been missing. Why could she not rid herself of the pessimistic certainty that she would regret this? Yet she knew she could not command his attention without paying the price. Which, she realized as she peeled away the shell to reveal the kernel, was what she really resented: that there should be a price. And that was a hangover from being left bankrupt once before.

She gulped champagne as though hoping to rust the ceaselessly churning engine of her mind. Chris had told her she thought too much, analyzed to obsession. But she was convinced that what was about to happen (which convinced her, once and for all, that it was) could be the rock on which her whole life would founder. Sex.

That was what it was, if she was honest. The relationship she was about to enter into was euphemistically named. Lovers. What had love to do with this? What lay—no, loomed—between them was a sizzling sexual attraction. Purely physical and please check your emotions at the door.

Well, she argued with herself, he has been honest with you, hasn't he? That is a rarity in itself. E for Excellence and Experience, as Chris said. *She* would not think twice! *She* would not think at all!

But what if it should turn out, as it had done with Derek, to be shatteringly disappointing? What if it *was* her? Chris had dismissed her fears out of hand. "There is no such thing as frigid women; only inept men." As Derek had been, leaving her with a dismayed emptiness and an "Is that all there is?" She had tended to agree with Dr. Johnson: the position was ridiculous, the pleasure fleeting and the expense indeed damnable. It had cost her her marriage. Or so she had thought until Chris, ruthlessly and scatologically comparing her lovers as to performance, had made Julia wonder if, after all, it had not been her fault but Derek's. That she had married a man who was a lousy lover. Well, she was about to find out.

"I hope you are thinking about me," she heard Brad say.

Julia pulled herself together. "Of course! Like, what do you do, for instance?"

"Whatever my mother tells me."

"I'll bet!"

"You'd lose!"

"You don't look like a mother's boy."

His face changed. "I'm not," he said roughly. "Now drink up."

"You wouldn't be trying to get me drunk."

"I would not!" His eyes moved from her face to the black chiffon through which her breasts gleamed. "I want us both to know exactly what we are doing."

He removed her glass from her hand when she had emptied it, set it beside his own, empty glass before turning back to her, drawing her into his arms, eyes gleaming from behind slitted lids. "For instance . . . ," he murmured, before putting his mouth to hers.

It was a deliberate assault on the senses carried out with the expertise of a seasoned campaigner, and what he began with his mouth he amplified with his hands. Nothing Derek had ever done had prepared Julia for this. She felt she was mounting a ladder, rung by exquisitely dreamlike rung, climbing the heights of physical intensity. He seemed to have vacuumed her confused mind before proceeding to refill it with concentrated essence of himself. It went coursing through her bloodstream and straight to her head, totally doing for her self-control. When at last he released her, she felt she had been given the merest foretaste of sublimity and was aflame with desire to know it all.

His sea-change eyes seemed to glow, bathing her in the heat of his potency. By now wholly under his influence, when he drew her up from the couch she offered no resistance, let him lead her obediently from the room.

THE BED WAS ENORMOUS, all silk hangings and piled pillows, turned down ready and waiting. He probably changes his women with the sheets, she thought, but this time the thought made her smile. She didn't give a damn how many there were. Just so long as she was one of them.

He saw the smile, was across to her in one stride. "Smiles like that should be used with care." He devoured her mouth once more, holding her helpless while his fingers pulled loose the pussycat bow, undid the tiny, self-covered buttons, finally pushing the dress over her shoulders so that it fell to the floor.

She saw his eyes flare, heard the sharp intake of breath as she stood before him in a single piece of black crepe de chine and her nylons. This time her smile was different. Then she raised her arms to place them about his neck before pressing herself against him like hot, melted wax. All coherent thought having fled, she was acting purely on instinct. The way he kissed her—wildly, passionately—told her she was

[24]

right. With a now supreme confidence she responded to his mouth, his hands and finally, when he had her naked under him in the big wide bed, his body.

THE BLARE OF A CAR HORN woke her to the dimness of a strange room, an unfamiliar bed; even more unfamiliar, a body lying next to her; the heaviness of a male leg across hers, the weight of male forearm across her breasts. Cautiously, she turned her head. A blond head buried in the pillows. Memory flooded and in a wholly gratified reaction she stretched gloriously, her body feeling strangely supple and marvelously *used*. There was an enormous carved mirror hanging above a walnut-and-ormolu chest; in it, she could see the bed reflected; two figures, sleeping male, wide-awake female. And how! she exulted. And how!

The very memory brought a tingle to her flesh. Not only had it been her first one-night stand, it had been her first *real* sex. Nothing she had ever experienced with Derek had prepared her for somebody like Brad Bradford; for what he had done to her, brought her to, time and time again. Oh, yes, Derek had indeed been a lousy lover; he had just not had any idea! The wrong man had turned her off. The right man turned her on—and into something she had not known she could be. Well, she reflected, I always was a fast learner.

Last night, for instance, she had learned more about herself in— what—three, four hours? (she had lost track of time as she had of everything else) than she had in all her twenty-six years. Had anyone asked the question she would have replied honestly: Yes, she did know herself; she had always made a point of it. Blunt, she thought now. And brittle. Last night it had snapped. The Julia Carey who had done that— yes, and *that*—was not any one of the Julia Careys she had thought she had known, yet not one of them felt either ashamed or surprised; only sat with smug expressions on their faces. Mentally, she stuck her tongue out at them, then became aware that Brad's body had changed, was no longer slack in sleep but pressed up against hers, warm, hard and eager.

"Good morning . . . ," he murmured, hands caressing. "How do you feel?"

"You should know."

A chuckle. "Like I do," he pronounced. He turned her to face him, his hardness pulsating against her stomach.

"You are insatiable," Julia murmured happily.

"Normal reaction in the male on waking, especially with a beautiful, naked female in his bed."

"Well, you did say natural was right so right must be natural."

His smile confirmed the rightness of her choice of words. "*We* are right. How about you, anyway?" He sounded surprised. "You were absolutely incredible; made me feel like a tiger. I lost count of the times you came."

"I lost count, track, time . . . everything."

He traced her mouth with a fingertip. "I was even more right about you than I thought."

And I hope I was wrong about you, Julia thought.

"You turned me on first look . . . and, baby, do you generate some heat yourself!" He smoothed her hair back, cupped her face in his hands. "I knew there were depths to you," he pronounced. "What you see and what you get with this one, I thought, haven't so much as been introduced."

"While I have to thank you for introducing me to a few things."

He laughed, but it was pleased. "You mean you'd never met them before?"

"Not until you, I hadn't."

He ran a hand down her sleep-warmed body. "You are like silk . . . inside and out!"

Julia stretched again, luxuriously, before curling up against him. "That's how I feel right now."

It was the truth. She had never felt like this before; as if her body were singing. She felt both adored and worshiped; both new to her. She mourned for what she had missed, not knowing it was there to be had. Chris was right; what a waste, she thought.

Brad's hands were moving, exploring, probing. "And you said *I* was insatiable!" he mocked gleefully, his eyes hot, his erection burning against her.

"Natural reaction in the female when penetrated by a potent male."

"So what are we waiting for?"

He was tireless, inventive, innovative. Derek had known only one way; Brad knew them all. With Derek, one orgasm left him limp; with Brad, he held off until she had come, thrillingly, again and again; had already attuned himself so acutely to her body's reactions that he knew when she began to peak and the contractions inside her body clasped him and thrilled him and then, as she felt him flood her, hot and copious, milk him until she both heard and felt the breath leave his

[26]

body even as the last drop left him and he shuddered and collapsed against her, his breath harsh.

"See," he murmured, his lips against her throat, "I told you."

AGAIN, Julia was the first to awake. Brad had moved in his sleep, now lay away from her, lying on his back, one arm flung out along the pillow, the other holding hers. The sheets were flung back, and his body was exposed to her avid gaze. It was as beautiful as his face: not an ounce of surplus flesh, and what there was smooth and tight and springy with the resilience of perfect physical condition. His chest was smooth, almost hairless, his stomach flat, and the bush of hair between his legs was as thick and yellow as that on his head, only it was a curly, golden fleece. Julia slid her fingers through it gently. His penis was smaller now, curled up—a thick, fat worm: when erect it was wondrous large, filling her as Derek's never had, and whereas he had never liked to let her look at him, even to making love with the lights off, Brad had lain under her eyes with pride in his maleness while she explored him, even as he had explored her, with the lights on, glad that she was worth looking at, happy to listen to him enumerating her delights and exploring every inch of them with hands, mouth, tongue.

Brad was a sensualist who luxuriated in the physical glories of the flesh. Derek had been a prude. With him, sex had been hasty, furtive and always done in the dark. A perfunctory caress here and there, then a quick, hasty mounting, a few convulsive thrusts and he had come, leaving her still at the starting gate. Brad had taken his time; led her slowly and deliriously upward to a peak which dizzied, before pushing her off into space. He had introduced her to the pleasures of the flesh; no, he had showered her with them. Never had she known a man so profligate in his giving.

He was deeply asleep, did not stir when she kissed, in gratitude, that part of him which had given her such undreamed of pleasure, but even as she buried her face in the golden fleece he muttered something she could not make out and heaved himself violently away from her, turning over onto his stomach. Odd, thought Julia. For a man she would have sworn had no sexual hangups, his refusal to let her do to him what he had so devastatingly done to her was a missing piece of the puzzle. Oh, well, she thought, he was more than satisfied with what I did do.

She realized she must find the bathroom. It was all mirrored. Naked, she faced a multiplicity of selves and realized the truth of them all, before standing under three shower heads in a driving spray of cool water for a gasping two minutes before lathering herself in silken bubbles in a cloud of steam. Wrapping herself in one of the sheet-sized towels she scrubbed her teeth with a new toothbrush before anointing her glowing body with handfuls of creamy liquid perfumed with Dioressence. She brushed her hair, skewering it into a pile on top of her head, then appropriated the silk kimono hanging behind the bathroom door. It was a man's, but she belted it tightly. In the bedroom, Brad still slept. Well, she thought on a giggle, he had used up a lot of energy.

She felt ravenous, longed for coffee. The clock said twelve noon. Brunch, then? But where? The living room was all tidy; no sign of her dress, but a definite aroma of coffee. Following her nose she found the kitchen. A set tray lay waiting on the butcher-block table. Wedgwood Napoleon Ivy china, Tiptree and Frank Cooper's Oxford marmalade, honey in the comb, butter, sugar, fresh cream. Coffee waited on its hot plate. She could also smell fresh bread. Opening a warming oven she discovered half a dozen morning-fresh croissants, and in the bank-safe-sized fridge, a jug of orange juice.

Carefully, she toted the heavy tray into the bedroom, laid it on the table by the window before drawing the curtains a little. A Grosvenor Street Sunday. People walking dogs, cars passing. The orange juice was deliciously cold; had never seen the inside of any tin. Then she poured her first cup of coffee, black and steaming, savouring the first mouthful after the citrus freshness of the juice. Delicious.

Everything, this morning was magnified, her senses acutely sharp. All of her was vibratingly, tinglingly alive! I am happy! she thought with stunned surprise. I am gloriously, ecstatically happy!

She demolished two fat croissants, thick with butter and heavy with chunky marmalade. She was beatifically licking her fingers when Brad stirred.

"Black, no sugar," Julia said promptly. She had already poured his juice.

"Back in a minute." He loped into the bathroom. When he came back, water-slicked and fresh, he clambered back into bed, piling pillows behind him, draining the juice thirstily, likewise the coffee. "Angel! Just the way I like to be woken." He eyed her over his cup. "But you are all bathed and fresh!"

The yellow robe against her hair was glorious.

"I borrowed your robe."

"Feel free. At that it looks better on you than on me."

"My dress has disappeared, you see."

"George will have taken it away to press."

"George—oh, the gnome."

[28]

"Come again?"

"The invisible provider of champagne, turner down of beds, maker of delicious coffee."

"That's George. He looks after the place—and me, when I'm here. He has a flat upstairs." He paused. "Do you want your dress? You are not planning on going?"

Julia's smile blazed. "I am not planning on anything."

"Good. Because I am." He handed her his cup. "How about a refill—and a cigarette."

She provided both. He patted the bed. "Come sit. We have to talk."

"That will make a change," Julia observed.

"Sassy wench," he grinned. "But I like you."

"I'd gathered that," Julia said modestly. "What did you want to talk about?"

"Us. Last night. Today. Tomorrow."

"All right."

"*You* are all right."

"Never better," Julia grinned impudently.

"Oh, you were marvelous."

"No—*you* were."

His smile was vanity gratified. Yes, thought Julia. He would expect straight A's. But then, didn't he deserve them?

"Didn't I say I was right about you?"

"How?"

"Your mouth." He traced it with his fingers. "A dead giveaway; doesn't go with the rest of you."

The gray eyes were clear as water. "I thought you had taken all of me."

His eyes adored her. "Even without a scrap of makeup you are ravishing."

"So ravish me!"

"And you said *I* was insatiable!"

He put down his coffee cup, drew her into his arms, settled her comfortably. "We have the whole day. I like to spend a whole day in bed—if it is with a woman."

"You've done it before," Julia said lightly.

"Many times. Haven't you?"

"Not with a woman!"

His eyes were intent, suddenly. "No—but with a man."

"No."

[29]

It was the right answer. He was gratified. "Good. Another first time."

With you, everything is a first for me, Julia thought. Please God don't let it be the last.

"You smell nice," he said, sniffing.

"Contents—and compliments—of your bathroom. It has everything."

"Not quite. I have you."

"Several times!"

"And more to come."

Their eyes met and they both laughed.

"You read my mind!" he said contentedly. Then, with a little frown: "I can't read yours yet, though . . . Your deeps are very deep."

"Well, you don't know me yet, do you?"

"Only in the biblical sense." He paused. "But in my experience it is possible to know somebody that way as you would never get to know them otherwise." Another pause. "You got to know me. In fact—sometimes I had the feeling you were ahead of me." His tone said he was not used to that.

"Only because you so clearly showed me the way."

"I did!" False surprise but deep pleasure. His ego was showing, but Julia's new, relaxed woman-self was able to handle it all, now.

"More coffee, I think." As she turned from him his hands seized the trailing sash and pulled; it came apart, allowing the robe to slip from her shoulders.

"Draw the curtains," he ordered. "That's better . . . I want to look at you."

The light was behind her as she advanced toward the bed, carrying a cup in each hand, the glow of the sun on yellow silk bathing her body in a flaring radiance. Brad's eyes matched it. "You have a glorious body. Renoir would have adored you."

"Better him than Modigliani," demurred Julia lightly, but expanding under his adoring eyes.

"When you came into the room Thursday night I couldn't believe my eyes! You certainly know how to make an entrance."

"So do you!"

He seized her in his arms. "Oh, come to bed!" he exclaimed joyfully. "I can't get enough of you."

THEY SPENT THE REST OF THE DAY in bed—talking, making endless, seamless, sensuous love, drinking wine, sleeping, waking to make love

[30]

again. It was the most intensely experienced day of Julia's life: the sex increasing in power and caliber as they became even more deeply attuned to each other. When finally they left the bed to shower—together—this turned into the most erotic encounter yet, water on skin arousing them to new paroxysms of sensuality. Then, sated unto exhaustion, they dressed—Julia's clothes having been returned looking brand-new—and went out to dinner, this time to a basement restaurant with red-checked tablecloths and candles in wine bottles, where they ate steaming platefuls of risotto al salto, both voraciously hungry, and drank a couple of bottles of wine. Then Brad drove her home to Kensington and stayed the night.

She was gone when he awoke on Monday morning, but on the bedside table was a Yale key. He stretched, bonelessly replete. Oh, yes, had he been right about this one! All that cool sophistication overlaying a whirlpool of passion. That body had been as voluptuous as had been hinted by her dress. The ripeness is all indeed, he thought smugly. But in the meantime, he had a day to get through.

She had left coffee waiting, and the water was boiling when he ran a bath. She had even provided him with a razor and shaving cream! There had been no trace of a man's presence on his first visit. He was whistling as he let himself out.

He called her at her office that afternoon to say he would be late picking her up; a meeting was taking longer than expected but he would be by about eight. It was nearer nine when he turned up, but the table was set and something smelled appetizing. And it was raining again. What the hell, he thought, one night in. But he was unprepared for the excellence of the meal she set before him.

"But you can cook!" he exclaimed, savoring the succulence of the veal in its sauce of white wine and capers.

"I can do a lot of things."

His gaze was thoughtful. "Yes, I guess you can."

That night, she sensed a subtle change in his lovemaking. It was still skilled, still passionate, still wholly centered on her pleasure, but there was a new dimension to it: tenderness. And he did not talk, as he had done before, telling her what he was going to do and why. He was silent, bemused, straining to reach the ultimate for both of them and, once he had succeeded, holding her afterward, cradled against him, making her feel cherished and vitally important.

He had a long-standing dinner engagement on Tuesday, but he turned up around midnight looking taut and somewhat strained. Julia did not question, only took him to bed. Just as they were drifting into sleep he murmured drowsily: "You are a marvelous woman, Julia. I am so glad I found you."

On Wednesday night, their last night, when he came in he handed Julia a small package. "Not to be opened till Christmas," he instructed. He took her back to the dining club. Their beginning—and their ending. But this time, Julia was conscious of strain. There were a lot of silences. Not uncomfortable, or awkward. Just—silences. She was aware of an intentness in his gaze, puzzlement in his eyes, but his face was always the attentive, devoted one she had become used to. That was what made him so irresistible, she decided. She had been wrong to condemn him as a nonbeliever. While he was with a woman he was her acolyte; made his time with her feast days dedicated to her worship. Once they were over—well, there was always another goddess, another fiesta. It was not women per se he worshiped; it was the woman he was with.

Later that night, having made slow, lingering love, they were lying in one of their silences when Brad suddenly reached out to switch on the lamp he had not long before switched off, remaining propped on one elbow, staring down at her with that intent, studying look she had noticed before. At her own, questioning look: "I just want to look at you—fix the image." He pulled back the covers, let his eyes travel the length of her, from the burnished hair, now loose and spreading over the pillows, to the rosy-tipped, full-bloom breasts; on past the swelling indentation of her waist and hips to the rounded yet columnar thighs, the triangle of silky fleece between them as red as her hair, the endless length of legs ending in long but narrow, high-arched feet.

Julia lay quiet under his eyes, willing her body not to clench because the look in his eyes was suddenly unbearable. He ought not to be looking at her like that. He was departing from the script, ad-libbing his own lines. The curtain was meant to fall on a last witty line meant to provoke laughter, not tears; their starring vehicle had been a sophisticated slice of life, not an intensely felt, seriously meant drama. She forced herself to look up at him, gave him a warm, contented smile when his eyes came back to her face, holding back with relentless self-discipline the tears that pricked behind her eyes; thankful for her years of practice at concealing her feelings. She saw his own lids veil his eyes as he laid his head, with a wordless murmur, between her breasts. She stroked the thick blond hair, trying to convey a warmth that was casual but not deeply felt, when what she wanted to do was let loose a sudden, swamping tenderness. After a while, she reached out and once more switched off the lamp.

[32]

It was dawn when he turned to her again, lying awake. She had not slept much, dozing fitfully, knowing he was awake too, but giving no indication.

"One last time," he said, in a curiously plangent voice. "My marvelous, beautiful Julia . . ."

It was like nothing that had gone before; he was so tender as to be reverent, worshiping her as if she were, indeed, a goddess, and it reached an intensity that was so exquisite Julia felt her nerve endings were being pinched; left them both silent and trembling, holding each other tight, faces hidden as though afraid to reveal what they felt.

That was not just sex, Julia thought shakily. That was love—or something like it.

HE DROVE HER TO THE OFFICE, but not right up to the door. Julia was composed, had herself in hand. What she wanted to do was hurl herself against him and beg him not to go. What she did was smile and say mischievously: "I am so glad you decided to go to that housewarming."

His own smile did not reach his eyes. Their blue-green was darker, as though a storm were coming. "As I am glad you decided to give me the benefit of the doubt." He took her hand, kissed its palm. "We had ourselves a ball, didn't we?"

"Several times." Her laugh covered the break in her voice, but the relief in his eyes knifed her.

"You are a marvelous woman, Julia."

"You are a superman."

"I enjoyed you so very, *very* much. I hope you enjoyed me."

Feeling hysterical: "Likewise," Julia managed to return.

Once more he kissed both palms, folding her fingers back on them.

"Have a good flight," she said quickly, feeling her smile start to break. She got out of the car, forcing herself not to run, closed the door carefully and walked—don't run, she told herself fiercely—away from him. She did not look back.

WHEN SHE GOT HOME that night, a florist's basket crammed with long-stemmed roses had been placed outside her flat. No card, but she knew who they were from. She took them in, stood them in the hall where it was coolest and they would last longest. Then she went to the drawer where she had put Brad's present. Christmas was still more than nine months away, but she could not wait that long. She tore off the gay wrapping paper. An Asprey's box. Raising its lid she found a miniature

[33]

black cat, exquisitely fabricated out of black pearls, with emeralds for eyes and the bow at its throat. A reference to the bow at the neck of her black dress and his affectionate naming of her as "Pussycat." She stood looking at it for a long time, then shutting the box she put it back in the drawer.

She had never been paid off before. It felt strange. *She* felt strange. Shaky and hollow and missing something. Like her heart. And it was not as though she had given it, either. He had taken it with him. Number one thousand, she thought numbly. A nice, round number. Lots of zeroes. Think of it as Chris told you to, she thought desperately. An experience. Be grateful for it. He has taught you much. But what a way to learn, she thought painfully. What a hell of a way to learn.

SHE WAS SITTING in numb silence, listening to the emptiness of her life, when the phone rang. She leaped for it. It was Chris.

"Want some company?"

"How did you know?"

"I know you, sweetie. I'll be right over."

She took one look at Julia and said: "You lost!"

"Utterly routed."

"He got to you?"

"Right where it hurts, and, oh, Chris, does it hurt."

"I warned you: you left it far too late, which is always when it hits hardest." To Julia's stiff, suffering face: "I take it, then, that he will not be coming back."

"It was never mentioned."

"Then he isn't."

Chris made for the drinks trolley. "A little fortifying while we conduct the postmortem. In fact, let's get stoned! My own ankles are twisted from that rocky road I'm struggling up with Tony. Let's drown our sorrows. What's this?"

Julia glanced across. "Oh—Jack Daniel's—bourbon. Brad drinks it."

Chris read the label. "God almighty! Ninety proof! This should petrify us!" She poured two hefty slugs. "To men—the bastards!" she said, before downing hers. When she had coughed and spluttered and regained her breath: "Whew! That's liquid dynamite! Goes with the rest of him?"

Julia nodded.

Chris sat down. "Well, at least you started at the top. I had to work my way up. Not many women hit the jack—or should I say sex—pot first time."

[34]

"It only means you've that much further to fall."

"Which is what you've gone and done?" Commiseratingly: "I can see he is all over you."

"God, I wish he was!" Julia swigged her Jack Daniel's.

"That's the way!" encouraged Chris. "Let's loosen our girdles and tell all."

"I told you before it began: I knew it would leave me hanging, but you were right about one thing. It *was* because of Derek I steered clear of men. He turned me off the whole bit."

"And Brad turned you on? Well, love, nature abhors a vacuum, you know. First chance that Mother gets she fills it—and you don't get asked what you'd like, either."

"I think I knew—subconsciously—that I was too—vulnerable. Capable of falling too hard too quickly. Emotionally immature."

"Well, you haven't exactly majored in experience."

Julia got up restlessly. "But it's all so—so stupid, Chris! I don't *know* him! Well—in one way . . ."

"Sexually? And in that way he made you privy to his all?"

"It was like nothing I've ever known," Julia said in a faraway voice. "Derek was useless, he just hadn't the slightest idea. Brad knows it all—and gave it all to me. At least I have learned what it is all about, but, God, Chris, am I paying for it!"

"We all have to pay up sooner or later—and look what you got for it! He sounds like the kind of a guy I've offered my eyeteeth for!"

"But I'm the one on the bonfire!"

"Even so, I wish *I* had ever had a Brad."

Chris got up to pour more bourbon. "What you are suffering from is a late awakening—the worst kind. You left it far too long. Ripe for the picking."

"Reaping, you mean. He's sliced me off at the root!"

"I told you that you should have availed yourself of the ample opportunities you've had! You'd have those calluses by now. You were newborn-babe virginal, love—emotionally, that is. It is Brad who has really taken your virginity. There is a hell of a sight more to that than losing your hymen, you know."

"Don't I," Julia said bitterly. She went to the drawer. "I got paid off too."

"Wow!" Chris breathed. "Asprey's yet!"

"For services rendered."

"No." Chris was decisive. "That's usually a check. This shows taste and thought and not a little appreciation." Openly envious. "You really did hit the jackpot, didn't you? And at first try!"

"The only one you ever get with him."

"So go and look for another one. Don't—repeat *don't*—sit and brood; that's strictly for hens." Chris drew Julia down onto the sofa. "Look, love, every affair has its own self-destruct built into it. A lot of them are straight 'Mission: Impossible'! You read the instructions on yours before you burned the tape: 'Good for a certain time only. Enjoy while you can; not reusable'. So you did—and he did. Now what you have to do is take your experience in both hands and go looking for someone on whom you can use it."

"I don't have your resilience."

"Oh, I've been bounced against so many walls I've no corners left—just angles." Quite firmly: "Take my advice: go find yourself another lap—and what's in it. Sort of hair of the dog. But no curs, mind."

Julia had to laugh. Chris was always a tonic.

"That's better. Now, let's have another one for the road. Mine's uphill all the way."

Julia went to bed in a haze of alcohol and exhortation. Chris should know. She'd been to the fire so many times she was a candidate for plastic surgery. Julia had never been able to stand the heat. Not for her being consumed by passion for another human being. Oh, no? asked her mind snidely. Then why are you mooning around like a lovesick teenager?

Because that's what I am, she told herself bitterly. I should have been doing this when I was seventeen. But I'll get over it. I will! I have to. You'll see. Once I get back into the old routine I'll be as good as new.

ONE NIGHT, about two weeks later, there was a spring storm. A powerful gale and torrential rain. It woke Julia, and as she stirred to consciousness she felt something behind her, something warm and solid. Brad! her heart sang. Then as she awoke completely she realized it was Willum; his "Chirrup" was sleepily grumpy. He had wandered in one day, inspected the place and decided to take up residence. Julia had named him Willum, after Pussy Cat Willum, and because it was a connection with Brad, who had called her "Pussycat." He had left his basket because of the storm, sought out her bed, seeking comfort and a presence. She put out a hand to stroke him. He was large and black with a white shirtfront and paws; under her hand he was a smoothly running engine, butting his head into her hand. You and me both, Willum, Julia thought.

She was still not yet cured; still wanting Brad, still missing him. Well, so it was taking longer than she had expected. It would still pass. Nothing lasted forever. Thank God, she thought, turning over, feeling Willum settle himself snugly against her. But as she drifted off to sleep again, she pretended it was Brad.

HE HAD LEFT LONDON with an unfamiliar feeling of regret underlying his contentment. Julia Carey's effect had been that of a tranquilizer, dulling the edge of his restlessness. She had turned out to be the least demanding yet most challenging woman he had met so far; had given him a game such as he had not enjoyed these many years, as well as the respite he badly needed; made him feel he was up to facing what lay waiting for him back home.

But he had not thought to find her still in his mind weeks afterward; not expected to find himself wanting—needing—more of the same. Once had always been enough; too many others waiting to be enjoyed. Why was it, then, that Julia Carey kept smoking around in his brain, like that perfume she wore—haunting, suggestive? She would keep materializing at the most unexpected moments: like when he was in bed—and inside another woman—and the feel of her—slender to the point of emaciation—made him contrast her unfavorably with the rounded, womanly warmth of Julia. Or when the frantic fever of another—all claws and teeth—made him recall the passionate yet unfrantic giving of Julia. She had never gone wild. He had always been conscious, even when he had her on the edge and could feel himself going, knowing there was no way to stop it now, that though she had given unstintingly of herself, there was still, deep inside her, some closed-off portion not yet open to him, and which, try as he might, had remained shut. Maybe that was why he was unable to file her away, in the past where she belonged, so as to be able to concentrate on the present, even the future.

He kept remembering how she had walked away from him that last morning. She had not looked back, had made him feel, uneasily, that for the first time he had not won a game. Yet she had been so bloody marvelous; so satisfying to be with, not only to have sex with, but to be with, talk to, or not talk to, it didn't matter. And it nagged at him that she had not asked, as they inevitably did, if she would see him again.

He had been aware from the start, of course, of a ruthless self-discipline. Which was no doubt why he now felt he had not succeeded

[37]

in breaking it down. He had always been conscious of a cool mind, even in the midst of their most heated exchanges. And while he liked independence in women, he didn't like them to be *that* independent! Like not needing him. What he wanted, he realized with astonishment tempered by a frowning unease, was a second bite of the apple. Most unusual. Normally once was enough. They came, they saw but as yet no woman had conquered. Yet he was rarin' to go at another chance to fracture that unblemished self-control, smash that smooth façade and see what really lay at the heart of her, because he knew for sure that she never really had come out from behind the smoke screen of those incredible eyes.

It surprised him, but it also confirmed his conviction that life still held much to be discovered. Especially about women. And with Julia Carey he was well aware that he had done no more than scrape the surface. It won't do, he decided finally, when the niggle became an itch which became an uncontrollable urge. I've got to go back and finish it properly; if I don't it will get worse, not better. And there are so many others just waiting to be found . . .

So he picked away at a slight snag in the negotiations he had gone to London to complete; eventually managed to make a slight hole which, his mother said irritably, he would just have to go back and mend—and properly, this time.

"Don't worry," he assured her truthfully. "This time I will do it right."

IT WAS JUST 10 A.M. when he arrived at Grosvenor Street, some six weeks after he had left it. He had a working lunch at 1 P.M. which would knit up the raveled sleeve of care. After that he was free. He showered, changed, drank a cup of coffee while he made his calls. When they were done he stood with his hand on the receiver, fingers tapping. He could call her . . . She could come here this afternoon. No. He found he wanted to have the element of surprise. The memory of that brisk "Don't call us, we'll call you" walk of hers still rankled. It had always been his policy to leave them laughing—but never at him. No: he wanted to savor the shock on her face when she opened her door.

But she was not at home. He was so put out he was furious. His women were always there, waiting. Penelopes all. He had made no other plans; these three days were to be spent with her . . . Damn. Could be she was working late, of course . . . He would give her till—he checked his watch—eight-thirty; an hour and a half. If she was not back by then, then the hell with her.

[38]

It was 9 P.M. when he drove back up Hornton Street. Still no lights. So be it. He would call Angela.

She was delighted to see him; ready and waiting and as full of gossip as ever, but he found his attention wandering; wished she would for God's sake shut up and let him think. Where was Julia? And with whom was Julia? By eleven-thirty he could bear it no longer.

This time the lights were on, but there was a car outside. Even as he drew up on the opposite side of the street her front door opened and a man came out, making for the car. In the light of the streetlamp Brad could see he was about his own age; dark hair, walked with jaunty confidence. He could have been visiting the lower flat, of course, but the surge of jealousy Brad felt still brought a mist to his eyes.

He stabbed her bell as if using a knife. He heard the little click of the entry-phone and then her voice: crisp, a little laugh in the resigned: "Now what have you forgotten?"

"Not a thing. How about you?"

Silence. Surprise, surprise! he thought with savage glee. Then the door clicked and gaped. He pushed it open, took the stairs two at a time. Her flat door was open. Pushing it wide he strode in. She was not alone. Sitting in a chair by the fireplace, where Julia was standing with one hand on the mantel, was a rosily plump, Kewpie-doll blonde.

Damn! "Hello," he said easily, including the blonde, who looked from him to Julia and back again.

"And goodbye, in my case," she said promptly, making to rise.

"Don't rush on my account," he said, but looking at Julia.

"I wouldn't dream of it," she assured him throatily, "but I will on Julia's."

"Christine Barnes—Brad Bradford," Julia introduced.

He advanced, holding out a hand, which the blonde took, eyeing him up and down with evident—and growing—appreciation.

"The improper Bostonian," she murmured impudently, gentian eyes all sparkles and bright lights. Her interest was candid, openly admiring. A sumptuous piece of candy floss, he decided. Who knew about him. Which was his surprise. He would not have thought Julia the all-girls-together type. As if she read his thoughts: "Julia and I go way back," Chris explained.

"I know the feeling," he said, smiling down at her. She was not more than five feet; pouter pigeon-plump, all bust and bustle.

"I live only a few streets away," she went on, her eyes adding, And feel free to call.

Fun, Brad thought, but no depths to drown in. Still, you could have lots of fun playing around in the shallows . . .

"I'll see you down," Julia said to Chris.

At the door: "I see why you had your doubts," Chris commented thoughtfully. Then, firmly: "Smother them. With that one, the pillows will be to hand . . ." Her look was one of honest envy. "I see what you meant. He *is* gorgeous, isn't he? Could I sink my teeth into him—except from the way he was looking at you he wouldn't even notice." But Julia was frowning. "Oh, come on now—no second thoughts? I thought you had taken the big fall."

"I've still got the bruises." Julia's frown was uneasy. "*And* only just got myself back under control."

"That's your trouble," Chris warned. "You can't stand the very thought of not controlling everything—and everyone. Just remember, whether you do or not, the games go on."

"I've already lost once."

"Just so long as you don't let him know it! And he must have enjoyed the game. Why else is he back for a return match?"

"That," Julia agreed darkly, "is what I'd like to know!"

But her face in the hall mirror showed her eyes that looked as if they had been loaded with belladonna, and her legs, as she went slowly back up the stairs, felt boned and rolled.

He held out his hands as she went in, his eyes crinkling in the way she remembered so endlessly. "Pussycat, pussycat, where have *you* been?" he chided.

"Well, the Queen has been at Windsor . . ."

He laughed as he pulled her into his arms. "Oh, how I've missed you! I hope you've missed me."

"I never expected to see you again."

That brought a scowl. "Why are you back in London?" she went on.

"Unfinished business." Something in the way he said it made her eye him narrowly.

He dropped his hands, stood back. "Did I interrupt something?" She looked puzzled.

"The man I saw leaving just now . . ."

Why, he's jealous! she thought, stunned, before her heart snapped its chains and went soaring. "I do have other friends."

"But is he a boyfriend?"

"How many girlfriends do you have?"

She held his eyes; his were angry. "Okay, so now we are even," he said curtly. Had he been wrong? She was so damned difficult to read.

[40]

But so desirable. That sweater and those pants showed off that luscious figure to perfection. "You don't seem very pleased to see me," he accused.

"Of course I am!" Keep it cool, she thought. Let *him* dangle and let *him* hope.

She was giving him what he termed her "white look": scarifyingly dispassionate. Yet those same eyes could melt you down. He supposed that was what had him hooked. Nobody looking at the perfect camellia would believe it could open to reveal the most luscious of hearts.

"You really are glad to see me?"

"Of course I am!" She relented, raised herself on tiptoe to brush his mouth with her own, but he caught her to him passionately. Is this what has me in thrall? Julia wondered as she felt him down to toe and fingernails. Is it the leash of passion that holds me tethered? In which case, surely the thing to do is wear it thin. "Yes, you are glad to see me." He ended on a contented note, satisfied by her response. He turned to the clock. "It's early yet! Let's go out. I feel like celebrating."

He took her gambling, something else she had never done, could not bring herself to do, even now. She watched him, wincing as he stacked chips worth a quarter's salary on random numbers that had no meaning, seeing them raked away without a qualm. When he urged her to try she refused. "I couldn't! I don't have your cavalier attitude to money."

"Look, it's my money."

"Even more so."

She saw his face set, the lower lip thrust out, but she stood firm. He changed his sulk to a wheedle: "Come on—for once in your life let go of things. When's your birthday?"

"July."

"No, which date?"

"The twenty-seventh."

He stacked a pile of chips on the number nine. It won. Picking up the two stacks that were shoved across to him he thrust them into Julia's hands, ignoring her protests. "They are yours and that's that," he said, brooking no argument. There were so many that Julia could not hold them all; several slipped from her hands to the floor. As Brad bent to pick them up he knocked against a woman leaning over to place a bet.

"Do you mind!" the peanut-brittle voice snapped and then suddenly became Turkish delight. "Brad! My God, what a surprise! How are you?" She embraced him enthusiastically.

"Sally!"

She was thirtyish, tall, rapier-elegant in black and gold, stunning but hard-edged.

"It's been an age. Why didn't you call me—oh!" Her eyes flicked from him to Julia and back again. "I see: otherwise engaged, as always."

Sublimely ignoring that, Brad introduced the two women. "Julia Carey—Sally Armbruster."

They nodded briefly; smiled: opponents' smiles.

"How is everyone back home?" Sally asked sweetly. "Your mother?" Even more sweetly: "Caroline?"

"Fine, thanks." Brad's overheartiness was matched by his briefness.

"Do give them my best when you go back."

"Sure . . ." He turned to Julia. "Ready? Let's cash in, then."

"Oh, must you leave? I thought perhaps—a drink?"

"We've already been there, thanks. Nice to have seen you again, Sally." Purposefully, he drew Julia away.

The glance Sally Armbruster flicked at Julia was hard enough to cut. "Goodbye—and good luck." There was no doubt as to her meaning. Well, I don't know what her number was, Julia thought as Brad led her away, but she certainly has mine.

Outside: "Let's walk," Brad commanded. "You still can, in this town."

"But—the car!"

"They know where I live."

His mood had changed, though she had been aware of exposed edges all night. Now, it was as if someone had thrown sand in his gears and he was furious at having to wait for an overhaul. He took her hand as usual, but they walked quickly, and in silence.

Sally Armbruster was a family friend as well, then. She knew his mother. And Caroline. Whoever she was. His wife? A patrician-sounding name, redolent of horses and dogs and subscriptions to *Town & Country;* Friday concerts and tea at the Ritz. It brought home to Julia, with the force of a blunt instrument, how little she knew of him; how small was the world which enclosed the two of them; how many were the women he knew. Of whom she was just one. Her scruples should have been drawing on their gloves, ready to leave; what they did was sit there, being stared out of countenance by a rationality that said if it was not her it would be someone else. But later, that night, he made love to her as if there had never been a woman in his life before.

ON SATURDAY MORNING they slept late. As soon as Brad
Julia knew the mood was still on him. Very carefully she
edges, likening it to the weather: bright but cold, th
without warmth.

When he suggested—in a way that was an order—th
drive, she did not demur. Just so long as he worked off l
she saw the car she knew that was his intention. It was
much above ground level, wickedly rakish and its speed no doubt
straight bat-out-of-hell.

Which was the way he drove it as soon as they hit the A23. Julia hated
speed and had a dread of breaking the law. She was tense with the
expectation of flashing lights and a siren, but Brad obviously loved it.
His face wore an expression she was familiar with: ablaze with triumphant *exaltation*—the way he looked when in the throes of orgasm.

Which was when she began dimly to comprehend that sex was, to
him, a means of escape from something. Someone? That through it he
took risks and in doing so found release. Something drove him. Uneasily, Julia realized there was more to him than the uncomplicated playboy with his good looks and money. He was playing games, all right,
but she had not understood that they were a matter of life and death.

They ended up on the cliffs by the sea, which was slate-gray and
sullen. Julia stood looking out at it, breathing deeply and pleasurably.
She had been born by the sea; only when she left it had she realized
how much she loved and missed it. The wind tore her hair loose from
its pins, and she buried her face in the sable collar of the suede car coat
Brad had tossed at her with a careless "Here, this should fit you." A
woman's, of course.

"Careful!" Brad pulled her back from the very edge. "That's a long
fall." He peered over with a jumpy nervousness. "Obviously you have
a head for heights."

"Haven't you?" Julia would have thought him game for any danger.

They had tea in a little tea shop in Hove; buttered scones and toasted
tea cake, the tea the color of well-polished leather. It was filled with
elderly ladies in flowerpot hats, monocled gentlemen wearing button-
holes.

"Like Florida," Brad commented thinly, glancing around.

"Yes, Hove is where you retire to," agreed Julia.

"God forbid!" Brad observed disagreeably.

"It happens to us all, eventually."

"Not to me it won't!"

The final piece fell into place with a click. That was why he was

[43]

moving on, living hard and fast, changing his women with his
—and she had seen how many of them he had. Always a new
sensation to replace the one that palled; a new woman to replace the
one that bored. It was only, she now understood, that it was because
she had managed to retain his interest that he had returned for a
second game. *She* was his unfinished business.

That night he took her dancing. Like everything else he did, he did it
superbly. But he was unusually distrait, even broody. He puzzled her.
This was not the Brad she had remembered. There was a sense of
something simmering between them, and his mood kept changing with
the traffic lights. He could flash from high to low in seconds. When, as
Julia was changing back at her flat, she had been kept on the telephone
for some time, his face when she returned to him had been a thunder-
cloud. He did not like her attention straying.

And that night he was violently passionate, almost punishing her, as
though bent and determined to make her cry uncle. Which she did not.

At times, she longed to say impatiently: "Oh, do grow up!" even as
she knew that their relationship precluded such taken-for-granted candor. He had made it plain from the start that it was physical. Body
rules, okay?

On the Sunday morning, the telephone woke them. Brad answered.
"Sally!" He sounded surprised, slid a glance at Julia she could not
read, said: "Hold on, I'll ask her." Covering the mouthpiece with his
hand: "Sally Armbruster is asking us around for drinks. Want to go?"

Julia knew him well enough by now to know he did; had he not he
would have refused without consulting her.

"Why not?"

The Armbrusters lived on a square off the Kings Road. A long
drawing room held a dozen or so people, all of whom Brad knew,
especially the women, who more or less sealed him off. Julia was given
a drink, expected to circulate, make small talk; knew she was being
stared at, surmised, whispered over. She felt remote and disconnected;
as though her plug had been taken out of its socket.

She found herself standing by the long windows, gazing blankly out
at the square. Sally Armbruster saw her standing there, came over.
"Another drink?" She was stunning in honey-colored silk top and
culottes, her tawny hair brushed back like a lion's mane.

"Have you known Brad long?"

"No. I hardly know him at all."

"Oh, still in the preliminary stages." A feline smile. "I remember
that stage myself. A real virtuoso, isn't he? Prime stud. He'd fetch a

fortune in fees." Her smile revealed sharp teeth. "We have all been serviced at one time or another . . ." Her hand gestured to the women, but as she gazed at Brad Julia saw her teeth catch her lower lip. "Underneath the boyish exterior is an even more boyish interior. Still at the toy stage." A brittle laugh as she gestured to the women once more. "Discards, all of us."

Her cat's eyes surveyed Julia with frankly jealous curiosity. "I was curious about you, I hope you don't mind."

"Why should I?"

"I have my reason, believe me, which you will discover for yourself, in time. Brad is an experience which leaves its mark. He has the lightest of touches—oh, yes, the lightest." She fixed him with a long look that was a compound of baffled longing and undisguised hatred. "One of these days somebody will mark him, I devoutly pray and hope. The thought of seeing him bloodied and bowed . . ." She drew a sharp breath. Turning back to Julia: "You don't say much," she observed, "but I bet you know your lines." She sipped at her drink. "Tell me, is your hair really that color? If not, do tell me who does it."

"Courtesy of my mother," Julia said.

"Ah, yes, mothers . . ." Sally glanced back at Brad. "Brad has one of those; a remarkable lady—Lady Macbeth, I mean. Lady Hester Bradford could make the Gorgon cry uncle."

"*Lady* Hester?"

"Didn't you know? Brad's mother is A for Aristocracy, daughter of a marquis, no less. She was a Conyngham-Bradford—*very* grand; her husband was one of the American branch of the family—both lots being awash with money. She'd cut your throat at the hint of more than an interest on the part of Brad, then hang you up so as to catch every last drop of blood. She has already chosen Brad's life partner. God help *her.*" Her eyes surveyed Julia with wicked knowingness. "Why am I telling you all this? I suppose it is the Tinkerbell in me." The tawny eyes flared. "In your own good—or should I say bad—time, you will find out what I mean. Don't hate me for it, if you can."

"I don't hate easily."

"Something else you'll learn. He teaches you." A sneer made her mouth twist viciously.

"Even Caroline. She comes on like the original vestal virgin but even she steams at the ears around him. Mother quenches all flames—not that she gives a damn who Brad consigns to the bonfire; just so long as her darling boy doesn't get burned." Her look was mocking. "You could well be his last bonfire." A theatrical sigh. "But he gives such a

[45]

lovely light . . ." With a last nod at Julia's black cat and a "Mine was a lion," she moved gracefully away and down the room.

Julia went back to staring out of the window. She felt nothing. Only sad.

"What were you talking about for so long with Sally?" Brad asked, as they seated themselves at their table in Le Gavroche.

"You."

"She was a long time ago." And long forgotten, said his tone.

"You owe me no explanations."

"I wasn't about to give you one. I just—wanted you to know, that's all . . ."

"Why?"

"Because *I* know Sally."

As she knows you, thought Julia.

"She's one hundred percent pure bitch," Brad went on, "and jealous as hell; not like you."

When she made no comment: "You aren't, are you? Jealous, I mean."

"I never have been," Julia answered truthfully, not bothering to add that she had never had cause.

"Not even with your husband?"

"No."

"What went wrong, then?"

"We weren't suited."

"Why marry him in that case?"

"I didn't know it until I had."

"But you were in love with him?"

"I thought I was."

Brad moved restlessly as though her answers were not definite enough for his purpose—whatever that was.

"Do you think there is a difference between loving and being in love?" he asked next.

"Yes," Julia answered. "One is real, the other romantic."

The little stitch appeared. "For a person who keeps her emotions in cold storage how come you generate so much heat?" he asked, almost belligerently.

"Perhaps because I tend to be sparing in their use."

"Is that your way of telling I am too free with mine?"

"No. I don't think you use yours at all."

"Oh, Sally *has* been at work, hasn't she!"

[46]

"Sally has nothing to do with it."

"Then why are you being so unpleasant?"

"I was paying you the compliment of being honest."

"It's only complimentary when you are not on the receiving end."

The scowl deepened. "What was it you wanted from me?" he demanded roughly.

"What you were offering."

She saw the little muscles on either side of his mouth—that sensual, senses-provoking, fire-leaving trail of a mouth—bunch. "I trust it came up to your expectations?"

That was very sarcastic for him.

"I have no complaints."

"Well," he said (bitterly?). "I did ask for the benefit of the doubt." The last word came out savagely before he thrust a menu at her. "Let's get off this." It was an order. "Let's eat."

WHEN JULIA LOOKED at the little crystal clock she saw it was 4 A.M. The dark night of the soul. Which was no doubt why she was lying here examining hers.

She had gone carefully and painstakingly over the charts which her mind, that meticulous keeper of records, had marked scrupulously, even in the midst of the most ecstatic of physical delirium; had traced the rising graph, upward from the first symptoms of a rare physical attraction, the marked climb of feverish response, the peaks of gratification. She had weighed the evidence of her pleasure, plumbed the depths of her involvement and come up with the only diagnosis she could (or was willing to) make. Infatuation.

But even as her mind had presented its findings so it had disclaimed all responsibility; had she listened to it instead of being urged on by her body none of this would have happened. As it was, it warned her she was in a situation she would regret having created; that it was time she removed herself from the source of the infection, otherwise it would only get worse, with the danger of becoming a raging epidemic of that most dangerous of all terminal diseases: love.

Which scared the hell out of her. For *this* man? This selfish, callous, careless, immature playboy with a propensity to kiss and run? It was just not *her!*

Oh, no? returned her mind scornfully. How come he only has to touch you for your bones to melt, then?

Sex, she answered herself bluntly. I was starved and he was handy. That is not my understanding of love.

[47]

Define love, her mind returned caustically.

But before she could, the phone rang. Brad stirred but did not wake; he slept like the dead. Who on earth could be calling at four in the morning? And then she knew. His mother, of course.

The voice confirmed it: "Brad, darling . . . is that you?" Imperious, carrying, commanding.

Julia dug Brad in the ribs. "For you."

Still feeling the dig Brad took the receiver. "Brad Bradford . . . Mother!" He sat bolt upright. His surprise, Julia thought clinically, had been in the oven too long. "Fine, yes, all squared away . . . What? Now? Today?"

His dismay was also overdone.

"Well, if I have to . . . Sure, there's always that seven thirty-one."

A plane, Julia thought, to rescue him; take him away from a situation he no longer finds comfortable. She could feel herself receding from him with the speed of light. He replaced the receiver, raked his hands through his hair and sighed: "I've been called back home. Something's come up."

I know, thought Julia. Your boredom threshold. "What a pity," she said.

"I've got to be at Heathrow for six-thirty . . ." A quick glance at the clock. "And on that seven-thirty plane."

"Can I do it for you?" Julia found herself asking.

"You're a doll! Would you?" He bounced out of bed, relieved and smiling. There was to be no "one last time" this time.

She managed to get him a seat—first-class—while he showered. She could hear him whistling cheerfully through the sound of the water. When he was dressed he turned to her. "Quick is best," he said briskly. His kiss, too, was practiced rather than passionate. He was eager to be gone.

Then he was.

$$\boxed{2}$$

game. scheme to defeat another; trick, cunning device

ALTHOUGH EVERY WINDOW in the dining room had been raised, the Boston summer was winning hands down, and of the four women and four men at the dinner table, one of them, a relentlessly chic forty-three-year-old woman who spent her time and a great deal of money trying desperately to look thirty-three, was obviously wilting under its assault. Her flesh gleamed with a fine beading of moisture, and her hair, upswept for coolness, was damp at brow and nape.

"Mother, you will simply *have* to install air conditioning," she complained at last, and yet again. "I simply cannot stand this Turkish bath the house becomes every summer."

"I have lived in this country for forty-five years," Hester Bradford returned imperturbably, "and I have never let the weather affect me in any way. Perhaps if you exercised a little mind over matter, my dear Bitsy, as a change from exercising your ire, it would benefit you in the long run."

"I am used to living in air-conditioned comfort," Bitsy retorted.

[49]

"I cannot abide it. It is the cause of more chills than can be counted, and even had I not to be careful because of my asthma I would still not have it in the house. You should have lived at Arun fifty years ago; then you would have had something to complain about." Lady Hester's thin lips smiled in fond reminiscence and Brad, seated at the other end of the table, raised his eyes to heaven. Noticing it, his fiancée, Caroline Norton, sitting on his left, kicked his ankle.

"Arun has changed a lot in the past fifty years, Mother," Brad's elder sister said. "It may be cool in summer thanks to the thickness of the walls, but it must have been hell in winter before the central heating was installed."

"Namby-pamby nonsense," Lady Hester dismissed. "I thought you had more stamina, Abigail."

"There is certainly more of her to look after," Brad said on a grin, but affectionately. He did not particularly like his younger sister, but he was very fond of his elder. Abby, he was fond of saying, was the Rock of Gibraltar.

"Since you never tire of telling people I weighed in at eleven pounds, is it any wonder?" Abby asked, but placidly. Facially, she was very like her sister—they were Bradfords both, down to the beaky nose and lantern jaw, but there the resemblance ended. At forty-four, Abigail Amory was as absentmindedly dowdy as her sister was obsessively fashionable. They both had the Bradford hair; gilt blond and heavy, but whereas Bitsy's was attended to by her hairdresser every day, Abby's was always skewered carelessly atop her large head with pins which kept falling out, causing her to tuck long lengths behind her ears. Bitsy was in Norell Parma violet with pearls; Abby's fifteen-year-old port wine velvet had a rent in the hem where a good six inches of stitching had long been undone, and a rip under the arm. But the rubies in her ears and at her throat were worth a king's ransom. Her tact was worth even more, Brad thought, as he heard her change the subject.

"So how was your trip?" she asked him.

"Tiring."

"You mean you worked nights as well as days?" Bitsy inquired with spiteful innocence.

"Be careful, Caroline," she went on mockingly, to Brad's fiancée. "Where Brad is concerned it is not an X which marks the spot; it is a woman."

"Oh, I know they stand in line," Caroline smiled easily.

[50]

"You mean lie in wait," Bitsy purred, lowering her individually planted eyelashes.

"I don't blame them," Caroline said simply. "I lay in wait for Brad myself."

And that, thought Bitsy, is the understatement of this or any year.

"Caroline knew a good thing when she saw one," Lady Hester said fondly. "As did Brad, of course," she added graciously. "And as the wedding is now only three months away we must finalize the last arrangements tonight. Did you have a word with your mother, Caroline, as I asked?"

"Oh, yes, Lady Hester. She said for you to go right ahead along the lines you suggested."

"Ordered, more like," Bitsy muttered under her breath. Next to her, her husband said from behind teeth bared in a smile: "For God's sake don't start any more trouble tonight. Your brother's home, your mother is happy, so please leave her that way. More important, leave me too."

As the butler appeared behind Bitsy with the wine he put his hand over his wife's glass. "No more for Mrs. Adams, Parkes."

Bitsy glared, but he turned his head and met her affronted stare with one of his own, which made her subside. Drexel Adams angry was a Drexel Adams to avoid. So she sulked instead.

"Did you get a chance to see John Holgate while you were in London?" Seth Amory asked. "I dropped him a line to say you'd be in town and to call you."

"I'm afraid I didn't have time to see Professor Holgate," Brad admitted. "It was all go this trip, Seth. Meetings all day from breakfast on, and more than a few went on into the night."

Bitsy laughed. "Is that what they are calling it now?"

Lady Hester turned her head to look at her younger daughter. She had the sea-change eyes she had bequeathed to her son, and they could be as cold as the North Atlantic when she chose. Right now they were frozen over.

"This dinner is to welcome my son and your brother back from a long and arduous trip abroad," she said in the measured tones of a hanging judge. "If you have no wish to participate in that welcome you have my permission to leave."

Bitsy attempted to stare her mother down and, as usual, failed. She flushed instead, threw her brother a look that sank right between his eyes, and subsided into smoldering silence.

"Now then, Seth." Lady Hester turned to her favorite son-in-law.

"This Professor Holgate, is he related to the Holgates of Winchester? My father was a friend of old General Holgate . . ."

"What's up with Bitsy?" Brad asked Abby, under cover of his mother's carrying voice.

"What has always been up with Bitsy," Abby answered calmly. "A severe dose of jealousy."

Brad's laugh was harsh. "Home sweet home. Nothing has changed."

"In six weeks?"

"I wouldn't expect it to in six years."

"If Mother has her way the next sixty will be frozen in amber."

Another harsh laugh. "Who is there in this world dares to cross her?"

Abby flicked a glance his way. "You are the only person who can make her change her mind."

"That's an entirely different thing. I learned at an early age never to thwart her." He picked up his glass, drained it, looked across to Parkes, who came over to refill it. "Maybe that's her trouble," he said gloomily. "Nobody ever has."

"Not if they know what is good for them," Abby agreed.

"What about what is good for *her?*" Brad asked.

Abby turned majestically to look at him in some surprise. "Have you been indulging in the rarity of serious thought?" she asked, wide-eyed.

Brad grinned. "All right, so tease if you like, but I do think now and then, you know."

"I should hope so. You wouldn't be mother's emissary if you didn't."

Brad drank more wine. "You mean hatchet man."

Abby let go a gentle sigh. "Ah, I see . . . More executions, this trip?"

"I'm tired of saying 'Fire,' " Brad said shortly.

"Mother is sixty-six," Abby said gently. "And her arthritis gives her a great deal of pain about which she does not complain. You know her; if she were able to do she *would* do. It is because she can't that you do." She paused. "Besides, you've known since you were old enough to know anything that you were heir to the throne."

Brad was staring into his glass. "What do I do to abdicate?" he asked, and in a way that had his sister looking at him sharply.

"Bad trip?" she commiserated. He was looking hagridden, she thought concernedly. There was a look in the sea-colored eyes that seemed aimed at the past; at something which had not only happened but left an unforgettable memory. A woman, probably. Didn't they say that a man's last months of freedom often provided the most memorable experiences of his life? He had only three months left as a bachelor. Obviously he was living them to the full.

"I've known better," Brad was saying. He was staring across the table at Caroline.

"Everything all right there?" Abby asked *sotto voce.*

"If it wasn't I would never know," Brad said sardonically. "Not *before* the ceremony."

"Look, if marriage is not what you want—"

"It's what Mother wants. Would *you* tell her otherwise?"

"She wouldn't listen," Abby answered simply. "You are the only one she has ever taken any kind of note of. She would tell me not to waste her time with nonsense or my own by making a fool of myself. But if *you* told her—"

"As you said, I'm the heir. It's incumbent upon me."

"But not the sort of sacrifice you care to make?"

Brad grinned. "You know me, Abby. I've never quite seen myself as a married man."

Abby grinned. "No; it's the women who've done that."

A shadow crossed the handsome face, but so briefly Abby wondered if she had been mistaken. "I'm not complaining," he said lightly.

No, thought Abby, and I wonder why. Brad had been spoiled rotten all his life and was not backward in coming forward with complaints. Why, then, did she get this feeling that he was suffering? And from something he could not tell anyone. Being fourteen years older than he was, she had been his buffer against his mother's possessiveness and his other sister's vindictiveness; they had always been very close. Abby had been the one he told his secrets to, confessed his troubles to, turned to for advice. Now, her instincts—and inside the two-hundred-pound bulk was an acutely sensitive and perceptive woman—told her that he was deeply troubled; that something occupied his thoughts and it was nothing to do with either his mother, his fiancée or his forthcoming loss of freedom. Yet something had been lost, she thought. When he thought he was unobserved he had a funny, puzzled, almost frightened look on his face. She had noticed it the moment she entered the house tonight. She glanced at her mother, still holding forth to Abby's husband. If she had noticed, no layer would have been left unprobed in her efforts to discover the whys and the wherefores. Which means, Abby thought, that she has not because around her he has been careful not to show it. Which also means, she thought with a suddenly hollow feeling, that it is serious . . .

Oh, my God, she thought prayerfully. Not Mother in one of her fits. I

don't think I could stand it. They scared the hell out of me as a child.
She could not repress a shiver at the remembrance of her mother in the
grip of one of her asthmatic seizures; the frantic rasp of laboring lungs,
the bulging eyes, the flailing hands. It had terrified her, and like Bitsy,
she had gone to extraordinary lengths to prevent them from occurring
once they realized that they were always brought on by emotional
upsets: in other words, by Lady Hester losing her temper.

All three Bradford children had tiptoed through childhood constantly terrified of causing their mother's ire, and thus wholly in sub-
jection to her monstrous emotional blackmail, most especially Brad.
Now, it made Abby distinctly uneasy to realize that if Brad was in some
kind of trouble and was not, as normal, turning to his mother for help,
then it was obviously something his mother would not like. Which also
meant, Abby thought on a sinking heart, that when she eventually did
find out, it would bring on the fit of her life . . .

HER EARLIEST ONES had been asthmatic; so bad that her doctors had
insisted on clean, country air. Her early life had therefore been spent
entirely at Arun, the vast Vanbrugh pile in Sussex that was the seat of
the marquises of Arun, her father being the sixth of his line. She was
his only child, her mother having died in the effort of giving birth to
her brother, who had also failed to survive the experience, and her
father never having remarried—entirely because his daughter prevented it. She wanted him all to herself. She adored him; blindly,
besottedly, with impassioned possessiveness. A big, blond (like all the
Conyngham-Bradfords) man, with the sea-colored eyes his daughter
inherited and passed on to her own children, along with his height and
his temper.

Lady Hester Mary Clarissa Conyngham-Bradford had a temper that
terrified, allied to an iron will and an imperious manner which brooked
no opposition. She was a dangerous person to cross, as the women
who tried to marry her father soon found out, but she could also
render you helpless with enormous charm—if it suited her. The only
person she could not manipulate was her father, but this only served to
make her love him more. She thrilled, with the admiring thrill of the
dominant, to a dominance stronger than her own, and worshiped him
for it. He was the prime concern of her life. Coming a close second was
Arun.

Hester gloried in her ancestry and its visible form, shaped in marble
and, from its hill, dominating the Sussex countryside for miles around.
It was huge, its interior as rich as its exterior: heavy with gilt and

[54]

carving, huge frescoes and echoing, marble floors. Its lofty corridors were lined with marble statuary, set among gargantuan furniture covered in crimson velvet, the walls behind hung with sumptuous Rubens nudes—of a size with their surroundings—glorious Titians, Veroneses and Caravaggios.

Hester had run it all. Every morning she did her rounds, attended by the house steward and the housekeeper, beginning with the lineup of servants in the great hall. Woe betide a spot on an apron, a crooked cap, a pair of grubby hands. She would then draw on a white glove, and this she would run across tabletops, window ledges, chairbacks as she made her progress through the rooms. That done, she would confer with the housekeeper, approve the day's menus, receive the wine steward and consult with the butler.

Her father left her alone to manage everything once it became obvious that she had a bent for organization bordering on genius. He would arrive from London on a Friday morning and say casually that he had invited a dozen or so people for the weekend. By the time they arrived, in time for tea, their every whim had been catered to: masses of freshly cut flowers everywhere, bedrooms stocked with magazines, books and cigarettes; unwrapped cakes of soap in basin and bath. They would not eat the same dish twice, and their individual preferences would be observed as to the kind of morning tea, the blend of coffee. The tennis courts would have been rolled, the croquet lawn mowed, the swimming pool cleaned and the horses groomed, and at dinner that night, Hester would preside over the hundred-foot-long dinner table, wearing the fabulous Conyngham-Bradford pearls, or the Russian emeralds, or the Indian rubies.

The Conyngham-Bradfords were enormously rich. In the late eighteenth century, the then marquis, desperately in debt, had married Clarissa Conyngham, the only child of an East India nabob. In return for her fortune, he had agreed to add her name to his for their descendants to bear.

At twenty-one, Hester Bradford was possessed of the confident aplomb of a woman of thirty-five, concealing behind her classic features the brain of a robber baron. Her favorite reading was the *Financial Times*, and it was on her advice that her father relied concerning his investments.

Presented at court when she was eighteen, she would have none of the young men who clustered round her, caught by her icy beauty as well as her fabulous fortune. She dismissed them contemptuously. Idiots all. They bored her, invoked only contempt. Her father was the only man she wanted, and she was determined to keep him. Especially when the Honorable Mrs. Helene Fortesque appeared on the scene.

She was a widow, fortyish, a *jolie laide* but sensuously sexy; she only had to stand still and breathe for the men to come running from all sides. The marquis was no exception. When he took to inviting Mrs. Fortesque down every single weekend and compounded his error by turning blind eyes and deaf ears to Hester's subtle disparagements and sly insinuations, she knew it was time to act.

The marquis was a bruising rider; it was the fact that Helene Fortesque was a superb horsewoman that had first endeared her to him. She was game for anything, he told his daughter enthusiastically; but all she saw was Mrs. Fortesque's game.

So one evening, when her father told her that next morning he would be riding with Mrs. Fortesque *à deux*, Hester realized from his manner that this was the day he intended to ask the gold-digging bitch to marry him. Over my dead body, she thought, except it was Mrs. Fortesque's demise she had in mind.

On making her rounds, she also made it her business to check that all was well with the horse that lady would ride; a high-spirited, bad-tempered colt Hester had insinuated would be beyond her. "My dear," Helene had replied amusedly, "the horse has not yet been foaled that can unseat me!"

That's what you think, Hester thought, as she handled the colt in a way that had its ears back and its eyes rolling. Then, making sure the groom was occupied with her father's big gray, Balthasar, Hester inserted, under the saddle of the colt, a carefully pruned, deliberately thorny rose stem. Once that worked its way into the tender flesh of the colt's back . . . She hoped the red-headed bitch would smash her ugly face in. But it was the marquis who got thrown. Once out on the downs, and after having accepted his proposal, Helene cajoled him into changing horses, eager to try her hand—and seat on the raking gray, whom not even Hester was allowed to ride. It was when his massive two hundred pounds settled into the saddle of the colt, driving the thorn deep into its back, that the animal went mad: leaving the ground on all fours, bucking and snapping so violently that the marquis, vaunted rider that he was, parted company with it, sailing through the air towards a massive old oak, which he hit with such force that he snapped his spine.

Hester's first task was to go out and shoot the animal (first removing the thorn); that done, she vented her temper on the hapless Mrs. Fortesque, so badly that she had to be restrained from physically attacking her. "It is all your fault!" she screamed at the distraught woman. "You would insist in riding Balthasar. You are responsible for this! I will never forgive you, never! Get out of this house, you murdering bitch. Neither my father nor I wish to set eyes on you again! Go on, get out . . . out . . . . *out!*"

Cowering in the hall, the servants saw the morning doors burst open and the weeping Mrs. Fortesque bolt for the stairs.

Hester had already ruthlessly rationalized everything so it became all Helene's fault. If *she* had not got her claws into Papa; if *she* had not persuaded him to exchange horses; *she* should be the one with the broken back, not Papa; therefore it *was* all her fault.

LORD ARUN was paralyzed from the hips down, from then on a cripple in a wheelchair. Hester nursed him herself, and without a word of complaint. Truth to tell, she was exultant. No other woman would want her father now; now she had him all to herself. Now he would never leave her.

Lovingly she tended to him, seeing to his every need with a dedicated devotion which had people shaking their heads. Lady Hester Conyngham-Bradford was not much liked, but by God, the county said, you had to admire the gel.

Her father tried to fight her. "You should not be devoting yourself to me, darling. You are too young, too alive . . . You should be thinking of marriage, children."

"Children! I don't want brats, Papa! I want you . . . dearest, most adored Papa."

"But it is not right!"

"Right!" Hester had scorned. "We are Conyngham-Bradfords, Papa. Who is to say what is right or not right for us?"

"But I am a cripple!"

She pressed a hand across his mouth with a vicious look. "You are not to say that word! You are incapacitated, that's all. And even then so much more of a man than any other I know. Oh, yes, dearest, most adored Papa . . . so much of a man."

He had smothered a groan in her white throat, his lips feeling its satin smoothness, his nose inhaling her scent. Always the same one. Floris Red Rose.

"But we should not, dearest, we must not."

"But we shall, shan't we, dearest Papa, and we will. You need *me*, Papa . . . who loves you better than anyone ever can or will. I can give you all you want and need, because I know what it is . . . my love."

He had groaned as she took his hand, placed it on her body, but more in passion than in despair, because he was a man of powerful sexuality and his daughter provided the most satisfying of disturbingly erotic thrills; her delicate yet strong hands were capable of producing in him feelings and sensations he had thought lost to him forever, though he still possessed some nerves capable of response. It was these nerves his daughter knew how to stimulate. From the first, when she had, while bathing him, made the first, oblique advance, he had been lost. And she knew it. "I am so much better for you than those drugs the doctors give you. You are a man of appetites, Papa, and it is my joy to be able to satisfy them—the ultimate in joy, Papa—for us both. I know what is good for you, and you shall have it, all of it, Papa . . . Just the two of us, forever and ever; you and I together, for always . . ."

It was afterward, when the guilty remorse set in, the sick realization that he was indulging in the most forbidden of sins, that he would suffer. It was a madness; but she tormented him to the point where he was conscious of nothing but desire for her. This was what frightened him. He had the feeling of being consumed; and while, every time it happened, he dreaded it happening again, he also longed for her to come to him, when he would throw his scruples to the winds and surrender himself to her in a way that had him gasping and shuddering under her avid mouth, begging for more, and more, and more. Afterward, he would remember and realize that it was the possession of him which mattered to her most; to know she had him completely in her control, body and soul. Desperately he invited young men down for the weekend. They came eagerly, compelled by her icy sensuality, the tall, lily-slender body in jodhpurs and clinging white silk shirt, her shingled hair bright as ripe corn above an exquisitely cruel face with enormous, sea blue-green eyes, set in a skin like porcelain. But she did not give a damn for any of them.

Avery, the butler, would relate confidingly to Forbes, the steward, how he had heard Lady Hester at the dinner table, ridiculing her suitors to her father in the most scathing of terms, savaging them with a mockery that shredded. He had once seen her slash a young man across the face with her riding crop, because he had touched her. "Nobody touches me!" she had spat at him. "Nobody!"

"She'll never get a husband that way," Avery had said, wagging his head. "Her tongue is too sharp and her contempt too obvious."

[58]

But Hester did not want a husband. She wanted her father. And was happy as she had never been because she had him. And all to herself.

Forbes was privately of the opinion that his master would not last much longer. He looked like a man who was being suffocated, so tightly did his daughter have him in her clutches, and all the while sucking him dry.

And then, one morning, waking after a night which made him cringe in remembered self-disgust, Lord Arun took the only way out, by means of the morphine he had secretly been hoarding.

Hester had gone riding, galloping to the far reaches of the estate, tingling with the glorious feeling of insuperable power. Everything had come about as she had planned. She was gloriously, deliriously happy.

By the time she was brought back, Dr. Hargreaves, an old family friend, after a discreet conversation with Forbes and Avery, the subject of which was never referred to again, had already signed the death certificate, which gave the cause of death as heart failure. It was Hester who took the handling. She went to pieces. When they told her, a sound started, low in her throat: a growl that escalated to a wild, shrill shriek which resounded through the great rooms; peals and peals of hysterical, abandoned howls of grief and temper. She threw herself about her father's bedroom in a paroxysm of abandoned fury, kicking and stamping, throwing things, rending her clothes, her flesh, screaming for her father over and over again. "Papa! Papa! Come back to me, Papa! I won't let you do this to me! How can you do this to me? I love you! Papa! Papa!"

It took two of the strongest footmen to subdue her, while the doctor administered a strong sedative, her breathing already tortured, rasping in her chest, her eyes bulging, her lungs heaving.

She came out of it dry-eyed and gelid. Insisted on sitting by her father's body; refused to leave when the undertakers came to work on it. She accompanied the coffin to the family chapel and remained with it until his funeral, two days later. Then she sat, silent, as her father's will was read. The title and entailed estate went to his heir: his nephew, son of his dead younger brother. Everything that was not entailed he left to his daughter, making her a fabulously rich young woman. But Arun was taken from her.

The new marquis approached her with trepidation afterward. "If you would like to take up residence in the dower house," he offered nervously.

Baleful eyes turned his way. "The *dower house!*" He might have said "workhouse."

"Dorothy thinks . . ." Dorothy was his wife, whom Hester regarded as a parvenue. "There will be the children, you see, and she has it in mind to change things . . ."

Once again his voice dried under her eyes. Privately, he thought his wife was right. His cousin Hester had been driven mad with grief.

"What kind of changes?"

His skin crept. "Well . . . it's a bit heavy, don't you know. Dorothy wants to modernize everything—"

"*Modernize!*"

He retreated a step. "Why not?" he asked, desperately defiant.

"Nothing has been changed here for generations. This is *Arun,* you fool!"

"Here, I say, steady on . . . It is my house now, you know. I can jolly well do as I like!" Stand up to her, his wife had urged frantically. Don't let her bully you, James. You know what she is like. If she has her way we'll end up in the dower house. *You* are the marquis now; don't let *her* tell *you* what to do.

Hester would have consigned him to hell had she been able; had toyed with the idea of getting rid of him, but he had two sons. Insupportable though the idea was of this po-faced prig and his tradesman's-daughter wife living and lording it at Arun, there was nothing she could do. The entail must stand. A silent scream choked her. Papa! Papa! Hatred rose like bile. Just because she was not a man. Why, she was as good as—no, better than—any of them! Just because they were the seed carriers, had that thing between their legs. She suppressed a moan. Mustn't think of that. But it was so unfair. Arun was *hers.* Well, she would show the lot of them! She would take her revenge for what had been done to her. She would show men what a woman could do. Loathing filled her as she stared at her cousin's pudding face, made her turn her back on him and stalk away at a furious rate, right out of the house and across the lawns. She did not see one of the mourners, a tall, cadaverously thin, solemn-faced man, detach himself from a murmuring family group to follow; at a distance, because although her beauty drew him, her character unnerved. So beautiful, he thought admiringly, but so proud. He followed, keeping station behind her, as she strode, in that head-high, long-legged way of moving that she had, toward the lake where the white swans sailed. She was like a swan herself, he thought, romantically for him because he was a prosaically minded man.

Her high, imperious voice, never lowered for anything or anybody, floated back to him as she said to the swans: "Not even for you, my lovelies. They have taken it all . . . all . . ."

How sad she must be, he thought. And how angry she was! He shivered deliciously. He had seen her talking to her cousin. How magnificent she was in a temper. Just then she must have sensed him because she looked over her shoulder. Her perfect manners perfectly disguised her annoyance, and he took her smile at its face value.

"I only want to say goodbye," he began diffidently. "My boat sails from Southampton tonight."

"Of course. You are from the American branch of the family, are you not?"

"Yes. Winthrop Bradford. We share a common ancestor, but you are descended from Sir Henry, who became the first baron, while I trace my roots back to William, his younger brother."

Hester considered his bony, long-nosed face. The only obvious Bradford traits were the blond hair and the height. Politely, because he bored her stiff: "Are there many of you over there?"

A surprised laugh, somewhat chagrined. "Indeed. We are a considerable clan. One of Boston's oldest families. We have lived there some two hundred and ninety years now." His swelling pride made Hester smile. Her own family had lived on this land for close on a thousand. "One never thinks of Americans as having ancestors," she said with callous amusement.

His pale face flushed. "In Boston they are all-important."

"Really! One always believes America to be inhabited by red Indians and gangsters."

"Obviously you have never visited my country."

No, and don't intend to either, Hester thought.

"I promise you, you would like it," Winthrop assured her. "Boston is its most civilized city, of course, the epitome of Englishness yet the cradle of our independence."

"Indeed! How very kind of you, then, to come all this way to my father's funeral."

"We are very proud of our English connections!"

"But surely you have abolished aristocracy."

"Not in Boston! Who you are is every bit as important—if not more —than what you are!"

Deliberately cruel because he really was the prosiest of ridiculous bores: "My father was of the opinion that you were inbred to the point of incestuousness." His bony face flushed. "It is true we tend to intermarry," he agreed stiffly. "My own ancestry comprises Adamses, Cabots and Lowells. My mother was an Adams."

Hester wanted to laugh in his face. Who in God's name were the Adamses? He made it sound as if they sat on His right hand.

"We take great pride in our ancestry," Winthrop was going on. "In fact, we follow just about everything English—except your laws of entail, of course."

Hester's interest was caught and held. "You have no laws of entail?"

"Not since Thomas Jefferson abolished them." Confidently: "We get around it, of course. In Boston we also believe in passing on our heritage intact. There are ways to prevent it from being dissipated. Look what happened to the Vanderbilts."

Hester, who neither knew nor cared, said slowly: "So . . . if I belonged to the American branch, I would have been my father's heir?"

"Of course! You were his only child."

Hester released a dazzling smile, came toward him and slid a hand through his arm. "How absolutely fascinating! Do tell me more . . ."

SIX WEEKS LATER, Lady Hester Conyngham-Bradford was listed among the passengers sailing on the S.S. *Mauretania* for New York. Six months later, it was announced in the London *Times* that Mrs. Winthrop Bradford III, of Mount Vernon Street, Boston, Massachusetts, and The Farm, Concord, Massachusetts, was pleased to announce the engagement of her eldest son, Winthrop Bradford IV, to the Lady Hester Mary Clarissa Conyngham-Bradford, only daughter of the sixth marquis and thus a distant cousin many times removed, of her fiancé.

Winthrop Bradford married for love. Hester married for Bradford & Sons, which, she discovered, was exactly what she was looking for. The American branch of the family were multimillionaires, even though they lived like the genteel poor. Spread all over Beacon Hill, the family fortunes had been founded in shipping and textiles, spread into banking and commerce, all of it run on the most ultraconservative of lines by the eldest male members of the family. Not until he was forty-five would Winthrop be allowed to sit in on the councils of power, even though he was the eldest son of an eldest son. Bradfords had to serve a long apprenticeship and prove their worth—and ability to make five cents do the work of fifty—before they were given any major responsibility.

Hester was outraged. What did a bundle of doddering old men—not one of them under sixty—know of the modern way of doing things? This was 1930, for heaven's sakes, and though there was a most inconvenient nuisance of a slump, even that could not last forever. Could they not see that this was the time to buy, not retrench! Companies were to be had for a song! But her husband's response, when she pointed this out to him, was horror and a nervous look over his shoulder as he beseeched her never to mention the matter when any of the uncles—or aunts come to that—were present. She should not be worrying her pretty little head about such things anyway. He had no idea that that same pretty little head could have sold him and his uncles at a very considerable profit. Hester fumed and planned. All that money doing nothing but biding its time in banks, earning the Great God Interest, the Capital worshiped as Sacred. They spent money as if it were their life's blood. Yet she stared amazedly at her first family dinner, when the aunts appeared in dresses that must have been made for their trousseaus and sporting several fortunes in jewels. Having thoughtfully appropriated her namesake's fabulous pearls, emeralds and rubies, Hester had no qualms about holding her own there, but she had not made it known exactly just how rich she was. She had handled the question of marriage settlements herself, instructing her lawyers as to how much should be divulged, making sure it was as little as possible. Hester had 95 percent of her enormous fortune entirely under her own control, and she used it to buy up several bankrupt companies. One had made guns until the War to End All Wars; the second had made silk stockings, the third milled cotton, the fourth aluminum products. They would all make more, once this slump was over. As it was bound to be, in time. Meanwhile, it was as well to be ready. That was the trouble with the Bradfords: they gloried in their past while distrusting the future. Hester, on the other hand, planned for nothing else.

First of all she made it her business to learn as much as possible about the workings of Bradford & Sons. She would have liked to remain at the dinner table with the men and join in the discussions; instead she followed the women into the drawing room—or parlour, as it was known in Boston—to be bored to tears by discussions about cooks and pregnancies and marriages and deaths. Hester was aware that she was expected to produce Winthrop's son and heir before too long, but she had no intention of rushing her fences. Her father had always told her, since she had begun to hunt: "Always walk over the ground first; know what you have got to get over before you put your horse at it."

She was therefore anything but pleased to discover, just three months after allowing him to take her virginity (and as in everything else, sex with Winthrop was a bore) that she was pregnant, even more angry when her child was a girl. Now she would be expected to go through the whole damned thing again. Her daughter was named, according to Bradford custom, after an ancestress—Abigail—and she was only a year old when Hester found herself pregnant again. Behind his proper Bostonian façade, Winthrop hid a powerful sex drive, but while sex with her husband was in no way to be preferred to talking about Bradford & Sons, Hester discovered that the postcoital Winthrop was much more amenable to being cross-examined about the family firm. He for his part was smugly satisfied at the sexy thing his wife was turning into. That he engaged neither her interest nor her emotions never entered his head; he only knew she was ready and willing every night, and that it was what she could extract from him afterward that mattered, he never knew.

By the time her second daughter—called after herself and an ancestress common to both branches but forever condemned to be called Bitsy after Uncle Brewster, on setting eyes on her for the first time, exclaimed: "Why, compared to Abby she's a little bit of a thing"—was born, Hester knew all there was to know about Bradford & Sons, most especially its share distribution, held in such proportions as to preclude any one shareholder from possessing a threatening majority. Which was exactly what Hester herself intended to have one day.

Hester's second daughter all but killed her. It took her a long time to recover. Her doctors warned her not to become pregnant for at least two years, which further enraged her against her husband. Everybody knew it was the man who determined the sex of a child.

And in the Bradford family, sex—in terms of gender—was all-important. The men ran everything. Hester knew that if she was to wield any power at all it would have to be done (ostensibly) on behalf of her son. So she ignored the doctors, got Winthrop to impregnate her again and miscarried at nine weeks. Of a son. By the time Pearl Harbor dragged America into the war, she had miscarried three times more; twice of sons. She was desperate, what with the war finally here. She was counting on it to reduce the plethora of male Bradfords—the younger ones, that was—somewhat. Her own son had to have no rivals. And he *had* to be born. Now was probably her last chance for some time. So when Winthrop, a naval reservist, was drafted, she saw to it before he left for Norfolk, Virginia, that his ardor was thoroughly aroused. And duly conceived once again.

[64]

SHE HAD MEANT to take it easy this time, really she had, but when Uncle Brewster, on learning that his only son, young Brewster, had been killed at Guadalcanal, the news brought on a heart attack, from which he died within twenty-four hours. This was closely followed by the death, also in the Pacific, where his plane was shot down, of Uncle Timothy's eldest, Lowell, and the news that Uncle Willie's eldest, Eliot, was missing over Guam. The old uncles were prostrate, under the attentions of their doctors. Hester sensed her time had come. By the time they were able to take stock, she had established herself in Winthrop's office down on Commonwealth Avenue, giving orders and issuing edicts.

Her own four factories she now took from under their wraps. All were at full stretch; the cotton machinery made army uniforms, the silk looms parachutes, the aluminum plant parts for airplanes. The armaments factory was churning out bullets. She had tight, warlong contracts and was making fat profits, took in her stride the protestations of enfeebled Uncle Timothy, now seventy-seven and deaf as a post, and Uncle Willie, crippled with arthritis; met no opposition in the shape of young Willie, 4-F because of his flat feet and thick bifocals. She was in her element: running everything. Bradford & Sons she dragged, kicking and screaming, into the twentieth century. When Winthrop came home on leave it was to find his wife in charge.

"Come now, darling," she told him briskly, when he made his displeasure known. "You don't think I have sat and listened and not learned all these years."

That she had not so much learned as improved upon hit her husband's amour propre like a sledgehammer, which young Willie swung his way when he enthused: "She's a dynamo, Uncle Win. Can she organize! There isn't a thing you can slip past her, either!" Pregnant or not, Hester took it upon herself to travel to every battle zone where a Bradford product was used by the armed forces. She lived and ate with the men, harangued the generals and admirals, distributed largesse to the admiring GIs and generally, thanks to a besotted photographer from *Life* magazine, became a household word. Her looks, her lineage, her indifferent bravery (she was Lady Hester Bradford, for heaven's sake! And as young Timothy observed to his wife in a letter: "If a Jap should get within bullet range of Hester she would only look at him and ask: 'But don't you know Who I am?' ") became a source of endless publicity. *So* good for business. When it was pointed out to her (by the man who drew the short straw) that not only her gender but her pregnancy precluded her venturing into deepest jungle, or spending hours in an unheated Dakota, or tossing in the confines of a cabin on a destroyer, she ignored him. This was all the most heaven-sent of opportunities. And anathema to the family. They dreaded opening their papers of a morning for fear of what they would find concerning her. And when she miscarried yet again they all pursed their lips and said "I told you so." But not to her face. Hester was relieved. It had been a girl. Now she had been saved waiting another dreary four months for something she did not want.

She was in her element: organizing, streamlining and steamrolling anything and anyone in her way. So famous did she become that it was front-page news when President Roosevelt invited her to the White House for dinner; pronounced afterward that she was "a most remarkable woman. I only wish we had more like her."

The Bradfords, who loathed him to a man, muttered among themselves that one was far too many. Hester had gone too far this time. Actually dining with That Man. When, in the spring of 1944, Winthrop told her he was being sent to Europe—no doubt to take part in the forthcoming invasion—Hester's practicality at once took account of the fact that he might not come back. It was therefore of paramount importance that she conceive her son. So she bathed and scented herself, left orders she was not to be disturbed, even for a call from the White House, and set out to become impregnated.

Winthrop had never known anything like it. Hester had him bedazzled, befuddled and beside himself, all but disemboweled by the passionate creature that was his wife. He came so often and so devastatingly he thought he was being blown apart, climaxing with a detonation he was sure could have been heard out in Brookline, but long past caring who heard his moans and cries, coming so deeply that Hester felt confident he was planting his seed with a trowel. The time was right: bang in the middle of her cycle. She would have her son this night or die in the attempt.

Which was how her husband felt as he staggered off to catch his plane. Sore and weary, his balls aching and his mind still wandering around in a daze, not knowing that the son he would never see was already clinging to the wall of his wife's womb. Ten weeks after he landed in England he was killed, along with the rest of the occupants of the pub where he was enjoying a quiet drink, when a V-2 blew everyone to pieces that were unidentifiable. What they thought was him was shipped back to Boston, to be buried—with honors—among his ancestors. Hester, who had risen from her bed for the funeral, reflected practically that he had done his real duty: left her his son. For son it would be. She never thought the word daughter. And this time she did take care; retired to her bed and a battery of telephones, from where nothing and no one was safe. This was her last chance. This time she would have her son. And did. On her father's birthday.

From the moment she laid eyes on him, Hester fell deeply in love for the second time in her life. Her son was a Conyngham-Bradford. No bony, long-nosed face here. He had her father's face. And eyes. And hair. So she gave him her father's name. Jonathan Winthrop Bradford V—Brad to the family—was, his mother devoutly believed, his maternal grandfather's reincarnation. It was, she thought prayerfully, a miracle. She fed him herself; no bottles for him as for her daughters. To feel her son sucking greedily, fists clamped on her breasts, was to be united, physically and emotionally, with her father once more. Her first orgasms since his death were the ones she had when feeding her son; glorious, exploding orgasms for which she came to worship him. She spent hours poring over his naked body, caressing it with her mouth, especially the tiny penis; could not bear to be parted from him. Her daughters she had never managed to tolerate for more than short stretches of time, handing them thankfully back to Nanny. Her son she never left. On returning to work she took him with her, placing his bassinet by her desk, locking her door when it came time to feed him.

WINTHROP HAD LEFT EVERYTHING to his wife, who had worked long and hard on him, so that there were, uncharacteristically, no strings. She inherited his 25 percent shareholding outright, along with the shares that had come to him from those uncles who had lost their heirs. By the time the last of the Bradfords came home from the war she had accumulated 55 percent of the A shares. But 65 percent would be better, she thought. So she set about getting it.

Her target was her cousin Amanda—widow of a Bradford but also one in her own right, and possessed of a 10 percent shareholding. (Her mother had been an emancipated woman for Boston.) A lushly, indolently sexy creature, she spent most of her time in bed—always with a man. Her husband had no sooner left for boot camp than she was being pounded by a lieutenant commander whose ship was in harbor for repairs.

She had no idea who made her pregnant; knew only it had to be terminated. But the abortion was botched; she ended up pleading with her cousin Hester for help.

In her dealings with a certain group of high-ranking officers, Hester had, in return for some fat contracts, set up a private clinic where the wombs of the daughters of Boston's Best could be scraped clean of any unfortunate deposits. Many a Boston debutante went down the aisle of Trinity Church without so much as a glance at Lady Hester in the Bradford pew, who had arranged for her to enter the clinic and be purified. Hester did not fail her cousin Amanda, who told her gratefully: "You saved my bacon."

"I rather thought it was your reputation."

"Whatever. I am really grateful. Anything I can ever do for you . . ."

"You can. Sell me your Bradford A shares."

Amanda looked shocked. "But I can't do that! Bradfords never—but never—sell their shares."

"Only to non-Bradfords."

"Oh, but the family would not like it," Amanda protested virtuously, wondering how much the traffic would bear.

"Just as you would not like it if it were to get out that you keep a house on Brattle Street in Cambridge for your—shall we say—assignations—with sometimes groups of men?"

Amanda turned pale. "How you do pry."

"No need to. Your—proclivities—are well known."

Bitch! thought Amanda venomously. How the hell had she found that out?

"I want your own 5 percent and the 5 percent that came to you through Brooks. I need an unshakable majority if I am to do what I intend to do with Bradford & Sons."

Amanda thought. "How much?" she asked finally.

"Market value."

"Oh, but to you, Hester, they are surely worth much more."

"It is their value to you which concerns us at the moment."

Amanda burned with discomfited rage. "I never did believe that holier-than-thou attitude of yours," she sneered. "You may have fooled the rest of the old fuddy-duddies in the family but I've had your number from the start!"

A thin smile. "My dear Amanda, tell me the name of the man who has not had yours."

Amanda ground her teeth. Pure, triple-distilled bitch, she thought. Armor-plated and with a clock where her heart should be. Who would not hesitate to ruin anyone who got in her way.

"Any transfer of shares has to be approved by the board," she stalled.

Another thin smile. "I *am* the board."

[68]

"Which is what you've always wanted, isn't it? Power to you is what sex is to me; you can't do without it."

"I have . . . plans." With indifferent cruelty: "The war was a godsend to us both. You in your small corner—or should I say bed?—me in mine. I aim to see the good times continue, and I want a free hand to do so. One way and another I intend to get it."

"What would I get for my ten percent?"

"Cash or shares."

"You are not going public!" Amanda gasped.

"Don't be stupid. I do not intend to burden myself with shareholders. The new issue I propose to raise will be family-held and carry no vote, merely dividends—fatter than you have ever had."

Amanda did not doubt it. She knew her cousin Hester by now. A combination of Adolf Hitler, Joseph Stalin and Queen Victoria. "All right. They are yours. But I want a lawyer friend"—one of her current lovers—"to look over any papers."

"As you wish."

So it was, when the remaining four members of the board to come back from the war sat down in the boardroom with those three members who had remained behind, Hester owned 65 percent of the controlling shares. When the meeting ended she owned 75 percent. Young Cabot Winthrop had seen a different kind of life while he was away from Boston and in the army; had no intention of returning to the old one. He preferred to sell his shares to his aunt Hester and build that yacht he had designed, use it to sail around the world . . .

"It would seem, Aunt Hester," young (thirty-two) Timothy remarked acidly later, "that Bradford & Sons also bears the depredations of the recent conflict." He talked just like his father, Hester thought derisively. Old Timothy had been a great admirer of Henry James.

"Hardly depredations," she replied crisply. "The figures I presented to you disprove that. Never have our resources been so ample or our order books so full."

"The cumulative effects of the past four years will take some time to run down."

"Which is why I intend to diversify. The war will be the cause of a technology explosion, mark my words. Bradford & Sons must be in the forefront. Leave it to me, Timothy, and we will be leading the parade."

"I would not expect you to be anywhere else," he sniffed sourly.

But, like everyone else, he had no choice but to hang on to his hat as he was swept along in Hester's tail wind. Scenting changes (she had a nose like a bloodhound, Timothy observed spitefully) she was ready

[69]

when the TV boom swept the country, already had a new plant churning them out by the thousands. She foresaw the need for houses and went into prefabrication; she realized the coming domination of plastics and built a vast new complex, and was full of plans for her venture into electronics. Profits zoomed off the graph. She built a new prestige headquarters downtown on land she had thoughtfully acquired many years back; the old Commonwealth Avenue offices were kept as a sop to the glorious past. She heaved out all the Victoriana and Edwardiana that cluttered the Mount Vernon Street house, replacing it with the superb old furniture that had been consigned to the attics. Nobody was surprised when it was written up in Boston guidebooks.

Hester was aglow with satisfaction. Everything was going the way she had intended. And she had her son.

Her daughters soon came to realize that while they could expect a judicious—if strict—impartiality from their mother, it was their brother who got the love. All Hester's children were brought up in the English way. They had an English nanny, an English governess until they were old enough to be sent to boarding school. Hester saw her daughters off with brisk admonitions as to good behavior and excellent marks. Her son she could not bear to part with. She had toyed with the idea of Eton even as she knew she could not bear to send him so far away. It would have to be an American school, alas, and her diligent inquiries resulted in her choosing to send him to Phillips Academy at Andover. It was, after all, the oldest incorporated school in America—founded in 1778. A mere stripling next to Eton but . . . He would be under her eye there. So Andover it was.

She never ceased to instill in her children the vital importance of their English heritage. Every summer she took them to Arun, to let them live it. All three adored it: Abby because of the horses, Bitsy because of its grandeur, Brad because it was at Arun that he made the glorious discovery of sex, when he lost his virginity to one of the maids. And in so doing, gave his mother the opportunity to seal her domination. The girl became pregnant, and it was Hester who saw the girl married off to a laborer on one of the estate's many farms, the child's paternity attributed to him. It was done so swiftly, so ruthlessly, that there was no gossip whatsoever.

That done, she saw to it that her son was made fully aware of what she had done—and why. It was to be the first of countless times when she would bail him out of a situation he created but later found untenable, and it planted, as she had intended, the profound conviction that in his mother he had the Protestant equivalent of the Virgin Mary. A true believer, he worshiped her. In his eyes, his mother was Perfect. He believed in her blindly, adoringly, totally. In his eyes she could do no wrong; she was Truth Itself; Mother Incarnate. She awed him, baffled him, ruined him.

He matured into a man possessed of an irresistible attraction to women; a blindingly handsome, ever boyish, callously selfish user of the sex, always taking, never giving—except of his prodigious sexual skills. On the rare occasions when he was stirred elsewhere than his loins, his mother always dug up such burgeoning feelings by the root. When he graduated from Harvard she took him under tutelage; he accompanied her on her trips, first as an observer and then, as he learned, allowing him to participate, little by little, in her various deals and power plays; showing him the intricacies of a takeover, the precise amount of pressure to be exerted, and where; the variations and kinds of manipulations necessary, the bluffs to be called, teaching him the shrewd and deadly skillful game she played—and invariably won. His impression of an all-powerful, all-loving mother was increased by all he saw and learned, which in turn served to increase her domination.

He was soon doing the majority of the traveling, leaving his mother to sit and spin from the center of the web, but always aware, from even the slightest vibrations, just exactly what he was up to—and with whom.

When her elder daughter came to her and said seriously: "Mother, Brad is getting a lousy reputation as a particularly nasty kind of Lothario," her mother smiled amusedly, already fully aware of her son's activities. "Vicious tongues," she dismissed. "I know my son, and if I am not worried I do not see why you or anyone else should be." Her voice icy with contempt: "If the women he takes are greedy enough—and stupid enough—to want more than he is willing to give, then that is their affair. I know that Brad is a honeypot where women are concerned; in that, too, he is so like my father . . ." The smile changed. "He was a devastatingly attractive man too . . . Oh, yes, such a man among men . . ."

And Abby had seen her mother's eyes light with that look they wore only when she spoke of her father, and knew she was wasting her time.

But the tales continued to come back: of messy divorces, several beatings, once even a suicide. And whenever it became necessary, Brad turned to his mother, hid behind her skirts while she dealt with the mess.

Lady Hester thoroughly enjoyed her son's sexual depredations. He treated women as she had treated men. Besides, it afforded her a sense of revenge against Helene Fortesque and all those other women who had sought to ensnare her father. Brad could have all the women he wanted, leave them for dead if he cared to, just so long as he did leave them in the end.

Fortunately, she had so blocked his channels that they did not run deep. If—and it was not often—he came to wonder why it was he could not seem to form a permanent relationship with a woman, his mother soon resolved any doubts. "I suppose you must marry one day," she would sigh regretfully, "but finding the right—no, the perfect— woman for you, my darling, is a positively Herculean task."

"I don't need one. I have you," he would answer, and she would touch his cheek and smile tremulously. "Flatterer . . ." Deeply, satis- fiedly, pleased.

But as he matured (in years) she began to turn her mind to the question of a suitable wife. She would have to be malleable, docile even, and eager to please (not Brad but his mother). He was thirty now; she had let him run riot and wreak havoc, but there was the question of the continuation of the line. Hester thought it very bad planning on the part of the Almighty to allow such a short life-span.

It was in the midst of her rigorous scrutiny that she became aware of Caroline Norton. She was the sister of Brad's oldest friend, Bradley Norton (the friendship had begun at Andover because of a mix-up caused by the similarity of name), and her father was a self-made millionaire. Eldridge Norton (originally Elmo Notorianni) had started in a Chicago junkyard; become the largest dealer in scrap on the Eastern seaboard. His wife, Eloise (originally Esther Schnautzer), was a social climber. M.A., Hester noted in her file. Mother Appalling. But the Nortons were very rich; had been the means of Caroline receiving a thorough polishing at the best schools, emerging as a Barbie doll– pretty, outwardly demure, inwardly rabidly selfish girl who, having once decided what she wanted, let what anyone else wanted matter not at all. And she wanted to become Mrs. J. Winthrop Bradford V. Her mother held the same ambition for her.

With Norton Inc.'s Dun & Bradstreet rating in front of her, as well as the company's current balance sheet, Lady Hester thought that Caro- line would bear further investigation. The mother, of course, would have to be kept in her place. Father, a rough diamond, was still worth a great deal. She accordingly invited Caroline to the farm for a weekend.

Well aware that she was up for election, Caroline spared no pains to give the right impression; made herself out to be a sweetly naïve, purely virginal girl, hopelessly smitten by Brad and both willing and necessary to do whatever was necessary to get him. Once she had returned to Philadelphia, Hester sounded out her son. "Such a pretty girl, though at times her sweetness made my teeth ache . . . but absolutely gone on you, my darling."

"She's all right," Brad conceded with an indifferent shrug. "Tends to cloy, though. Lemonade rather than champagne . . ."

"Always the best thing to satisfy a thirst," pointed out his mother. "And with the kind of settlement her father is willing to make you can drink champagne every day for the rest of your life!"

But Brad's face was unsmiling.

"Darling, you must marry *some*time. Caroline is pretty, not *too* bright; she will dress really well by the time I am finished with her—and eradicated all traces of her hideous mother's influence; she will give you no trouble. All you have to do is give her your name and then children. Once she is occupied with them your life is your own to lead; only do be discreet, darling; the Nortons are so frightfully *nouveau riche.*" Now he looked sullen.

"You are my only son, dearest. Would you have those awful prigs of Timothy's take over, or those hellions of Eliot's? All I have done has been for *you*, my darling. *Your* children. If I was prepared to fight death to have you, the least you can do is be willing to share your life for me."

As always, guilt overflowed.

"Is it that you don't find her attractive enough? I know how high your standards are—"

"She's all right, I suppose, just—no excitement, no depths . . . and I don't love her."

"But, darling, *that* would never do! People in our position cannot afford to marry for love; marriage is far too important."

By the time she was through with him he was convinced that Caroline Norton would do perfectly. All he had to do was give her his name and his children. Nothing was said about giving himself.

So he did his duty. A formal courtship, followed by a formal engagement, the whole to be rounded off by a grand (Boston) wedding, the arrangements for which Hester kept firmly in her own hands.

"Oh, that snooty, hard-nosed harridan!" Eloise would explode, arriving home from a hard-fought session. "Christ, but she's a hoity-toity bitch!"

"You want me to marry her son, Mother," Caroline reminded snottily. "Your grandchildren will be the great-grandchildren of a marquis. Isn't that what you've always wanted?"

"But not to have to crawl through shit to get it!"

Caroline winced. "Don't be vulgar."

"With what this is costing your father I'll be what I damn well please! We are paying through the nose for your right to be called Mrs. J. Winthrop Bradford V. Marriage settlements indeed! Blackmail, more like!"

"I want Brad and I'm going to have him," Caroline warned in an ugly voice. "Don't start sticking that nose in where it is not wanted."

"You are far too crazy about that sexpot. You'll have to put your foot down once you are married."

"Don't worry. I intend to put my stamp on a great many things once that ring is on my finger."

"Just so long as you keep in your hand the one through his nose."

Once I can get it away from his mother, Caroline thought now, glancing at her fiancé, who had been in an anything but loving mood since his return from Europe. Something had obviously hit a snag. With any luck some woman he'd had designs on had torn them up and thrown them in his face. Caroline was under no illusions that Brad would like nothing more than for her to do that, including his ring in the confetti. She smiled to herself. What he would like and what he would get bore no relation to each other whatsoever. Besides, in this matter—as in all others where Caroline Norton was concerned—it was what she wanted that mattered.

3

game. the state of a game; manner of playing a game

IT TOOK JULIA SOME TIME to realize she was pregnant. After Brad's brutal jettisoning she had holed up inside herself, going through the motions of living but making them automatically, feeling nothing, noticing nothing, especially the fact that she had missed two periods. Even then she did not feel any shock, only a dull apathy. Nevertheless, she sat down with the calendar and her diary and worked back. The last time she had been with Brad had been right in the middle of her cycle. Yet she had taken her pill—hadn't she? No, she found, when she checked. She hadn't. The cycle was way out of whack. Like everything else, she thought. That was the effect he had on me. Like nothing else before or since . . .

When Chris asked her what was wrong, noticing the paleness, the thinness, the silence, which was even more marked, Julia told her. Chris threw up her hands in horror. "You are what? In this day and age? What in God's name were you thinking of?"

"I wasn't thinking at all, you know that."

Chris shook her head. "Oh, Julia, Julia . . . To think I always considered you the most intelligent of women. A teenager would have known better." An exasperated sigh. "Well, inexperience—innocence in your case—will do it every time. What's done is done." Pause. "Now we have to undo it."

Her voice was sympathetic, her words ruthlessly practical.

"I know," Julia said dully.

"Do you?" Chris's voice was persistent.

Julia nodded. "Yes. I've thought and thought. I can't have this baby. I'm not ready for it—emotionally or any other which way." Her voice hardened. "It was a mistake."

"Then leave it all to me. I know exactly how to put it right."

"Whatever you say," Julia said.

She went along obediently, doing as she was told, offering nothing but her body for surgery at the private clinic she entered on Friday afternoon. She was in the theater at 8 A.M. and by eight-thirty was back in her room, her womb scraped as clean as her scarified emotions. She came to at ten o'clock, conscious of a dull grind in her lower back and an empty ache in her heart. This was not happening to her! Not eminently practical, nontaker of risks *ever* Julia Carey. She would wake up in a minute, find it was Monday morning and raining and she had overslept.

Only it was no dream; the small hospital room, the hospital smells and noises, were all too factual, like the ache in her back and the fact that she was bleeding. She knew she should feel relieved, was grateful for Chris's warmth and comfort when she bustled in later, but all she felt was cold and numb. Chris took one look at her face; the empty eyes, the blank expression, and went to find a doctor.

Julia went home next morning. The bill, when presented, amounted to exactly what she had won when Brad had placed the bet for her. So, she reflected unemotionally, it had not cost her a penny. In money, that was.

She took a week off work and holed up like a wounded animal, sleeping most of the time with the aid of the pills the doctor had given her. That way she did not have to think. When she was awake she paced the floor like a caged tiger. She was being punished, she reasoned. For straying from her course, for not behaving as she ought to have behaved. Had she not warned herself she would regret it? She should have stayed the way she was. Safely dead. Not wanting, not needing, not anything. Not as she did now. Wanting Brad. Needing Brad. Even now, in spite of everything. If he had come through the door she would have hurled herself at him.

At the end of that week she still could not face work so she took another week's leave—doctor's orders, she said—and went up to Yorkshire. Back to her roots. Somewhere with no reminders of Brad, gone along with the seed he had spilled so copiously and carelessly. She would gain strength from her experience, never make those mistakes again. She would start a clean, new page. As for the old one, that would have to be burned.

SHE TOOK WILLUM WITH HER, buying a cat-carrying case, which he hated, yowling and scratching with such power that once on the highway she made sure all the doors were locked, the windows shut, then let him out. He took station on the rear window ledge, still howling his displeasure and spitting at the passing cars.

The weather was glorious: hot and sunny. So sunny that the little cottage looked drab in the bright light of the sun. So she drove into Whitby, bought whiter-than-white paint and spent two days decorating the kitchen. Which showed up the living room. So she took down the old curtains, stripped the old soft covers, bought yards and yards of sleek cotton satin in a pattern of nasturtiums on almond green and set to, with the aid of her sewing machine, to make new ones. She felt driven by a compulsion to work, work, work. She turned her attention to the garden, spent hours digging and hoeing and weeding, exhausting herself so completely that she was usually in bed by eight o'clock, where a pill would give her ten, sometimes twelve, hours' oblivion.

She walked too, long lonely walks along the cliffs or the beach. One afternoon, it clouded over suddenly and a sudden squall of rain had her soaked by the time she had made her way back to the top of the cliff path. She had her head down against the driving downpour and so did not notice the car parked outside her garden gate until she was right on top of it. A gray Bentley Continental. She stopped dead, was gazing at it stupidly when she heard: "Hello, Julia."

Brad was standing behind the gate. She transferred her stare to him.

"You are soaked," he said quickly. "You had better come inside and dry off."

She brushed past him without a word, up the path and in through the front door. She went straight upstairs to the bathroom, where she stripped off her sodden clothes and toweled herself dry, wrapping herself in her toweling robe, another around her hair. Then, feeling weak suddenly, all of a tremble and hollow inside, she fell onto her bed. Her heart was pounding and nausea threatened. I am not playing any more games, she thought painfully. I can't. I don't have the strength anymore. Rage surged like molten lava. Who the hell does he think he is? Picking up and tossing down. Well, I won't let him! I daren't, she thought desperately. Oh, God, why did he have to come back . . .

When she was able to, she went downstairs, hanging on to the banister. He was standing by the diamond-paned windows, staring out, the brightly blond head touching the old beams. Hearing her, he turned around. As their eyes met, before she jerked her own away, the old treacherous flicker of melting delirium coursed through her veins, turning her blood to something heavy, hot and molten. She stalked into the kitchen without a word. Her hands were shaking badly as she filled the kettle. A cup of tea, she thought.

He did not follow her; when she peeked through the door she saw he was sitting on the sofa, Willum on his knees purring like an outboard motor, eyes slitted with pleasure.

That won't be me this time! Julia thought, blind with rage. How *dare* he take me for granted! How *dare* he! She wanted to rampage into the sitting room and scream her head off; ask him what the hell did he think he was playing at, what did he think she was—a ball to be bounced against a brick wall! She was sick and tired of him and his death-and-destruction games! Instead, she went back to the sink where she splashed cold water on her stiff face. Her legs seemed to have been filleted and her stomach was on the boil.

When she went back into the sitting room with the tray he stood up, dislodging Willum, who protested crossly, to take it from her, careful not to touch her. The look he gave her was furtive, very wary. Julia fell into a chair.

"What do you want *this* time?" she demanded abrasively.

"To see you; talk to you."

"About what? Anything we had to say—or anything else for that matter—was said last time; and how come you knew where I was?"

"I made Chris tell me."

"You had no right to ask and she had no right to tell you!"

He looked taken aback. "I insisted she did," he said stubbornly. Uneasily: "You look awful," he said. "Have you been sick?"

"None of your business. *Why* do you have to talk to me?"

She tried to lift the teapot and found she couldn't. He did it, pouring two cups, setting one before her.

"About us," he said.

"Us? Since when was there ever an 'us'? You were always your only concern."

He flushed. "It wasn't a pleasant surprise this time, was it?"

"Third time unlucky," Julia snarled.

Now he paled. "You don't mean that."

"Try me!"

"Julia, I've flown three thousand miles just to see you; I'm not going to blow it again."

"All you have ever blown is your own trumpet!"

He looked to be reeling under her onslaught, but he refused to give way. "I have never stopped thinking of you since I left; not for one moment."

"I never had *you* down as a thinker!"

"You didn't have me down as a lot of things, I know that. But what you did have me down for was dead to rights. You took me at my face value—which was nil." He stared down at the old Tabriz rug Julia had bought at a country auction. "In material assets I can muster ten figures in as many minutes; in spiritual assets I guess you could say I was bankrupt." He raised his eyes to hers. "You gave me the courage to pay my debts."

Julia stared at him blankly. What on earth was he on about? He was not making sense to her, concentrating as she was on holding herself together. She found it hard to hear him through the roaring surf in her ears; it kept bringing him forward, then taking him away. She could see his lips moving but could not hear what he said. She closed her eyes, took deep, calming breaths, forced back the bile rising in her throat.

She looked awful, Brad thought, shocked and frantic. Gaunted and wasted. The bones of her face protruded and there were heavy, thumb-print smudges under the beautiful eyes which were, he saw through his own, blurred eyes, regarding him with hatred. Oh, God, he thought, for the first time in his life conscious of something he had done. What have I done to her? I've got to make her understand. I've got to! Seeing her like this, ill and suffering, too vulnerable for his comfort, he longed to reach out, touch her, comfort her. But did not dare. The fascinating maze that was the Julia Carey he had thought he had come to know was in no way this wasted, burning-eyed, racked-with-pain woman. But he knew he loved her. More than ever. As he had never loved in his life before. Never even known what it was to love. Not like this. Even though he knew she was paying for his pleasure. Oh, God, he thought again, agonizedly. What have I *done*? Despairingly: "I know you doubted me from the start; took me for what I was offering and beat me at my own game. You think I'm superficial, don't you; capable of no more than shallow puddles of meretricious sex."

"I think you are spoiled rotten," Julia answered callously. "Little boy sulk when he could not have what he wanted and then, when he got it and didn't want it anymore, ran to his mother and asked her to dispose of it for him."

"Then why did you give it to me?"

"Because it suited me to!"

"Jesus, but you are cruel!"

"*I* am cruel!"

The whiteness went red. "All right then, let's have the truth between us."

"Truth! Whose truth? Yours, of course. The kind that says no feelings, if you please; no kind of emotional—spiritual as you said—involvement; just callous use and mindless sex. That way you can pick up, discard and pick up again. Women are pieces of pasteboard to you, aren't they, in the games you play? Well, I am no card! I am flesh and blood and pain and suffering, you bastard. I'll be damned if I'll play any more games with you!" Her voice had risen. "I thought I could play you at your own game—me! I forgot that when anyone enters your gambling hell they leave their soul at the door. Like the fool I am I took mine in with me! And lost it! But for that I blame myself. I should have heeded my own warnings, but what did I do? I stupidly compounded my mistake by letting you think I knew it all! I have taken your consequences. I think I will dispense with your truth, thank you very much!"

His face was by now a white, stricken blur, mouth open, eyes anguished, and when he put out a hand, said in a trembling voice, "Julia, for God's sake," she struck it away violently. "No more! No more, I tell you! I can't take it. Just go away and leave me alone!"

She clapped her hands to her mouth as bile rose, but it would not be contained. She staggered to her feet, stood swaying for a moment then reeled from the room. He heard her stumbling up the stairs and then the sound of painful, pitiful retching. He raced up the stairs after her. She was crouched over the lavatory bowl, corpse-white and shiny, shivering and gasping. Her forehead, when he touched it, was cold and clammy before she jerked it away. "Go away . . . ," she gasped, dry heaves racking her, "go away and leave me alone . . . no more . . . I can't take any more . . ."

"Oh, Christ, Julia!"

She slid sideways then, eyes going up and back, her head hitting the floor with a thwack! Kneeling down he lifted her carefully. Her head

[80]

lolled back as he got her into his arms, but her body was so light as to be hollow. What had happened to her? This was not *his* Julia, firm-fleshed and solid.

Across the passage was another door; he kicked it open. A bedroom; sloping roof, dormer window, heavy, brass-railed bed. He laid her on it, covering her with the squishy-soft duvet. She had lost consciousness, and when he picked up her wrist her pulse was sluggish, fluttering like birds' wings.

For a moment he hovered distractedly; then: Phone, he thought. Doctor. In his world, that was the only thing you did when you were sick. He ran downstairs. The doctor's number was among those on a list pinned to the back of the kitchen door, along with the dentist, plumber, electrician. Trust Julia.

The doctor was a woman who reminded him of his mother so much he felt at once relieved and comforted. She spent a long time upstairs while he paced and chain-smoked. When at last she came downstairs she lowered her bag to the table, fixed him with a ruminative gaze and said: "What ails her is not strictly physical, though there is evidence of a recent and drastic weight loss; she needs feeding up. However . . ." Her eyes, like his mother's, were hooks that held you fast. "What she is suffering from is shock—the severe, emotional kind. What can you tell me about that?"

"Only that I caused it," he admitted miserably.

"Are you her husband?"

"No."

"How did you cause it, then?"

"I arrived unexpectedly."

"Ah . . ." said the doctor. "I think you had better tell me exactly what happened."

When he had done so she nodded. "Yes, I could see she had been living on nerves and pride, with the result that she has very little of both left. I prescribe rest and rich feeding. Lots of beefy soups, eggs scrambled with cream, toast soaked in butter. I've sedated her for now so she will sleep for at least twelve hours. When she wakes, I want you to see that she eats. Are you staying here?"

"I am now."

"Good." She took a prescription pad from her bag. "Take this to the chemist in the village; one tablet every four hours. Do not allow her to get up. She will try; she has a strong will. That is what she has been living on. Resist it. Impose your own."

"That's easier said than done."

"Not in her present state. She is physically and emotionally drained. That's the trouble with absolutes: no give in them."

"You are quite sure there is nothing physically wrong?"

"Apart from malnutrition, no. It is her nerves which are mangled. She has suffered a severe emotional battering; they are far worse than the physical kind, you know. A black eye heals far quicker than a lacerated mind."

He saw her out to her car—a battered Rover. As she drove off she looked at the Bentley, then at him. "Give her an easy ride too," she advised.

When he went back upstairs Julia was deeply asleep, her hair fierce against the white of the pillow, her dark red lashes lying on her cheeks like scratches; the hollows in her cheeks would have held water. For a long time he stood looking at her, then on a sigh, he turned away, went downstairs, picked up his Burberry and left the cottage.

JULIA SLEPT FOR FOUR DAYS, waking only to eat, under protest, thick broths and fresh farm eggs rich with butter and cream, drink eggnog with brandy in it. The doctor came to check on her daily, expressed herself satisfied with progress. She it was who found a local lady to cook and clean, Brad being useless at everything except boiling water. Mrs. Collier cooked like a dream and with Yorkshire taciturnity saw and heard all but kept her mouth shut.

On the fifth morning, when the doctor came downstairs she said, "She'll do. But keep her in bed for another couple of days. No strenuous activity. She's slept herself out but she can read or watch television. And keep up the feeding. She is many pounds underweight."

Brad had kept out of Julia's way. Mrs. Collier had taken the trays up and down. He had done the shopping, though, coming back from the nearest large supermarket with several cartfuls of goodies, a lot of them expensive specialties intended to tempt Julia's appetite.

SHE GOT UP for the first time on Sunday, the doctor helping her stand on weak legs. "I feel so rubbery."

"You have been ill."

"I am never ill!"

"That's why—"

Julia shot a glance at the doctor's placid face, and when she heard, "I think we should talk now," she looked anything but forthcoming. "You are out of the woods physically," the doctor continued. "The rich diet should do the rest. It is emotionally that you still need care and attention." Gently she pushed Julia down into a chair, sat herself down on the bed. "A doctor acts in the same capacity as a priest. Much of our time is spent listening to people's troubles. So often we find it is the mind which is making the body ill."

Julia said nothing.

"What we are told is sancrosanct," the doctor went on calmly. "My diagnosis is that you have been punishing yourself; for what sins only you will know. My prognosis is that only by confessing them will you gain your absolution."

Julia had been staring down at her hands. It was only when she felt the doctor shove a wad of tissues into them that she realized she was weeping.

"That's better," encouraged the doctor kindly. "Tears not only cleanse the eyes, they launder the soul, and I am of the opinion that you have come to regard yours as irredeemably blackened."

Julia burst into racking sobs.

"It is all to do with that Adonis downstairs, isn't it?" the doctor mused. "He *is* a handsome one, and no mistake, but handsome is rather than handsome does?"

Julia could only nod.

"Tell me all about it."

Disjointedly, between sobs, going back and forth in sequence, Julia poured out what had been lying so heavily on her spirit.

"I was so—so shocked and angry to see him again. I had never expected to; did not even want to. I just—went for him. He deserved it. I was determined he should not get off scot-free." Julia wiped her eyes. "I should hate him for all he has done to me, but in spite of everything I find I can't hold on to it."

"Why should you hate him? You went along of your own free will. I suspect it is yourself you hate, for losing your—shall we say amateur—status? For allowing yourself to become involved again though you had abjured men after your disastrous marriage, which was a mortal blow to your self-esteem—wasn't it?"

Julia nodded.

"All failure hurts, but in your case it annihilates. Why is it so necessary to be perfect?"

"Nobody loves a failure."

"Ah . . ." The doctor's voice was soft. "Is that what you were taught to believe? To strive for standards that are impossibly high for any human being? You are hard on people, aren't you, but even harder on yourself." The doctor mused in silence for a while, then went on:

[83]

"From what you have told me, your husband resented your success, which was rapid as against his studying struggle; the fact that you were the breadwinner mauled his pride; he resented it, while you re-arranged your priorities and found he came a long way down the list. He failed you, in your eyes, then betrayed you by finding another woman—the kind you perhaps despise? The kind who is content to have a man and no more."

"He said I wasn't one," Julia wept. "Typically and selfishly male; he meant not the kind of woman a man will want: docile, malleable, eager to please . . . I am not and never will be. I tried it and look where it got me."

"Was that why you accepted Adonis's offer? Because you felt you were not a woman in the masculine sense of the word? You saw it as a chance to prove your husband wrong."

"I had had opportunities before," denied Julia, "and took none of them."

"Because they did not appeal, that's why. He did. So powerfully you were incapable of resisting. Had you really wanted nothing to do with him you would have sent him packing like all the rest."

The doctor abstracted the sodden tissues and handed over a fresh supply. "The self which responded so passionately to him was the one you had put under lock and key; his effect was to set it free; then, when you saw that the woman you were was still not enough to prevent him from leaving you for others, you engineered your own punishment."

Over the tissues, Julia's eyes widened and fixed.

"In my work, I deal with so many women who 'forget' to take their pill. No woman 'forgets,' Julia. Not if she really wants to prevent conception. It will be the one thing she will *never* forget. I think you sought punishment for his abandoning of you the first time, to the extent that you would never so much as look at another man."

Julia's face was a study in white.

"It is all very complicated, I know. Human behavior usually is. Our motives are not always the ones we decide they are." The doctor eyed Julia keenly. "He, of course, assumed you were pregnancy-proof?"

Julia nodded.

"Tell me about your relationship."

"Nothing to tell. It was sexual; end of story."

"Only you became inescapably emotionally involved as well."

Julia's silence was her answer.

"Are you in love with him?"

[84]

"That's the trouble," Julia said despairingly. "I shouldn't be! Not with a spoiled brat like him!"

"Whom you cannot get out of your mind."

"I can't account for it—any of it! It is not like me at all. Why should I be so besotted with someone I regard with contempt? It is desire, that's all . . . sexual need. I have the urge to sample what he peddles—and so well!"

"You think so?" The doctor obviously did not agree. "Or is it that you keep telling yourself so? I think you love him very much. Why else are you in this state? You say you grieve for the child you aborted, but you were acting within your character, which is practicality incarnate. You had not expected to be so violently disturbed emotionally. But then, emotions do disturb you, don't they? They are so intractably arbitrary; will not do as they are told. If you had no feeling for this man you would not feel so guilty at having aborted his child. No woman grieves for the loss of a child by a man she hates. And are you not shielding him by keeping silent about it? What is that if not love? You are doing what he has come to expect from women. Yet I can tell you that this week has given him much to cope with too. Whatever his feelings for you they are not casual; he too, is involved in a relationship he cannot discard. He has returned to you twice, now: right out of the character you have depicted. Have you not wondered why?"

"For a little more practice."

"No. If he was still that kind of man he would have gone when he saw you were not capable. Found someone who was. Instead, he has stayed here, worrying about you, anxious for you, biting his nails to the quick and smoking like a chimney."

Julia's mouth opened.

"Meet him halfway—if you still wish to meet him, that is."

"That's the trouble. I don't know if I do. I am so confused . . ."

"Then tell him so. He has come back to tell you something: let him tell it. Then decide what to do."

The doctor rose. "You have a decision to make. My advice is, put him out of his misery too."

"I'm scared."

"So is he. That is why it is so serious. You are the strong one, you realize that. But do not assume that because hitherto he has shown none he does not possess any strength of his own." The doctor laid a hand on Julia's shoulder. "Be kind to him," she advised. "He has discovered that he loves and needs you very much."

IT TOOK JULIA a long time to bathe and dress, so depleted was her energy. On going into the bathroom she found an enormous bottle of bath oil perfumed with Dior-Dior. Brad must have bought it. She poured a generous libation, soaked in scented bubbles until she could delay no longer. He was downstairs, waiting for her.

She put on a pair of sage-green trousers and matching sweater, avoiding the sight of her body in the mirror. Brad had said she was a Renoir; now she *was* a Modigliani . . . The trousers gaped at the waist, hung on her hips. She was only glad the polo neck of the sweater hid the empty saltcellars at her collarbones. Her face too, was tautly pale. She applied blusher and a bright lipstick. A death's head looked back at her. She wiped it off again, applied a soft rose. That was better.

BRAD WAS ON HIS HAUNCHES in front of the bright fire, placing fresh logs. He heard her coming downstairs, rose and turned, but Julia was stock-still with astonishment. Every bowl she had was in the room, bursting with flowers, making it a bower. Roses, lilac, freesia, tulips. On the coffee table was a pile of the latest magazines, next to them an enormous box from Charbonnel et Walker. And in the corner was a brand-new television set—color, in place of the old black-and-white portable.

Her eyes reached Brad. His face was more nakedly vulnerable than she had ever seen it; the brass-bound confidence badly pitted. Apprehension, even desperation, was writ large, and his smile was too bright, like a star about to go nova.

"I think a drink, don't you?" he asked quickly. "The doctor said you could, now."

"All right," agreed Julia, tearing her eyes away.

"Come and sit down by the fire."

He piled cushions behind her back solicitously, careful not to touch her, before going into the kitchen. Julia drew a shaky breath. The very sight of him still had the power to undo her, but she had, it seemed, rid herself of her accumulated store of bitterness, leaving a vacuum waiting to be filled. But she was also conscious of a gulf as wide as a seismic fault. What happened now would be either rescue or disaster.

He came back with a bottle of champagne in one hand, two glasses in the other. Julia's heart sank. He could not be *that* obvious. "You are sure your name is not Charlie?" she asked waspishly.

"Nope. It's Jonathan."

"So that's what the J stands for."

[86]

"Right. Jonathan Winthrop Bradford. But as I said . . ." His eyes met hers. They begged. "Brad to my friends."

Something in the way he said it caused her eyes to probe his; what she saw there caused an explosion inside which blew up the debris of Monday's earthquake. Her hand was trembling as she took the glass he held out. "What to this time?"

"How about the beginning?"

"Another one?"

Stubbornly: "I said *the* beginning. The others were false starts."

As their eyes met again her heart tried to leap her rib cage and fell back stunned.

"Were they?" She forced steadiness into her voice.

"Weren't they?"

"Well . . . I remember you saying you didn't like endings."

"I hate them! I thought this one was the end of me! I mean that, Julia. That's why I'm back—had to come back." He drew a deep breath. "No more games. From now on, truth between us. We weren't before, were we? Truthful, I mean. Not until you were on Monday."

Julia opened her mouth but he jumped in quickly. "You were dead right, of course. I had already realized the truth of what you told me." He paused to gulp champagne. "How do you feel?" he asked next.

"Much better—thanks to your care and protection," she added.

"Self-protection, you mean. If I haven't got you I haven't got anything."

This time Julia's heart got as far as her throat and stuck there.

"That's what I came back to tell you." In a rush: "That it isn't a game any more with me either."

Julia could not have taken her eyes from his if she had tried.

"When did it stop being a game with you?" he asked.

"When you went back, that first time."

"Me too, only I didn't—wouldn't—realize it. But that's the reason I came back, of course." He dragged up the old pouf Julia had recovered to match the chairs. "What we were playing was a game of Truth or Consequences; my coming back to you was a consequence; what you told me Monday was the truth." He gulped more champagne, refilled his glass. "You were so sick because I had got to you, hadn't I? The way you had gotten to me?"

Julia nodded mutely. She could only follow where he led.

"Even so you had me dead to rights. I was never a thinker—only acted; but since you, I've changed. Thought about someone else besides myself. Even dreamed about them. You, Julia. You haunted me all the way across the Atlantic, have never left me since. I've dreamed about being with you the way it was that first time. Not the second; I did that in, didn't I? Really blew it when I made a run for it. But for the first time in my life I was out of my depth." He paused to stare into his glass. "Like I said, I'd always stuck to the shallow end."

His knees were touching hers because he had edged forward as he spoke, lost in the intensity of his feelings; his words hurried as though he had to get them out while he still had the courage to do so.

"I came back to ask you if you would—take me on. I need you, Julia, more than you know. I won't blame you if you don't trust me, but I trust you. With my life. I did use you, take you for granted, expected you to be waiting and willing each time. For that I am truly sorry. It is the truth when I tell you I need you more than I have ever needed anything or anyone—that to think of life without you is to think of death."

"How do you think I feel?"

"Do you? You have such a tight hold on your emotions; at least I thought you did until Monday, but you weren't yourself then."

"No," Julia said in a clear voice. "It was because I *was* myself—my real self. Not the sophisticated piece of machinery you thought me. I am *not* experienced, not worldly-wise, not—" Her voice snapped.

"So all this"—his hand sketched her gauntness and paleness—"*was* because of me?"

"Yes."

"Thank God! No—I don't mean I'm glad you were sick, I mean I'm glad I was the cause of it—because it means I did get to you."

"Without even trying."

The glasses went flying.

"Oh, Jesus, Julia! I've lain nights on this lumpy old sofa and thought of nothing but you. I was so scared when you went for me; thought I'd finished us, until I realized you were so sick." He held her as though she would break. "So thin and frail," he fretted. "One good grip and you'd fragment."

"No I won't. Not anymore. You are the right shot I need."

"I felt like shooting myself!"

Julia, too, felt she had been exploded from a cannon and was soaring, soaring upward. She could only hang on to Brad, feel him hold her safe. Everything was happening so fast, but for once in her life she didn't give a damn. All that mattered was that Brad needed her, wanted her.

Under her cheek his heart was pounding like a trip-hammer and he was as shaky as she was. "I feel drunk," he said with a little laugh, "and it's not on two glasses of champagne."

"I'm light-headed myself."

"You are light all over! I don't like you skinny, my love, it doesn't suit you. I'll have to fatten you up."

"What for, the kill?" teased Julia, only to see his face go out like a light. "I was only joking," she faltered in bewilderment.

"I'm not," he said. "I want you should be the Julia I first met when I take you home. Bowl them over the way you did me." He held her so close it was as though he was trying to melt into her. "I want it all to be so different from now on. I'm tired of the way I was living—" He broke off to kiss her. "It will be different, you'll see," he vowed vehemently. Over her head his face was set. Then he fell to kissing her with a passion that was, for the first time, desperate. "Oh, how I've missed you. With you it was like with no one else." But she felt him applying the brakes. When he would have put her away reluctantly she would not let him.

"You don't have to treat me like china, darling, I won't break. I am still the same woman, you know, only less of her. And I've dreamed of being with you too."

"But you are so fragile . . . it would be like taking advantage of a child . . ."

"I am no child." Julia kissed him to prove it.

"You are quite sure?"

"Positive. I want to make love. I need to, right now. Please, love me, Brad; love me as only you can."

He pulled her to her feet then swooped her up into his arms, before making eagerly for the stairs. But he still made exclamations of distress at the sight of her meager flesh, the hollows and protruding bones he remembered as cushions of satin flesh. His own clothes went everywhere as he flung them off before sliding under the quilt to join her, gathering her to him. "This is really our beginning," he told her, mouth and hands readying her, evoking the quivering, greedy response that was already clamoring for him.

How many lonely nights had she lain and remembered how it had been; his touch, his mouth, his body. Her own fingertips remembered the feel of him; the resilience of firm flesh, the wide shoulders, the roundness and erotic curve of his buttocks, and finally, as he entered her, the silkiness and pulsating power of his penis, deep within her, flesh within flesh. She locked her legs around him in a way that made him utter a thrilled little laugh and exclaim: "Oh, Julia . . . Julia!"

[89]

before he went wild, unable to hold back at the feel of her, warm and tight, her inner muscles contracting and caressing him into frenzied thrusts that made her feel he was trying to lose himself in her. For the first time she felt his trouble in withholding, and she squeezed him, letting him know he did not need to. But he struggled manfully until, unable to stop, she felt his buttocks tense and the little tuft of hair at the base of his spine bristle before his whole body erupted into her, hot and copious, his orgasm wild and lengthy and ecstatic, as were his cries. Finally he fell forward, totally spent, his skin hot and slick under her hands. "Oh, my God . . . ," he gasped, "that, my love, is what it is all about, you and I, but more me than you this time. Give me a little while and I'll make it up to you, I promise."

"No need," Julia told him gratefully. For the first time she felt she had really possessed him, though she herself—strangely—had not come. It was the very first time he had failed to bring her to orgasm, but it did not matter. What mattered was the way he had come; more devastatingly than he ever had. It satisfied her emotionally in a way that was totally different from her usual physical satisfaction; in some inexplicable way, even n.ore gloriously fulfilling. "We have all the time in the world now," she said contentedly.

His breathing had slowed, but his voice was blurred with felicity when he murmured: "Just so long as we can spend it together."

He settled his chin in the hollow of her shoulder, as he always had, body warm but no longer urgent against hers, yet conveying an immensity of loving. "Now I can sleep," he sighed. And did.

THEY WERE MARRIED, very quietly, at ten o'clock in the morning by a judge at the American Embassy in Grosvenor Square. Chris and an embassy official—a college friend of Brad's—were witnesses. Julia wore pale cream; a Jean Muir dress and jacket of pure silk, with a wide hat of pure silk straw, its crown a mass of tiny Pinocchio roses, rosy pink with a touch of flame, matching the posy she carried. Brad was glitteringly handsome in a new gray suit. Afterward, the four of them adjourned to the Connaught for—literally because Julia had been unable to eat a thing—their wedding breakfast. From there, they went straight to Heathrow to catch their flight to Boston.

As their flight was called Chris hugged Julia hard. "So long, Mrs. Bradford, and the best of luck—especially with Mother Dear. How much has he told you, by the way?"

"Not much, but every word was done in gold leaf. She is obviously very—special, only son and all that."

"Which is no doubt why he gets away with murder." Chris frowned. "Why do I have the feeling that where everyone else is concerned she is a hanging judge?"

"Not to Brad," Julia said quickly. "To him she is Mother Incarnate."

"I always said the Virgin Mary gave the rest of us an impossible image to live up to." Bluntly: "There's a screw loose somewhere, Julia. Tighten it, is my advice to you." She paused. "He still doesn't know about the abortion?"

"No."

"Why not?"

"That was the past. The future is all that matters. I burned that page."

"Along with your boats?"

"I am doing what I want to do," Julia said ringingly. "It all reduced to a single choice. Brad—or no Brad."

"You have changed," marveled Chris. "All I recognize about you these days is your face!"

She turned to Brad, who embraced and kissed her. "Take good care of her," she warned jokingly, "else you'll all be running around Boston crying 'The British are coming' all over again."

Brad laughed. "As if I would dare do anything else."

He glanced at his watch, impatient to be gone. Just then, he was drawn aside by an obsequious airline official, giving Chris a chance to murmur: "You've got a tiger by the tail there, love. Go with it—and him. As for the rest—well, you remember I advised you to go get yourself another lap? This is in the lap of the gods, sweetie." She fluttered her eyelashes at the hovering embassy official. "But right now, it's somebody else's lap I'm interested in."

Julia boarded the plane laughing.

THEY HAD THE FIRST-CLASS CABIN to themselves. Julia suspected Brad had bought every seat; the way the flight attendant brought champagne at once confirmed it, along with her murmured "Congratulations."

It was all so totally different from her first marriage. That had been the whole bit: white, church, bridesmaids, because Derek's mother had been tearful at the thought of her son getting married "miserably," as she put it, in a registry office, as had been suggested, in her ruthlessly practical way, by Julia's aunt. "A sheer waste of money," she had said disgustedly. "Not the way I brought you up, Julia. All this needless expense for one Saturday afternoon!"

And then it had been two weeks in Marbella for their honeymoon. This time, Julia had no idea where—or even if—Brad would take her. He had a pile of cables on his lap now, going through them with a slight frown, making notes with a gold pen. Julia examined her new rings; her plain gold wedding band and the enormous topaz set in diamonds which had been her surprise engagement ring. "Matches your hair," Brad had told her. Smiling to herself she looked up to find Brad watching her.

"What's the matter?" he asked.

"Oh . . . a momentary flash of disbelief, I suppose."

"About what?"

"That it has all really happened; that I am here, Mrs. J. Winthrop Bradford, on my way to Boston, Massachusetts. It has all been rather quick."

"That's the best way," Brad said curtly. "Things go sour when they hang around."

"Don't you feel any sense of—well—wonder, that this has all come about?"

"No; all that matters is that it *has* come about."

"But you are so used to all this." Her hand gestured to the empty cabin, the champagne, their cases—including her new crocodile dressing case that had been one of his wedding presents. "It is brand-new to me; nerve-racking as well as exciting."

"Nerves! You!"

Julia opened her mouth to say: "But that me is not the real me," then shut it again. She would just have to show him.

"You are not having second thoughts?" he asked, his lips pursed in the way that said he was not best pleased.

"Don't be silly. It's just that it is taking me all my time to cope with the first ones. I'm a new bride, darling, bear with me."

"But you've done it all before."

She withdrew from him. "Not like this."

His smile told her he had relented. "Good. I want it all to be first time for you."

"What's Boston like?" she asked after a moment.

"Nowhere else. You'll see."

BUT JULIA THOUGHT, once they reached Beacon Hill, that it was all like London, only once removed. The airport, the journey from Logan, had not had the feeling of a foreign country about it; the language, of course, she told herself. And besides, she had seen streets like these so many times on television, ditto the enormous American cars, the drug-stores and the drive-ins and the hot-dog stands. Beacon Hill was different: old, quiet, very dignified. It brought back Kensington for some reason, and when they turned into Mount Vernon Street and she saw the cobblestones, the gaslight, the iron boot scrapers, she could have been still in London—except it was definitely once removed.

The Bradford house was large, double-fronted, front door and shutters painted a glossy bottle green. A brass plate bore the name *Bradford* in copperplate script, and the knocker was in the shape of a lion's head. Julia lifted it while Brad brought out the bags. A butler opened up. His impassive face broke into a smile as he saw Brad coming up the steps behind Julia. "Mr. Brad, sir! We had not expected you, but it is a pleasant surprise. Nice to have you home again, sir."

"How are you, Thomas?"

"Very well, sir. I trust you had a good trip."

"No complaints."

The butler stepped back, allowing Julia to enter a high, wide and handsome hall, its floor like a chessboard, a fine old staircase curving up one wall. It smelled of polish and the masses of white flowers in brass bowls which Julia was to learn were called dogwood and native to New England. There was not a speck of dust anywhere: everything glowed, reeked of tradition and age and a set and certain way of life. This was a house run to perfection; there would be no raised voices here.

"Anybody home?" Brad asked.

"Mrs. Amory and Mrs. Adams are in the back parlor, sir, awaiting your mother's arrival. Her plane has been delayed through engine trouble, unfortunately. She is due back at around six o'clock."

"In that case, you can be the first to know," Brad said. Turning to Julia: "This is Thomas, who has been with us all my life. This is Mrs. Bradford, Thomas. We were married in London this morning."

Thomas's impassive face betrayed nothing but pleasant welcome. "Good afternoon, madam."

Just then, a door at the rear of the hall opened and a bone-slender woman stood poised for a moment before exclaiming: "Brad! We were just this minute talking about you . . . wondering where you were and what (or should I say who?) you were doing!" She skimmed across the floor, arms spread in extravagant welcome.

"Bitsy!" exclaimed Brad.

His second sister, Julia thought, fixing a smile. She watched brother and sister embrace, caught over Brad's shoulder the sudden look of

[93]

surprise in Bitsy's eyes—Bradford eyes, as sea-changeable as those of her brother. She smiled into them but there was no answering smile; only sharp surmise, which changed to stunned, disbelieving shock when Brad introduced them.

"Married!" Shock echoes ricocheted.

"This very morning, in London."

"I don't believe it! You are engaged to marry Caroline Norton! The invitations came from the printer just yesterday!"

"Not anymore. I am married, Bitsy. Julia is my wife."

There was a hint of steel in Brad's voice and Bitsy's eyes narrowed, only to flare wide in unholy glee as she asked: "And Mother? Who is going to tell Mother?"

Julia glanced at her husband. His jaw was tight and there was a queer look on his face.

"Have you thought what will happen?" Bitsy demanded gleefully. "Do you realize what her reaction will be?" Bitsy was gloating. "She will have a fit!"

"That, my dear sister, is the understatement of this or any century," a voice boomed, and Julia swung, as Brad did, to see a large woman sailing across the hall like a galleon into battle.

"Abby!" This time the gladness in his voice was genuine.

"Well, dear brother, now you've gone and done it," she said, but affectionately, and the smile she turned on Julia was warm, if curious. "Welcome to Boston, Julia. I'm Brad's eldest sister. The one with her mouth open is Bitsy. Welcome again."

"Thank you." Julia found herself warming to this sister; Bitsy had evoked no such response. No wonder Abby was Brad's favorite. Bitsy was obviously a bitch. Brad had already thrown out the casual aside that Bitsy was jealous. Another understatement, Julia thought now. She hates her brother's guts. She turned her eyes to her husband, now talking urgently to Abby, who was listening and frowning. No doubt enlisting her support. Bitsy, on the other hand, would probably take an ax to those supports already in place. Which was when that lady observed, with unpleasant surprise: "You are the very last thing we expected. When Brad left for Europe he was engaged to someone else."

"I know." Julia held on to her cool.

"But didn't care?" Now there was contempt, and also anger. Bitsy obviously did not like being surprised by her brother this way; it left her ill prepared for battle.

Now Julia manned her own guns.

"Brad told me it was more or less engineered by his mother."

Bitsy's face took on an affronted stare. Then she laughed. "Oh, do tell her that," she urged. "She would be *most* interested."

Which was when Julia knew she had made an enemy. Oh, great, she thought. Not five minutes into the house and already in the rough. She turned away from Bitsy and moved to where Brad and Abby were still conferring in low voices.

". . . do my best but this is one time where I can't—won't—guarantee results," Abby was saying. "This time you've really gone and done it—" She broke off and said with that overheartiness which always betrays a topic: "Well, now, Julia, I'll bet you could do with a nice cup of tea." She put her arm through Julia's. "There's just Bitsy and I right now. Mother is still over the Atlantic and not due to land until six o'clock, but it will give us time to get acquainted."

Brad smiled at his wife but Julia could see that his mind was elsewhere. That little stitch she knew by now denoted displeasure was rucking the space between his blond eyebrows. His smile was also mechanical; he saw her but her image was not strong enough to derail his train of thought.

Abby led her into the back parlor, which made Julia's working eye glow. Terra-cotta walls hung with portraits of long dead Bradfords. Copley? Gilbert Stuart? A carpet which picked up that color with medallion insets of chocolate brown and sharper, lemon yellow. Four tall windows along one wall hung with cotton satin also of rich, milky chocolate brown, bound in terra-cotta. A fireplace of white marble, ablaze with those same white flowers she had noticed in the hall, placed in copper bowls and crystal vases; candles in engraved storm lanterns, and a tall gilt mirror hanging above a massively carved and gilded table on which stood a fine ormolu clock under a glass dome. Opposite, an oval vitrine housed a collection of superb English porcelain. July sunshine made the room glow.

Abby drew Julia toward a sofa upholstered in golden yellow figured damask. She was warm, friendly, direct, if somewhat overpowering because of her size, but Julia felt she had met a kindred spirit. All three were strikingly alike in their coloring and eyes, but Abby and Bitsy had the bony, long-nosed American Bradford face; Brad's classical handsomeness came from the English branch of the family.

"Come on then," urged Bitsy, sitting down on the matching sofa. "Do tell . . ."

"Nothing to tell," Brad shrugged, but coming to sit by Julia and take her hand in his. My comfort or his? she wondered. "We met, fell in love and found we couldn't do without each other. So we got married and hope to live happily ever after."

"Which leaves Caroline where?" Bitsy asked wide-eyed.

"That's my business," Brad snapped.

"When were you married?" Abby asked, not having heard the earlier exchange in the hall.

"This morning, in London. Ten A.M. London time."

"Good God! Then this is a honeymoon."

"Once everything is squared away."

Bitsy's laugh cracked like glass. "I rather think it is a triangle."

Abby leveled her a glance that was a blunt instrument before saying: "Tea, please, Thomas," to the butler who came in.

It came on a heavy gallery-edged tray of what Abby told Julia, who asked, was Paul Revere silver, though the silver spirit kettle, teapot, creamer and sugar bowl were English. She watched while, in true English fashion, Abby warmed the pot before spooning in what smelled like Earl Grey from a silver caddy.

"Go on," Abby chuckled, observing her. "You expected tea bags and cookies, right?"

Julia had the grace to blush.

"Surely Brad has told you Mother is English." Bitsy exclaimed.

Again Abby saved it. "Forty-five years in these United States haven't even scratched the surface. Mother is and always will be an expatriate."

As if to drive home the lesson, there were English-type scones bursting with currants, a feather-light sandwich cake, and petits fours Julia recognized as coming from Fortnum's. She drank two cups of Earl Grey gratefully, clutching at this reminder of home as at a lifeline, answering Abby's kind questions and doing her best to ignore Bitsy's constant sniper fire.

Finally, sensing Brad's rapidly fraying equanimity, she laid down her cup and saucer saying gratefully: "That was the perfect introduction to Boston. Thank you, but now I would dearly love to go upstairs, unpack and then have a cool shower and change."

"Fine!" Brad said heartily, with overquick alacrity. "You go on upstairs and take a leisurely time about everything, while Abby and I go to meet Mother."

Julia glanced sharply at him. He evaded her direct glance and putting an arm about her shoulders proceeded to draw her from the room. "We'll have to rough it in my bachelor room for now, I'm afraid. Nothing is prepared, you see. You don't mind, do you?"

Of course, he still had to tell his mother and was taking Abby along

[96]

as bodyguard for that occasion. Julia's heart turned turtle and quietly sank.

"Whatever you say," she said, swallowing hard.

He took her up the lovely old staircase and along a corridor to a door which opened into a large sitting room off which was an equally large bedroom. The bathroom opened off that. The furniture was American, and lovely, especially the superb old four-poster, and the quilt was a work of art. "Done by a Bradford wife God knows how many generations ago," Brad said carelessly. He also had a dressing room lined with sandalwood cupboards and shelves.

"There's plenty of room," he was saying, sliding back doors and rattling hangers. "The bags are here but I'll send someone to unpack for you."

"Will you be long?" Julia asked, facing her problem head on.

Brad's shrug was uneasy and his back was to her. "Hard to say . . . Traffic can be hell to and from Logan at this time of day . . . I'll get back as soon as I can. It's just that Mother always likes to be met . . . You know, family customs and that sort of thing." He turned to face her, face and voice elaborately casual. But Julia knew him by now. He was preparing himself for Armageddon. Her heart threatened to choke her. Dear God, she thought. What sort of a mother has he got? They are all terrified of her. She moved blindly to where her cases had been laid on their trestles just as someone knocked. "Hello, Rose," she heard Brad say—relievedly. "Come to help?"

"Miss Abby thought Mrs. Bradford could use some."

"Rose looks after Mother," Brad said, as Julia looked at the elderly, thin-faced maid, neat as a pin in a silk dress of clerical gray under a spotlessly white apron and cap. "How long is it, Rose?"

"Thirty-two years this very summer, Mr. Brad."

Her smile made Julia warm to her, as did the South London accent.

"Rose will see you all right," Brad said affectionately. "As you've always done me, eh?"

"Lady Hester likes everything to run smoothly," Rose answered composedly, but with a twinkle in her faded blue eyes.

"You might give my wife a few hints," Brad grinned, but purposefully. "This house runs to a schedule," he explained to Julia. "Mother is keen on oiled wheels and all that."

"I am always willing to learn," Julia said, smiling at Rose. And anxious to please. Had the circumstances of her marriage been less shocking she would not have given a damn. But Brad had jilted a fiancée to marry her and she was anxious to dispel, from the start, any

[97]

hint of the gold digger. Rose, she thought, was the perfect place to begin. A direct line to Brad's mother.

"I'll be up later," Brad said now, his mind already elsewhere. Well, he wanted it this way. Let him deal with it. Anger burned.

"It's awfully hot, isn't it?" Julia said, feeling moisture bead.

"I'll turn up the air conditioning. Mr. Brad won't go without it in the summer, but I'm afraid the main rooms of the house don't have any because of Lady Hester's asthma; it affects her breathing."

Asthma! Brad had not mentioned that . . .

"You will get used to the heat in time," Rose said kindly. "And the winters too. In America, even the weather tends to go to extremes."

"Do you get back to England very often?" Julia asked.

"Every year, madam. Lady Hester spends every summer at Arun."

"You are a Londoner aren't you?"

"Born in Clapham, but evacuated to Arun during the war, to one of the estate farms. When I was fourteen I went to work in the house as a parlormaid, and I used to give Miss Jelks—she was Lady Hester's maid in those days—a hand. When she retired I took over."

Rose was unpacking Julia's bags with the skill of long experience, hanging up the new clothes with the labels which, Julia thought, should pass muster: Rive Gauche, Elle, Gina Fratini, Bellville-Sassoon . . .

"Would you like me to run you a cool bath, madam? Lady Hester found them a sovereign in the summer, always."

"That would be lovely."

As she undressed: "Lady Hester isn't an invalid, is she?" Julia asked casually.

"Good heavens, no!" Rose sounded amused. "She broke her hip last year when a horse threw her, but she does not let that stop her—or anything else, come to that." Rose tested the water with her hand. "There, I think you will find that very refreshing."

It was; the water was just right to the perfect degree: just this side of cold, and it was refreshingly perfumed with a lovely green fragrance which also softened it. Julia trickled silky water over her and let her body relax, even if her mind would not leave its treadmill.

So the fit, then, would be of anger. Bitsy—and in their own way Abby and Brad—had made that plain. Lady Hester would be anything but pleased even with her precious son. And as for her daughter-in-law . . . Well, Brad had told her enough to make it plain that it would be up to her to prove herself. Any cracks in the structure she would have to set to and mend herself; it was up to her to prove she was to be welcomed rather than withered, and one thing she had learned from this instructive afternoon was that in this particular family, all roads led to the Mecca that was Lady Hester Bradford. If you knew what was good for you made your pilgrimage.

She lay for a long time, thinking, thinking, finally clambered from the bath with a start when she realized the clock set into the wall said six o'clock. Lady Hester's plane should, if it was on time, be landing right now . . .

ABBY HAD VETOED THE IDEA of meeting their mother in the VIP lounge.

"You've got to deprive her of her weapons. You know what she's like. Whatever kind of scenes she makes in private, in public she is never less than the perfect mother-general. Take the advantage; tell her in front of a couple of hundred people. She'll look daggers but she won't be able to stick them in you." She shook her head at his taut face. "What *were* you thinking of?"

"Freedom," he replied, eyes turned inward. "You know damned fine if I'd asked her first she'd have blocked it. Caroline was her idea, not mine. I don't give a damn for her. Come to that, I don't believe she cares for me as much as my name. Julia knows nothing about the Bradfords; all she knows is me—Brad Bradford—and it's me she loves. She's not like the others, Abby. Not Julia. And I'm not the same when I'm with her. Besides, I happen to be in love with her. And that's a first too."

Abby saw his face had set into the old, intransigent stubborn-lipped look he wore when at odds with his mother and was set on defying her. Except, thought Abby, he never defied her over a woman before. Another first and, she only hoped to God, not the last. But if Mother's previous reactions to his defiance were anything to go by . . .

When Lady Hester's plane landed, they were in the forefront of waiting families and friends. As always, she was escorted by an obsequious airline official. Lady Hester believed in flying the public airlines (first-class, of course). It was good for her image, as well as for public relations. The Aristocrat not afraid to mingle with the Common Man. Now, when she saw not only her expected son but her elder daughter waiting for her, she greeted them warmly, offering Abby a cheek, but kissing her son on the mouth, like a lover.

"Dearest boy! And Abby too! To what do I owe this signal honor? And aren't you back early, my son?"

"I had a very good reason to come sooner."

She was walking arm in arm with him, as tall as he was, but infinitely more commanding. The crowds fell away before her as though they sensed her presence.

"No problems, I hope." Lady Hester frowned, alerted by his tone of voice.

"*I* don't think so. I hope you won't either."

She regarded him from eyes that held a hint of displeasure, then she smiled and patted his cheek. "Do I ever find displeasure in my adored son?" she asked.

"There is always a first time," muttered Abby.

"Abigail, do not speak as if you did not wish to be heard," commanded her mother. "Now, tell me, what has brought you back so soon?" she asked her son.

Brad took a deep breath. "I got married," he blurted.

Lady Hester stopped dead in her tracks before turning a slow-motion face to her son.

"I got married," repeated Brad, but not so strongly.

Lady Hester's marble face let a couple of heartbeats go by. "Married?"

"In London."

"London!"

"Today."

"Today."

Lady Hester was repeating each word he uttered in measured, unemotional tones. And then suddenly her laugh was an indulgent one. "You are, as they say in this country, putting me on."

"No, I'm not," Brad said. "I'm married, Mother. As of this morning. Legal and binding."

"I refuse to believe that Caroline persuaded you to elope . . . The invitations are ready to be sent out this very week, and I have spent a great deal of time and effort on the arrangements—"

"I didn't marry Caroline," Brad said.

Lady Hester's face took on a look that had Abby retreating a step backward. Brad's arm was held so tight by his mother that he could not move.

"You did—not—marry—Caroline?" repeated Lady Hester slowly.

"No. I married somebody else. An Englishwoman. Her name is Julia Carey." Before his voice failed him: "She's back at Mount Vernon Street, waiting to meet you."

Twenty seconds ticked by. Twin spots of color had appeared on Lady Hester's high cheekbones, and her carefully rouged mouth had tightened, even as her hand tightened on her son's arm. For a moment she was quite rigid with shock, and then she was drawing a deep breath, reasserting all her iron will over her instinctive response to throw back her head and howl. In a voice that was remarkable for its calm she said: "Dearest boy, you have chosen the strangest place to convey to me what must be the most important piece of news you have ever had to tell me in your life." Her face turned, stiffly as though it had rusted, so that she could look at her elder daughter. And I know who put him up to it, flashed silently between them. Abby forced herself to hold the baleful eyes, and when her mother said simply: "We will walk to the car," she fell in obediently behind.

Not until the luggage had been loaded, Ames in his driver's seat and Abby in the jump seat facing her mother and brother did Lady Hester speak again. "Now," she said, "you will tell me everything."

As Brad did so, she forced herself to remain calm, when what she wanted to do was take her large alligator bag and beat him over the head with it. She wanted to rant, rave, scream, rend, tear, in her anguish. She wanted to drum her heels, howl her fury to the four winds. Fool! she screamed silently at her son. Witless, mindless, sex-mad fool! Yet another part of her mind listened coolly to what he was telling her, eagerly, proudly, defiantly, about some woman who according to him was a combination of Helen of Troy, Eleanor Roosevelt and Madame de Pompadour, and it was this part which rang the warning bell.

When Brad had finished, sat looking at her with that tilt to his chin which meant he was away with the bit between his teeth, she selected the right smile—amusement tinged with besotted resignation—and sighed: "I can see she has got you struck all of a heap, darling, but— don't you think you have been a might careless? I do not care for myself—you know that, though I must admit to being hurt that you chose not to take me into your confidence—but have you given a moment's thought to what Caroline must be feeling? It all looks so *shabby*, dearest. To jilt a woman is in the worst possible taste. And not the act of a gentleman. It is also exceedingly bad-mannered and I had not expected it of you. I had not believed you could be so selfish."

Sitting silently in the jump seat, Abby flicked a glance at her brother's face. It was tight, white and losing, as his mother steadily and deliberately drained his pride and pleasure, its command of itself. As always, Hester Bradford had the power to reduce something of which he had been both proud and happy to something cheap, tawdry and best put away out of sight. God, but she was strong! Abby thought. She could feel the command emanating from her mother's slender figure,

[101]

too tall, now, for the meager weight she carried. Not once had she kissed him, said: "If it is what *you* want, my darling, then I am happy for you." Oh, you bitch, Abby thought, feeling her brother's deflation and unease. For God's sake, Brad, she's not an icon! Tell her to go to hell. That choosing a wife is your business; that your life is your own business; that you are thirty years old and you don't want to marry your mother!"

Abby must have made some sound at the shock her instinctive thought had produced, because her mother turned her head to look at her. The two women stared at each other, and so perceptive was Hester Bradford that she seemed to read Abby's horrified thoughts. Her eyes flashed a warning. Be silent! they told her. I will deal with you later.

"It has all been so hasty," Brad's mother said, turning back to him with sad finality. A shudder of distaste rippled through her. "So hole-in-the-corner, as though you had something to be ashamed of—"

No; but he will have by the time you are through with him, Abby thought.

"I trust there was no—specific—reason for such unseemly haste?"

"There was not."

At once, Lady Hester changed tack, warned by the note in her son's voice. "Forgive me, dearest, but you do see how it will look? What people will think?"

"I don't give a shit what they think!" Brad said in a strangled voice, his use of the obscenity a measure of just how hard he was trying to stand his ground against an adversary who had programmed his every move.

Worse and worse, Lady Hester thought, as she realized that far from being pressured into this hideous misalliance, he had been the one to instigate it. Even so, it would not do. How dare she? How *dare* she? She will pay for this. I will destroy her, whoever she is. Let her think everything in the garden is lovely—for now. Once I get behind the plow . . .

She sighed once again, saw how it clouded the bright eyes, and leaned on the hilt a little more.

"Well, my dearest boy, if it is what *you* want."

"More than I have ever wanted anything in my life."

Abby closed her eyes in despair as she heard the plea in his voice. *Don't*, Brad, she willed. You are letting her spoil it all. You are letting her win—as usual. Lady Hester cupped her son's chin with her hand, leaned forward and kissed him on the mouth again, lingeringly, again like a lover. "I can see you are head-over-heels and if she is your choice, then I am sure I shall come to love her too. But before I meet her I must know something about her. I want you to tell me *everything*. Start at the very beginning, from the moment you first set eyes on her . . ."

JULIA WAS STANDING in front of that section of the wardrobe Rose had appropriated for her when Rose came back to help her dress. Julia decided to go for broke. "I need your help and experience, Rose," she said frankly. "This is a very important night for me. Which dress shall I wear? I have to look exactly right, as I am sure you will understand."

Rose was unhesitating, her hand going straight to the dress she thought perfect. "The yellow silk, madam."

It was the kind of dress one wore in one's home. Cut on elegantly plain lines, it had a becoming cowl neck and long tight sleeves which buttoned up the forearms but hung in loose batwings from the shoulders, a narrow silk belt at the waist.

"It is a family dinner tonight, madam, and as such, then this is exactly what I would wear." She smiled at Julia and it was warm and encouraging. "It is also your color, having that red hair and all."

"Right," Julia agreed gratefully. "The yellow silk it is." Casually: "Is Lady Hester interested in clothes?"

"Only to the extent that she is never anything less than perfectly turned out, madam. She is a perfectionist, in clothes as in everything else."

Julia felt that added another thousand feet to the height of the mountain she had to climb.

"Just be yourself, madam," Rose advised, no expression in her voice, ever the perfect servant. "Lady Hester is very quick to spot the slightest hint of artifice." Pause. "And she is very protective of her son."

Watching Julia's expression in the mirror, "I am sure you will look very nice, madam," Rose said stolidly. "The yellow silk is just right and will pass muster with no difficulty." Diffidently: "And if you like, I could dress your hair in keeping."

Normally, Julia took no more than a few minutes to sweep a classic French pleat atop her head, but now she agreed at once. Rose was telling her quite plainly that she was on her side; that she wanted Julia to succeed.

Rose had talented hands. Soon Julia had an Edwardian-type cottage-loaf hairstyle, the heavy mass safely anchored with heavy pins. It gave her an elegantly old-fashioned look; gave her dignity and a fetching simplicity.

"Thank you, Rose," she said gratefully.

Rose smiled. Just then the telephone buzzed and Rose answered. "I'll be straight down," Julia heard her say, then as she cradled the receiver: "Lady Hester has arrived, madam. I must go and see to her. If I have a minute I will come back and help you to dress."

Julia stared at her reflection. Now! she thought. But her hands were steady as she made up her face; not too much: the art was to apply it so that you did not look as if you were wearing any at all. She used a tinted moisturizer, a blusher to highlight her high cheekbones, shadow only slightly deeper than her eyes, and three separate coats of mascara. No powder. That way her face retained a youthful sheen. A rose-bronze lipstick toned in perfectly with the yellow silk. There, she thought, surveying herself in the pier glass. That should pass muster.

Brad came in just as she was spraying L'Air du Temps. One look at his face and her heart contracted. It was white, tight-lipped, his eyes blazing queerly in a blind sort of way. Oh, God, she thought. What on earth has she said to him? And as she met his eyes she read their message, went across to him instantly. "You look frazzled, darling. Was the traffic bad?"

"Lousy." His voice was thick. "All of it—lousy . . ." His arms punished her, revealed an inner desperation. His kiss was the same. And he was ravenously aroused.

"I know what you need." Slipping from his arms she went to lock the door, then she went across to strip the quilt from the bed.

"You read my mind," he said thickly.

No, your face, Julia thought. It confirmed a theory she had formed: that sex was her husband's way of working off pressures, especially those exerted by his mother. Well, she thought practically, as the yellow silk—and everything else—came off, some men drink, others beat their wives. Surely this is the best way. But she was aware, on a deeper level, of resentment that she should be no more than a sexual sounding board. You are married, Julia, she reminded herself. And a little voice whispered slyly: Yes, and didn't Aunt Charlotte always say that was nothing more than legalized sex?

They were lying in sated silence, all Brad's tenseness gone, when someone knocked at the door. "That will be Rose," Julia sighed. Brad lifted his head, looked at the bedside clock. "Hell's bells, it's way past seven o'clock!" He was out of bed and loping for the bathroom.

Rose made no comment at the sight of the rumpled bed, the ruined hairdo. She merely waited while Julia sat down at the dressing table again before doing it all again. Then she placed a chiffon square over Julia's hair as she dropped the yellow silk over her head, after which Julia did a restoration job on her face. When Brad came out of his dressing room in shirt and trousers his eyes glowed: "You look fabulous!" he said with deep satisfaction.

"Due in large measure to Rose."

Brad flashed her a smile. "Thanks, Rose."

"If there is nothing more I can do I will go and see to Lady Hester."

"Fasten these for me, will you?" Brad thrust out his shirt cuffs, links dangling.

Julia smiled up at him as she did so. "This is all so *married!*"

"We *are* married!" The truculent set of his face harked back to half an hour before, which meant, she thought, that his mother had not been of the same opinion. Brad's last words reinforced it.

"This is important, Julia," he emphasized, as they prepared to go down. "For my sake—do it right."

For your sake? Julia thought, as she preceded him through the door. What about mine?

BRAD LED HER not into the parlor but into another lovely room, all soft rose and pinky-white, and Julia saw with a shock that all the family was present except for her mother-in-law.

Majestic in bottle-green velvet—badly creased and sporting a tear in the skirt—Abby sailed across to them. She had emeralds the size of quarters in her ears and a necklace that must have weighed several pounds. Julia had not put on any jewels—not that she had more than the black cat and the string of pearls that had been another of Brad's wedding presents. Obviously it was to be a family dinner.

It was Abby who introduced Julia to those members of the family not yet met—the sons-in-law. Brad made no protest as Abby bore her off, only headed for the drinks tray.

Abby led Julia first to where Bitsy, soignée in palest blue crepe, was standing with a tall, dark man with a satyr's face and an air of boredom.

"Julia, this is Drexel Adams, Bitsy's husband. Your new sister-in-law, Drex."

He bent over Julia's hand. "And a very lovely one."

"Mr. Adams," Julia acknowledged politely, staring straight into boldly admiring eyes.

"Drex to friends and family, please."

Abby bore her on. "And my own better half. Seth, say hello to Brad's wife."

Julia had to tilt her head. He must have been six and a half feet tall and thin with it; he stooped too, no doubt to avoid door lintels, which was also probably the reason for the head of thick, old English sheep-dog hair. But his face was gentle and his smile transformed it into something impish. He had an unexpectedly beautiful voice, as dark as his eyes, when he quoted: " 'Whenas in silks my Julia goes . . .' " And as his large hand enfolded hers he bent down to kiss her.

"Seth has a quotation for everything," Abby explained complacently.

"We had no Paul Revere to warn us this time," he said, twinkling down at Julia from his great height, "but it would have been to tell us to get ready to welcome your lovely face, my dear." He raised his champagne glass. "I drink to you. Health, wealth and as much happiness as is possible."

"Thank you." Julia unfurled in the warmth of her first unstinted welcome.

"No, it is you who do us the kindness by bringing among us your lovely face."

"I told her Brad could always pick 'em," Abby boomed.

Julia turned to find that Drexel Adams had come across, was holding out a glass of champagne. His eyes blatantly undressed her. "How does it feel to be Mrs. Apollo Belvedere?" Under the suavity lay sandpaper.

"I wouldn't know," Julia returned. "Why don't you ask her?"

She saw his eyes, so dark a blue as to be navy, flare suddenly, like his smile, and his laugh was appreciative. Before he could say more his wife was there, sliding her hand through his arm in a "down, boy" way, the eyes she focused on Julia hard with dislike. "We were just wondering where you have decided to go for your honeymoon," she drawled.

"We haven't—yet," lied Julia, the word not so much as having been mentioned.

Bitsy's lashes lowered in the way Julia knew meant the sting had been unsheathed. "Well, I suppose you could always utilize the arrangements made for the other one."

Abby, who had heard that, said trenchantly: "Since that's your foot in your mouth, sister dear, you'll just have to chew on it," before bearing Julia away. " 'The great mind knows the power of gentleness,' " she heard Seth say to nobody in particular, and turning her head Julia had the satisfaction of seeing Bitsy's flush.

[106]

"You will have gathered that my husband teaches English literature," Abby said. "That was Browning, by the way. I know them all too." Then: "Don't mind Bitsy," she said firmly. "She is well named: she has a little bit of everything, including jealousy."

What a nice lady, Julia thought. No wonder Abby was Brad's favorite sister. "A Rock of Gibraltar," he had said to her, "and every bit as unshakable." Bitsy looked as though she defended every square inch of territory; Abby, on the other hand, looked serenely confident that hers was inviolable. As for their husbands . . . Drexel Adams was a sharper, Julia decided. Too smooth by half and all done with somebody else's plane. Seth Adams was the only one who looked as Julia had expected a Proper Bostonian would be. But the sixty-four-thousand-dollar question, she thought, is what I am—and why; why Brad had jilted a fiancée so precipitously, and for what kind of woman.

Looking for her husband, she found him standing back to the fireplace—and watching her. His smile was a whip, urging her on, before he beckoned Thomas to bring him more champagne, after which he turned to check the clock. It was five minutes to eight, and Rose had told Julia that dinner was always on the stroke of eight o'clock. Surely her mother-in-law was not going to come in only to sweep them all off to the dining room without so much as a "How do you do." But Brad had made it emphatically clear that she had to win this one, even though he had pitchforked her into a situation she felt was strewn with mines. And his own continual checking of the clock added to her inner sense of unease and the growing conviction that her husband was terrified of his mother.

And then, even as the lovely old bracket clock chimed the hour, the double doors opened and everyone turned to face them. For a moment, Julia wondered hysterically if all the women would curtsey, for the woman standing in the doorway was majestic in every sense of the word. Julia saw at once where Brad got his eyes and his long, lean elegance. His mother was all of six feet tall; intimidatingly grand, radiating an aura of presence and authority. Which still did not prevent Drexel Adams's stage whisper: "My God, she's gone into mourning already!" from sounding loud and clear.

Lady Hester's black was stunningly elegant: a slip of thin silk under an overdress of transparent chiffon, goffered frills at throat and wrist. A five-stranded dog collar of pearls centered with an enormous sapphire framed in diamonds, encircled the no longer firm flesh of the throat; matching teardrops swung from her ears under hair that was as white as freshly blued sheets, cut short and crisp to spring away from forehead and nape. Her face was eagle-imperious, the eyes sharp enough to slice and blazingly bright. Her mouth was thin-lipped but artfully rouged so as to appear fuller. Her skin was remarkably unlined and her maquillage, delicate, the bones revealing what must have been breathtaking beauty. Her expression was commandingly arrogant, and her voice, as she tapped the silver-knobbed cane on which she leaned, was equally so, as she demanded: "Well, my son. I am waiting to be introduced to your wife."

Brad was at her side with a speed that would have won him a gold at any Olympics. His mother held out a hand; he kissed it, then her—on the mouth, Julia noticed, his mother's hand going to his face and holding the kiss until Julia's face began to burn. Then, when she let him go, he offered her his arm, which she leaned on before making progress across the room, everyone respectfully silent. He led her to the big old Georgian armchair Julia had noticed nobody had sat in, placing at her feet a footstool on cabriole legs. She handed him her stick, which he leaned against the chair. That done, she smiled at him again in a way which made Julia clench her jaw, before giving him a little nod which said: *"Now you may proceed."*

This is just not true! Julia thought. Do I bend the knee, or what? Her husband's expression, as he came toward her, made it clear she should bend *everything,* and the grip he took on her elbow propelled her along so urgently that she caught her heel in her gown and staggered. She heard Bitsy's smothered laugh and could have killed them both.

"This is Julia, Mother," Brad said, in a subservient voice. Julia stared into eyes that Brad had inherited, but much more penetrating, seeming to dissect her by way of peeling back the skin. She forced herself to meet them head on, refusing to grovel. She had never done that to anybody and, by God, she never would! She held the gaze unwinkingly.

Which was when Lady Hester smiled, making Julia jerk, as though a restraining hold had been loosened. "Come and kiss me, child," she said, proffering a cheek. Julia recognized the perfume as she touched her lips to the papery cheek. Floris. Red Rose. As she went to straighten, her chin was caught by long, powerful fingers which held her still while the eyes scrutinized her with a force that rendered her helpless. Now you know who I am, they said; let me see who you are.

"Yes, you are a beauty and no mistake," Lady Hester pronounced, sounding satisfied. "My son did not exaggerate. Welcome to Boston, Julia. I hope you will be very happy with us."

Us? thought Julia.

The smile Lady Hester bent on her was overpoweringly gracious.

[108]

"Brad, dear boy, a chair—here, by me," she commanded without looking at him.

"Thank you, darling," Julia countered in a clear voice, establishing her own dominion.

Lady Hester now held out a hand, much as a surgeon would, expecting the right instrument to be slapped into it. In her case it was a pair of half frames placed there by her daughter Bitsy, who had taken up station behind her chair, in the age-old lady-in-waiting position. So that was her function in this household, Julia thought.

Donning them: "I have seen hair that particular color only once before," Lady Hester commented, with that stunning rudeness Julia had only encountered with the aristocracy; she had the voice too. High, somewhat hooting and carrying; the kind that never saw fit to lower it because inferiors would never be capable of understanding what it was saying anyway. "She was remarkable too."

Julia was seething. Why not prod me for fat content and be done with it? That Brad should have let her in for *this!* She *would* kill him. And then Lady Hester took the steam right out of her anger. "My dear," she said warmly, "how happy I am that my son has chosen an *English* bride. My own, beloved country means so much to me." Suddenly her eyes actually twinkled; a whole Milky Way. "Now I shall not feel so outnumbered."

Julia blinked, bathed in the warmth of enormous charm focused, with unerring accuracy, right where she was hurting most.

"I remember how it was when I first came to America," Lady Hester reminisced. "One feels one is being weighed in the balance and found wanting . . . but I can see why my son wanted you."

"You are very kind," Julia murmured.

"I am rarely kind, my dear, but I am *always* honest." She broke off as Thomas bent in front of her, proffering a single glass of what looked like tonic water. "Certainly not." Lady Hester waved it away. "Tonight I shall drink champagne with the rest of you."

"Now Mother, Dr. Venner said—" Bitsy began.

"I am well aware of what Dr. Venner said, just as I know what I am going to do. Champagne, if you please, Thomas."

Turning back to Julia: "My wretched arthritis," Lady Hester said on a moue. "I am forbidden alcohol. But not tonight. I cannot very well toast my son and his new bride in Vichy water, can I?"

Thomas approached with her champagne. "Ah, that's better. The Taittinger, Thomas?"

"Indeed, my lady."

Lady Hester reached for her cane and tapped it on the leg of her footstool, not that anyone was looking elsewhere. She raised her glass. Everyone followed her example. "To my son and his wife," she said. All drank. It was as though general amnesty had been granted. Everybody relaxed. Julia was utterly confounded. The Dragon Lady had metamorphosed into the Sugarcane Fairy. Under the spellbinding charm she found herself opening out, running eagerly to fetch the conversational ball to lay it at her mother-in-law's feet, basking in the warmth of an approval ungrudgingly given and unstintingly voiced.

"Brad always set great store by good looks; in that direction he is remarkably susceptible," Lady Hester remarked on a note of satisfaction, which made Julia think she set great store by physical presentation, much as the Spaniards did. To be *guapa* was to be forgiven all the rest.

"I was susceptible to him," she answered honestly, to be rewarded by an approving smile.

"I have yet to meet a woman who was not. In that respect he is like my own father. That is he, over the mantel."

Julia turned obediently to look at the portrait she had noticed before but not wished to be seen staring at. It was Brad, but fifteen years on, and with an air of authority, command and maturity which as yet Brad lacked. Only the smile, all lady-killing charm, was the same.

"I adored my father," Lady Hester said in the voice of the confessional.

"Brad is astonishingly like him," Julia said.

"Which is why I also adore him."

Eyes met and held. Julia felt she was being instructed. She nodded slightly, and was again rewarded by an approving smile.

DINNER WAS AS SPARKLING as the champagne, though Julia was not really conscious of what she ate, only that it was perfectly cooked and beautifully presented. The conversation was equally digestible. Every now and then Brad, across the table, bathed her in one of his Turkish-bath smiles as his eyes telegraphed the message "Keep it up!" Which on the one hand offered feeling of relief, tempered on the other by dismay that he should feel it to be of such vital importance. It made her wonder what his reaction would have been had things gone the other way.

She watched him with his mother during dinner, saw how she touched him constantly, possessively, proudly. Whenever her eyes met those of Julia they seemed to say: Is he not beautiful, my adored son? Is he not to be worshiped by us both? No wonder he is spoiled rotten, thought Julia, which brought another thought to mind. Amid the plethora of family pictures in the drawing room, nowhere had she seen one which could have been Brad's father. Parthogenesis? she thought sourly. Because the Bradford family was a matriarchy, and it was in this capacity that Lady Hester questioned her, with gentle but ruthless insistence, as to her background, her family, her upbringing, her education, her work. No detail was too small to be inquired about. Julia felt she was being given the thirty-third degree.

Well, it is only natural, she comforted herself. If my son had brought home a total stranger and introduced her as his wife, when you thought he was happily engaged to another woman, I would be suspicious too. Which was another thing. Apart from Bitsy's spiteful allusion, Caroline Norton's name had not so much as been mentioned. It was as though Lady Hester had ordered her name erased, instructing that Julia's should be written in its place. Yes, thought Julia. Nobody does anything around here unless she says so.

Sally Armbruster had been right about the power: this was a formidable *grande dame.* But Julia had since learned that Sally had been fatally flawed in Lady Hester's eyes. She had already been possessed of a husband.

Studying her mother-in-law, Julia could see how Sally would regard Brad's mother as a killer. Had she not killed her hopes? Behind the effortless charm was a skeleton of steel. Julia did not doubt for one moment that her mother-in-law could be entirely ruthless when she chose. It made her thankful that what was coming her way—for now anyway—was approval.

Glancing around the room Julia decided to get up from the microscope. Everyone was flushed, not so much with wine as with relief. Which made her wonder once again, unease returning, what they had actually expected. She found herself looking down at her yellow satin pumps to check for signs of blood. And as she looked up caught Drexel Adams's sardonic eyes. She stared back. He was the first to look away. Don't concern yourself with the opinions of the rest, she told herself. Lady Hester's is the one that counts. If Brad wants you to fall into line, then get down on your knees with the rest of them.

As with everything else, Lady Hester decided when it was time to break up the party. "Long past my bedtime," she announced, before allowing: "But on an occasion such as this . . ."

It was eleven-thirty. And such was her power of command that the leavetaking was very different from the greeting. Julia found herself kissed by both wives and husbands, but it was Abby's approving "Well done," murmured into her ear, that pleased her most. Until Brad turned on her a smile that promised his own, special reward.

Which was when Lady Hester said with brisk finality: "I must keep my son from you for a little while. Business, you understand." A dry tease to the voice: "I must know if he did any work at all while he was in England."

Brad went with Julia to the foot of the stairs. "I shan't be long," he assured her. "I don't want to be. Wait until I can come and show you."

Julia floated upstairs. Rose was waiting for her, and Julia thought she read approval in her smile too. Well, she thought, as the yellow silk was lifted over her head, don't they say servants know everything?

It was only now, with the first high hurdle behind her and she still safely in her seat, that she realized how intent she had been on surmounting it. All of a sudden she was exhausted, the release of tension having the effect of sandbagging her. But her first sleep, though dense, was disturbed. Voices filled it, resounding like echoes. "She's a real Dragon Lady . . . cut your throat and hang you up so as not to lose a drop of blood . . . What do you do? What my mother tells me . . . My God! Mother will have a fit! . . . How does it feel to be Mrs. Apollo Belvedere? . . ."

She came out of it to find Brad sliding into bed, heard him say: "Hey! What's all this tossing and turning? You are not having a nightmare *now!*" He pulled her to him, all warm and ready and eager.

"Jet lag," lied Julia, turning to him gladly.

"Poor pussycat. I'll soon have you purring."

Julia's last thought, before all control fled, was that maybe Brad should report to his mother more often.

NEXT MORNING he kissed her awake. "Rise and shine, we have things to do, places to go."

"Where?"

"Shan't tell you till we get there."

Julia sat bolt upright. "A honeymoon?"

"Well . . . it's going to be short but I'll do my best to make it sugar-sweet."

"How long?"

"Only till Monday night."

Disappointment sprouted leaks. "Four days!"

"Mother had arranged certain—things—not knowing about us, you see. I'm more or less booked, all appointments firmed. It's a deal, and a big one, but suddenly we've got competition from an unexpected quarter. Nothing for you to worry about but it means I shall have to leave you for a while."

"So soon!"

"You won't be alone," Brad said quickly. "Mother has all sorts of plans. And we do have these four days."

Think yourself lucky, his tone said. He bounced out of bed with a playful slap on her bare bottom. "Up and at 'em, wench! Breakfast in this house is always at 9 A.M. and punctuality is one of Mother's things."

Lady Hester was already down, seated at the breakfast table, wearing a pair of large, tinted spectacles and reading a pile of mail. The glasses were whipped away as she raised her face to her son's kiss—on the mouth, as usual. To Julia she proffered a cheek. This morning she was bandbox-elegant in a black-and-white dogtooth suit—Chanel, Julia noted—braided and *très chic*. Pinned to one shoulder was what Julia came to recognize as her trademark: one, fresh red rose.

Brad went to the array of silver dishes on the sideboard, helped himself to scrambled eggs, tiny sausages, strips of bacon, button mushrooms and grilled tomatoes. Julia settled for an egg from a clutch in their special container.

"You are not dieting, I trust," Lady Hester asked disapprovingly.

"No, just not very hungry."

"A good breakfast starts the day well," instructed Lady Hester. She poured coffee from a Georgian silver pot.

"All is arranged," she said to Brad as she handed him his cup: Spode, willow pattern, the twins to Julia's own set. "Now, as to Tuesday . . ."

Julia buttered toast, played with her egg, not really wanting either, listening to mother and son talking of things about which she knew nothing; felt wholly excluded.

"If necessary, you'll have to go where he goes," she heard Lady Hester say. "If McCauley gives us the slip the Dunham boys will get to him and that will never do. I want that split to become a schism; that way we can divide *and* rule."

"Okay," Brad answered, with easy but total confidence, "will do."

Julia drank her coffee, feeling supernumary, remembering her dream of the night before. An omen?

"Hey!" She felt Brad's foot nudge hers.

"What? Oh, sorry, daydreaming . . ."

"Had enough to eat? Want more coffee? If not, then let's be on our way."

"Way! But I haven't packed or anything."

"I took the liberty of ordering Rose to do it for you," Lady Hester said.

"But—"

"Rose knows exactly what you will need. By the time you come back I will have engaged your own maid. All you have to do is go off and enjoy yourself."

Julia felt Brad pulling her chair back, rose uncertainly, feeling she was being sent through the mail. Thomas entered the room. "The car is waiting, sir."

"Fine. Bags loaded?"

"Yes, sir."

Brad turned to his mother. "See you Monday night, then."

Her embrace was disconsolate. "Home so briefly . . ." She proffered a cheek to Julia. But her "Enjoy yourselves" was a command.

Julia was quite sure she would do anything but. To be bundled off like a parcel, with no say as to her destination, was not her idea of a honeymoon. She had not been so much as consulted.

She sat, stiff with sullen grievance, as Brad drove the car—a big station wagon—through traffic that whizzed past like angry bees. As they crossed a river: "That's the Charles," Brad said. And a few moments later: "And this is Cambridge, where Abby lives." A casual nod of the head: "That's Harvard."

Soon they had left the groves of academe and were out in the country, and it was then Julia saw the sign: "CONCORD 20 M." Her sense of grievance burst into flame. They were going to the farm! A *farm* for a honeymoon? Cows and plowed fields and some old farmhouse! She was so outraged she was speechless. So this was his mother's idea of a honeymoon.

Brad had a smile on his face and was either unaware of or indifferent to the smoldering coming from the adjoining seat. It was a lovely day; he had wound the windows down, had his elbow propped on the door, hands negligently on the wheel. At least he was dressed for the country, Julia fulminated. Checked shirt and jeans; she had put on an elegant town dress in milky-coffee linen, nylons and high heels! A fine start to a honeymoon this was!

Then she noticed the beauty of the countryside. Lots of green grass, white picket fences, cattle, horses, the smell of hay.

[114]

"Not far now," Brad said comfortably. He glanced at her. "The sun is shining, why aren't you?"

"If I knew where I was going—and to what—I might have something to shine on!"

"Wait till you see it; you'll love it!"

That's what you think, Julia thought. She had expected to be taken somewhere special, glamorous. Step back on board the magic carpet that had brought her here.

"Mother was positive it was just the place." Brad went on blithely.

For what? Julia thought sourly. Me to come to my senses?

They were climbing a hill, topped it and as they did so she caught her breath. "Oh . . ."

Brad's glance was alight with laughter. "Told you. You expected some dirt shack and scratching chickens, didn't you? I could tell by that cloud hovering over your head." Spread before them, in a slight hollow, was a scene like an illustration from Louisa May Alcott. Sprawling white-painted house, ancient old trees, a stretch of water that must be a lake—or at least a large pond; ducks swimming on it, horses grazing, the smell of fruit trees, newly cut grass.

"Oh, but it's beautiful!"

"Go on. You really did expect the worst, didn't you?"

Julia had the grace to laugh, if it was shamefacedly. "Well . . . I didn't know what to expect."

"This is the farm. Where we Bradfords came from. It's special to us; here's where we took root in America, played our part in helping it become the United States. John Adams is a remote ancestor of mine—umpteen times removed—but we are proud to be descended from a Signer. Where else would I bring you for our honeymoon?"

"Angel!" Julia threw her arms around his neck just as he turned the car onto a wide expanse of smoothly raked gravel. Almost at once, the screen door at the side opened and a woman came out to the top of the steps. Oh, no! Julia thought, hugging herself. She was right out of a Norman Rockwell cover: stout, gray-haired, pink-cheeked, wearing a gray print dress and a voluminous white apron. Her smile was a beam.

"Here we are, Annie!" Brad called enthusiastically. He bounded from the car and up the steps to hug her. "Annie has been with us forever," he said, turning to Julia as she came up.

"So this is Mrs. Brad . . . My, but you're a pretty one. I mighta known."

"Where's Jonas?"

"Here . . ." He too was pure Norman Rockwell—or was it Grant

Wood? Striped overalls over a gray work shirt, a bony New England face, dry, laconic voice. He and Brad wrung hands.

"Jonas is Annie's husband. He runs the farm, she runs the house." Julia shook hands.

"Come on in then," Annie bustled. "Coffee's fresh and I baked you a pecan pie."

Ohhh, thought Julia, breathless with delight, it was all so *American!*

Once over the threshold, she stopped dead in her tracks. The sun poured in through a large window at the top of a flight of stairs, mellowing a fine old highly polished woodblock floor scattered with what she recognized as handmade rugs of venerable antiquity. An old grandfather clock ticked comfortably and, as at Mount Vernon Street, there were flowers everywhere. A couple of golden retrievers padded up, plumed tails waving, raising themselves to paw at Brad eagerly, whining with pleasure.

"Hey, here, Jack . . . hello, Jill, old girl." Brad patted them both and they whuffled with delight, panting and snorting. "Poor Jack is blind but Jill sees for him, don't you, girl?"

Jack's milky eyes saw nothing, but he shoved a cold nose into Julia's hand and she let him sniff and imprint her, doing the same with Jill.

"I'm dressed all wrong!" wailed Julia, of her linen dress, her high heels. "Let me get changed and then you can show me *everything.*"

Their room was a delight: high, wide and brilliant with sunshine, with a four-poster big enough to sleep four into which you had to climb by means of a small pair of steps covered in Turkish carpet. The furniture was old and beautiful, every bit of it Early American, and the quilt which covered the bed was a superb example of the skill of the early New England women; as were the cushions in the rocking chair. And the samplers on the walls had been done by Bradford children with names like Abigail and Sarah, Priscilla and Prudence.

"Oh, but this is gorgeous!" breathed Julia. "Pure *Saturday Evening Post.*"

"Told you it would be a nice surprise."

Jonas came in with the bags, and Julia seized hers. As she had known, it was filled with trousers and shirts, flat shoes. Quickly she changed into jeans and a shirt like Brad. "Now," she said eagerly, "you can show me the rest of this magical place . . ."

JULIA FELL IN LOVE with the farm. This was all American, not quasi-English like Mount Vernon Street. It sprawled, like an aging beauty with her girdle off. The original saltbox, now forming the heart of the

[116]

house by way of the enormous living room, had been added to over the centuries: a wing tacked on here, an annex there. Flights of stairs wandered off in odd directions, some of them ending in rooms with sloping ceilings, right under the roof. All the furniture was antique, and lovingly cared for; everything smelled of polish and flowers and summer. Julia examined portraits, obviously primitives by itinerant painters—no Copleys or Gilbert Stuarts here as in Boston—and reverently handled Paul Revere silver, Sandwich glass.

"Oh, all this is absolutely gorgeous!" she enthused to Brad, who watched her, smiling indulgently. "How did you know?"

"I know you—besides which, Mother said it was the perfect place."

Julia felt a cooling of her joy. "Mother's got a very sharp eye when it comes to understanding people," Brad went on. "Every word you said last night would be noted down and gone over—and she was right, wasn't she? You do have this thing about the past . . . and the farm is *our* past. This is where the Bradfords celebrate Thanksgiving and Christmas and—oh, all important occasions. So, where better to spend *our* honeymoon?"

Julia felt ashamed of her suspicions. "Angel!" she cried, throwing her arms about him. "It is perfect."

"Let's go see the rest of it, then."

It was a dream. White fences, green grass, leafy trees, spirited horses, cattle, some sheep, even a couple of goats, corn rustling in the slight breeze, a man on a minitractor mowing grass, another spraying cranberry bushes. "This is a working farm, you know," Brad explained. "We market a considerable cranberry crop."

"Is there a village nearby?"

"Sure. Bradford, a couple of miles away. We'll go there. You'll just love the church; it's a clapboard copy of a Wren church in the City of London."

Arms about each other's waists they walked over the farm's entirety. Brad showed her the trees he'd climbed as a boy; the secret places where he used to hide from his sisters; the pool where they'd swum in the summer, the hills where, in the winter, they had raced their toboggans.

He had also brought a pocketful of sugar lumps for the horses, who trotted over to whinny at them. Normally nervous of horses—all paving-stone teeth, rolling eyes and hot breath—Julia nevertheless held out sugar lumps on a flat palm and shivered deliciously as velvet muzzles delicately scooped them up, leaving her palm damp.

"Oh, I could live here forever!" she cried, weak with pleasure.

[117]

When they finally went back to the house, Annie had lunch waiting, and Julia ate for the first time in her life scrod and shoofly pie, with a zeal that had Brad protesting laughingly: "Hey, I know you still have weight to gain but not too much. I don't go in for fat women."

Afterward, they retired upstairs to the big four-poster for a nap, awoke to make slow, greedily absorbed, luxuriant love, after which they took another stroll before dinner, coming back to sit out on the porch in rockers, nodding back and forth in the sweet-scented evening, drinking applejack that Jonas had made, sniffing the delicious smells wafting around the corner from the kitchen at the back of the house.

After dinner they sat in the living room listening to music, Julia on the floor by Brad's knees, his hands taking the pins from her hair, letting it spill over her shoulders and down her back, finally tugging at her hands to pull her up and lead her upstairs to the big four-poster, made up with fresh sheets smelling of lavender and sweet herbs, where once again they made contented love before falling into sleep as into a well.

Never had Julia felt so tranquil, so secure; Brad's tyrannical need of her she was able to accept with a slumberous complacency which amazed her; normally she could not stand being crowded, but his own mood was so sunny, as though he had taken his cue from the weather. Out here in the country, he amazed her by his contentment in doing nothing and counting it everything; watching her with indulgent amusement as she made daisy chains, picked wild flowers, got to know the horses. But mount one she would not.

"You'll have to, sometime. All the Bradfords ride. Abby's a centaur. And as for Mother . . . It will be expected of you."

But Julia was preoccupied with her own expectations, feeling more confident about them now, after these four blissful days. Nobody called, nobody came. They had themselves all to themselves. It was the most perfect—if one of the shortest—of honeymoons.

On Monday morning: "Oh, darling, I have so enjoyed every single minute of our stay in this enchanted place. Can we come back often?"

"Sure . . ."

"It is so peaceful here."

"You are sure you wouldn't get bored?" His tone, his look, said he probably would.

"Never!" she denied. "Nobody could possibly be bored in this magical place."

"Okay, we can come out weekends, and, as I said, Thanksgiving and Christmas are mandatory; the house bursts at the seams then."

"Oh, yes, please, darling." She kissed him, meant to be her gratitude, which he at once turned off on the road he wanted to take, after which he kissed her soundly (his gratitude?) before bouncing into the shower, whistling loudly over the hiss.

I am a *wife!* Julia thought gleefully, hugging her knees. She felt a belonging, to and by, such as she had never known with Derek; realized that in spite of all her inner strictures against doubts, she had still packed them with her luggage; still, *au fond,* disturbed by her out-of-character emotional recklessness. Now, she had no doubts at all. She had done the right thing. Brad had transported her, not only across three thousand miles of ocean but into a new life—yes, *life,* she thought; not the living death that had been, she now realized, her day-to-day (and emotionally hand-to-mouth) existence. She would be a good wife. She would not make the mistakes with Brad she had made with Derek. She would take him as he came (and he came in any one of a thousand and one varieties) and his mother too. She would tread carefully, as he so obviously wanted; she would repair the damage her collision-course crash into the Bradford family had created and prove to them all, not only his mother, that Brad had done the right thing in marrying her.

It was going to be another glorious day. A last swim in the pond, a last walkabout; a last lunch and siesta and all *that* implied. She was grateful for these four days; felt they had given her the respite she needed. Whatever came her way, now, she felt up to handling. Throwing back the covers, she went into the bathroom to join her husband.

They left at five o'clock, after hugs all around and "Don't be too long, now, in coming again" from Annie and Jonas. Julia turned in her seat for a last, memorizing look. Then the car topped the rise and went down the other side and the farm was behind them. Turning, she faced whatever lay ahead.

4

game. scheme to defeat another; trick, cunning device

"DO I LOOK ALL RIGHT?" Julia asked anxiously.

Abby, who had come upstairs to give moral as well as physical help if need be, stood back and said fervently: "Julia, you look marvelous. Black is your color, all right. You've got the skin for it."

"Brad likes me in black," Julia confessed.

"And out of it too, if the way he looks at you is anything to go by." Julia blushed.

"It was awfully nice of Bitsy to show me where to get this dress," she said hastily.

"This is an important party. A summons from Mother is not to be ignored. The Family—by which I mean everybody including second cousins—only meets for births, marriages and deaths. We haven't sat forty to dinner since Bitsy got married. And you are now married to Brad." Abby frowned. "You really should have some jewels, though. That neckline is made for an important necklace. I had thought perhaps maybe Mother would give you the Bradford diamonds but I suppose a week is not long enough 'on approval.' Have you anything of your own?"

"Only the pearls Brad bought me as a wedding present."

"Let's have a look."

But she shook her head. "No . . . They don't look right." Her hands went to her neck.

"Oh, no, Abby, I couldn't . . ."

Abby was wearing emeralds, right for her gilt-blond hair and sea-green eyes, but Julia was horrified at the thought of wearing a fortune around her neck.

"I can borrow something from Mother."

"Borrow what, from Mother?"

They both whirled to see Lady Hester standing in the open doorway.

"I am lending Julia my emeralds so I was hoping to borrow something from you."

"There is no need for Julia to borrow jewels," Lady Hester dismissed. "I have brought her her own."

Abby winked at Julia. "Not the Bradford diamonds!" she exclaimed.

"What else?" asked Lady Hester haughtily. "These are traditionally given to the bride of the eldest son," she said to Julia. "As they were given to me, now I give them to you."

Opening the large red velvet box she was carrying, she held out for Julia's inspection a dazzle that blinded. Julia drew in a sharp breath. "Oh, but they are exquisite."

"Made in France in 1798 for Abigail Bradford," Lady Hester said. "And very pretty. Not to be compared to the Conyngham-Bradford diamonds but first-quality stones nevertheless, and charmingly set en tremblant."

The necklace was a garland of flowers made out of diamonds, with tiny dewdrops on their petals which trembled liquidly whenever the wearer moved. There were matching earrings and a bracelet comprising a further half dozen flowers. Julia stood while Lady Hester put them on, finally standing back to survey her.

"Yes," she said finally, on a satisfied note. "Very presentable, Julia. Very presentable indeed. Black is your color, undoubtedly."

She herself was in pale blue, with a necklace of sapphires that were the size of marbles, pear-shaped solitaires in her ears and a matching cabochon on her left hand which made Julia wonder how she managed to raise it.

"Now then, I wish you to receive with me, Julia. That way I can introduce you to everyone. Abigail, you will, as usual, work in conjunction with Bitsy and see that everything flows. Seth and Drexel will look after the solitary ladies—thank God they get fewer every year—while Brad will fill any gaps. We are only forty to dinner so that is not too bad."

Julia wondered what Lady Hester's idea of a large dinner party was, only to be answered.

"At Arun, we usually sat one hundred." A sigh for the Good Old Days, then a brisk "Now then, down you go, Abigail. Julia and I will follow in a moment."

Abigail, resplendent in bronze faille—for once miraculously free of rents, holes or stains—swanned out, leaving Julia alone with her mother-in-law.

"Now then, Julia." Lady Hester sat herself down on the chaise longue and regarded her daughter-in-law like headmistress to pupil. "There is no need to be nervous." I do not allow it, her tone said. "This is merely the Family. I had to undergo the same formal inspection myself when I came to this house as a bride. The American branch of my family, being a cadet branch, tends to place an exaggerated importance on ancestry—something like the Shintoists in Japan." Her tolerant smile of shared amusement said that this of course, was quite ridiculous; it was quite enough to know one had them, but being such a young country, indulgence was called for. "Now, as to tonight's events. Dinner is family only, and all senior members. Later on, I shall give a series of small dances for you and Brad to which the younger element will be invited along with their friends. For tonight, I must ask you to bear with me and entertain a great many prosy old bores who are nevertheless part of the Family. Most of them suffer from one infirmity or another and several of them are quite deaf, especially the remaining three great-aunts, the sisters of my husband's father. They do you great honor by coming here tonight; they are all well over ninety and seldom leave Louisburg Square these days. Cousin Timothy is the senior male member of the family, being the son of my father-in-law's brother; he is still known as 'young' Timothy though he will never see sixty again."

Lightly, trenchantly, Lady Hester took Julia through a brief sketch of those Bradfords she would meet later, culled from the Hill, from Brookline, from Cambridge and from Chestnut Hill. Cleverly she illumined them in Julia's memory by some telling descriptive stroke, so that Julia could put a name to the one with the rabbit's teeth, another to the one with the ear trumpet; be able to distinguish between the three great-aunts by the color of their dresses—the only colors they ever wore, a habit begun by their mother, who could never tell the difference, and pick out the Saltonstall wife from the Adams and Cabot wives.

"You will have it much easier than I did," Lady Hester said. "Boston in 1930 when I arrived was very different from Boston now, in 1975. They were so suspicious of anything non-Bostonian that they were all but xenophobic. Lack of confidence, of course. But then, with only three hundred years of history . . ." Lady Hester's smile said, What else could be expected from such parvenus? Julia, who by this time was juggling desperately with names and faces, smiled dutifully but longed to say: "But isn't that exactly what I am? I have absolutely no history whatsoever," even as she wondered if her mother-in-law was not getting in her little digs. You are being oversensitive, Julia, she admonished herself. She is being helpful, not hurtful. Be grateful!

Lady Hester glanced at the clock. "Now we must go down. I always allow half an hour for drinks before dinner at eight and it is now seven twenty-six. My fetish for punctuality is well known in the family. I *never* keep people waiting and I expect them to return the compliment."

Rising to her feet, and without so much as a last glance in the mirror, unlike Julia, she swept from the room.

As they went downstairs Julia saw that the house had been transformed—and willingly—for the occasion. It was ablaze with fresh flowers, massed in silver bowls, great epergnes, crystal vases. The chandelier sparkled and everything else gleamed. Brad was in the hall conferring with Thomas—who would have two attendant footmen and the assistance of Roach, Bitsy's butler, as well as the three maids, crisply fresh in their black silk dresses and starched frills—and as his mother and his wife came down the stairs Brad advanced to meet them, smiling.

"Well, I must say you two look most resplendent." He kissed Julia lightly on the mouth, his mother on the cheek.

"You don't look so bad yourself," Julia retorted impudently, her eyes dwelling proudly on his blond handsomeness, always set off to advantage by black tie.

He smiled at her but said to his mother: "Everything is perfect. I've just checked."

Lady Hester nodded. "I would expect nothing less."

Brad's eyes dwelled on the diamonds sparkling at Julia's white throat, and she saw something like relief in them. "Nice," he said, nodding at them. "Now you really are a Bradford."

And watching him that night, Julia began to get her first inkling of what it meant to be one. Standing between his wife and his mother, he greeted the Family with either a handshake in the case of the men or a kiss for the women, and always the light quip, the easy aside, the right compliment. He received the congratulations pleasantly, introduced Julia with just the right amount of pride and/or deference or triumph. He glittered with the confidence of one who was long used to all this, while Julia struggled to connect faces to the little hints Lady Hester had given her, forcibly restraining her shock or surprise or amusement at some of the family members, especially the three great-aunts: Henrietta, known as Hetty; Sophronia, known as Sophie; and the youngest, Louisa, known as Louie; all were tiny, amazingly spry, and dressed in the style of the turn of the century, in dresses that were almost as old as they were, so fragile that the material, some kind of paper taffeta, had split at the worn seams. They wore a great deal of lace that was as yellow as old newspaper, but were much hung about with old-fashioned jewels of superb quality. They all giggled as Brad kissed them, first their hands, then their cheeks, like royalty, and fluttered and flirted up at him before tottering off to greet "dear Abigail" and "young Hester."

"Young" Timothy was stout, bald and too pompous to be true, and as Julia was seated beside him at dinner she had to look interested while he bored her to tears by telling her in great detail what was wrong with England's present government. Brad, on the other hand, was seated next to a dangerous-looking blonde wearing a dress that was obviously held up by willpower, displaying a tan and a pair of magnificent breasts which Brad, to her jealous eyes, seemed to be admiring far too much. Racking her brain Julia could remember only that she was married to a Bradford cousin, but which one she could not for the life of her recall. There were just too many of them, she thought fretfully. She had been flung into a deep end forty people deep and was floundering, hopelessly out of her depth. One or two of the most telling faces—the rabbit teeth, the ear trumpet, the unforgettable old aunts—she had no trouble remembering; the rest were merely faces. The dinner—plain and simple on account of the age of many of the guests who had difficulty coping with complicated dishes, went down untasted, but the wine, a superb Montrachet with the fish and a fine, big St. Julien, she perhaps imbibed too freely, because as they got up from the table—all of them because, as there were further guests to come there was no time for the gentlemen to linger—she felt a distinct buzz. Coffee was an ordeal. Each and every one of the females took turns to come and "chat"; a delicately conducted but nevertheless thorough third degree. Julia desperately gulped black coffee that was made English style and therefore much stronger than the American type, while she answered the same questions over and over, keeping a constant smile on her face and her voice pleasant. By the time she had answered the last probing question she was ready to scream, but it was then that Brad came across to say: "Sorry, Cousin Dodo, but I'm afraid I must pluck Julia from you. We have to greet our other guests."

"Do we have to do this often?" Julia asked desperately as he bore her away.

"No, thank God. But this one is an absolute must. It's a Family Rite. Chin up, sweetheart. You are doing it fine and dandy. Everybody is talking about you. The women approve and the men are envious. More important, Mother is happy. Keep up the good work." He nodded at the diamonds. "The fact that you have got these already is proof that you are no longer on approval, and don't think that fact hasn't been noticed. Mother is the matriarch of this particular clan and the others tend to follow her lead. You've taken the family prisoner; now do the same thing with Proper Boston and we are home and dry . . ."

The rest of the evening was a blur of more new faces; once again Julia found herself under inspection by some very imposing dowagers; the younger women tended to congregate around Brad. The champagne flowed, and she availed herself of it recklessly, seeing as it was Dom Pérignon '47; the orchestra had begun to play, and the conservatory, where the reception was held, was massed with flowers and people who wandered in and out from the house; large expanses of glass in the roof had been opened to the night air but it was still very warm. Julia found herself glowing, slipped away to powder her nose and pay a visit and overheard two women talking about her:

"—good-looking," one of them said, in that funny accent with the neighing, nasal "aaa" sound.

"Brad always did go for looks," the other replied.

"Nobody seems to know who she is, though. Lady Hester is not saying a word, which means there is nothing to say, knowing her." There was a sneer in the voice as it went on: "Which also means she is *not* Lady Hester's choice. Whatever happened to Caroline Norton?"

"Last I heard she was crying her heart out back home in Philadelphia."

"Wouldn't you, if your man had been stolen just as you came up to the finishing line?"

"Well, it was a shock, to say the least. Hester Bradford has not shown so much as a crack but I'll bet she gave him hell!"

"Well, she seems to have taken to her daughter-in-law. Why else tonight? If she hadn't taken she'd be back on the plane heading for home."

"Even so, I wonder what actually made him *marry* her?"

"Not because she is pregnant, surely. Not in this day and age?"

"No? What about Charlotte Ford? Discount nothing, my dear, until you see the bill."

There was another wicked giggle. "Oh, she'll be the one to have to pay that. I mean—did you ever know Brad to?"

They both laughed and then their voices faded.

Julia waited a moment or two then left the bathroom. Fortunately the bedroom was empty and she made her escape unseen. She went rapidly along the corridor to her own bedroom, where she looked at her hot-cheeked face in the mirror.

Steady on, Julia, she told herself. All this is perfectly natural. Brad jilted a longstanding fiancée for you—a nobody, as that harpy said. Don't get uptight about it. You are doing fine. Brad said so. You are wearing the Bradford necklace. Wear a smile too. She repaired the slight ravages eating and drinking had done to her makeup, sprayed fresh perfume and, squaring her shoulders, went back downstairs.

"There you are!" Abby pounced. "I thought you had retired from the fray."

"Chance would be a fine thing," Julia answered lightly.

Abby laughed. "It would be a mistake. You have made a hit. The women like your modesty—and your honesty—and the men are quite content just to look at you."

"All of them?"

Abby narrowed her eyes. "Nobody ever gets one hundred percent of the vote," she said. "But I'd say you've got a good ninety and that's not bad." She took hold of Julia's arm. "Now come and say good night to the old aunts. It's ten o'clock and curfew time for them. Old Doremus has got the horses outside and he's a Tartar about them standing too long."

"Horses!"

"The aunts don't approve of the internal combustion engine. They use the carriage they always used, and as it is just up the hill the horses —as old as the aunts are, I'm sure—can just about manage it, in summer that is. Come winter and we visit them." The aunts were being draped with ancient velvet trimmed with ermine by a solicitous Brad, and obeying his silent instruction, Julia went out with him to see the three old ladies handed into their carriage by an equally old coachman who scolded them with the familiarity of many years' service for keeping his precious horses—two of them—standing.

The door was shut, hooves clattered on the cobbles, and the carriage rolled slowly away up the hill. Brad let out a sigh. "I swear they look exactly as they did when I was five years old. They used to feed me chocolate digestive biscuits on the sly when Mother took me to visit them."

"They never married?"

"No. Uncle Eliot was the worst Brahmin of the lot—convinced nobody was good enough for his daughters. I think he always had his sights on the Prince of Wales but he got stolen by another American much later on. He was a dreadful old snob; simply adored mother because she was a real blueblood. She told me he did his damnedest to marry his daughters off to some penurious duke or something like but the fact is they just didn't take and while he was rich he was also mean and wouldn't fork over enough of his millions. So they just stayed at home getting older and older . . ." He slipped an arm about her shoulders. "Be glad you live in the Boston of today instead of seventy years ago."

"Just so long as it is with you I don't mind where I live."

"Sweet . . ." He bent his head to kiss her and she would have clung but he released her briskly to say: "Right, let's get back to the party. All the older ones will be leaving soon and then we can relax. I swear Boston is the last city in the world where the mere fact of years carries so much weight . . ."

She had always known Brad loved parties, that he was a social animal, and watching him later, always the center of a convivial group, his cheeks slightly flushed with champagne, his sea-change eyes vividly bright, she could see how elemental it all was to him.

"Yes, he is handsome, is he not?" her mother-in-law's voice asked softly. "I have watched you watching him, Julia."

Defiant with champagne: "A cat may look at a king."

Lady Hester laughed. "That's what I like about you, Julia," she said. "You have a boldness which reminds me of myself." She leaned forward. "We are also the two best-dressed women here." She nodded across at a representative group of the old guard: ladies of indeterminate age wearing dresses that must surely have come from a thrift shop, and aglitter like Christmas trees with diamonds. "In Boston," Lady Hester said, "it is a compliment to say of a person: 'He (or she as the case may be) still has the first dollar he ever made.'" She nodded, rose to her feet and saying, "Now I must get back to work," went across to join them.

She was, as Sally Armbruster had said, a work of art. When she was not watching her husband, Julia watched her mother-in-law—and learned. Julia was not a shy person, but she was a reserved one, and large gatherings were not to her taste. It was obvious that to Brad they were the breath of life, which meant they would not be infrequent. So she forced herself to go to people, to offer herself up to their curiosity, to give of herself. It was purely an effort to please, and she had to quell an inner stricture which prodded an instinct to shrink away. Julia had always hated to be an object of speculation and curiosity, but she had a ferociously strong sense of duty and was always prepared to pay much more than lip service. So she circulated, chatted, laughed at jokes, smiled at wit, essayed a few quips of her own and every now and then caught her mother-in-law's gaze, felt the slight nod of approval she gave like a shot in the arm. Her dress was much admired, black velvet cut tight to the body with a swath at the hips and a small fishtail, its deeply square décolletage forming a superb setting for the Bradford diamonds, something else which was much commented on. It was as though her mother-in-law had given her a medal.

And then people began to leave.

"Now don't forget. You are dining with us on the twenty-second. Eight o'clock and black tie. We are looking forward to it."

"So am I," Julia lied brightly.

"Best evening in a long time," another face said. "Bradford parties are always better than anyone else's."

"How nice of you to say so."

"As usual, staying to the bitter end—except that in this house it is always sweet."

"You are very kind."

"Goodbye, and thanks a heap."

"I'm so glad you enjoyed it."

Julia shook hands and smiled till her face ached, and when finally, the front door was shut on the last one, and Parkes was locking up, she heaved a sigh and closed her eyes.

"Come with me, Julia, I know the very thing," Lady Hester commanded, sweeping Julia along with her as she went back into the Rose Parlor. There, she took off her shoes and lay down flat on the Aubusson so that the curve of her spine was stretched flat and hard against the floor. "Come along," she said. "It is a sovereign remedy when one has been on one's feet all night."

Julia laughed suddenly. What the hell, she thought. It was all a part of this crazy dream her life had suddenly become. Kicking off her satin pumps she stretched herself out by her mother-in-law. After a moment: "You are right," she murmured amazedly. "It does feel good . . ."

Brad came in and stood looking down at them. Upside down, his face was still handsome, Julia thought sleepily.

"That was a good idea, inviting Muffy tonight," he said to his mother. "I know you don't like her but by tomorrow she'll have tonight laid out like a blueprint which any layman can understand."

It was then that Julia connected name to face and realized that Muffy was the blonde. So there had been a reason for Brad's attention! But have what spread out? And then like a light switch Julia's brain was illumined. Some story had been concocted as to why Caroline Norton had been jilted; some save-face hype that this Muffy, evidently the family gossip, would have all over town next day.

"I cannot stand the woman," Lady Hester said, her eyes still closed, "but she has her uses."

Julia filed that away too.

Bitsy and Abby came in, their husbands trailing behind. They were staying overnight. Abby laughed. "My God, Mother, how *do* you do it? Once I get down I can't get up again!" "I can," Bitsy said, and did so, now that the evening was over careless of her Norell pink silk taffeta and five strands of perfectly matched pearls.

"I," said Abby, "am going to make my own sovereign remedy for evenings like this. A cup of tea."

Julia's eyes flew open. "Oh, Abby . . . !"

"Come on then. It has to be drunk in the kitchen to be right . . ."

Julia had never been in the kitchen, now she looked round at the gleaming white-tiled walls, the red rubber block floor, the enormous marble-and-zinc-topped table in the center of the room, the hanging ranks of old but lovingly cared for copper pots, the huge old-fashioned hotel-type gas range with its whole series of baking, roasting and stewing ovens. The refrigerator was the size of an English wardrobe, and the kettle Abby put on to boil was of the eighteenth-century copper type.

"You hungry?" Abby asked.

"Starving!" Julia replied happily.

"How about . . ." Abby inspected the contents of the refrigerator, took out a cold roast of beef, half carved, the meat bright red and beautifully marbled with fat.

"On rye?" Julia asked hopefully.

"Bread's in that china crock over there."

Abby placed butter, salt and English mustard on the table and while Julia sliced the bread, she carved the beef, making American-type sandwiches: thin slices of bread and thick slices of beef piled into a three-inch-thick wedge. The tea Abby made was hot and strong. "Irish tea," she said as she shoved a cup across at Julia. "We had a cook called Delia when I was a kid and she taught me how to make tea."

"And who taught you how to make these sandwiches?" Julia mumbled through a full mouth.

"I did!" It was Brad. He swooped up a sandwich, perched himself on the table and wolfed happily. Suddenly, Julia was overcome by a feeling of such happiness as she had never known.

"This is the best part of the evening!" she proclaimed.

"Isn't it though? I never seem to enjoy food when I've got to give thought to a conversation I'm holding," Abby agreed.

" 'S'easy," Brad said, taking another sandwich. "You get your partner to talk then you can eat and listen."

Bitsy came tip-tapping in with her quick, staccato walk and said: "How in God's name you can eat when you weigh what you do, Abby—"

"Leave off the nagging," Brad said roughly. "If you want a cup of tea pour one; if you don't, good night."

"I came for a glass of milk," Bitsy bridled.

"So pour it."

She did so, in frigid silence.

"Mother gone up yet?" Abby inquired, pouring more tea.

"No. She's talking to Seth and Drex." Bitsy turned to her brother. "And she wants you," she added pointedly. "Like now."

Brad at once slid off the table, strode to the sink, where he rinsed his hands and wiped his mouth.

"Don't wait up for me," he counseled Julia. "Evenings like this always wind Mother up. She'll talk for hours, but it's Saturday tomorrow so we can sleep late." He bent to drop a swift kiss. "You were great. Take a ten-dollar raise, Mrs. Bradford."

He went out, followed by Bitsy, who sniffed at Julia as she passed.

Julia poured herself more tea. "What exactly does Brad do—his work, I mean?" she asked Abby eventually.

"Mother's dirty work. I don't mean underhanded or dishonest stuff; I mean the unpleasant kind. She used to do it herself but she can't handle the traveling. Brad spends his time visiting Bradford & Sons wherever it happens to be, handling crises, settling disputes, hiring and firing and dispensing justice as well as handing out praise. He's good at it, damned good. He handles people well and he's got a good brain behind all that charm and dazzle. Believe it or not, he was a straight-A student all his young life."

"I do believe you," Julia said.

Abby's smile was apologetic. "Of course you would," she agreed. "You'd be surprised how many other people wouldn't, though."

"I know Brad is clever," Julia said quietly, "and that he goes to some pains to conceal it."

Abby raised her eyebrows. "You are no fool yourself if you've twigged that already."

Slowly, and with some care: "I know that there is much more to him than the golden boy he comes on as," Julia said. "He's—complicated."

Abby was silent. "Julia—" she began when to her vexation her husband put his head around the door.

"Ah . . . I thought as much."

"Want a cup?"

"No, thank you. I've just had a nightcap with Drex. I am now about to seek my bed. Can I persuade you to share it?"

"I thought you'd never ask," Abby replied with alacrity, rising from the table. Her eyes rested on Julia with a look that said plainly: "Another time, okay?" and Julia contained her disappointment behind her smile. If anyone was going to lighten her darkness it was Brad's older sister.

"You did splendidly this evening, Julia," Seth said warmly. "*Tout* Boston will be alive tomorrow with talk of the elegantly beautiful Mrs. J. Winthrop Bradford V, as the columns will have it."

"Don't tell me you read them!" Julia joked.

"*They* are the way *I* relax," he said.

"Liar!" said his wife. "Good night, Julia. My husband was right. You did indeed do splendidly. Sleep late tomorrow. You deserve it."

Rising from the table, Julia went to wash the cups. Abby had replaced the beef and the butter. Now Julia put away the bread, and with her usual practiced efficiency rinsed the plain white kitchen cups and saucers and matching plates, the utilitarian kitchen cutlery. Switching off the lights she went back through into the hall. There, most of the lights were off. In the distance, through the Rose Parlor, she could see the servants clearing away the last remnants. There was no sign of Brad or his mother and Bitsy and her husband had disappeared too. Slowly, she went upstairs, and in her bedroom she found Rose waiting.

"Congratulations, madam, I hear you were a great success," she said.

That, more than anything, set the seal of approval on Julia's evening. "Thank God for that."

Rose helped Julia undress, brushed her hair, which made Julia purr like a cat.

"Aren't you tired, Rose?" she asked drowsily.

"No, madam. Working for Lady Hester I have learned not to be. She will not be up for some time yet."

"But it's midnight."

"Even so. Parties seem to leave her restless; she always spends some time working after them. And I rested earlier on, while you were all downstairs."

"That means my husband will not be up for some time either, then, I suppose," Julia sighed.

"I doubt it, madam. You will get used to it in time. We are, by now."

Just so long as everybody gets used to me, Julia thought, once she was in bed, physically tired but sure that the evening, in spite of her initial dislike of the whole thing, had gone off so well. I did my duty, she thought drowsily. She can't say I didn't try. Nor can Brad. He said it all depended on me . . . But her last thought before drifting off into sleep, was: And he still hasn't told me why.

"YOU WILL UNDERSTAND, of course," Lady Hester said with the brisk finality of one who expects nothing else, "that having no idea of my son's marriage, this trip—of vital importance—was arranged in accordance with my understanding of his known commitments. It cannot, now, be disarranged without causing a great deal of hassle, as they say over here. I am quite sure, however, that you are not the kind of woman to complain because her husband devotes a good deal of his time to his work."

"I knew from the beginning that Brad traveled a great deal," Julia replied levelly, aware that she was being weighed in the balance and determined not to be found wanting.

"I knew you would be sensible," approved her mother-in-law. "And you shall not be left alone to mope, I promise you."

In fact, Julia felt she was the target of a remorseless campaign, pressed home with total disregard for anything but winning. Lady Hester had been born with a field marshal's baton in her knapsack and, like all good generals, was the recipient of superb intelligence. Julia was left in no doubt that Lady Hester had studied a blueprint of her with great care and an attentive memory, because Julia was taken in hand and the task of shaping her into a Bradford wife was begun.

Obviously under her mother's instruction, Bitsy took Julia under her wing as far as shopping was concerned: the "right" shops, charge accounts, where one went personally, where one chose goods from a selection sent to one's home. Julia discovered that in Boston, the name Bradford bore the same connotation as H.M. the Queen did in London. Lady Hester's patronage was the equivalent of a royal warrant.

Abby undertook her cultural instruction; the Friday concerts, the charitable organizations, the museums, the intellectual side of things. And it was this which Julia preferred. She took care to spend as little time as possible in Bitsy's elegant but chilly designer desert in Louisburg Square, where indifferent cocktails but 200 proof gossip was dispensed. She preferred Abby's large, untidy house in Cambridge, where her children—two boys at Harvard and a girl just beginning her freshman year at Radcliffe—made her casually welcome.

There was always a good deal of laughter in the Amory household, an atmosphere of warmth and happiness. The children had no hang-ups about openly displaying their affection for each other, and as there were also several dogs and a couple of cats who made their own way through the melee with good-natured indifference, Julia always enjoyed any time spent in the enormous kitchen, where everyone ate at the vast butcher-block table—heartily—and talked the same way. Julia adored the long discussions on art and music and politics. Winthrop, Abby's eldest, had political ambitions while Seth, Jr., was a budding novelist and Charley played the piano well enough to consider music as a career. It was a happy house.

Not so Bitsy's. Bitsy was her mother's daughter and emulated her in all things. It was obvious that Bitsy longed to be a *grande dame*. Her house was impeccably run along the same lines as Mount Vernon Street, but her sons, impeccable preppies both, reminded Julia of nothing so much as store-window dummies. They never ran down stairs two at a time, they never whistled or sang, they never left anything lying around, never teased the long-serving servants. Bitsy's sons, Bradford and Drex (short for Drexel), were good-looking boys with all their father's élan and their mother's elegance, but they had one fatal flaw. They had no charm. Abby's two hulking boys, on the other hand, lived in jeans and sweatshirts, Charley ditto, never had a hair *in* place, would not have been seen dead in the clothes the Adams twins wore, but could have charmed the birds off the trees. Abby and

[133]

Brad shared the Bradford charm; it had totally escaped Bitsy and thus her sons.

Knowing him well enough, after a few weeks, to be able to do so, Julia commented on this difference one afternoon while walking with Seth, who was her favorite guide to Boston, around the Old Granary burying ground, where she absorbedly inspected the graves of Paul Revere, John Hancock and John Adams—the latter an ancestor common to both Seth and the Bradfords.

"Yes, there is a clear demarcation," Seth agreed. "Abby and her brother are what we call English Bradfords; Brad and the present marquis bear a strong resemblance. Bitsy is an American Bradford." With dry amusement: "We New Englanders are not known for our mirth and jollity, you know. This is Puritan country."

Julia smiled mechanically, her mind still chewing on the point she wished to make. "Nor has Lady Hester become Americanized in any way after so long in this country."

"Indeed no! She has Anglicized us." Seth bent to peer at a badly worn gravestone. "A most remarkable and redoubtable lady. Very strong. The kind of women we men tend to label 'masculine-minded' —for our own protection, of course."

Another quick smile, but returning to the point: "And yet, though Brad looks so much like her, he does not seem to have inherited her strength; only her charm . . ."

Seth pursed his lips and shook his head. "I would not go so far as to say that," he disagreed courteously. "It is that around his mother, Brad tends to tread very carefully. They are very close, as you know."

"I know," Julia said.

"He is the most precious thing in her life and Brad is very aware of this." A sidelong glance. "She has told you, I am sure, of the risks she took to have him?"

"Yes."

"And that he is her own father's reincarnation?"

"Oh, yes." Julia took a deep breath and plunged. "But not so much as a word about Brad's father. The house is filled with photographs of the marquis, but I have yet to see one of Brad's father. It is as though he never existed. Abby is the only one who ever talks about him."

"Abby was closest to him and, as the eldest, has the best memories. Bitsy was always closest to her mother, whom she emulates, as you will have realized. As for Brad"—Seth paused, then went on—"it is his mother who has loomed largest in his life. He is well aware of his importance to her and his—handling—of her is based on that awareness. It took a great deal of courage on his part to marry without his mother's approval. To me, that is indicative of just how much he loves you." Another pause. "And needs you."

His eyes were warm. "I have admired you very much, Julia, as I have watched you take things in your stride which would have thrown a lesser woman. You have tact, discretion and a great deal of patience."

"Not really," Julia admitted ruefully. "Sometimes I astonish myself with my own forbearance."

"You are a mature woman for your age. How well you have coped, under pressure."

"I want to do this right," Julia said carefully. "It is important to Brad that I do."

"Of course," Seth agreed simply. "But you are what Brad has needed."

"Rather than Caroline Norton?"

There, she had said it.

"Brad never loved her; he was doing his duty, no more. I do not blame him for finding he could not do it and then refusing to do so."

"Why then do I get the feeling that everyone blames me?" Julia asked.

He looked surprised. "Do you? I can assure you that Abby and I—"

"Not you or Abby, but—Bitsy and—"

"Bitsy is jealous of her brother," Seth said candidly. "Always has been, always will be. Always she has had to compete for her mother's love with him, while he has never had to compete for anything."

"I can believe that," Julia said.

Seth looked at her keenly. "You think, perhaps, that Lady Hester, in spite of what appears on the surface, does not, *au fond,* either like or approve?"

"She has never been anything else than generous towards me," Julia replied, very, very carefully.

"That is because you are on trial," Seth explained kindly. "You have married her Beloved Son; you must be *seen* as well as *felt* to be Right. She will not be other than generous until she has made up her mind about you. You will know when that happens."

"How?"

"It will be very obvious," Seth told her dryly, "but I do not think you need worry. I have heard nothing via Abby, who has it from Bitsy, who invariably reports back what her mother has said. You are not complained of, Julia; on the other hand nor are you extolled; you are merely accepted, and that, in my opinion, is worth much more." Seth

[135]

paused. "Had it been otherwise you would have felt Lady Hester's displeasure by now. I am sure I need not elaborate on its—power. Lady Hester looks to her son: if he is happy, so is she. And Brad, may I say, has never seemed happier to me."

"You think so?" Julia was vastly relieved; the certain surety of her honeymoon had evaporated in the fierce heat of Brad's absence, to leave a residue of greasy doubt.

"You do not think he has gone away on this trip with pleasure!" Seth looked at her and laughed. "That is not how he expressed his feelings to me!"

The look in the quizzical eyes had Julia blushing.

So did Brad, when he called her that night to describe, in scatological detail, how much he was missing her.

"Darling, this is an open line," protested Julia uncomfortably, not used to such frankness in or out of bed.

"Who cares! I've got steam coming out of my ears, and if I didn't call you at night I just wouldn't sleep. As it is, I dream of you when I do."

"Do you, darling?" That touched Julia more than anything.

"I'm not used to the celibate state, you know that," he went on, bursting her lovely bubble, only to blow another when he continued: "But I'm struggling, even if I am building up a head of steam which is the result of almost three weeks' abstinence."

Which reassured Julia no end. She went to sleep with his "three weeks' abstinence" ringing the peal in her ears. For a man of Brad's sexual appetite it was a sacrifice of mind-bending proportions, and the most satisfyingly reassuring thing he could have said. She still missed him though, more than she had ever missed another human being in her life. It amazed her how much of a fixture he had become in it already. She missed his presence, his gaiety, his warmth, even his untidiness: he always hung up everything on the floor. She missed him in bed, but not only the sex; she missed the warmth of him. Brad was better than any hot water bottle or electric blanket. He radiated warmth, always slept wrapped around her, following her across the big bed when she moved, so that she always awoke with him entwined, his erection pulsating gently.

But no matter what her inner loneliness, outwardly she was careful to present a cheerful, smiling face, put a curb on her forthright tongue. She had made that mistake with Derek, and with Brad's mother monitoring her every look and movement, she was sure, she was mindful of every p and q.

If Brad wanted her to walk on eggshells around his mother then she would not break so much as one piece. Her unexpected eruption into the Bradford enclave had made a big enough hole in the fabric of things; not until that was mended so that you would not even know there had been a break would she exert her own authority. For now, she was on approval. She did not kid herself, in spite of received kindness and concern shown, that she had been accepted, no matter what Seth had said. She knew that Bitsy watched and hoped for her mother to find the flaw which would result in Julia's being returned as unsatisfactory.

But instead, what Julia received was praise. "I think you are a brick," Lady Hester told her warmly. "Not a word of complaint after three whole weeks. But then, you are a wholly self-sufficient young woman, are you not? As I am. I see myself in you in so many ways, Julia." A complacent yet coolly surmising appraisal. "I wonder if that is why my son married you."

Julia had to prevent her jaw from dropping. The complacent arrogance was so sublime as to be ridiculous—except it wasn't. And it sowed yet another seed of doubt. *Was* that why Brad had married her, Julia Carey, of all women? Because she reminded him of his mother? And reminding, would also be expected to treat in the same way, smooth away all obstacles in his path, heap praise when necessary, always temper complaint with tenderness and above all love: without query, without doubt, without end? Always and ever love?

She found she did not like it; she did not like it at all. She wanted to be married for herself, not because she reminded her husband of his mother; but all the same, she found herself studying her mother-in-law, as if searching for vital clues.

There was no doubt that Lady Hester Bradford was a masterpiece. Nothing—but nothing—escaped her notice, no matter how small. Woe betide, for instance, a smeared cup, drooping flowers, the slightest film of dust, imperfectly prepared food. Nothing escaped the still beautiful, exquisitely made-up eyes.

Every morning, at the breakfast table, at which Julia was expected to be present because Lady Hester considered breakfast in bed slovenly unless one was ill, she dealt with her considerable pile of mail with brisk dispatch, marking notes on the top of the piles of letters before dividing them into various categories with which her secretary would deal later. All this before she left for a full day at the office. Then she would turn to the day's menus, crossing out or initialing approval as the case might be. And still found time to inquire keenly of Julia what her program for the day was, expressing approval, tinged with surprise, when Julia told her she was going to take the car and explore beyond the city. She had practiced driving the big American cars with Winthrop or Seth, Jr., beside her, until she felt confident enough to tackle Boston itself—a nightmare, since, she was told, Bostonians obeyed no traffic laws except their own.

But it was the big Rand McNally atlas she pored over, and once having discovered that American cars practically drove themselves, which left her free to concentrate on the bewilderingly unfamiliar road signs, she took to exploring farther and farther afield. Finally, one bright morning at the end of Brad's third week away, she set off for Concord and the farm.

Annie was delighted to see her, made her warmly welcome. "I knew right off you was taken with this place." And she commiserated with just the right attitude about Brad. "My own sister, she married a travelin' man; never did see him but once a month all her married life." A chuckle. "But then, Mr. Brad was never one for stayin' in one place too long."

"What was he like when he was a boy, Annie? You have known him all his life, haven't you? Tell me about him."

She knew that warm, comfortable Annie would tell her what she shrank from asking her mother-in-law, wanting to know the truth rather than a fairy tale. Annie loved Brad, that was obvious, but unlike his mother she was not blind to his faults. To Annie, Brad was human, not godlike.

"A right varmint," chuckled Annie, her hands busy rolling dough for biscuits. "Always up to some mischief. The times he fell from a tree or window or even a horse . . . He's had more broken bones than a butcher shop! The more danger there was the more he liked it— especially if his mother took agin it; she only had to say no for him to go right off and do it!" A reminiscent sigh. "He could always get around her—still can, for that matter—around anybody. He's a real charmer, is Mr. Brad. But he has a good, kind heart. I don't set no store by what some people says about him and his ma . . ." She broke off, looking vexed, as if her ready tongue had slipped its moorings.

"I know they are very close," Julia said.

"Oh, Lady Hester sets her clock by Mr. Brad!" Annie looked relieved, as though Julia had absolved her.

"Well, with no father." Delicately, Julia led where she wished Annie to follow.

"A right shame. Such a nice man, Mr. Winthrop. A kind heart, just like his son, though he was mighty careful with money. Not like Mr.

Brad; he'd give you his last cent. But it ain't right when a boy don't have a pa. There's things a man can give a boy no mother can; things a boy needs . . ." She broke off again, her hands busy cutting out round, fat disks of dough. Julia maintained her interested silence until Annie went on: "But you can't fault Lady Hester for lookin' out for her boy; some says as how she looks out too much, but him bein' born only months after his pa was killed and her takin' to her bed to have him. And for a woman like her that's as big a sacrifice as can be made. I guess maybe his ma saw him as a sorta substitute."

"She could have married again," Julia said.

"Oh, she didn't lack for offers, but she wouldn't have none of them. Gave all the love she had to her boy. Only the very best was good enough for him from the minute he was born. He's been the heart in her body ever since."

Julia pondered over Annie's words later, as she wandered the paddocks. All that Annie had told her confirmed her own judgment: between Lady Hester and her son was a bond so close, so tight, that when Julia pressed close she felt it push her back. So far, she had respected it, ever conscious of the unusual circumstances surrounding her marriage. And after all, so far she had no cause for complaint as to Lady Hester's treatment of her. She treated Julia as she treated her own daughters: somewhat brusquely, expecting to be obeyed, but with kindness. Only to her son did she show love, and far too much of that, in Julia's opinion. She was by now firmly convinced that Brad feared his mother. Why? Never once had she heard them argue, never did Lady Hester raise her voice to her son; never did she do less than concern herself absorbedly and lovingly as to his happiness and well-being. Yet she was smothering him, Julia was sure. She was the cause of his rootlessness, his restlessness. It was when the leash chafed that he turned to Julia with his tyrannical needs. Yet never did he explain it in words. And never did Julia feel confident enough of him, sure enough of herself, to ask him.

It was a puzzle; one she did not yet understand, and in the face of her lack of firm instructions, she could only obey the one Brad had given her: to do it good and do it right. In other words—do as she was told. She would have preferred cards on the table. Lady Hester was a forthright woman, and in likening Julia's character to her own she must have realized that Julia was equally forthright. Yet not once had she said: "Well, Julia, you are not what I wanted for my son, and certainly not what I expected, but if you are what Brad wants, then it is up to you to show me you are right for him, because his is the only happiness I care about." But she had never sent for Julia so they could talk alone; never instructed her, as a possessive mother might have been expected to, in what was expected of her. She had merely left Julia alone. Waiting for me to make my own mistakes? Julia thought, as she wandered through the rustling sweet corn. And then, when I have made enough, damned myself in her eyes, will she move in and me out? More important—will Brad do as she tells him? She ended up at the pond, sat herself down on its edge, throwing the bread she had brought to the ducks.

Why do I feel so suspicious? she thought. Is it because of what Sally Armbruster told me? Because of what Drexel Adams said about her being in mourning? Why do I feel on trial? Because you have been married four short weeks, she told herself. For God's sake, Julia, give it time. You always were far too impatient. Not for the past three weeks I haven't! she answered herself roundly. How many brides could let their new husbands disappear to God knows where for three weeks only a week after they were married? Hundreds of thousands of them, during the war. But Brad is not in the army and there is no war. Oh no? her other self answered snidely. That's what you think.

Then she started as a smooth voice drawled: "Alone and palely loitering, Julia? Except in your case I know what is ailing you."

Looking around and up she saw Drexel Adams, dressed to kill in pale gray slacks and navy blue shirt, a navy blazer hooked on the fingers of one hand, over his shoulder. And suddenly she knew who it was he reminded her of; always had, since their first meeting. The young Cary Grant. Same dark good looks, same cleft chin, same insouciant charm. She had always been a fan of Cary Grant.

"I thought Seth was the literary member of this family." She teased with a smile, glad of company.

"I have been known to read a book or two in my time." He lowered himself to the grass beside her, first hitching up his immaculate pants. "I was in the neighborhood so I thought I'd drop in. I always do if I'm near. It is a lovely place, isn't it? The sort of place that soothes the most savage of breasts." As he spoke, his eyes lingered over Julia's own breasts in a way that had her freezing. "Looks like Brad is going to be away longer than we thought," he went on sympathetically.

"Too long for me," Julia retorted crisply.

"Of course, new bride and all. But this is a very big deal. Worth millions. If Brad pulls it off he'll wear a whole new bonnetful of feathers in his cap. Gift of his mother, of course." The dark eyes mocked even as the smile commiserated. "These deals are hell on wives."

"You speak from experience, of course."

"I *always* speak from experience—and a propos of that, how are you finding yours, of Boston and the Bradfords, I mean."

"Everyone has been most kind."

"Not difficult with someone who looks like you."

"How is Bitsy?" Julia asked deliberately.

"Doing her charity bit, today. I'm having a day off. I do, from time to time. Tell you what, why don't we go and have lunch someplace. I know a lovely old inn not ten miles from here."

"Annie is preparing lunch, thank you."

"Then may I join you?"

"I am sure Annie will have enough," Julia replied obliquely, no longer sure now, remembering what Charley—the family gossip—had told her about Drexel Adams: that he was a philanderer, and that Bitsy wore herself ragged keeping track of his affairs. "She's incredibly jealous, you see. Poor Aunt Bitsy. She loves him, alas, while he only married her because Milady"—her name for her grandmother—"wanted him to. I believe he cost her quite a lot of money . . . His branch of the Adamses are as poor as churchmice."

Now, he smiled into her eyes as he said: "Not only Annie."

Time to put a stop to this, Julia thought, and said bluntly: "Don't get your hopes up."

"They are not the only thing that is up."

She was on her feet in an instant. Brother-in-law or no, this was too much! But his hand caught hers, held her fast. "Don't run away, please. So lovely to be so lonely."

"Only for my husband."

"Won't you look on me as a substitute?"

His cheek almost robbed her of words. "There are no substitutes for Brad."

"Lucky man—but it is a fickle thing, is luck. A lady, of course, like our redoubtable mother-in-law." He tugged at her hand, smiled penitently. "Will you stay if I promise to behave? My excuse is that Brad is not the only man taken with you: you have very taking ways."

"And all I need, thank you."

"I know that, alas. You have me at your mercy, Julia."

"Then be thankful I am inclined to bestow it."

An appreciative laugh. "No wonder Brad is so besotted. I never envied him before, but you really are something else. Good to look upon, good to listen to, and all that cool brilliance . . ."

Julia removed herself firmly from his fingers. "Brilliant enough to do you the kindness of forgetting this conversation."

"I wouldn't, if I were you. You need friends."

"Is that what you are trying to be?"

"If you will let me. I make a better friend than an enemy, and you already have one too many of them." He lay back on the grass, propped on his elbows, and the blue eyes were hard as they regarded her. "Don't let the heavy hand with the sugar fool you. There is poison at the bottom of the cup. You are not what she wanted for Brad; most certainly not what she will allow him to have." The pity in his smile made Julia feel sick. "You don't think he has been sent so far for so long because of a mere business deal, do you? She herself had it sewn up weeks ago. You are the one getting the runaround, Julia. She is testing you. And when Brad comes back she will test you again—and again, until she finds the one that will break you—"

Stomach churning: "I don't believe you," Julia lied.

"*I* don't lie."

"If Brad goes away again I shall go with him."

"Try it!"

"I am his *wife!*"

"Of course you are. That's the trouble."

When she could steady her voice: "Why are you telling me all this?" Julia asked.

"Because you are too lovely to be done to death so young. Courageous too. But hopeless and helpless against her. She never fails. So devious she can stab you in the back while smiling into your face. And you without the slightest idea . . . You are an honorable person, you see. You play fair." He shook his glossy head. "She doesn't. She plays whichever way is necessary to win. You are clever too, and strong—which is why Brad married you, of course—but she has got him hopelessly entangled in her silver cord and he will never be free. I know her, Julia. I have twenty-odd years' tenure in this family so I know what makes Hester Bradford tick—and I use that word advisedly because she is an electronic marvel. The things I could tell you—"

"At a price, of course."

"Nothing comes free."

"I wouldn't have you as a gift! I don't need you or your spurious concern, Mr. Adams. I can manage very well on my own."

"The times I have heard people say that!"

As Julia stalked away from him at a furious rate, "Don't say I didn't warn you," he called after her, and spitefully.

Not once, but twice? Julia was thinking as she all but ran from the pond. Sally Armbruster *and* my own brother-in-law. He had his own ax to grind, obviously, but . . . What had Lady Hester done to him? The venom in his voice had dripped when he spoke her name.

Her long legs lengthened their stride as the terrors he had named took shape and substance over her head. He had put both feet through her painstakingly painted picture of Life with Mother. Chris's "There's a screw loose somewhere" came back to haunt her.

Was there poison in the cup? If so, she had not tasted it. Was Lady Hester out to get rid of her? If so, she had not shown even the slightest sign of it. True, she had expected Julia to measure up to her, rather than gently shown her how. And had not Brad said to her: "I need you, Julia. If only you knew . . ."? And then not explained why. While she, ever anxious not to make waves, had forborn to ask. Was she rescue? Did Brad regard her as some form of protection against his mother? If so, why? That he was afraid of her Julia knew, but she had come to the conclusion that it was because Brad was afraid he was going to be killed by kindness. Lady Hester adored her son; that was the lesson for this and every other day; she was also possessive of him, but had she not, according to Seth, arranged his marriage to Caroline Norton? If she wanted him to herself why arrange for him to marry any woman at all? No . . . If Lady Hester wanted to be rid of her it was because Brad had had the temerity to spurn his mother's choice and make his own. And Julia had learned enough about her husband's relationship with his mother by now to know that that was something nobody ever did if they knew what was good for them. Besides, Drexel Adams had his own problems, but his cynical assumption that there were occasions when brides—no matter how new—could—and should—seek comfort elsewhere appalled her. No wonder Bitsy went around wearing an expression that said she was damned if she was going to suffer alone.

No; it was obvious that what Lady Hester was doing was testing her; making quite sure she was good enough for her beloved son. And what I have to do is show her I can take whatever she cares to throw at me; that not only am I good enough, I am the best he will ever get! And isn't that what Brad wants? For me to *prove* he made the right choice? That I am no brass-faced hooker or double-dealing gold digger but an ordinary woman who loves him?

But why hadn't Brad explained? Why hadn't he sat her down and said: "Look, Julia, about my mother . . ."? Truth to tell, sometimes she was not at all sure that what she was doing was either the best or for it.

I'll ask Brad, she thought, more calmly. As soon as he gets back I'll have it out. I'll put it to him straight. Put what? she thought. What do

[143]

you ask him? What is between you and your mother? Why are you in thrall to her? What exactly is the hold she has on you? She found her heart sinking at the very thought. Brad would hit the roof!

Annie came into the hall as she entered the house. "Did Mr. Adams find you?" she asked. "I told him you was down by the pond."

"Yes; he came to tell me I have to return to Boston," Julia improvised.

"Mr. Brad comin' back?" Annie's face lit.

"I hope so," Julia said fervently. "Oh, Annie, I hope so."

SHE WAS STILL WORRYING at the bone when she got back to Mount Vernon Street, so that she did not notice the bags in the hall, but Brad must have been watching because the parlor door opened and there he was, arms outstretched.

"Brad! Oh, darling . . . Brad . . ." She hurled herself into his arms, burying her face in his chest and so missing the surprised yet relieved look on his face as he said: "You missed me, then?"

"Missed you! I've been dead without you!"

"I was about to send out the dogs myself. Where *have* you been?" Teasingly but intently: "Don't tell me you've taken a lover already."

"I've been at the farm."

"Oh . . ." Relief was in his voice. "The farm . . ."

"I can find my way there now . . . and I love to go there because it reminds me of you. I had to do something to take my mind off things."

"I won't tell you what *I* had to do!"

"I am not being left behind again!" Julia said, dead set and determined. "I don't give a damn if I have to sleep in a suitcase, I am going with you in future. No more separations, do you hear? I absolutely refuse!"

"I won't give you an argument on that," Brad said happily.

"I know green suits me but I draw the line at being a grass widow!"

His laugh was exultant as he swept her off her feet and whirled her around.

Lady Hester was in the parlor. Of course; Brad was home, therefore, so was she. And I hope she heard my every word, Julia thought, but shivered nevertheless.

"Cold?" Brad asked, concerned.

"No; that was a shiver of delight," Julia lied easily. Her eyes went over him enviously. "I can see you've been soaking up the sun."

"In between soaking up my tears."

Lady Hester's laugh tinkled. "A fine pair of lovebirds you two are."

"How was California?" Julia asked. His last call had been from Los Angeles.

"Three thousand miles away."

Lady Hester gazed at them and sighed. "I can see my son is not going to be fit for work, in which case I might as well not ask it of him. You are on your own till Monday." Her smile was pure indulgence. See, Julia told herself. It *was* spite, pure and simple.

"Let's go back to the farm." Exorcism was called for.

Brad's eyes glowed. "A second bite of the cherry."

"I want all of it," Julia assured him.

HE DROVE WITH ONE HAND on the wheel, the other around her, dropping kisses on her avid mouth every time they stopped for a light, his foot down all the way.

"So it was Mr. Brad back, then?" Annie exclaimed delightedly.

"You knew I was coming?" he asked in surprise—and something else.

"Only hoped," Julia told him.

"I've been hoping for three whole weeks." He scooped her up in his arms. "You've got your weight back!"

"Every lost pound."

"That I have just got to see."

Which led on to touch and ended up in a deliriously endless bout of lovemaking which left them both sticky with exhaustion.

"God, Julia . . . I've missed you like hell. I never knew it was possible to miss anyone so badly. Like being hollowed out. I've been reduced to hand jobs for the first time since I was learning what it was all about. Tell me you've missed me too. I need to know you have missed me."

"It's been a desert without you. I'm parched for you."

"It's crazy but it's true, isn't it? The way I'm crazy about you. I thought I was before but I know I am now."

Never had Julia felt more worshiped or adored, and she took it to her cracked self-confidence and used it as plaster. Whatever was between Brad and his mother (and now was not the time to go into it), there was no doubt as to her importance as his wife. He had demonstrated how much he needed and wanted her. And that was all that mattered. To *know* that she was loved. *Then* she could show his mother.

They slept late next morning, not having been able to leave each other alone all night. For the first time, Brad had no erection when he awoke.

"Jesus, Julia," he groaned into the pillow. "What have you done to me? I don't think I can move." He lifted his head to regard her. "How do *you* feel?"

"Deliciously sore." Sexual candor now came easily.

"Well I'm fucked out and that's the truth."

"I can see what you meant about three weeks' abstinence!"

"I've never gone so long in my life, let me tell you!"

"But isn't it marvelous when you end your fast?"

He pulled her down to him. "You are a marvel."

"So are you . . ." Julia reached out to pat his for once flaccid penis, but with a light "Careful, it might drop off!" he was out of the bed and making for the bathroom. It was always the same. He would *not* be handled. He liked her to caress the rest of his body with her hands and mouth, but he would never let her get him into her control. Well, Julia thought, with his mother controlling everything else I suppose *he* needs to feel in control somewhere. Like of me, for instance.

Julia was quite sure Lady Hester had heard her say she refused to be left again, because Brad stayed at home for a good long spell, during which they began to build a life together. Julia was in seventh heaven. He spent all his time with her when he was not working; they attended dutifully the formal dinners Lady Hester gave to introduce them as a couple to Boston society; they went to the ones given for them, but as much as possible, they preferred to be only with each other.

Whenever the family gathered, Julia took scrupulous care never to be left alone with Drexel Adams, to the extent that she found Bitsy watching her with narrowed eyes, while Drexel's sardonic smile said plainly: "Don't say I didn't warn you. At least give me the credit for that."

At the beginning of August, Lady Hester left for her usual month at Arun, made no demurrer when Brad said firmly he was taking Julia to Martha's Vineyard for their vacation. Bitsy took her husband and sons on a Caribbean cruise, while Abby and the Amorys went, as usual, to Cohasset, where the Bradfords had gone for generations.

Martha's Vineyard, on the other hand, turned out to be Julia's idea of paradise. From the moment the boat left Woods Hole, she knew this holiday was going to be perfect. She was surprised at the size of the island, even more surprised when, instead of to a car, Brad led her to a couple of bicycles.

"The terrain is perfect for this particular mode of transport," Brad told her with a grin. "Don't worry about the bags. They'll be waiting for us at the cottage."

And Julia discovered that even the most traveled roads had bike paths, that they were flat and thus easy to ride, and it was glorious to pedal along the shore from Oak Bluffs, the warm breeze in her face, the sea glittering with sunlight, the sand inviting and Brad, by her side, whistling cheerfully.

The "cottage" turned out to be a Victorian gingerbread, built on a former tent platform, its veranda a mass of plants in pots, others hanging from the shingle roof. Their bedroom opened out onto a small balcony, and the garden in front was decorated with patterns of white stones and brilliantly gay flowers. Rockers upholstered in patterned chintz were placed all over the veranda, and it was a matter of descending the front steps, walking down the garden path, across the road and you were on the beach. Inside, it was filled with cane furniture, a marvelously comfortable Victorian brass bed and a plethora of Victorian pictures. The kitchen was small but well equipped, and a "girl" from the village came in to do the cleaning.

But the cooking Julia did was not what she had expected: for instance, Brad showed her how to slow-cook clams in heaps of seaweed. Quiet nights were filled with the smell of fires—both of wood and of seaweed—and salt air.

They swam—Julia was rarely out of her bikini—sunbathed, water-skied, wind-surfed, at both of which Brad was skillfully adept, but Julia learned fast, though she never really became as good as he was. She preferred the boat, the *Hester*, which they used to sail right around the island and across to Nantucket. They played tennis on the court belonging to some friends of Brad's, at which he always trounced her, and at night, Scrabble, at which Julia always trounced him.

And could not leave each other alone. It was as if bonds had been severed with a knife. They made love anywhere and everywhere; on the boat, in the sea, on the screened veranda, once in a hammock under some trees. It was only in the second week that they sought company other than each other's, and Brad began to accept the many invitations that came their way. They went to parties and clambakes, to riotous drives in sand buggies over the dunes. Julia's skin deepened to ripe apricot while Brad took on the darkness of a Caribbean pirate, against which his body hair, turned white by the sun, glowed as though phosphorescent.

One night, they sailed over the sound to Nantucket to a party held in the skeleton of a house being built over the sea on stilts, invited by a college friend of Brad's, which resulted in their first quarrel.

"You didn't have to dance so much with Chuck Cabot," Brad complained disagreeably as he tied up the boat.

"I danced with other men too."

"Not the way you danced with him. From where I stood it looked like he was trying to get inside you."

"Darling, you know you are the only man who ever does that."

"Am I?"

Julia stiffened, but a look at Brad's sullen face was enough to tell her the whole story. He was in a mood, and there was no telling when he would fall into one of them. They littered his immediate vicinity like shell holes and he had to be guided past them most of the time. Now, it was obvious that the one he had fallen in was a deep one; one he would never succeed in getting out of without her help. Oh dear, she thought. And it had been such a good party; she had never been off the dance floor; had not for one moment given houseroom to the idea that Brad would mind. Now she read the signs.

There was a queer look on his face to match the odd note in his voice.

Julia smothered an impulse to laugh. Jealousy! Surely he could not be so jealous that he suspected her of being unfaithful—after the goings over he gave her daily—sometimes twice, sometimes thrice!

"Where would I get the energy—or the time?"

A reluctant grin spread. "Well . . ."

"He was only being nice to me."

"He's never nice to anybody unless he wants something!"

"Well, I don't want him, if that is what you are thinking."

"Prove it!"

She did.

Afterward: "I'm sorry," he apologized. "It's just that—you mean so much to me I can't stand the thought of you and any other man."

"There is no other man. Not now, not ever."

"Forgive me for being jealous?"

"Of course I do." A long pause. "But why, darling? You have absolutely no need."

"I can't help it . . . it's the way I feel about you . . . what you do to me . . ."

"But surely you know you mean everything to me."

"Do I?"

"Of course you do."

[148]

"Then why don't you ever tell me?"

"But I do!"

"Only when I tell you first!"

Julia felt stricken. She had not been conscious of the omission but obviously Brad was. So many times he would come up to her, put his arms around her and say: "Guess what?" and she would ask: "What?" and he would say: "I love you." Or, suddenly: "You'll never believe it!" he would exclaim, making Julia ask instantly: "What?" Only to have him grin and say: "How much I love you."

She had never been one to make overt demonstrations of affection; they had never been made to her by her aunt, who had an abhorrence of openly expressed feelings. Bad taste, was her thinly given verdict. But Brad, she reminded herself, had been brought up in an atmosphere of openly and constantly expressed love. He expected it. She snuggled up closer. "I promise to do better. It's just that—well, I don't have your spontaneity. Maybe yours will rub off on me."

"It won't be for want of trying!" He rubbed himself against her to prove it.

"One more time?" asked Julia.

"*All* the time . . ."

SHE WAS AT A LOSS to understand his uncertainty, his need to be shown. But she went along with it, ever mindful of his mother's influence and determined not to be found wanting should comparisons be made.

"I guess it is that basically, we are totally different," Brad said later, showing he had not dispensed with the subject. "You are cool, efficient, modulated, always under control."

"Not *always!*"

But his glance was speculative. "Sometimes I wonder . . ."

"I know I don't have your impulsiveness. I think that's what carried me along with you; a sort of wild beat."

In an odd voice: "I guess I've always ridden the dragon," Brad said.

"What does that mean?"

He was on his feet. "Nothing! Come on, race you back to the house!"

He was mercurial; a complex mixture of combustible gases. At times, his restlessness would not let him sit still. His emotions were fierce; quick to erupt, and he could act without a second thought. Always sure, Julia thought, of his mother's back up. And expecting the same of me? Swallowing her propensity to think first, she followed where he led, even if she occasionally shut her eyes. And she knew him well enough

[149]

by now to know when to tread carefully. She was, she thought, giving way all the time. Ever mindful of Drexel Adams's long spoon, she was careful to give Brad no cause for complaint. She knew they lived under a magnifying glass; even here, away from everybody, she realized she was still walking on tiptoe. She would not be the one to rock this boat. No matter how big the swell, she was bent and determined to prove herself a good sailor.

Which was probably why, she realized reluctantly, she had not yet openly broached the subject of his mother's influence. Here, away from it, just the two of them, wholly immersed in and by each other, Julia felt she possessed Brad as she had never done in Boston. Here, he was all she could want in the way of a loving, passionate, tender, concerned husband, anxious for her happiness, solicitous of her welfare, eager to give and happy to receive. Here, she felt that if she tried to plumb the depths of her own love, her line would not be long enough. Here, with Brad twenty-four hours out of every twenty-four, she never tired of him, or grew impatient with him, because here, he was a different man. He seemed to have left the complications of his nature back in Boston, along with the other Brad Bradford who walked so carefully around his mother, and here, too, Julia lost her own constraint, became once again the Julia he had met and been so deeply affected by, in London. Here, for the first time, she felt she was seeing the real Brad, the one inside the many layers of self-protection he had acquired over the years. Here, he was nakedly open with her, talked to her as he never talked in Boston. For instance, about their unlikely partnership.

"You are mental, I am physical," he said one night, after a bout of the most shattering sensuality which had left Julia feeling she had been offered a glimpse of paradise, so fulfilled did she feel. "Yet, to me, you are very—therapeutical. With you, physical exchange such as we gave each other a few minutes ago is an expression of faith; in me and with me. I like that. I need it."

"With you, it is the culmination of love."

He was silent, then said softly: "Yes. Love." Turning to face her. "I never loved till you, Julia. Never knew what it meant. Thought it had all to do with sex."

Julia smiled.

"All right, so we do find each other sexy, but you are so much more than a desirable woman, Julia. You turn me on—God, don't you—but it's come to me this past couple of weeks that I like being *with* you; that your presence—calms me, soothes me—comforts me, if you like. You

[150]

have great depths; I thought that from the beginning. Even now I don't know what lies at their bottom, but what makes you different from the others is that I want to find out."

His voice, his expression, were quiet, serious. Never had he opened himself to her so freely. Julia felt her throat tighten.

"I need you. I guess that's what I'm trying to say. You've become so necessary to me . . ."

"And you to me."

"Have I?" Even now, there was a question in him.

"Yes. More than any other human being ever has been. I never thought that would happen to me, but—the more I have the more I want. Whatever you are—and I too still have a lot to learn—it is what I, too, want and need. I suppose—after Derek—I never allowed anyone, male or female, to get too close. There was no stopping you. You took me over. I felt it that first night. I suppose that's what frightened me."

Brad sighed. It was a release. "Yes. It is frightening, isn't it."

"To give yourself over—completely—to another human being, is taking a chance," Julia said honestly, "but I don't regret it."

"You are sure?" There was still something—a doubt?—in his voice.

"I am positive. This time alone was what we needed, so that we could —find each other again."

"You felt it too?" Now there was eagerness in him.

"Yes." The door to honesty lay wide open. "Back in Boston—you were another Brad, one I was not sure about. You had a life about which I knew nothing and sometimes felt excluded from . . ."

He made a sound in his throat and pulled her closer.

"But here, just the two of us, you are the Brad I fell in love with, always will love." There was laughter in her voice now. "No matter how many other Brads there are."

"I guess we are all several people, depending on who we are with."

That was his first admission—no matter how oblique—that around his mother he was the Brad *she* wanted. But when Julia waited for him to tell her why, he did not.

"But we can tell each other everything," Julia prompted, "can't we?"

Brad's hesitation was just that second too long. "We will always tell each other everything," he promised.

But he still did not tell her about his mother.

THEY RETURNED TO BOSTON after Labor Day, deeply tanned and deeply content, both feeling they had somehow repaired any recent snags in the fabric of their opinion and feeling for the other. Never had Julia felt so sure of herself and her marriage, never had Brad felt so certain he had done the right—the only—thing.

It was therefore all the more shocking that the quarrel which erupted their very first night left a rent that let in a very bitter draft.

There had been a family dinner to celebrate everyone's return from vacation; much talk of what had been done, who had been seen, how things looked. Even Bitsy's edges had been smoothed: she was actually quite affable as she bade Julia good night to return to Louisburg Square. And it was as she watched Abby, Seth and their children drive off back to Cambridge that Julia thought: I wish we were leaving to go to our own house.

She was brushing her hair, Brad scrubbing his teeth in the bathroom, when she spoke with unthinking confidence: "When will we have our own house, Brad?"

"What's wrong with this one? God knows it's big enough."

"But not ours. This is your mother's house. Your sisters have their own houses; that's different."

"They also have families."

"So will we, one day."

"I thought we had agreed: time to play first."

"I know, but—"

Brad appeared in the doorway, a scowl on his face. "You don't like living here?"

"I didn't say that. I said I would like my *own* house one day." Lightly, warned by his tone: "You know what they say about living with Mother."

"No, I don't. What *do* they say?"

"That it never works."

"You think this isn't working, then?"

"I didn't say that either."

"Then what *are* you saying?"

"That I would like my own house, one day. Is that so strange?"

"This is already our house—well, mine, anyway."

"Yours!"

"When I married, Mother made it over to me."

"You never said!"

"You never asked."

Angry now: "As you asked me?" Julia seethed. She slammed down her brush. "When I said a house of our own I meant exactly that. This is your mother's house, no matter whose name is on the deed!" Helplessly: "I was thinking of something smaller, for just us two."

[152]

"It suits me living here. I was born here and I'll probably die here. Bradfords—eldest sons anyway—always do. Besides, it means I can keep an eye on Mother. She is not getting any younger and there is always the threat of her asthma." Brad paused. "You've never seen Mother when her asthma hits her. It's scary. When it does she always wants me with her. What would happen if we moved away out to Brookline or somewhere? How in hell would I get to her as quickly as I can here?" The scowl deepening: "She did offer to move out, as a matter of fact, but I wouldn't hear of it. Mother is pushing seventy and in spite of coming on like she's indestructible she's much more frail than she seems. Surely you don't begrudge a few out of the years and years we've got ahead of us spent with a woman who has never for one minute denied me—or you, come to that—as much of her own time as was needed."

The scowl was a storm front and the voice as lowering as a heavy cloud. Julia had done the unthinkable: disparaged his mother.

"And don't tell me she gets in your hair or interferes all the time," Brad went on viciously, "because she is the last person in the world to do that. Mother never interferes."

She doesn't need to, thought Julia. You already do exactly as she wants.

"You don't answer," Brad threatened.

Julia turned away. "Let's forget it," she said tonelessly.

"You started it!"

"Then let's end it!"

Julia stared at her taut face in her dressing table mirror. Frail? she thought. Hester Bradford is about as frail as a Sherman tank. But another piece of the jigsaw had fitted into place. Her asthma—scary or not—was a prime weapon when it came to controlling her son. Brad obviously believed totally that his mother was only putting on a brave face—and, like everything else she did, for his sake. Oh, yes, she had offered to move out, quietly confident that Brad would not allow even the thought. And what a master stroke, to make the house over to him now; to put him in charge of everything—especially her. Binding him even more tightly with that unbreakable silver cord of hers. Ostensibly giving him total freedom but in reality giving him no more than another few yards of movement. Oh, Brad, Julia thought, shivering in the cold because that was where she felt she had been shoved; Brad, *Brad.* Why can't you be honest with me; why can't you *tell* me what it is between you and your mother? Because there is something; something I don't know and don't understand . . . I only know it has to do with your fear of her, because you are afraid, so afraid you are terrified. Of her dying? Is that the threat she holds over you? Of leaving you to cope alone? Is that why you won't move out of this house, away from her? Because you daren't? Bitterly she realized how well she understood his fear. Because she had her own. The few words she had said a moment ago had all but unleashed a storm; it would take only a few more—the words she longed to ask—and she would unleash the Apocalypse. There was an invisible line behind which Brad withdrew when it came to his mother and not even his wife was allowed to cross it.

SHE WAS THEREFORE decidedly taken aback when, a few days later, Lady Hester said out of the blue: "I have been thinking, Julia; it really is time you and Brad stopped roughing it in his rooms. They are really single quarters. This is an enormous house; why don't you take a look over, choose a suite of rooms and redecorate? It was your profession, after all. It would—keep your hand in, shall we say?"

Julia could not say anything, only goggle. What *did* she use? Osmosis?

"Brad will have to go on another trip in a week or so—and alone, I am afraid." The sea-change eyes bore a look that said she had heard what Julia had said about being separated and it made not a blind bit of difference. "The countries he will visit are no pleasure trip, believe me. Arab countries never are. You will be forced to hibernate in your hotel room. Much more sensible to occupy yourself here."

"I would very much like to have a place of our own," Julia said, mind working furiously.

"Then by all means do so. And I know how you like to be kept busy."

"I miss Brad," Julia replied, again truthfully, but thinking: so she had noticed. She never missed a trick where her son was concerned. I wouldn't put it past her to have Brad's rooms bugged, she thought. Well, she won't get the chance with our new ones . . . Which was when she knew she would do it.

"I should like to do what you suggest very much," she agreed.

"And it shall be our little secret, eh? A nice surprise for Brad when he comes back?"

"How long will he be away?"

"About a month." At Julia's openly expressed doubt Lady Hester laughed indulgently. "My dear Julia, this is the United States. One merely has to express a preference and it is done. Workmen really do work in this country. A month is ample time for all you will have to do, believe me. And I am giving you *carte blanche* to make a home within a home. Brad simply will not hear of moving elsewhere; he insists my age makes his presence mandatory!" The smile was even more indulgent: more, it was triumphant. "But a mother must accept relegation," she continued gaily, "so I am doing the best I can."

"And you had better be grateful" remains unspoken, Julia thought. But at that, it was better than what they had, and she would make it perfect.

She inspected the house from top to bottom, found exactly what she wanted on the third floor: a series of connecting rooms which were filled with light, gave a lovely view of the Common and could easily be transformed into a self-contained suite. When Lady Hester stoutly if painfully made her way up the several flights of stairs (she had flatly refused to countenance the installation of an elevator) she commented: "I remember these rooms. They used to be used by the young bachelors when I came here as a bride. There were a lot of them in those days." A sidelong glance: "It will be very quiet up here, but perhaps that is what you want. A love nest?"

"Just a place of our own," Julia answered.

But she plunged happily into color schemes and designs. Lady Hester let her choose from the furniture in the other rooms, raised thin eyebrows at Julia's final choice. "I can see you have an eye for a good piece," she said, and something in the way she said it made Julia think: Why, the sly old thing . . . It was obviously a reference to Brad. But at that, she was right.

She also gave her cards to various specialty stores, and certain "little men" who could provide expert workmanship and fast delivery. She also recommended the decorator. All the planning gave Julia just what she needed. Something to *do*. It was only when she returned to work that she realized just how much she had missed it, and when Brad told her resignedly he had to leave on an extended trip she was able to say convincingly: "Oh, darling, *must* you?"

"Sorry, but I do. And I can't take you—not where I'm going. It would be nothing but hotel rooms in a dozen different countries."

But there was something in his eyes, his voice, which Julia, her mind on her plans, failed to notice. As well as the tightening of his mouth, his lowering look. She would give him such a lovely surprise, she was thinking. So she missed the storm warning. Kissed him goodbye in a way that had him cold-eyed and flinty.

"I'll call you every night," he said.

"Hmmmmwhat? Oh, yes, darling, please do . . ."

The moment the door closed on him she was at her drawing board.

This time, his absence passed with the speed of light. Her days were gloriously filled; every minute crammed with activity. Bitsy gave her the name of a marvelous little man on Washington Street who kept the most exquisite of bibelots, and Abby recommended a lady who made—by hand—sumptuous cushions in your own materials. She also knew an Italian lady down in Boston's North End who ran up curtains that could not be bettered by any of the specialty shops—for whom she worked anyway, but if you went direct you got them at half the price. Bostonian thrift, Julia thought, ran deep no matter how rich the family.

Once the workmen were in, the bathroom was completed in a matter of days, including the enormous tub Julia had bought from a demolition contractor who had retrieved it from a derelict mansion down in Back Bay. It was to be a surprise for Brad, who always complained that baths were too small. The basin matched it. Both were decorated in a pattern of spring flowers and miraculously uncracked. Julia managed to match them with cachepots into which she placed rare plants from another shop recommended by Bitsy. The window blinds were in the same pattern. The floor and walls were cork, and the shower had a nozzle which could be adjusted a dozen different ways. It was a bower of greenery and reflecting mirrors; a place in which to spend hours. When Brad did come home—unexpectedly and sooner than he had indicated—Julia was busy hanging the floor-to-ceiling voile which stretched across the windows under the taupe linen curtains, which were lined in cream silk; when the sun shone through them it filtered the light to a glow which was easy on the eyes.

"If you can spare him five minutes, your husband's home," he said jokingly—but not too jokingly.

"Brad! Darling—oh, you were not supposed to see all this until it was finished . . ."

"Too late." But he looked impressed as he gazed around their lovely sitting room: all taupe and white with touches of lemon; a subtle interplay between the polished cotton in the upholstery, the linen of the curtains, the slubbed silk of the cushions; the rich velvet of the big armchair made specially for him. And when he saw the bathroom he flipped. "Wow! Where did you get that tub! I can stretch right out in that . . . Angel!" he enthused.

"You approve, then?"

"Do I!" On a sigh: "I can see you didn't miss me *this* time."

"Want to bet?"

But it was true, she reflected guiltily, as he once more took his favorite route. She had not. She had been too busy.

LADY HESTER'S BIRTHDAY fell at the end of October—Halloween—and it was celebrated by a family dinner party. "When we were kids it coincided with trick or treat," Brad told Julia, and had to explain what *that* meant to a non-American.

Drexel Adams was more explicit. "You celebrate Halloween in England, don't you? And you had witches too. Right here, of course, is where we burned so many of ours."

Julia ignored him. She felt that much more secure now. But she had still chosen her birthday present with great care. She had found it in an antique shop on Washington Street, quite by chance. It was a Victorian fob watch: her mother-in-law never wore a wristwatch and had her sleeves cut to above-the-wrist length on all her clothes. It was done in diamonds and filigree, the bow worked in the shape of an H.

When Lady Hester opened the box she exclaimed in delight, "My dear, how exquisite! And Victorian!" An arch glance, a hint of a brittle smile.

"I had it cleaned and it keeps perfect time," Julia offered.

"I am sure it does . . . I know how *efficient* you are, Julia . . . such a dedicated worker, darling," she said as an aside to her son. "It has been nose to the grindstone all the time you were away. We only saw her in the dining room. *So* single-minded. Pin it on for me, darling," she asked him, and he fastened it securely to the shoulder of her coffee lace dinner dress.

"So me, don't you think?" she pronounced, gratified, before turning to the rest of her presents; a negligee from Bitsy, all ruffles, in chiffon bound in satin; a new briefcase from Abby in shiny crocodile; a Chelsea figure—a milkmaid, from her Amory grandchildren; chocolates—Bendicks Bittermints, from Drexel Adams; a first edition of Thoreau from Seth; a handsome, leather-bound appointments diary from the twins. Brad's present was a capacious crocodile handbag from Asprey's. "I could see your other one was showing its age."

"As I am," sighed his mother, on a moue.

"Nonsense! You are ageless."

She cupped his chin, kissed him lingeringly on the mouth. "Dearest boy . . ."

ON SUNDAY MORNING they went for a long walk; the leaves were turning and falling.

"How well you named this season," Julia commented, her arm in his, their hands clasped.

"No—you did. It's an English word you no longer use, that's all. Read your Shakespeare if you don't believe me!"

Julia was so astonished she stopped dead.

"I do read sometimes, you know," Brad said, his grin not quite masking his shortness of tone. "And you don't get into Harvard by money alone anymore."

"Darling, I didn't mean—"

"I know you didn't, but I just need to prove now and again that you aren't really the brains of this marriage."

"Who says I am?" Once more Julia was astonished.

"You'd be surprised," was all he would say, adding: "As I was, when I saw what you'd done to the house."

"I'm so glad you mentioned what I said about the house to your mother," Julia said happily.

"I didn't."

"You didn't! Then how—?"

"Mother knows everything," Brad said on a shrug. "Don't ask me how but she does." There was a pause. "And she was right, wasn't she? You really did enjoy doing it."

"I loved it," Julia enthused. It had been different, decorating her own place instead of someone else's.

"Mother said you were really wrapped up in your work."

"I always did enjoy it, you know that. I'm the kind that has to be busy to be happy, I suppose."

"You miss it, then?"

Too late she saw her error. "Not when you are home," she answered quickly.

"You are not bored at all?"

"Not around you I'm not."

"But when you are not around me?"

"Well . . ." Julia trod cautiously. "I suppose I get something from work other people don't. I like to feel I am doing something useful."

"That sounds like something your aunt would say," Brad said disagreeably.

Actually, it was, but Julia didn't tell him so.

"She always said hard work was its own reward," she agreed lightly.

"So—when I'm away you'll look for more work?"

"Well—Bitsy did say—just to advise her, you understand. And Abby says she's been meaning to do something about her own house for years—"

"Like burn it down and build anew," Brad said sardonically.

[158]

"I don't think she intends to go that far," Julia laughed.

"It's how far you intend to go that interests me."

Instinct made her say: "With you, if you are going away again."

The way his face relaxed told her she was right. "Not just yet," he admitted. "But before the end of the year I'll have to do at least six weeks in Europe."

"Then I come too. No being left behind ever again, do you hear? Whither thou goest, and all that jazz."

The way he pulled her to him, kissed her, told her she had said the right thing. She was glad she had never mentioned the boredom of her first time alone, when she had nothing to do except fritter her time away. It was no use: she was work-oriented. She found no pleasure in paying boring calls, attending the same old receptions and soirees, meeting the same people, listening to the same gossip. Getting down to work had been, in some strange way, a reaffirmation of her worth; not just Mrs. J. Winthrop Bradford, as Proper Boston thought of her, but Julia Carey, Interior Designer. And in spite of Brad's being back she was not going to turn down the opportunity of proving her worth to Bitsy; with Abby there was no need: Julia had the feeling she knew.

A week later, poring over patterns for a suggested scheme for Bitsy, Julia was sought out by her mother-in-law.

"I need your professional opinion, Julia."

"Of course. On what?"

"These."

They were pictures of an interior that had seen better days—obviously a hotel, once.

"It must have once have been rather splendid," Julia said, "but a long time ago."

"As a matter of fact it was; before the First World War it was the height of grandeur. I have acquired it as part of a large property holding. There is talk of demolishing it but I rather like the idea of owning an hotel. I could rechristen it the Hotel Bradford."

"That would cost a great deal of money."

"That is no problem. What I want to know is if you think it could be done—should be done, come to that. If you think it is worth rescuing."

Julia examined the photographs more closely: the lovely scrolled ceilings, the spacious rooms, the elegant staircase. "How many bedrooms?"

"Fifty—and a dozen suites. Small, but select is my aim."

It was all neglected and had been allowed to decline; paint was shabby, gilt peeling, carpets worn, the colors years out of date.

"You would have to junk an awful lot," warned Julia, "but on the other hand a lot of this stuff is priceless. I mean, will you look at those bathrooms? Baths and basins like that go for a fortune nowadays. I'll bet those surrounds are mahogany."

"They remind me of the ones at Arun," Lady Hester reminisced, "or rather the way they used to be at Arun. My cousin's wife went mad with her modernization. I would not want such wanton destruction with my hotel. It must be done with care—and with love. I need someone who can rejuvenate it without making it look its age, if you know what I mean. Successful face-lifts should go unnoticed." Looking at the photographs, "I want something 'special,'" she decided. "Something— unique. On the lines of the Connaught—not a hotel; more an English country house . . ."

"That *will* cost you!"

"I am prepared to pay for what I want; but it has to be right, and right means perfect."

Dinner was announced and the papers put away.

Over the ensuing days Lady Hester kept harking back to her hotel. It was plain it was her present "pet project," and from the figures being bandied back and forth there was no doubt she intended to spend lavishly; whoever redesigned the interior would be able to let themselves go.

It was when she heard the names being considered that Julia felt her first pang of envy: wished her first "If only it were me . . ." Which drove her to her drawing board to make a series of sketches of the way she saw the reborn hotel. They were good: she knew it, she *felt* it. But she had no "name." Unknowns were not handed commissions like this on a platter.

She was therefore not prepared for her mother-in-law's producing those same sketches—which she had stoically thrown away—one night before dinner.

"I hope you do not mind, Julia, but your maid brought me these; she thought they were of importance . . . Naturally, seeing as they are ideas for my hotel."

Caught red-handed, Julia could only bluff it out. "I was only idling. What you said stirred up some ideas."

"To good use, evidently. These are exactly what I had in mind. Why did you not say straight out you would like to design my hotel?"

Conscious of Brad listening intently, Julia squirmed, remembering their conversation of not long before.

"Had I known you seriously wished to be considered I would of

[160]

course have asked you to prepare sketches, but I was under the impression that marriage had preempted your career."

"It has!" Julia leaped to her own defense.

"I think not. Otherwise—why these?"

"You did ask my advice."

"And I obtained it. These are something else again. Come now." Lady Hester was at her most indulgent, which was when Julia felt at her worst. "These are obviously well thought out and exquisitely prepared; these are no idle sketches, these are a bid for recognition if ever I saw one—and quite rightly too." At the last minute the ax swung away. "These meet every possible criterion."

Julia had to prevent her jaw from swinging.

"You are a very talented lady, Julia, and just think, we can keep it all in the family!"

Julia dared not look at Brad. "But—" she began feebly, head down against the force-ten gale.

"How long would it take, do you think?"

Julia gathered her befuddled wits. "Well . . ." She grabbed the first figure that came to mind. "Six months at the very least—possibly longer; certainly not less."

"Hmmmm . . . We are now in mid-November. Could it be done for next spring, do you think? I should like that. A May opening. Paris in the spring—at the Hotel Bradford."

"Paris!" Julia's heart leaped, like a homing salmon.

"Did I not tell you it was in Paris?"

"No. I had assumed it was here, in America."

"Oh, no. That sort of *fin de siècle* is wholly European. The hotel is in Paris, on the edge of the Bois de Boulogne." Lady Hester cast gloating eyes over the sketches once more. "It is uncanny," she marveled, "how you have captured the very *essence* of my thoughts. One would almost think you had been listening at keyholes . . ." One of her tinkling laughs. "But you have obviously devoted much time and thought to my pet project and I am very flattered. This hotel *is* important to me—very important. It will bear my name, after all. But there are one or two queries in my mind . . . As to these suites, you are of course quite right to incorporate the smaller, single rooms into them, but—"

Julia left her chair, went to sit by Lady Hester on the sofa, both of them poring over the sketches, leaving Brad sitting stone-faced and out of it. It was only when, coming up for air, Julia happened to catch his expression that she realized he was anything but pleased; she had forgotten that he could not bear to be overlooked and overrun, and it

[161]

was just then that Lady Hester turned to her son to exclaim: "What a clever wife you have, darling. Brains *and* beauty; the unbeatable combination. And so obviously first-class at her job—which she was prepared to give up for even *my* son!"

"It was no wrench," Julia lied through her teeth, feeling it like a tooth being yanked. "But as the hotel is in Paris it would be a wrench leaving Brad; it was bad enough when he left me behind: six months apart would be unthinkable—and unbearable. However, if you really think my designs are what you want, then by all means feel free to use them as a base for the designer you eventually choose to work from. You could perhaps tell him the ideas were yours."

Lady Hester patted Julia's cold hand. "Such self-sacrifice. So kind . . . But if that is what you really want . . ."

It was not until they were in their own rooms that Brad let loose. "Jesus, all that long-suffering, nobler-than-thou smog made me sick! Why didn't you come right out and admit it! You'd give your eyeteeth to do that hotel!"

"And be separated from you for six months! You'd like that?"

"What I like isn't at stake here and you damn well know it!"

"Oh, for God's sake grow up!" Julia snapped, still smarting from her uncharacteristic bout of self-sacrifice and furious with him because he was its prompter. "Don't you *ever* think of anyone but yourself?"

"Do you? Why else did you spend so much time on those 'sketches'?"

"What your mother said piqued my interest. I was a designer for quite a few years, you know."

"And you would actually hand over your precious designs to Mother and let her take the credit for them? Come off it!"

"All right then, shall I go back downstairs and tell her I've changed my mind; that I will do the hotel and not see you for six months? Is that what you want?"

The quarrel in full spate, they backed off and stared at each other.

"Do you ever think of what *I* want?" Brad asked in a queer voice.

"For God's sake, haven't I just proved it?"

"Have you?" Brad asked, still in that queer voice. "I wonder."

"*You* wonder! How the hell do you think I feel?"

"What do you want—really? Be honest."

Something in his voice drew the truth from Julia like a cork from a bottle. "I'd like the hotel and you to be in Paris with me."

"Suppose it was possible?"

Her look was quick. "How possible?"

"Just—possible. Would you do the hotel?"

"Would I!"

"You did say no more separations—remember?"

"And I meant it. That's why I turned down the hotel."

Now, something in her voice and attitude brought him over to her, to put his hands on her shoulders, stare down into her eyes. "Really and truly?"

"Really and truly," confirmed Julia, ruthlessly repressing an astonishingly sharp pang.

"It would be the chance of a lifetime."

"I know that." Julia clung to her stoicism.

"And you would really give it up for me?"

"I married you, didn't I?"

"Angel!" Brad swept her into his arms.

When at last she came up for air: "What was that for?" Julia asked breathlessly.

"For being a good girl. We are going to go to Paris together!"

Julia goggled. "We are what?"

"Mother came up with the idea. She's really gone bananas on your sketches, and when she first told you about the hotel she thought maybe you'd ask for the chance; but when you didn't she realized you meant what you said about not being separated—*really* meant it. So she's sending me to Paris for six months."

Julia gasped, then flung her arms around him. "Oh, darling Brad, how fantastic! Why didn't you *say?*"

"Because I wanted you to say first."

Julia felt a cooling of her joy. "You mean you wanted me to prove my love?"

Unabashed: "You know me; I have this thing about needing to be first."

Disengaging herself: "So you were testing me?"

"I'm jealous of anything that takes you away from me—no matter how. I just wanted to be sure that when it came to me and the hotel I still came first, that's all."

Still unable to understand: "*Why* are you so insecure? If anyone is loved—and shown to be loved—it is you. Your mother—"

"I am not talking about my mother; I am talking about you: my wife. About us—our relationship."

He was curt, hard, emphatic, and something in his stance warned her of its importance to him. She still didn't understand it but moved, suddenly, by what she could only classify as sympathy, she turned to him again. "You will always come first with me. First, last and always. Is that what you want to know?"

His voice was muffled when he said against her hair: "All the time. I love you so, Julia, and need you the same way. I never needed any woman before; it's new and strange to me and sometimes I think I can't handle it. Before, I never saw it as anything else but want. Want I could understand; I thought need was beyond me—until you."

"Oh, my love . . ." Julia smoothed back the thick fair hair from the boyishly handsome face.

"Am I? Your love, I mean?"

"Like no one else before or since."

"And if it ever came to the choice—"

In a microsecond Julia knew, beyond a doubt, that she would hesitate, and in the next ruthlessly steamrollered over that doubt to answer: "It would be you, my darling. It would always be you."

It was only afterwards, Brad heavily asleep in her arms, that she stared aghast at what she had never expected to find, and wondered what the hell she was going to do with it.

THEY EXPLORED THE HOTEL TOGETHER. It was already gutted inside, the ugliest parts of the decor stripped away, the proportions of the lovely ceilings revealed, the elegant marble fireplaces, the finely designed windows. All these had been incorporated into Julia's designs, over which Lady Hester had gone with a microscope and a pocket calculator. Costs had been calculated to five places beyond the decimal point.

It was when they got to the top floor, where workmen were still busy on the last suite, that Brad eyed the enormous Belle Époque bed in which many a grand *horizontale* had entertained her lovers, to murmur: "Could we have some fun in *that!*" He swung on Julia, eyes alight. "Why don't we do that? Stay here, right in the hotel. You'd be on top of your work and the office is not too far away. It would be such fun!"

Fun! Is that all you ever think of? Julia thought tightly. I've come here to work—and damned hard at that. Already, seeing the actuality of things, she knew she had been wrong to agree to six months; there was at least nine months'—probably a year's—work here. What had she been thinking of? But by the time Lady Hester had turned her around and around, and Brad had given her a few spins, she had obviously not been thinking clearly. That would have to change, for a start.

"Oh, come on, Julia!" Brad urged impatiently. She could be so depressingly practical at times—always the wrong ones. This was

Paris! They were only months married. Now was the time for fun! The seriousness would come later—much later. He had thought he had broken down that no-pipe-dreams, no-trips-to-the-moon mentality of hers. And she could cope, handle pressure. She would get the job done. But now, looking at her, he knew what she was thinking. Sleeves were being rolled, nose positioned at the grindstone, deadlines placed on the altar.

"You'd be right on top of things," he added as a sop.

I would indeed, Julia was thinking—or rather calculating. And there would be so much to watch. This had to be done right. Perfectly, in fact. Not only did she have to reach her mother-in-law's exacting standards, she herself was under inspection. There was no margin for error.

"All right," she decided swiftly, "let's do that."

THEIR DAYS fell into the ordered, regular pattern Julia loved. They would breakfast together before Brad departed for his day, dollar signs already rung up in his eyes, then Julia would descend to the ground floor, where she had set up a corner as her office, in which the manager-designate was already at work.

He was a Swiss, a forty-five-year-old charmer named Pierre Chambrun; twenty-five years in the hotel trade and multilingual. Lady Hester had prised him away from the Georges V. Julia thought he was a treasure. He was calm, authoritative, fast-thinking, unflappable. From the start, he and Julia melded, and as he knew Paris like a native he was a gold mine when it came to information—from the best shop from which to buy silks to the one which could supply the most esoteric of bric-a-brac.

"He's heaven-sent!" Julia exclaimed to Brad happily. "God knows how I would have managed without him."

She plunged headfirst into a maelstrom of work, surfacing at the end of each day high on adrenaline and accomplishment.

Lady Hester called regularly, and Julia also made weekly reports in writing. She was careful to keep her mother-in-law informed on all aspects of the work as it proceeded, while she herself watched the budget, hewed to the timetable, kept an eagle eye on the workmen, chased suppliers and haunted the shops for the right lamps, the perfect mirrors, the only china.

She had designed a dining room in the most flattering shade of pink; muted but with silvery overtones, its mirrors also tinted so as to give any woman the most flattering of reflections. She hunted down the

[165]

little bibelots which would give her rooms character, endow them with personalities. The right base to match the right shade; exquisite enamel boxes for cigarettes, beautiful frames of silver or peacock-blue enamel or carved coral and iridescent mother-of-pearl, into which guests could place their treasured photographs. She strove mightily to avoid the impersonal, to create the ambience Lady Hester demanded; something intimate and intensely private; not a hotel but a home.

Each suite—there were no rooms—had its own individual decor, and nowhere was the name of the hotel to be seen except on the handwoven writing paper, kept in its color-of-the-suite folder of watered silk. She went miles to lay her hands on the right thing, often to Brad's displeasure as time went on.

"But I've made arrangements to spend the day at Neuilly," he would complain. Or: "But you know I booked a table at Maxim's!" when Julia had to beg off because now was the only time she could look at a certain article.

"I'm sorry, darling; if I don't go today"—or tonight—"I might lose the chairs"—or the chaise longue or the portrait or the mirrors. And he would scowl and sulk and complain that this was not what he had come to Paris for. Not to be neglected.

"Nor did I come to Paris to play," Julia would say patiently. "I am up against a tight deadline; your mother is dead set on opening in May, though I've told her I don't see how. You go, darling. There is no need to forgo your pleasures."

"Don't think I won't!" he would snap rudely.

And more and more he took to going places on his own; more and more to coming in later and later, often to find Julia deep in exhausted sleep and inclined to protest: "Not now, darling . . . I'm tired. I've had a fourteen-hour day and I have to be up at seven in the morning . . ."

Until one night he jackknifed out of bed, snarling: "Maybe *I* should make an appointment!"

Julia found him on the chaise longue in the sitting room, wrapped in a quilt, stiff with hurt outrage.

"Darling, I'm sorry. Please try to understand. I've had a horrible day. The wretched carpenters erected the paneling in the wrong room and it had to be taken out again. I didn't mean to snap at you, but I do get short-tempered when I'm worried."

"What have you got to worry about?"

"You know very well! We are behind schedule. We are not going to be able to open in May and your mother has set her heart on it. Every time she calls she reminds me."

"Then tell her you can't do it! You are a clever lady but even you can't work miracles!"

"I've tried—but she only laughs and says, 'Oh, now, Julia, if anyone can do it you can. Paris in the spring, remember? You agreed to that.' "

"Well, didn't you?"

"I said I thought it could be done by then. I was wrong. I don't think it can."

"Tell her so, then!"

"Contradict your mother! I've never seen even you do that!"

"Then work twenty-four bloody hours a day! See if I care!" And he humped the quilt around him, turning his back.

Julia stormed back into the bedroom, slamming the door. Of all the childish, selfish men! Did he never think of anyone but himself? Let him sulk if he wanted to. She needed her sleep.

Next morning he was not speaking, but Julia was staring at a letter from the manufacturers of her special silver-rose paint, telling her the batch had been spoiled in the mixing and would have to be redone. Oh, my God, she thought to herself, reaching for the telephone. When she put it down again, Brad had gone.

She went with Pierre to the paint factory that afternoon, and on the way visited a gallery he knew which specialized in fine china. Porcelain being one of Julia's "things," she spent a soothing and satisfying couple of hours wandering blissfully around, got back to find Brad in a foul temper.

"Where the hell have you been?"

"I told you, didn't I—about the mix-up in the paint?"

"You told me sweet nothing! The only person you ever talk to is that smarmy Swiss bastard!"

"Oh, don't be ridiculous."

"You are the one making yourself ridiculous with that little creep!"

She noticed he was in dinner jacket and black tie. "Are you going out?"

"I am! You were invited too, but it's far too late for you, now. I'll make your excuses—as usual!" he added, before slamming out.

Oh, God, the Flambard dinner, Julia remembered. Brad would be talking business all night while she sat and listened to the women talk fashions, scandal and trivia. No thank you, she thought. A soak in a hot bath and bed.

She was soaking blissfully when the phone rang. It was her mother-in-law. She sounded cock-a-hoop. She had, she said, heard that the Marquise de Montreuil was disposing of her twelve Louis XVI fauteuils, had managed to do a deal she wanted Julia to clinch. "Perfect for the lobby," Lady Hester trilled happily. "Exactly what you told me you were looking for: right color, right period, right everything. Now do not fail me on this one, Julia. She has agreed to see you tomorrow night and seal the bargain; she knows you are coming. Unfortunately, she has a dinner engagement so cannot see you before eleven o'clock."

"So late!" exclaimed Julia.

"It cannot be helped. I want those chairs; you understand me?"

"Yes . . ."

"Take Pierre Chambrun with you. He is very knowledgeable about furniture. I want to be sure she is not selling something not in perfect condition. Get him to give them a careful scrutiny."

"All right," Julia agreed obediently. Anything for peace.

"Now then, tell me, how is everything else going. . . ."

After twenty minutes detailed cross questioning—God help the size of her phone bill, Julia thought—she was finally satisfied, hung up with yet another admonition as to the importance of the chairs. "She is a mercenary old harridan but they are worth every penny if they are perfect—as they are supposed to be—and they once belonged to Marie Antoinette!"

Julia was asleep when Brad returned, and next morning, for some reason, she overslept, so that he was gone when she awoke. Oh, hell, she thought. She had meant to pour oil on troubled waters.

She told Pierre about the trip to Versailles and he showed surprise. *"Those* chairs!"

"You know of them?"

"Who does not? I believe Paul Getty once tried to buy them but with all his millions would not meet her price. They are priceless, of course."

"Well, I don't know what my mother-in-law has paid, but she is another hard bargainer so I shall be most interested to see them."

Brad returned early that evening; came to find Julia where she was engaged in an earnest discussion with the plasterer's foreman, who was haggling over the price for overtime.

"Aren't you finished yet?" he scowled. "Come on, you know it's the Embassy reception tonight."

Julia clapped a hand to her mouth. "Oh, no . . ."

"Now what?"

She told him about the phone call, the chairs, her late visit to Versailles.

"That's not right," he said derisively. "Mother would never forget an important reception. You've got it wrong."

"I have not! She was most specific."

"That can't be."

"Why should it be always me who gets it wrong? Your mother must have forgotten about the reception in her delight about the chairs."

"Mother never forgets anything to do with business."

"She must have. I told you: she was absolutely insistent."

"So you say!"

"Are you calling me a liar?"

The workmen were goggling, Pierre Chambrun had withdrawn to a discreet distance. Brad yanked her into the still unfinished lobby. "I am saying that something, somewhere, is a figment of somebody's imagination."

"Which *is* calling me a liar—*me*—never your precious mother!" Julia's simmering temper erupted. "Why should I want to make up stories?"

"You tell me!"

Julia marched to the nearest telephone, snatched up the receiver and thrust it at him. "Call her—go on, call her! Ask her to tell you what she told me!"

"Don't think I won't!"

But Lady Hester was not at the office, not at Mount Vernon Street, not at the farm. Nobody knew where she was.

"Very convenient!" Brad slammed down the phone. "With no way of checking—which you knew all the time—that leaves you your way out!"

Julia's eyes flashed. This was too much! "Brad, I am not going to brawl with you. I have had a long, hard day and it is not over yet by a long chalk. I am too tired to argue anymore."

"These days are you ever anything else?"

"Obviously it has escaped your notice that I work very hard; but then, nothing penetrates your self-righteousness, does it?"

Brad's face took on a queer expression. "That's a funny word to use. A Freudian slip, no doubt. Penetration on your mind."

Julia went white, then red.

"Is that a guilty blush?" His inquiry was menacing.

"I have nothing to be guilty about!"

"Don't play innocent with me! I know you've got something going with that smarmy Swiss bastard; have ever since we got here!"

"Now who is inventing fairy tales? Pierre Chambrun has *never* been anything but unfailingly kind and helpful to me! Use your common sense—what little you have, that is! *Think*, for once! It would be more than his job is worth, and for another, we just don't fancy each other! You are acting like a fool."

"I am well aware of your opinion of my thought processes," snarled Brad, "but I do engage my mind sometimes; I wouldn't be holding down this Paris job if I did not. You are not the only capable person round here, you know."

"I was not aware I had ever said I was."

"Maybe not said, but, by God, have you ever implied it!"

"I have done no such thing!"

Some stunned, far-off part of Julia could not believe what was happening. They had quarreled before—more and more lately—but not like this. This was open warfare. "You are letting your imagination run away with you," she said in the calm voice of reason.

"*My* imagination! You are the one making up tall stories."

"Why in God's name should I invent a trip to Versailles at ten o'clock at night?"

"So you can spend time with your lover, what else?"

Julia's hand met his red-with-anger cheek with a hard crack. "Have you lost your mind? I don't take lovers!"

"You took me."

"I fell in love with you!"

"At first sight, no doubt!"

"No, at first night!" Julia drew a deep, calming breath. "Use your reason, please. I spend a great deal of time with Pierre because we work together—work, do you hear? He helps me in ways you cannot."

"Helps himself, you mean!"

Breathing hard: "I don't tell you how to run the Paris office!"

"Not yet you haven't."

Julia stopped dead, stunned from that particular missile. When she could: "Brad, what are we talking about here?" she asked, in a completely different voice. "It's not just twelve chairs and Versailles, is it?"

"You bet your life it isn't—and it's been coming for weeks, ever since you divorced me and married your job."

Julia's jaw dropped.

"It gets the time you should be devoting to me."

"Devote!" Julia's voice soared. "Devote! Since when have you become my religion! I am your wife, remember—not your mother! And you won't get from me the uncritical, unquestioning worship you get from her!"

"How can I when you are giving it all to that Swiss bastard!"

"For the last time, Pierre Chambrun is not and never has been my lover!"

"Liar!"

"And as for devoting my time to my work," Julia swept on regardless, "that is something you have never been able to understand—or accept. Or is it that your mother played it down, made it appear like some dilettante exercise!"

"Then why did you manipulate her into giving it to you?"

Julia lost her breath. Gulping: "When I *what?*"

"Come off it! You got this job by sliding under the door and you know it! I know you were bored, restless—that I wasn't—our marriage wasn't—enough for you. You are greedy, Julia. You want it all . . . So you schemed and plotted and manipulated . . . You fooled me, by God, in more ways than one. You are not what I thought you were at all!"

"*I* wasn't! I suppose you haven't lied to me from the beginning—never once told me how your mother has you in some sort of an emotional cell—locked and barred! I've gone tippy-toe around her from the day I set foot in Boston—and all to please you. I agreed to take this job to please you! All I have ever done, from the start, is try to please you. Don't you dare make *me* the villain of this piece!"

"And don't you dare blame my mother!" His voice, his face, were ugly, made her take a step back, but: "I'll be damned if I will let you blame me!" she flung at him.

Brad regarded her with something like implacable hatred. "Are you coming with me to the Embassy reception or not?"

"Are you deaf?" Julia seethed from behind clenched teeth. "Your mother wants those chairs. Her orders are for me to get those chairs. *Now* do you understand?"

"Only too well!" He turned on his heel and strode away, toward the elevators.

Julia tottered to the nearest pile of carpet and sank down on it, legs trembling, hands too, stomach churning. She hated rows, and this one had erupted so quickly, so devastatingly. What in God's name had got into Brad? Pierre Chambrun? It was too laughable! All he had to do was think for thirty seconds. But if he had done that he would have realized that interior design was not something you could do on weekends or free afternoons. He just had no idea of the minute and careful dovetailing necessary on a job like this. The enormity of it all.

Anger surged once more, had her on her feet and making for the elevators. She would get this settled—made clear to him—once and for all.

The clothes he had shed lay in a trail all the way across the bedroom floor to the bathroom. She could hear water. But when she went to open the door it was locked. She hammered on the wood. "Brad! Open this door! Do you hear me? Open this door at once! Stop acting like a spoiled brat. All this is stupid and uncalled for. Let me in so we can talk it out calmly. We must settle it one way or another!"

Silence.

"Brad!" She beat an impotent fist on the door. "Please. You've got it all wrong, honestly. I swear there is nothing between Pierre Chambrun and me. And I *do* have to go to Versailles for those chairs."

More silence.

"Oh, go to hell!" Anger, fright and her deep sense of hurt ignited in a final explosion of rage. "Sulk like the spoiled brat you are! Go whining to your mother! I am sick and tired of you both!"

She slammed out of the room, stalked down the corridor at a furious rate and out to one of the balconies overlooking the Bois, where she rested her hands on the iron balustrade and shook. When it stopped, she leaned against the wall, closed her eyes. Something was wrong, did not fit. How could Lady Hester have forgotten something as important as an Embassy reception where the cream of French industry would be gathered? Had her triumphant acquisition of the chairs obliterated all other considerations? It was not like her. She could normally think of a dozen things at once. And where had she gone? If she had been there, she would soon have put Brad right as to priorities. Work always came first with her, as it did with Julia. You never argued with your boss. And it was because her mother-in-law was also her boss that Julia was bent and determined, teeth gritted and muscles straining, to work a twenty-four-hour day seven days a week to see this hotel completed on time; *because* she had been overoptimistic as to the opening date; *because* she would never admit defeat to her mother-in-law. She had seen Lady Hester's reaction with people who failed. This was not just the designing of a hotel; it was the whole structure of her marriage. Only now she realized how desperate she had been for Lady Hester's whole-hearted approval which, even now, she had never actually felt was forthcoming; been always conscious of a reserve, a lingering doubt, a whole series of qualifications. And because she sensed that Brad was even more desperate for it; his obsessive need for her to succeed had seeped through her very pores. Which was why Julia had worked so hard, to the total exclusion of everything else. So that Lady Hester would have her hotel ready for opening by the end of May. Which is what I have to get Brad to understand. Her resolve sent her back to the bedroom. The bathroom door was ajar now, the interior a mess, left for her to clear away. Also as usual. Seething, she picked up clothes, stuffed wet towels in the hamper, closed drawers and replaced caps on bottles, resentment simmering. She was sick and tired of picking up after him, of trying always to please. "Yes, dear," "No, dear," "Three bags full, dear." She slammed a door shut viciously. Yet niggling away at the back of her mind was a little alarm bell warning that she *had* relegated him; she *had* spent more time with Pierre Chambrun than she had with her own husband, even if it was purely in the course of her work. Brad was obviously insecure, which her impatient ignoring of him had obviously aggravated. She put her hands to her head. She felt she was being sundered: Brad and his needs pulling one way; his mother and her insistence on a May opening pulling the other. This row had lasted too long; it had been simmering for days before erupting tonight. Face it, Julia, she said out loud to her reflection in the bathroom mirror. Rescue is called for. Quickly she pulled off her own clothes, turned on the shower. She would wear her newest dress, a Madame Grès original classic of heavy white crepe; once she had the chairs she would join Brad for the remaining hours of the reception, show him she was making her amends, wanted to make things right with him. Guiltily now, she recalled those nights when she had repulsed him, genuinely too tired after a twelve-hour day but which he, being who and what he was, had taken as rejection because she was getting it elsewhere. Oh, you *fool!* she flung at herself. That is not the way to keep your husband happy. Sex might be a pleasure to you but with Brad it is a *need*. It's time to do some fast and fancy footwork, my girl, before you are dropped from the chorus line; worse, before Brad satisfies that sexual overdrive of his elsewhere, because you know damned fine he will, if you drive him far enough . . .

Pierre made no reference to the row; he was courteous, as pleasant as ever, but he did drive them as quickly as possible to the lovely old house where the marquise lived, not far outside the park. She must have been eighty at least but was painted and coiffed like a forty-year-old. She was disposed to talk, insisted on each chair's being examined while presenting yards of proof as to their provenance.

"For my old friend Hester Bradfor' I give only my best," she said grandly, insisting that they stay for drinks, embarking garrulously on a long, endless story about how she first met her friend, which led to her reasons for selling the chairs, asking where exactly they would go in the hotel, anxious that they should be treated with the greatest care.

Julia tried not to fidget, not to keep on looking at the little crystal clock, embellished with cupids, that stood on the carved-marble mantel. It was way after midnight when they finally managed to extricate themselves. Brad would never expect to see her now.

"Can you make it as fast as you can to the Embassy?" she asked Pierre.

"*Bien sûr, madame.*"

But he was not quick enough. As luck would have it, even as they turned into the Embassy gates, another car was coming out. At its wheel was Brad; snuggled up close was a striking brunette. His attention was on her, focused on her in a way Julia remembered. Then the cars had passed. But it was enough for Julia to turn to stone.

Pierre, who had also seen, merely drove the car right around and out again, before driving back to the hotel. When Julia got out of the car, deaf, blind, dumb, he only pressed her hand. He saw her to the elevator, stood until the doors closed on her. Only then did she lean back against the wall and shake.

WHEN THE PHONE RANG, she lifted her face from the sodden pillow and reached out an eager hand.

"Julia?"

She sat bolt upright, her hands smearing away tears.

"What have you to tell me?" Lady Hester demanded crisply.

"The chairs will be delivered to the hotel tomorrow," Julia answered tonelessly.

There was a brief silence, then: "Are you all right?" Lady Hester asked dubiously. "You sound—strange."

Julia covered the receiver and cleared her clogged throat. "Sorry . . . a frog in my throat."

This time the silence was startled before a very smooth: "I hope *not*, my dear." That was so unusual for Lady Hester—whose sense of humor needed glasses—that Julia, in spite of her misery, had to smother a laugh. "But you do sound *distrait*," her mother-in-law went on disapprovingly.

"I'm all right," lied Julia, "just tired."

She glanced at the clock. Almost 3 A.M. Nine P.M. back in Boston. And Brad not back yet. If he was coming back. "It's been a busy day," she went on, brimming with a need to give a little tit-for-tat. "They all are, these days, so much to do and so little time to do it in."

"Now, Julia, I trust you are not going to belabor me with that May business yet again!"

"Of course I'm not! I just want you to know that I am doing my best."

"I had expected nothing less."

"We will open on time," Julia promised recklessly. "If we have to work round the clock."

"You are not blaming me for that, I hope."

"Of course not. I—"

"It was no instruction of mine that you work yourself into the ground."

"If you wish the May opening to stand there is no alternative!"

The silence held its breath. "You misunderstand me, Julia. May was a suggestion, no more."

"It did not sound like a suggestion to me; more an order."

"You did misunderstand me, then."

"I am sure I did not."

"And I am sure you did. Do not brangle with me, Julia. I am always most precise when it comes to dates. Do not blame me if you are finding yourself in difficulties."

"I did not say I was in difficulties!"

"Kindly lower your voice," she was commanded icily. "I can hear you quite well; there is no need to shout."

"I am not shouting."

"Are you calling me a liar?"

"I never so much as uttered the word!" What the hell? Was she hearing clearly? Sometimes the lines across the Atlantic sounded as though the conversation was being held underwater. "Can you hear me properly? Is the line clear?"

"When you rant and rave like that anybody within hearing distance can hear."

"I—am—not—shouting," Julia enunciated distinctly.

"Now you are being ridiculous. I am *not* simple minded! Merely speak clearly and controllably. There is no need to be so over-wrought."

"I am not overwrought!" She can't be hearing what I am saying, Julia thought. "We seem to be at cross purposes," she said clearly.

"I am most certainly not cross! You are the one in a temper!"

"I am not in a temper!" But Julia could feel it, already badly frayed by the night's events, slipping its tie.

"You are shouting at me again!" Lady Hester admonished.

"Once and for all I am not shouting and I am not in a temper!" Julia said from between teeth all but clenched. "You keep picking me up the wrong way."

"Are you accusing me of being stupid as well as deaf?"

"I am not accusing you of anything!" But she wondered whether perhaps her mother-in-law was deaf. Woe betide anybody who mentioned her glasses.

"Let me speak to my son," was the next imperious command.

"He is not here."

"Not there? Where is he, then?"

"At the Embassy reception—the one you seem to have forgotten when you ordered me to go for the chairs."

"I did not forget it! Now you are putting words into my mouth. What on earth is the matter with you tonight, Julia? You seem to be upset about something—"

"You gave me the impression that the chairs were all that mattered to *you!*"

"You *are* calling me a liar!" The hurt was palpable, as was the shock. So was the sudden rasp of tortured breathing. "Oh, Julia . . . Julia . . . what have I done that you should say such things to me—"

"What things? What are you on about?"

"Oh, cruel . . . cruel." It was a moan, ending in a gasp.

"I don't think you can hear me properly. Shall I hang up and call you back?"

"I think you have called me enough. You have hurt me deeply, Julia. That you, of all people . . ." A rasp of indrawn breath. "That I should have to suffer this from you . . . I had not thought it of *you,* Julia."

"Oh, for God's sake!" Julia's nerves snapped.

"Ah . . . do not blaspheme!" It was a broken cry.

"I see no point in continuing this conversation," Julia said, enunciating distinctly.

"It is only upsetting you and I don't want—"

"You don't want!"

This is ridiculous, Julia thought, alarmed now at the tortured sounds coming from the other end of the telephone. She had been warned, by all and sundry, that Lady Hester's asthma was something to be avoided at all costs. She had thought it was a clear case of emotional blackmail, but the rasp of difficult breathing, the strain in the voice, the labored heaves, made her take fright. As if she did not already have more than enough to contend with . . .

"I will call you tomorrow," she said, still speaking slowly and clearly. "With a better line we can have a sensible conversation."

"I *am* sensible! How dare you accuse me of being out of my mind?"

Oh, my God, Julia thought, frantic by now. She's gone bonkers! Fright spurred her on to say hurriedly: "I am going to hang up now. I will call you tomorrow morning, your time." She replaced the receiver before she could change her mind, sat staring at it in frightened fascination. What on earth had she thought was being said? Not what actually was, that was for sure. I'll straighten it out tomorrow, she thought. I can't deal with her now. Not with Brad still out . . . He's all I can think about right now.

She was still lying wakeful with the beginning day lightening the windows, when the bedroom door crashed open. She shot bolt upright, her mouth opened to scream, then saw it was Brad. A Brad she did not know. Scarlet with rage, and advancing toward her with clenched fists. "You bitch!" he flung at her. "You lying, deceitful, conniving bitch!"

Julia stared at him, robbed of her voice.

"You have all but killed my mother, you bitch! She is in the hospital with a severe heart attack—brought on by you and your filthy tongue!"

His handsome face was ugly with rage, the sea-change eyes glittering with a light that had Julia shrinking back against the bedhead.

"What did my mother ever do to you that you should spew filth all over her? She took you in, didn't she? Welcomed you, did her best for you!" His voice shook with rage—and something else. Terror? Julia had never seen him like this, did not recognize him, know him.

"I could kill you, you foulmouthed bitch! By Christ, I *will* kill you—"

"I don't know what you are talking about," exploded from Julia like a bullet.

"Are you denying you spoke to my mother on the telephone earlier?"

"No, of course I'm not, but it was a bad line; she couldn't hear me properly—"

"Oh, she heard you all right! Every lousy, stinking word. What was the matter? Had she interrupted your lovers' idyll? What was he doing to you—your fancy Swiss paramour?"

"I was in bed alone!"

"Like hell you were!"

"I was—and she did mishear me! Nothing she said to me made sense; it must have been a bad line."

"Jesus Christ, what excuses you do dream up!"

"I'm telling you the truth!"

"You wouldn't recognize that if it came up and spat in your face!"

"I have never told you anything else."

"Liar! All I have ever had from you is lies; you yourself are one big lie! Everything about you is fake. In bed alone! You were with your lover, as I knew you wanted to be."

"I went to Versailles to get the chairs. Ask the marquise if you like; she'll tell you."

"How? She isn't there. She's in Monte Carlo."

Julia stared. "But—I saw her—talked to her—"

"Liar! Her house is shut up for the winter! There were no chairs; they were your cover story."

"But your mother called me and gave me explicit instructions as to when I was to go and see them—"

"She called you to see how the reception had gone. It is no use denying it. There was a witness—"

"No; not then, I mean before—earlier—"

"Mother called you once and once only. Bitsy told me that. She was there, you see. All the time Mother spoke to you. She heard every word Mother said and the word chairs was not one of them!"

Julia stared at him and for a moment all she could hear was a ringing in her ears; she could see his mouth moving, see his handsome features contorted with rage, note also with a clinically detached eye that there was terror written all over him, and then as if with an audible click, everything seemed to fall into sync and she knew she had been set up. The out-of-sync telephone conversation had not been a bad line: it had been deliberate, for the benefit of Lady Hester's witness. Every word she had said had been taken, twisted out of context and used against her to produce a self-inflicted bout of asthma. It was emotionally triggered, wasn't it? Sickened, she stared at the picture in her mind's eye. She would go *that* far? Make herself ill? She felt chilled as death.

That indicated a hatred that was terrifying.

"What's the matter? Why are you looking like that?" Brad's voice penetrated her cone of silence like glass breaking.

"She set me up . . . ," Julia whispered. "She must have worked on it for months—the hotel, the time limit, Pierre Chambrun—everything." Appalled, she stared into the horror picture. "How well she had come to know me; she must have been studying me like a manual all this time . . . She knew I'd give my all to my job . . . And she was the one put Pierre into your head, wasn't she?"

"People were only too keen to let her know what was going on over here!"

"People?" Julia shook her head. "Oh, you fool," she said despairingly. "You blind, bemused fool—"

His open palm met her cheek, rocking her head back.

"Yes, where you are concerned I am a fool! You've lied to me and cheated on me, but no more! My mother warned me about you. She said you were not what you seemed and, boy, was she ever right! And as for you being set up, that's even further proof of your sick, twisted mind and hatred for her!"

"*My* hatred for *her!*" Julia flung back her head and laughed. It made him hit her again.

Julia felt the pain as her teeth drove through her lip. Lying on her back she met his blazing eyes defiantly. "Yes, her hatred for me! Sally Armbruster warned me she brooked no rivals—even your own brother-in-law, Drexel Adams, warned that she was out to get me."

"Liar! Rotten, scheming, cheating liar!" Once again he hit her; she saw stars, heard a ringing in her ears. Blood dripped onto the silk sheets.

"My mother had you dead to rights from the start. She said you were a false image; that you were too ambitious to be a wife; you wanted the Bradford money, didn't you, you wanted entree into the world that would produce commissions. You couldn't sink your teeth into the hotel fast enough, could you? Mother told me you'd go for it. I didn't believe her, but she was right—as usual. Where you are concerned she has been right all along. And as for Drexel Adams, Bitsy told me you'd been trying it on with him—"

That brought Julia upright in the bed, dazed with pain, teeth aching, cheek on fire, but her voice pealing like bells. "And what the hell were you doing last night with that brunette? I saw you with her as you left the Embassy. I went there with the idea of making it up to you but all you had on your mind was making it with her! Don't you accuse *me* of cheating, you unfaithful bastard! I went to Versailles and hared back to put things right between us and when I saw where you intended to put yourself I came back to the hotel and to bed alone—alone, do you hear! I was the one who was fooled—then and before—from the day I met your bloody awful bitch of a mother, in fact! I'm the one who has been fooled, led like a lamb to the slaughter! She must have been

[179]

splitting her sides at the fool I have been where she is concerned—you too, come to that!"

"Liar!" Once again his open palm cracked across her face, rocking her back against the bedhead. "Whore!" Another slap. "Cheat!" The performance was repeated. "Don't you dare lay such names on *my* mother! And don't let me lay eyes on you ever again! As of now we are through. Get the hell out of my life and stay there, but I warn you: if my mother dies I'll come looking for you and kill you, do you hear! I'll kill you!"

But Julia was past hearing—or feeling—anything. She was unconscious.

WHEN JULIA DID NOT APPEAR for work as usual, next morning, Pierre Chambrun went up to see why. He took one look at the bloody, swollen, closed-eyes face, the stained sheets, and reached for the telephone. He knew a doctor who earned a fortune by dealing only with those cases where discretion was worth its weight in the gold he was sometimes paid, and having been in the hotel business for so long Pierre knew that there was nothing that could not be covered up if you had enough money to bury it deep enough.

The doctor tended to Julia's cuts and bruises, stitched her mouth where it was cut, inside and out, gave her a sedative and said he would call that evening. There was no sign of Brad; his bags were gone, all his clothes. Nothing but discarded hangers and an empty bottle of aftershave. Pierre read the signs. Before Julia slid into a drugged sleep he managed to get Chris's telephone number from her and when he went to his office he briefly told the foreman that Madame Bradford was indisposed—a virus—and would not be able to work for at least the next three days; he himself would be in charge until her return to work. That done, he closed and locked his door and called London.

Chris arrived that evening, and meeting her at Charles de Gaulle, Pierre gave her a succinct précis of the situation.

"Fortunately the workmen are gone home for the day so they will not see you. This must not get out, you understand. If Milady Bradford should be the subject of gossip then I am the subject of unemployment."

"I know the script," Chris told him grimly, but she was still appalled when she saw the battered face of her friend. She said nothing, only whisked away all mirrors and set to, along with Pierre Chambrun, to get Julia back to some semblance of normality so as to be able to return home.

After three days her face, though reduced in size, was still multicolored, so the doctor bandaged her. "I will say it is an infectious virus which produces pustules—something like smallpox," he told Pierre dryly. "There will be no one within hailing distance when she is carried to the ambulance."

And that was how it was done. Julia was taken from the hotel wrapped like a mummy, and once in the ambulance, she was unwrapped again, a huge pair of sunglasses placed over her blackened eyes, and a large hat pulled well down over her face. Pierre had a discreet word with Air France and Julia was allowed to board the plane well in advance of the other passengers. Had it not been for Julia's injuries and blank state of mind, Chris would have enjoyed everything hugely. It was just like the movies!

Chris took Julia to her own flat, where, once in bed, she retreated within herself as well as under the bedclothes, writhing in abject humiliation yet unable to stop going over the previous five months with a fine-tooth comb, sifting for errors and/or omissions, seeing how naïve and overconfident she had been, even in the midst of her doubts, how spellbound by Brad. A sex junky! You could not get enough of him physically even though you had such persistent doubts about him, she told herself scathingly. You were warned and still you didn't take any notice! Serve you bloody well right!

But still she could not stop herself from weeping for hours on end when she was not lying blankly staring at nothing.

Lady Hester had had her investigated, of course, and by professionals. All those casual questions, all the trails she had laid. All of which Julia, ever mindful of Brad's requirements, had obediently followed, eager to fit in even while she had been fitted up. The hotel had been a setup, Brad's tenure at the Paris office all part of Lady Hester's own grand design.

Brad. She saw him so clearly now, with hindsight. Sally Armbruster had been so right. He did mark you. Once her physical scars had healed she would still be scarred inside, where they never faded, sometimes never healed. He did leave you with nothing but despairing hate. No wonder he ran. Deep down he *knew*, he knew what his mother was doing to him, but he was either unable or unwilling to cut himself free. He was not his own man any way but sexually. Hence the compulsive womanizing. Hence the hasty, secret marriage. But why me? Julia agonized. Had it been rescue, as Drexel Adams had said? Had he seen in Julia a woman strong enough to fight his mother for him? Then why didn't he say so? Julia asked herself tormentedly. Why didn't he tell me exactly what was wrong, *why* it had to be me? I thought he wanted me to give way to her, to fit in with her design. Why didn't he say he wanted me to stand up to her, take her on, if that was what he wanted? Yet it can't have been what he wanted else he would not have got so uptight when I asked for our own house. Oh, God, I just don't understand, she thought despairingly. Him, her, any of it. Truth between us, he had said, lying in his teeth. The only truth he knows is hers and that is made up of lies. Every word she says, no matter how twisted, is gospel to him. Not for one second did he believe me. He never did believe me, from the start. Then why, dear God *why*, did he marry me? What was it he wanted from me? And why wasn't he able to tell me what he wanted in the first place? What is it she has got on him, because there is something, I know it. I *feel* it. Something so horrible he couldn't even bring himself to tell me, his wife, not even on the island, when we were so close, closer than we had ever been, before or since . . . That was when he could have told me, that was when I hoped he would. That is when I should have known.

Over and over and over she went through every moment of the past five months, looking for clues, finding none able to show her the true picture, no matter how horrible, putting together only the one that showed a man wholly dominated by his mother to the extent that their relationship was symbiotic. She had some insight into his very soul, because from other people, Julia had learned that Brad was first-class at his job, that he could be a very tough customer, that he ran things with no mistake, that he was, in some quarters, even feared and always respected. Yet this tyrant was the same man who was putty in his mother's hands. Julia had been astonished when, at one of her Boston dinners, she had sat next to a man who had talked of Brad with both awe and admiration. "Nobody's fool," the man had said, "and when it comes down to cutting a deal always manages to come up with the high card. His mother now, she had some fearsome reputation, but her son has taken it over and seems in a fair way to beat it." Julia had stared across the table at her husband positively in a state of shock. Brad? Ruthless? Hardheaded? Tough? This same golden boy who was a sexual stud of epic proportions, a highly strung, emotionally arrogant schoolboy with a capacity for endless sulks, who scurried at his mother's skirts like a lapdog? She had known he was complex, but now, she felt like Theseus—and she had no string with her.

"I told you there was a screw loose," Chris said sadly a few days later.

"Yes—mine! I cringe when I think of the fool I've been. How she must have been laughing at me! Watching me blithely set up my own destruction."

"I'd say he did a good job there," Chris said bitterly, eyeing Julia's still wrecked face, the livid bruising, the swollen mouth, the blackened eyes.

"He was programmed to do it. He was in such a state of terror he did not know what he was doing. How could he think straight after the way his mother had twisted everything?"

"Twisted! She's got it plaited!" Chris sighed gustily. "Well, now we know."

"Do we? We know she controls him, every which way, but *why*, Chris?"

"Because she's jealous, of course!"

"It is more than that, I am sure . . . something else . . . some . . ." Julia raised her hands helplessly. "It's murky," was all she finally said. "Whatever it is, it's that something nasty in the woodshed." Bitterly: "And it is my own fault for not insisting Brad show me what was inside."

"You can't take all the blame," Chris protested. "He left you in the dark, didn't he? Is it any wonder you fell over things?"

"I also had blinkers on. I thought I could handle it all with my clear, cool rationality. Me, I-am-the-great Julia Carey with her common sense and her capability and logicality. I overlooked the fact that when emotions come in the door they fly out the window!" Julia brooded silently. "Well, I've learned that the hard way." Abruptly: "As Hardy always said to Laurel—that's another fine mess you've got us into." She got up restlessly, went to the window to stare out. "I can't cope with emotions, Chris. They scare me. I drop them, fumble them. I should have paid more attention to my doubts. All we ever had in common was sex. He knocked me sideways physically; that in itself should have been warning enough!"

"Well, I have my own blame to bear," Chris said nobly. "I told you to go with your feelings, didn't I?"

"It wasn't love," Julia went on. "It was physical enslavement." Savagely: "Well, I'm free now, and I'll never—never, do you hear?—be put in chains again by any man!"

Why didn't I do a lot of things? she thought. Because I was not capable of thinking straight; not around him. Where he was concerned I became something I did not either know or understand; did things I would never have done normally.

"What happened with the hotel, anyway?" Chris was asking curiously.

"Well, Pierre more or less broke the door down—"

"Oh, I know about that. After all, it was he who called me. No, I mean about the commission."

"A visit from her Paris lawyer, instructing me to quit forthwith; that another designer had been appointed; that I was to take myself off. I had no contract anyway, no signed anything. It was a 'family' arrangement. All part of her plot. Like poor Pierre. She used him too. Anything and everything is grist to that woman's mill."

"He was fired too? For what?"

"Engaging in an unethical relationship with me."

"When? Where was the proof?"

"It turned out a private detective had been keeping watch. According to him, those times when we had gone to various suppliers or speciality shops had in reality been visits to a small hotel on the Left Bank."

"What?" Chris's voice screeched.

"Oh, yes. Signed affidavits from the hotelier."

"For how much of a bribe, I wonder."

"As she once said to me, money, is the least of my worries."

"Blimey!" breathed Chris. "She thought of every last thing."

"Mind you—she had to settle with Pierre. He did have a contract and he threatened to sue. That would have meant trouble she doesn't want. It was easier for her to pay him off."

"He seemed like a nice man," Chris said.

"He was. Very distressed about it all. The only good thing is that he took her for every cent he could, so I haven't got that on my conscience. And he's gone home to Switzerland. His family run a hotel in Lausanne."

"And you? What are you going to do?"

"Once I'm presentable I shall look for another job."

But before she could get around to that an air freight company delivered a large crate. In it was everything she had left in America.

"See," she said to Chris with an acid smile, "I've been expunged."

It was only when she finally did start looking for a job that she found she had also been blacklisted. Every job approach met with failure, no matter where she tried, how small the companies got. It was only through a "friend" who had always considered Julia a rival that she discovered Lady Hester had let it be known that Julia had fallen down badly on her first solo commission: run up unacceptable costs, failed to meet deadlines—and had an affair with the hotel's manager-designate.

"God almighty, that bitch!" Chris exploded. "She's done for your career, Julia! How are you supposed to live?"

"She would rather I died."

"But how are you to support yourself?"

"I thoughtfully brought my jewelry with me. The pearls, the black cat, my engagement ring. They must be worth quite a lot. I shall sell them."

"Let me have a word with Tony first. He's C.I.D.; used to work the Hatton Garden division. He'll be able to help."

And through him Julia got a fair-sized check, enough to live on for quite some time if she was careful and still could not get a job—not as a designer, anyway. She was coming home after yet another unsuccessful interview when suddenly, the crowded tube carriage blurred, her ears rang and her knees buckled. She came to with her head on her knees and a concerned-looking man kneeling beside her.

"You went out like a light," he said. "Keep your head down . . . that's right . . ."

"It's these overcrowded carriages," a nearby woman said indignantly. "They don't pack sardines as tightly!"

"Take your time. I'm getting off at the next stop," the man said kindly.

When Julia got off at South-Ken her legs still felt rubbery but she managed to make it back to Chris's flat. She put it down to not eating— or sleeping either. But the same thing happened two days later—this time indoors.

"It's the doctor for you," Chris said decidedly. "Remember what happened before?"

"It's just reaction," Julia said. "I haven't been eating enough, I suppose. I never do when I'm worried."

"We'll let the doctor decide that."

He said it was probably strain, gave her sleeping tablets, which Julia later flushed down the toilet. As she let him out a letter was lying on the mat. It was from Lady Hester Bradford's lawyers—the family lawyers. She was being sued for divorce on the grounds of her adultery with one Pierre Étienne Chambrun.

She took the papers to her own solicitor, who told her she was being divorced under American law—"seeing as you were, technically, married on American soil at their embassy. Do you wish to contest?"

"No. I want my freedom, too. Do whatever they want, I'll sign where I'm supposed to. Just do it as quickly and painlessly as possible."

It took six short weeks, during which time she discovered she was pregnant. When Chris found her throwing up for the fourth morning in succession she said: "I should have twigged from the start. Didn't you notice your periods were missing?"

"I had other things on my mind. Besides, I was on the pill. No, I am sure I didn't forget."

"You must have. A lot was happening, love."

"I took it every night before bed: it was habit . . ."

"But your hours were all to hell. I know there are occasional failures but I'll bet you happened to forget one night. That's all it takes, you know."

"Once, twice. It makes no difference now."

"To what?"

"I am having this baby. It will be the only one I shall ever have."

"Oh, now, Julia . . ."

"Once is coincidence, twice is happenstance; three times is a no-no. Never again, Chris; I mean that. *Never* again."

"You'll have to tell him."

"Why? I am divorced, practically. By the time I have this baby I shall long have been single again. He dumped me and my baby. This child will be mine, and only mine."

That night, in bed, she made her plans. She would go up to Yorkshire. She still had the cottage, normally leased for summers; she would keep it for herself now. With what she got for the jewelry . . . She reached for pad and pencil. Yes, she was very good with money; she could manage easily until the baby was born, even for a while afterward. She could do it and to spare, even taking into account all she would need for a new baby. When it was a few months old she would think about a job. It did not have to be in interior design. She was skilled with a sewing machine; she could always set up as a dressmaker.

She felt thrilled with resolve; eager to set plans in motion. She felt she was no longer wandering in limbo. And she always did best when she had a goal to work toward.

SHE LEFT LONDON a week later, and the first thing she did was ask Dr. Mead if she would look after her during her pregnancy. She examined Julia in her calm, methodical way, pronounced her fit, if underweight— "but that won't last long and I do not like my mothers to become too

ungainly. It will be a spring baby; sometime in May, I should think."
She smiled down at Julia. "How do you feel about being a mother?"

"Excited . . . contented, somehow. I had always intended to have
children but—well, after this second debacle had not expected to have
any."

"One cannot always foresee how things will turn out," the doctor
said in her placid way, "which does not prevent one from trying, of
course."

"This will be my only child," Julia said.

"One should not let one's failures block one's path either."

"I've had two on the trot." Julia began to get dressed. "I am not
emotionally oriented; I do better with the material—the factual. I shall
stick to it in future." She paused. "I will have it all right, won't I? I
mean—that abortion—"

"Was skillfully done. You should have no trouble. But I think a time
of rest is prescribed. Time to prepare yourself for your baby. You will
be able to manage financially?"

"Yes, if I am careful."

"As I am sure you will be."

She booked Julia into the cottage hospital and for attendance at the
prenatal clinic. She also recommended relaxation classes. "Childbirth
is a natural thing and I believe in assisting Mother Nature, not counter-
manding her. You do not smoke and that is a good thing. You may
drink in moderation and take gentle exercise: you like to walk; do so,
but not until you exhaust yourself. Nothing strenuous. Do not eat for
two, and come May we shall see a happy, healthy mother and baby."
Her wise eyes considered Julia thoughtfully. "What about the baby's
father?"

"I have not told him and I'm not going to. This baby belongs to me
and me alone. That I discovered I was pregnant as I was being divorced
I take as some sort of a sign. I want nothing to do with my husband or
his mother—especially her. She would take the child from me."

"Surely not!"

"If it suited her, she would. It does not suit me. This is my child, Dr.
Mead—mine!"

CHRIS CAME UP to spend a weekend and marveled. "You are blooming
like one of your plants!"

"I feel it. They say pregnancy makes you bovine and I do feel contented. Come and see what I've been making."

Chris eyed Julia under pretense of admiring the cobwebby shawl, the

[187]

beautifully made layette. She did look in full bloom: she had gained weight, her skin was glowingly radiant, her eyes clear and calm.

"You do seem to be managing," she said relievedly.

"Perfectly. I have a budget and I stick to it."

"I wish you would teach me; I can't stick to one even with glue!" Tongue in cheek: "I'll teach you how to handle men!"

"Thank you, but no, thank you. I do better on my own."

"But won't you be lonely?"

"Of course not! I'll have my baby."

In early February she received her final divorce papers. She was no longer Mrs. J. Winthrop Bradford. As she put them away in the steel box where she kept her personal papers, she felt only a glad, clean relief. The last threads had been cut. She really was free at last.

AS THE YEAR PROGRESSED, so did her pregnancy, tranquil and trouble-free. She went up to rest every afternoon, taking a book or a magazine, invariably falling asleep eventually. She found she slept a lot. One afternoon at the end of March, she was awoken by a loud knock on the front door. Now what? she thought. She was not expecting visitors. Chris was not due for another couple of weeks and Dr. Mead visited on Fridays. Going to the window she peered out. A large American car stood at the gate. She recoiled so quickly she banged her hip on the dressing table. Fear tightened every muscle. She could not see who it was because they were under the front porch. She would just have to go down and find out.

He was very large, wrapped in a suede car coat against the keen wind. His Latin-dark face broke into a smile as he said: "You Julia Carey?" Not a New England accent.

"I am."

"Thank God! I've been to every rose cottage in every village for miles around."

"What do you want with me?"

"If you'll invite me in—and give me a much needed cup of coffee seeing as your motorway cafés dispense sump oil—I'll be glad to tell you."

Julia did not move. "Who are you?"

He handed her a card. Marcus Levin, Levin Enterprises, with an address on Wardour Street. "I have a proposition to put to you," he went on blithely. "Strictly business," he added on a grin. "Couldn't be anything else in your condition." But he sounded surprised.

"What kind of business?"

[188]

Promptly: "Interior design."

"I am not working right now."

"It's not right now I am interested in."

He was blandly, cheekily confident, but these days Julia regarded anything from the other side of the Atlantic with deep suspicion. Smiling into her cold, closed face: "Look, I realize you don't know me, but if you'll let me inside I'll do my best to remedy that."

"Who sent you here?"

"Nobody. But you could say your work brought me."

"Which work would that be?"

"Oh, several remarkable interiors you did. I want you should work for me—well, with me, more like."

"You are looking for a designer?"

"Nope. For you."

"How did you hear of me?"

"I didn't. I saw and asked. Then I started looking. You are a hard lady to find but I don't give up easily."

"The world is full of great designers and I was never more than small fry. Why make such a thing about it?"

"I have a motto. Nothing but the best."

Still Julia regarded him unsmilingly.

"Look, lady. I realize you don't know me, but if it's references you want I can supply them by the yard. Check me out all you want. I'll stand up to anybody's inspection."

"Don't think I won't," Julia promised.

"So can I come in out of the cold?"

Reluctantly, Julia stepped back, allowed him in. Stooping as he entered he exclaimed: "Say, this has to be old."

"Seventeenth century."

"I'll say. People were much shorter then. Maybe I'd better sit down. Mind if I take off my coat?"

Under it he had a T-shirt and jeans. The T-shirt was emblazoned: "Don't knock sex; just don't get knocked up." Julia bit her lip.

"Say, this is nice." He surveyed with approval the low, beamed ceiling, the white walls, the brick fireplace, the leaded windows curtained in bright cretonne. His gaze came back to Julia and once again he flashed his smile. "Black, two sugars," he hinted.

In the kitchen, where the Aga gave off a comfortable warmth, Julia went over what he had said, which she intended to check. But if it was a genuine commission . . . Be careful, she counseled herself. Say nothing, discover all. But that hairdo, that T-shirt. No way was he her usual run of client. Still, the weirdest of people had money these days. What could he possibly want her to design? A disco, maybe? A chain of sex shops? Whatever, she thought, as she spooned coffee into the percolator. A commission means money and if it is genuine—and if he is genuine—then it is not to be turned away. You need every penny you can get your hands on, God knows. But don't do anything or tell him a thing until you are sure he is bona fide. And go over every inch of those yards of references. You've got plenty of time to check him out down to the name of his hairdresser, which, for your own protection and that of what you are carrying around, is a must. Don't be played for a sucker a second time. That woman is capable of anything, as you well know, and if he comes up clean—well, then that's a horse of a different color.

When she went back in he was stretched out in the big chair, long legs crossed.

"Mind if I smoke?" he asked.

"No. But I don't, thank you."

"Sensible lady. In your condition, and all."

"You said you had seen my work," Julia prompted.

"Made it my business to after I'd seen the Hotel Bradford."

Julia said, very carefully: "The what?"

"The hotel you did in Paris; it's the talk of the town. Going to be a grand opening come fall. There was a spread in *House Beautiful* or some such magazine."

"And did it say they were *my* designs?"

"No. It said Lady Hester Bradford had done it."

Julia's astonishment made her burst out laughing. "Talk about gall!"

"So I found out after I'd asked around. I mean, I know the lady is supposed to be capable of anything—and I mean anything—but I could see a professional had been at work."

"You know her?" Julia asked narrowly.

"Of her—as who doesn't? Anyway—I made it my business to ask around." Bluntly: "Look, I know all about your hassle. There were plenty to tell me all about it; but I'm not interested in the past. It is your future talent I'm after."

"Hang on," Julia said slowly. "Are you telling me that the Hotel Bradford is being done over according to *my* designs?"

"Absolutely."

At Julia's angry flush: "Something I should know?" he asked delicately.

"I was fired from that job. The hassle you spoke about. Later on I heard another designer had been appointed."

"Many were called but none were chosen. It was that dining room which made me sit up and take notice. Scuttlebutt says the food will match up. Look," he said again, with heavy finality. "I don't give a damn about why you got bounced. It is your talent I'm after. I want you to design for me."

"What?"

"Whatever I can come up with."

At her puzzlement: "I want you should join my stable." He laughed at her expression. "No, I don't run girls. The T-shirt is a joke." Julia found herself flushing slightly under all-too-knowing olive-black eyes. "I run talent. I have a pop star, a racing driver, a dancer, a couple of actors—even a tennis player. I spot their talent, invest in it, get them started, then, once they make the big-time, take twenty percent off the top of everything they earn." He sighed. "Mind you, I hadn't known you were pregnant. Still, that only lasts nine months." A shrewd glance. "I'd say not more than another couple with you. And it will give me time to get things set up."

"You are assuming an awful lot."

Modestly: "I haven't explained the whole as yet."

"Then by all means do so."

Julia listened critically; it all sounded too good to be true. She said so.

"I kid you not," he said in that same blithely confident tone. "I like money; I intend to make a lot; likewise you."

"But—I got—bounced—as you said, from my last commission."

"That's down the drain. It's what I can get out of the tap that interests me."

Julia thought. "So you would provide contacts, find me suitable commissions—and premises from which to work from, then, once I got going, take 20 percent."

"Right."

"What kind of commissions?"

"The best. No penny-ante jobs. I'm thinking about other hotels, prestige office blocks, restaurants—that sort of thing."

Julia thought again. "I should want a proper, legally drawn contract; I did Paris on a handshake and look what that got me."

He looked horrified. "Are you telling me you didn't get paid?"

"It was a—and I quote—'family affair.' "

With the bluntness she was to come to expect of him: "I know you were married to a Bradford," he said.

"Are you sure you don't know them?" Julia asked suspiciously.

[191]

"Of them—mostly the old lady. Was it her hand you shook?"

Julia nodded. He sighed. "That figures. She's known as a barracuda."

At last, thought Julia. The perfect description.

"So she is using your designs for free!" Marcus Levin whistled. "And after she'd fired you without compensation. You've got grounds for a suit."

"She'd soon cut them from under me."

"Not if you hire a good lawyer."

"I can't afford one."

Marcus leaned back and regarded her contemplatively. "Tell you what: as a small proof of my good faith, I happen to have a friend who is a *very* high priced legal eagle. If I could get him to tell you how you would stand regarding a possible suit, would you be more—amenable?"

Julia levered herself up. "I can hear the coffee," she said, avoiding a direct answer. She had to think about that one. A successful suit would mean more money, and she could use that. But could she trust this ageing hippie? The thought was tempting. To be one up on Lady Hester Bradford. She *was* using designs that did not belong to her. It had been purely family; nowhere was there so much as anything resembling a contract. Also quite deliberate, of course, Julia pondered. The last thing she would expect would be to be sued. She would not think for one moment that I would actually dare to take on the great, the famous Hester Bradford. Which was when she decided she would. There was money at stake. And while this Levin was doing what he could for her she would have Chris get Tony to run a check on him. If the C.I.D. didn't find anything on him then he had to be clean.

When she went back: "Tell you what," she suggested. "Put the case to your lawyer friend; see what he advises. If he really knows his business—"

"He does!"

"—then I'll go along. I have uses for anything I could get."

"Okay, give me the facts."

She did so, leaving out the personalities.

"Hmmmm," he frowned. "Seems to me you got the heave-ho for entirely different reasons; nothing was said about your work being at fault."

"I can show you the letter I received through her Paris lawyer," Julia offered.

He read it, asked: "Can I take it to show?"

"As long as I get it back."

"Sure thing."

He tucked it in his shirt pocket. Picking up his mug: "Hey, this *is* coffee," he approved.

"Tell me more about your plans," Julia prompted.

"Well, the way I see it . . ." He expounded—thrillingly.

Julia felt excitement lay hands on her and squeeze, but "Sounds all right" was all her now even more cautious self would say.

"Why don't you think about it until I get back to you on this other thing?"

"All right, I'll do that. How long?"

"Couple—maybe three—days?"

"Fine."

"Give me your phone number," he said, bringing out his cigarette pack and a pen. As he wrote it down: "Perhaps I should have yours," Julia said. "And some names I could contact—those yards of references you spoke about."

"Don't have one—always on the move," he said disarmingly. "Don't worry, you'll hear from me." He grinned. "And about me. The whole scam." He tucked the pack away, leaned back and asked comfortably: "So when's the baby due?"

"Middle of May."

"So . . . if we say what—six, maybe eight weeks after that you'll be ready for work?"

"If I have a base to work from."

"Any particular location?"

"A 'good' address is essential."

"Such as?"

"W.1, S.W.1, S.W.3, S.W.7—those districts."

"Okay. I'll have a look-see what's available."

He was wholly amiable, effortlessly agreeable, yet Julia knew he would get exactly what was wanted. The Hollywood persona covered a Pittsburgh drive.

He drank a second cup of coffee while they discussed pros and cons, and he must have felt the thaw because he said as he rose to leave: "You've decided I can be trusted, then?"

"Let's see what your lawyer friend comes up with; then we'll see."

"He will—if there's anything to come up with, that is."

"There is," Julia countered, and he grinned, stuck out a hand. "It's been a pleasure," he said. "I'll be in touch."

Julia watched him saunter down the path to the big, flashy car. One thing was for certain. He was as different from Brad as Boston was from Las Vegas. Thank God.

HE CALLED HER four days later. His lawyer friend was of the opinion that she had a very good case. Whatever the other reasons for her dismissal, disapproval of her designs was not one of them—an opinion confirmed by the fact that they were still being used.

"You want I should instruct him to pry the old lady loose from your fee—and whatever else the traffic will bear?"

"Only if it can be with the minimum—repeat—M-I-N-I-M-U-M," she spelled, "trouble."

"Why else do you think my lawyer friend charges such high fees? If you retain him it's precisely because you don't want that very thing."

She heard nothing for two weeks, then, to her astonishment, he turned up at her cottage one afternoon waving a check. Julia read the zeroes and fell into a chair.

"Mr. Levin! How on earth—"

"Marcus—and I gather the old lady was mad as hell, but she paid up."

"But how?"

"A letter. My friend writes the last word in letters. He can make the most innocent suggestion sound like the most hideous threat."

"He didn't threaten her!" Julia's heart raced.

"Come now. We both know better than that. He merely—threatened to threaten. And such is his reputation . . ." His grin was knowing. "Which reminds me: how did mine check out?"

"Everything you told me turned out to be true," Julia replied coolly.

"I knew it would. Me and my lawyer friend both have reputations to lose if this goes wrong. You don't tangle with old lady Bradford unless you are sure of your facts, and believe me, he could get a jury to acquit Judas."

Julia stared at her check. "Does this include his fee?"

"He did this one as a favor to me; he owes me one."

Julia let out a slow breath. She was rich!

"I also have something else for you. Take a gander at these and let me know what you think."

He handed her a sheaf of realtors' particulars.

WHEN CHRIS CAME UP the following weekend she was agog with curiosity. "Who and what and how is this Marcus Levin?" she wanted to know.

[194]

"Looks like a Mexican bandit, talks like a hippie but you saw Tony's report. He is genuine." Julia shook her head. "And does he get things done."

"Ah, but is he worth doing?"

Julia burst out laughing. "Chris, you are hopeless."

"No, just running out of it where Tony is concerned. This Levin is loaded, then?"

"He doesn't lack the necessary wherewithal, that's for sure."

"Right, when do I meet him?"

They took to each other at once, so much so that Julia was convinced that should she offer them the double bed they would hop into it with alacrity. Chris remedied this on their return to London.

"My dear," she purred down the phone. "I can't begin to tell you—"

"Then don't."

CHRIS TOOK to giving premises the once-over and reporting to Julia, entering into things with zest and, as she told Julia—"an eye on the opportunities."

In the middle of April they found the perfect place.

"Brook Street—Bond Street end; needs doing up but just right for your purposes." Marcus drove Julia down to give final approval. The shop was small, but it had a workroom above and above that a small flat. "Endless possibilities," Julia approved. The lease was signed and, back home, Julia started in on plans for the remodeling, which she gave to Marcus when he came up, Chris with him.

"I rely on you two to keep an eye on things—if you can take your eyes off each other!" Julia teased.

As May came, she was carrying all before her. "Are you sure it is not twins?" Marcus quizzed.

"It feels like an army—and kicks like a mule."

"You don't look bruised; in fact, you look very tasty."

No you don't, Julia thought. Stick to Chris. She is more in your line; she is used to it. Marcus was a flirt. And, according to Chris, a flitter. "No permanent boarders," she sighed to Julia over the phone.

"Then enjoy while you can," Julia advised crisply, wondering how Chris could in the first place. But then, Chris had never had any difficulty in leaving her emotions outside the bedroom door.

"I am!" Chris was saying. "I haven't had such fun in an age . . ."

Fun? thought Julia, and shuddered.

"He's a tiger," Chris went on, purring herself. "I'll show you my scratches sometime."

"How is the shop coming along?" Julia interrupted.

"Right on schedule. All the alterations are in hand and should be done by the end of next week. Then the decorating can start."

Marcus said the same thing when he came up that weekend. "Everything proceeding apace," he said contentedly. "And you—how are you proceeding?"

She had not seen him for a couple of weeks; he had had to leave the country for a while. "One of my stable having teething troubles," he had explained on a shrug.

"I am getting to the stage where I wish I could board one and ride into the sunset."

"You have a wicked, witty tongue," he said on a grin. "But I like you."

She knew he did; wondered if it was her condition which conditioned his response to her. She felt like a house end; had never subscribed to the (to her) fallacious belief that a pregnant woman was at her most beautiful; that was yet another con on the part of men, seeing as they were responsible for the condition in the first place. But she was aware, hugely swollen belly or not, that Marcus found her attractive. He flirted continually, and yet always gave her support—moral, physical, emotional. His hand was always there to fetch her up out of a chair; he would not let her do what he could do for her; he bore with her irritability, her seesaw swings of mood, the nearer her time came. And he always kept her right in the middle of things in London so that she felt, although far away, she was still a part of them. She was always glad to see him; always sorry to see him go.

He came up the weekend before she was due to go into the hospital, bringing a set of full-color photographs of the state of play at the shop, a large box of Turkish delight—for which Julia had developed a craving —and the good news that he was already on the trail—still quite cold as yet—of her first commission. And that was all he would say; he helped her upstairs for her afternoon rest and then went back downstairs to watch the horse racing on television.

As usual, Julia fell asleep. It was the pain which woke her; somebody had affixed a vise to her back and was proceeding to tighten it. She also realized the bed was soaked. Heaving herself up she reached for the stick by the bed and thumped on the floor. Marcus came up the stairs on the double.

"I think you had better call the hospital," Julia gasped, arching.

He also called the doctor, who was there before the ambulance, sent it away again when it arrived. "This baby is going to be born at home."

And it was astonishingly quick. Marcus held her hands, not complaining when she wrung them. He wiped the sweat from her face with a damp cloth smelling of eau de cologne, held the basin when she was sick, supported her with an arm around her shoulders when the doctor commanded her, "Push! That's right . . . hard . . . hard as you can . . . push . . . push . . . ," grunting and straining, making sounds like a pig as her body pushed her daughter from her, squalling indignantly.

Miraculously free of all pain in an instant, Julia levered herself up on her elbows.

"What is it?" she asked eagerly.

"You have a daughter—a redheaded one." The doctor lifted the squalling baby to show Julia, before swiftly and efficiently cutting the cord, clamping it and handing over the naked child; slippery, the amniotic fluid drying to a powdery finish, the baby protesting furiously until Julia cradled her in her arms. Then she peered up at her mother uncertainly—from her father's eyes.

"Oh!" Julia drew in a sharp breath. "She's beautiful," she said in a wobbly voice.

"Not quite your hair," Marcus considered. "More red-gold than red. But she's a beauty—like you."

"I think a nice cup of tea," the doctor said to him briskly.

"Coming right up." He got up from the bed, bent to kiss Julia's surprised mouth in a way that had her holding his eyes, reading the message there that things were different now—because she was different now, toward which he would act accordingly.

Weighed on the kitchen scales, Jennifer—but christened once and for all Jenny-Wren by Marcus, registered at exactly seven and a half pounds. When Marcus brought her back upstairs to Julia she said amusedly: "You carry her like an expert."

"I'll have you know I've been a godfather in my time; expect to be again, come to that."

Chris was godmother, along with Dr. Mead. Jenny slept through it all, slumberous even under the trickle of water.

"Is she all right?" Julia asked anxiously. "She seems to sleep all the time. I have yet to hear her cry the way she did when she was born."

"You have a placid child," Dr. Mead told her smilingly. "Be thankful."

"Thankful! I am blessed."

Once Jenny had been fed—Julia was feeding her herself, not only because Dr. Mead urged it but because she wanted to—Julia hung over the cot, bemused and disbelieving, in the grip of a love that welled from her, uncontrollably, like a spring gushing from broken rock. It was nothing like the undemanding fondness for Derek, the wild, compulsive, undeniable response to Brad; this was different: absolutely unshakable, part of her very self; so deep it was bottomless, so wide it encompassed all and every part of her life.

"I think you are in love," Marcus said, coming up to investigate her absence.

"No . . . not *in* love—just—love." Julia bent to tuck in a stray edge of blanket. "It's a funny thing, but—for the first time I begin to comprehend just how Brad's mother felt about him. I didn't know—how could I?—before. I never had a mother, was never close to another human being in all my life until him; but having Jenny has left me open to so many new thoughts and feelings. Jenny is so wonderful. So—bonded to me. I see now how easy it is to become ferociously possessive of that bond; be willing to do anything to keep it from breaking. I remember Abby once telling me that the hardest part of having children was knowing how—and being able—to let go." A sigh. "That's what Brad's mother could never do. She used to say he was her life. I never understood till now just how true that was." Somberly, gazing down at her daughter. "God forbid I should ever do to Jenny what was done to Brad."

"Are you going to tell him?"

"No."

"Why not?"

"I don't feel I need to. In some strange way Jenny has *really* freed me from him. I thought I would never do more than hate him; now I feel terribly sorry for him. Poor Brad. He has no one and nothing. He is tied to his mother but hates it; can't stand being her creature but has not the strength to stand alone. I am the lucky one. I have come out of this with Jenny. The slate is wiped clean at last."

"Is that how you prefer your life—clean, but empty?"

Julia turned to face him. "Marcus—"

"Don't say no at this point, Julia. Right now you are overflowing with emotions, all focused on Jenny, but you know where that can lead if all your other channels are blocked. You may be a mother now, but you are still a woman—with a woman's needs."

"That's just it," Julia said. "That's where I went wrong before; I took what my first husband said as an unshakable truth—whereas it was no more than his opinion. I tried to be like other people and accept that I needed what they needed when the truth is that I don't. My need is not to need. Do you understand me? I do better alone, Marcus. I function better, feel better—more myself, more—whole—than with someone else. I just don't like being involved. Don't like to feel—entangled, I suppose; caught up in another life and responsible for it. For their happiness. I believe it is because while I am willing to accept—and gladly—one hundred percent responsibility for myself—and for Jenny —I am not up to accepting it for other people, especially one other person. And I am not the kind of woman who can divorce her actions from her emotions. It is all or nothing, with me, and frankly, all things considered I find I prefer the nothing. That clean slate you mentioned."

She faced him honestly, openly. "I'll be your business partner, Marcus. I will work for you and do well for you; I'll be your friend and I will allow you access to my life as that friend—but that's all. If that is not enough for you—well, I will respect your decision."

But Marcus was not so easily put away. "Oh no you don't," he said with unruffled calm. "I won't let you. Like I said, right now you are so involved with Jenny you can't see around her; that is only to be expected. But there will come a time. And when it comes I intend to be here. A man must take his chances as and when he can. I wanted you from the first time I set eyes on you—pregnant or not. Getting to know you has only made me want you more, and I think you are saying no only because you won't allow yourself to want me. You got an emotional reaming from your pretty-boy ex and that takes time to get over. Okay, I'm a patient man. I've learned how to wait." He tilted her chin with a big finger. "You, on the other hand, still don't know anything about love—but I intend to be the man to teach you." He smiled into her eyes. "Now, come on downstairs. I've got something to tell you about your first commission . . ."

5

game. contest played according to rules
and decided by strength or good fortune

"BUT YOU HAVE ONLY been back a month!" Caroline Bradford
whined, rabid with resentment. "I hardly ever see you; no sooner do
you come home than you are off again. I'm sick and tired of being left
alone."

"It is only three days, for God's sake!" Brad said impatiently.

"I can't stand it when it is twenty-four hours. Sometimes I think you
do it deliberately to get away from me!"

"When all you do is nag and whine when I'm here, is it any wonder?"

Caroline bit her lip. She knew that tone of voice. It meant she was
treading on badly worn patience, which in turn covered a fragile temper; but her resentment had built up a full head of steam, based on the
fact that she could not stand it when his time and attention were not
given over wholly to her. She had been obsessed by and with him ever
since her brother Bradley had brought him home for the weekend. The
teenage Caroline had taken one look and been blinded.

At twenty, Brad Bradford had all the brilliance of a bronzed Apollo.

She had wanted him instantly and ravenously; her heart had thumped and her stomach churned and the place between her legs had burned. Never in her life had she seen such a beautiful man or wanted one in so sexual a manner.

But he did not see her except as Bradley Norton's kid sister. He was always polite, friendly, but unaware. And had driven her mad.

She had spied on him from then on, whenever he came to her father's Main Line estate. She would trail him and her brother when they invited girls back to swim or play tennis; tracking them with the dedication of a Daniel Boone to the most secluded parts of the grounds, hiding behind bushes to watch, dry-mouthed and shivering with sick excitement that spread fire through her loins, as Brad, inevitably and skillfully, seduced the girl. Caroline would clap her hands across her mouth to throttle her own moans at the sight of that beautiful, masculine body with its tight, firm buttocks and that thick, stiff member rearing from the clump of hair between his legs, which he would drive into the girl with convulsive thrusts, she moaning and gasping and heaving beneath him, her legs over his shoulders, her hips grinding furiously.

She had dreamed about being that girl; fantasized ceaselessly; had written him long, impassioned letters which she later burned.

She had a snapshot of him which she carried on her person at all times: he was standing on the board of the swimming pool, in brief swimming trunks, his hands on his hips, a little half smile on his lips proclaiming his awareness of what bulged under the thin silk.

When she went away to school, she began to plot and plan as to how to get him, and as her body began to fine down and her face to produce a sugar-candy prettiness, she ruthlessly made herself over into the kind of girl she had seen him with; a bone-slender fashion plate, immaculately turned out and coolly sexy. She dieted obsessively, spent hours on her face and hair and nails, and when at last she came out, poised and pretty, she was all ready to begin her campaign to become Mrs. J. Winthrop Bradford V.

She had studied him for years; knew his habits, his tastes, his opinions; had deliberately struck up friendships with the girls he had bedded—transients all, passing through his life like guests in a hotel—so as to gather even more information.

She knew he liked the hard-to-get ones, so that was how she played it at first. It made no difference. She was firmly fixed in his mind as the kid sister of his best friend; scrupulously he maintained a distance that drove her frantically into the role of aggressor—still to no effect. She raged and despaired over his power to dominate her every waking thought; tried to provoke him into jealousy by dating the men who did want her. All to no avail.

She used to cry herself to sleep at night, racked with unsatisfied desire; she masturbated constantly, only to be left frustrated and edgy. It was *him* she wanted; she wanted *him* to do to her what he had done to all those other girls. It became more and more difficult to restrain herself from begging him, pleading with him to put her out of her misery; knowing she could not; not if she wanted him forever. His discard rate was high and she intended to become a fixture.

When, out of the blue, his mother invited her to the farm for a weekend, she realized instantly that she was being looked over; understood at once that if she was to get Brad Bradford it would only be via his mother.

She had a native shrewdness that was, for the most part, unsuspected, as she was regarded as being not very bright; it was instinct that told her Lady Hester was the one to convince as to her suitability to be taken into the Bradford family. And when, by dint of careful eavesdropping, she discovered that her father's fortune was the foundation on which any negotiations would be built, she went to work on him. If buying Brad was the only way she would get him then thank God her father was a millionaire.

When Brad finally asked her out, she knew she had won. She also knew she was still only one of many women; that he was still conducting his transient trade. Well, let him, she thought. For now. Once we are married that will all change. Once I put into practice all I have learned . . . She had voraciously read every sex manual she could lay her hands on, becoming an expert in theory if not practice, because virginity was mandatory in a Bradford bride. Soiled goods were always sent back by return mail. Caroline was thankful she had preserved her own—and quite deliberately so as to allow Brad to be the man to take it. When, after some six months' decorous courtship, he at last asked her to marry him, it was with the air of one doing no more than his duty. Caroline ignored that, only sighed tremulously, fluttered her false eyelashes and said emotionally: "Oh, yes, Brad, yes . . . yes . . . !"

"You are quite sure? You understand what kind of a marriage this will be? I don't want you to be under any illusions, Caro. In our world people don't marry for love. Ours will be for material advantage and dynastic claims. I am not going to lie to you and tell you you are the love of my life because you are not. I've never been in love; don't expect to be. Love doesn't enter into this arrangement."

Caroline's smile did not waver though she raged inside. "I know what is expected of us," she answered demurely.

"Just so long as we don't get in each other's hair. I'm being absolutely honest when I say I'd rather not marry at all, but it is incumbent on me. I am the Bradford heir, so it is my duty to provide the next one. I'm sorry to be so cold-blooded but I want you to know from the start what sort of a marriage ours will be. I don't regard you as my property and I hope you won't regard me as yours. What I am saying is that we will do what is expected of us—but outside of that our lives are our own to lead."

You mean you will go on leading yours in the way you always have, thought Caroline. No way! I am not giving you a license to hunt in or out of season. But she smiled guilelessly and said adoringly: "I do understand, Brad. Honestly I do. I know what is expected of us and I am sure we can make a go of it—be happy together."

Brad's sigh was one of defeat. "Okay. We'll make a stab at it." He hesitated. "But if, while we are engaged, you come to feel it is not enough—well, then, I'll quite understand. You are awfully young—"

"I'm twenty-two. That's old enough." And I've wanted you since I was twelve, she thought. I've watched and waited and learned; by the time I'm through with you you won't even look at another woman.

The formal announcement was made, to be followed by two engagement parties: one in Boston, the other in Philadelphia. The wedding was set for six months hence, in October. In most of the months between Brad would be traveling. Caroline saw him off to Europe with complacence. One last fling, she thought, though he doesn't know it yet.

And when he came back he was all sunny smiles and declarations that he had missed her; seemed content to spend time with her, listening to her prattling on about the wedding arrangements; choosing the invitations, the decorations for the church, the bridesmaids and ushers. Until suddenly his mood changed; he became silent, withdrawn, short-tempered, disgruntled about something. And then he was off again. Caroline, who knew his every stance and expression, also knew it was a woman. Well, let him, she thought. I've got his ring on my finger and the church booked. Once that ceremony is over, then, by God, I'll have that ring through his nose. Only he was back within days; in a black mood and snappish enough to make her flee to her mother in tears. His own mother must also have said something because he came to her shortly afterward, all apologies, and for a few weeks was all she could have hoped for. Until he presented an entirely new mood. Silent, withdrawn, staring into space, tending to go off on his own—and not with a woman.

"You have to understand, Caroline," Lady Hester said soothingly, "a man shortly before his marriage is a man about to lose his freedom, and that has ever been most precious to Brad. Bear with him, try to understand."

And her own mother said trenchantly: "You are his fiancée, Caroline. He can't go too far. Remember that."

So when, one afternoon, her mother came home, white-faced and incoherent, after an urgent summons to Boston, Caroline could not at first take in what she said.

"Married! Brad married! Don't be stupid, Mother. He is engaged to marry me."

"He's jilted you, you fool!" her mother screamed. "Don't you understand? He's gone and married someone else on the sly—not so much as a word to anyone. Came back with her to Boston yesterday—taken her off to the farm on a honeymoon! He's dumped you, the bastard! Everything is ruined—ruined! Oh, the shame of it all! How those po-faced biddies of Rittenhouse Square will laugh down their long noses."

It was Mrs. Norton who had the hysterics, took to her bed, weeping and wailing and proclaiming she would never get over the shame of it all. Caroline, after her first, inner convulsion, went upstairs to call Lady Hester.

"Yes, it is true," she was told. "We must talk, Caroline. Can you come up to Boston tomorrow—in the afternoon? To my office in the Bradford Building. And tell no one. No one, you understand."

"I'll be there," Caroline said.

Lady Hester, seated behind her big desk, wasted no time. "What's done is done. Now it must be undone."

"How?" asked Caroline.

"Leave that to me." Lady Hester gave Caroline a long look. "I notice you do not ask why." A smile. "I thought you would not. You are still bent and determined to become my son's wife?"

Meeting the all too knowing eyes: "Yes," Caroline said.

"Good. I intend you to be." Briskly: "I repeat. Leave this to me. Do nothing. Return to Philadelphia and maintain a dignified silence. And keep your mother gagged. Return Brad's ring to him—no letter. Silence will make him feel worse. The rest I will deal with."

"How long?" Caroline asked, not bothering to beat about the bushes; not with Lady Hester's eyes staring at her through the leaves.

"Six months; anything less would be—dangerous."

The two women exchanged a long look. "Why?" Caroline asked baldly.

"This woman is not suitable. I will not have her as my son's wife. You are what I intend him to have; what he *will* have. In time, Caroline, you will replace this—aberration."

Caroline did not doubt it for one moment. She had always known she had been picked quite cold-bloodedly, but just so long as she had, the reasons were unimportant. She returned to Philadelphia and, in the face of the gossip, the scandal, the whispers, which had her mother privately prostrate and publicly proscribed, maintained a dignified silence.

But she followed Brad's activities. She knew—via Bitsy's malicious spite and love of gossip—where Brad went, the state of his marriage, how his wife spent her days. She bided her time and kept herself ready, marking off the days on her calendar, waiting for the call she knew would eventually come. Almost six months later it did. She had a call from Lady Hester.

"It is done. I have done my part, Caroline. Are you ready to play yours?"

"And waiting."

"Good. I'll be in touch."

It was Eloise Norton who told Caroline how it had happened, agog with greedy delight and satisfied spite. "You'll never believe!" she bubbled to her daughter. "Brad Bradford has left his wife! It's true; I don't know all the details but I gather it has to do with the old biddy's heart attack! Anyway, Brad gave her the boot! Which makes me happy on both counts; it's time somebody gave that snooty bitch a dressing down and that double-dealing son of hers got his comeuppance."

Caroline said nothing, just waited. Sure enough, she had another call from Lady Hester.

"I think it is time you came to see how I was," she said without preamble. "Tomorrow, four o'clock—and don't be late. It is important you look your best."

Caroline had her hair done, a facial, a manicure; wore one of the suits that had been destined for her trousseau, a Pauline Trigère heather tweed which flattered her hair and eyes. At exactly four o'clock, as she was admitted to the Mount Vernon Street house, Brad was about to leave it, just coming down the stairs.

He flushed when he saw her.

"Brad . . . oh, Brad, I'm so sorry." Caroline went up close, raised herself on tiptoe to brush his cheek with her lips, letting his nostrils get the full frontal assault of her Miss Dior, which he had always liked and associated with her.

"*Anything* I can do," she assured him plangently, letting her eyes suffuse with tender love, aware, as she drifted slowly up the stairs, that his own watched her. Lady Hester was sitting up in her four-poster, in a room awash with flowers and get-well cards. She looked pale (no rouge) but her voice was as crisply commanding as of old when she asked: "You saw him?"

"Yes."

"Good. It is up to you from now on, then. He is very vulnerable at this moment. Ripe for consolation of the right kind and a shoulder to cry on. He is full of self-pity and even more confused; feels he has been double-crossed. In that mood, if you play your cards right, he is yours."

"How did you do it?" Caroline asked, fascinated.

"With care, every consideration and a great deal of patience."

"What has happened to her?"

"Do not concern yourself in that direction. I have disposed of her; that is all you need to know. Now I must end the marriage. Hold yourself in readiness. He will call you. Maybe not for a while, he is very —down—right now, but in time. I know my son: he will bob to the surface eventually. When he does, be there." Lady Hester fixed Caroline with a penetrating stare. "Can you do it?"

Now it was Caroline's turn to smile. Lady Hester laughed. "Yes. We understand each other, do we not?" A satisfied intake of breath. "And that is how this will remain. Our—mutual understanding?"

Oh, yes, thought Caroline. I understand only too well. I am what you will allow Brad to have—no more. And I can have him only if I keep my mouth shut. Lady, I'll wear a gag if it means that eventually I'll get rid of you.

AND FOUR MONTHS LATER, Caroline Norton became Mrs. J. Winthrop Bradford V at a big Boston wedding, Mrs. Norton being completely outgeneraled by Lady Hester when it came to making the arrangements. She was given to understand that Caroline Norton was, like Grace Kelly of Philadelphia, marrying above her station; moreover, one could not compare some two-bit principality with the Bradfords.

So once again Philadelphia played second fiddle, and three hundred guests arrived at Trinity Church one bright April morning at 11 A.M. to await the bride. Exactly two minutes before she did, Hester Bradford made her entrance, stunningly elegant in crisp navy silk and a hat that drew moans of envy from every woman present except Eloise Norton, who felt it set off her own lemon-drop yellow quite well. All in all, thought Eloise, it had been an uphill struggle, made even worse by having to shove Hester Bradford up it backward every step of the way, but the end result was certainly worth it.

The church was ablaze with candles and brilliant with flowers. Eloise had dug her toes in there; she didn't give a damn what they did in England or Boston; this was an American wedding and the church would be decorated the American way. That Hester Bradford had ruthlessly cut away much of the beribboned extravaganza Eloise had planned made her frown for a moment, but this was soon smoothed away when a Boston Brahmin wife complimented her on the state of the church. "So charming." Wait till you see my daughter, Eloise thought triumphantly, and even as the thought appeared so did Caroline. As she came slowly down the aisle on her father's arm, he uncomfortably conscious of his gray morning suit, matching those of the ushers and groom, Eloise felt her bosom swell. She still thought the bridesmaids would have been better in the pastel chiffons she had wanted, rather than the old-fashioned ivory silk Hester Bradford had chosen, but she had to admit they did look charming, a good match to the four ushers, chosen for height and similarity in looks: all white Anglo-Saxon Protestant perfection. And what was wrong with a flower girl and a ring bearer? she thought indignantly. They were most certainly not tacky, as Hester Bradford had said with a flare of the nostrils. A flower girl dressed like Little Bo-Peep and a ring bearer like little Lord Fauntleroy, that was what Eloise had wanted. They were not what she had gotten. Nor had she won over the flowers: Lady Hester's instructions to Winston's had been exact: rosebuds, white, of a uniform size and of a virginal purity tinged with the merest maiden's blush of pink; no—repeat no—smilax; every thorn to be stripped and the leaves to be polished.

But as her daughter came down the aisle, Eloise swelled like a turkey cock and went just as pink with pleasure. The battle over the wedding dress had been long and hard fought, but Eloise had to admit, albeit grudgingly, that the old bitch had been right. The dress was not dull at all; under the glow of dozens and dozens of candles, its pure white, pure silk organza gleamed with the purity of innocence, its skirt full and spreading, rustling over the red carpet Lady Hester had specified.

The bodice, of Alençon lace, was tight, outlining Caroline's firm young breasts, the sleeves, also of lace, tight to the wrist. Her veil was also organza, sheer and filmy, falling in a twenty-foot train at the back, to just below her breasts in front. Under it, her face was flawless; clear-eyed, radiant, thanks not so much to the expertise of the minions of Miss Elizabeth Arden but to Caroline's sense of triumph. The fact that she was wearing the Bradford tiara, a glittering heirloom of first-water diamonds and teardrop pearls placed there by Lady Hester herself, was a measure of her confidence. So that when Brad caught sight of her, and she saw the way his eyes widened, his breath jolted, she was able to smile at him serenely, casting her eyes down demurely as they turned to face the bishop and she felt the possessive grip of his hand on hers. Now! she thought. Now he is *mine!*

Afterward, at the Ritz Carlton (Mount Vernon Street would be uncomfortably tight with three hundred guests) there were quails' eggs, poached salmon flown in from the Arun estates in Scotland, Maine lobster, guinea hen in aspic, marbled ribs of Scotch beef, pêches à la provençale, and plates of those delectable petits fours from Fortnum's, all washed down with limitless quantities of Dom Pérignon '47.

When Caroline went up to change, Eloise whooped with joy. "At last!" she hooted.

Caroline frowned. "Do be quiet, Mother," she remonstrated. "Remember who and where you are."

Already she was settling into the persona of Mrs. J. Winthrop Bradford V, and that night, in their honeymoon suite at the Stanford Court, where they stayed before leaving on the *QE2* for a six-week cruise, Caroline put into practice all she had assiduously learned.

"My God, Caro," Brad said when he could afterward, chest heaving, "I never dreamed . . ."

"I have kept it all for you, darling. Only you. I knew we would be together someday, even when—"

"That was a mistake!" Brad overrode her roughly. "The worst I ever made. Mother was right, as always. It was hasty and ill judged. I was thinking with my cock; that's always fatal."

"I heard she was very beautiful," Caroline said innocently.

"Skin-deep! Underneath she was pure carbon steel. Jesus, was I ever wrong about her! An ambitious, coldhearted bitch who played hard-to-get, and once she had got me turned her attention to what really interested her—her career. When Mother showed me the way she had manipulated that whole Paris deal! And then turned around and said Mother had manipulated her! God, but she was clever. Even to telling

[208]

Mother she did not want a fee for the job! That she would do it as a gesture of good faith. Faith! Christ, the only thing she believes in is herself! And then she turns around afterward and threatens to sue! I would have let her, but Mother didn't want any bad publicity. And God knows the bitch had almost done for her once already."

Caroline hid her face in her husband's shoulder. "Hey . . ." Brad was touched. "No need to cry about it." Poor kid, he thought, ego inflating, she really does love me. It was as well he could not see his bride's face, though he felt her body trembling. It was alight with laughter.

THEY CAME BACK TO BOSTON splendidly satisfied with each other. Brad was once more in possession of a restored and repaired ego, which Caroline took care to keep in perfect condition. There was no trace of Julia left when they took up residence on Mount Vernon Street. Everything she had done had been obliterated.

Caroline and Brad now occupied the master suite, which Lady Hester had insisted on vacating. "It is Brad's house, he is its master, therefore he has the right. I shall bestow myself at the other end of the hall. I feel I need someone near me now, after that heart attack."

Oh, clever, clever, admired Caroline. By seeming to confer on her son the status of head of the household she was only reaffirming her own. Caroline held her peace. She had no intention of living with her mother-in-law forever, in spite of this latest clever maneuver. But there was plenty of time now.

And then things began to change. Brad's old restlessness returned. Caroline was furious when she saw, in spite of all her sexual expertise, that it was still not enough to keep Brad on the straight and narrow, but outwardly she displayed not so much as a sign that she even knew, though for the life of her she could not understand why. She took care always to look good; she fanatically observed the maxim that thin is beautiful, she was—under her mother-in-law's guidance—elegant enough to be acclaimed as "the elegantly soignée Mrs. J. Winthrop Bradford V, acknowledged leader of Boston's Young Married set." In desperation, she turned to her mother-in-law, who raised her eyebrows and said impatiently: "My dear Caroline, you wanted to marry my son on any terms. I saw to it that you did. But marriage, so they keep saying, is a partnership; not a slave state. Don't be a fool. These women mean nothing to him and you are his wife. Which was all you ever wanted anyway."

Meeting the terrifyingly lucid eyes, Caroline knew that her mother-in-law had been aware, from that first weekend, of exactly what Caroline was after, and that it had been no more than a situation which suited her plans when she set about destroying her son's first marriage so as to install Caroline as the bride in his second. She knew Brad did not love Caroline; in fact, it suited her that he did not. It was because he had loved Julia Carey that she had had to go.

That none of the other women lasted, that Brad always came back to her in a way as to shackle her even more tightly to him, only increased Caroline's torment. He would be tender, thoughtful, gently passionate, as though some inner restlessness had been assuaged. He would make love to her every night in a way that satisfied her ecstatically. He would compliment her on a dress, her hair, buy her surprise gifts, take her sailing or skiing or to parties and theaters—until she saw the edges begin to singe again and she would know he was about to burst into flame.

Now, staring at him as he brushed his hair, shrugged into his jacket, checked that he had wallet, keys, credit cards, she knew he was on the hunt again. He had made love to her last night—something to keep her on the hook. She wished she were able to refuse him, tell him to get the hell away from her, but he only had to touch her and she was lost; clinging to him passionately, covering his face with wild kisses, sobbing and crying out his name at her climax, telling him she adored him and worshiped him and begging to know why was he so cruel to her.

Last night, for the first time, he had tried to tell her how it was with him. "I know I'm a bastard sometimes, but I did warn you, remember? Way back when. I told you I was not easy to live with. It's some— unsatisfiable thing in me, I guess. Some restlessness I can't control."

"From what I hear you were never restless with *her.*"

She had felt his body tense. These days he never so much as mentioned *her.* "We won't talk about that," he said curtly. "It's over and done with—dead—as she might as well be."

"But I never so much as look at another man; why must you have other women?"

He removed his arms from her, moved out and into his own bed.

"You've never loved me, never!" Caroline wept.

"Love!" his voice was ugly. "Jesus Christ! I've had enough of so-called love, thank you. It's a con, the whole damned thing! I'll stick to sex, thank you; it's a hell of a sight more honest."

"But don't I give you all the sex you need—and with love? Have I ever refused you?"

"Christ!" he exploded. "Did you ever think that it's because you never have that I get bored!"

Caroline gave a cry like a wounded animal.

"I know you by now, Caroline, in all the ways there are. The first—excitement has gone. There's no challenge anymore, no more mysteries to solve. Not like—" He bit off whatever he had been going to say.

Caroline shot upright, tears dribbling.

"Not like *her*, you mean!"

"All right then—if you want the truth! No—you are not like her—no other woman ever has been or will be; she was as deep as you are shallow—is that what you wanted to know? She had depths I never plumbed—I never knew her—not all of her, all she was—if you must know I think she's a mystery even to herself; now are you satisfied? And a man who meets that likes to think he is the one to solve it! The fact that I never solved her, that she was a challenge that never ceased to needle, makes no difference to the fact that she was a coldhearted, double-crossing bitch who was still the most passionately giving woman I've ever known; does that answer your question?" Without waiting for her answer he flung himself out of bed and into his dressing room, slamming the door behind him. Caroline screamed: "Bastard!" after him, following it with the pillow, before collapsing in a welter of tears.

Now, SHE REGARDED HIM with hatred. Something had murdered her feelings for him when he had spoken of his first wife in such a bitter yet anguished way. He still thought of her, still wanted her. Now, when she said to herself, "I hate him!" it was meant; cold and deadly. In spite of everything she had not been able to make him love her; not been able to put him under her lock and key. No. Julia Carey still had that, the bitch! He had demeaned her beyond repair when he had compared her lack to his first wife's perfection; proved to her that after almost two years of marriage, he was still, deep down where he had thrust it out of the way, not wholly over her effect on him. The fact that nowadays he never mentioned her name where once he had been so free in his denunciations of her served to confirm Caroline's belief. How many times has he made love to me while fantasizing I was her? she thought now. How many times has he said my name outwardly but hers inwardly, in silence? Bastard! she raged. Faithless, cheating bastard! I'll get him for this, see if I don't. And that archbitch his mother. Between them they have used me, screwed me up and thrown me away.

She conveniently forgot that in order to get Brad she had not cared how it was done. She only knew that in the end, she had failed to get him. No wonder his mother encouraged his infidelities; they suited her. She did not care how many women he fucked so long as he did not *love* any of them. That was what she was terrified of; why she had destroyed Julia Carey. Because Brad had loved her.

Just as she knew he didn't—would never—love her. Anything and anyone was grist to her mill, just so long as what came out was the concentrated essence of her hold on her son. Well, Caroline thought, now is the time to strengthen mine. I'll come off the Pill. I won't tell him but I will. I'll have a child. I'll chain him to me that way. He won't find any way out of this marriage because I'll block every exit. Getting up, she brushed silently past him and into their bathroom, where she took her pills from her cabinet, carefully and deliberately expelled each one from its individual plastic pod, flushed them down the lavatory, replaced the empty trays in their box, which she put back in the cabinet. Him and his time to play, she thought. Two years was long enough, and his mother had been dropping hints lately about settling down to responsibilities. I'll give him responsibilities, Caroline thought, staring at her stiff white face in the mirrored wall. I'll break his back with them!

"READY?" MARCUS ASKED, poking his head around the door, then on seeing how Julia looked came around it and into the room. "My, but don't we look something else this evening."

"You approve?" Julia was wearing gray; a velvet suit with a hip-clipping jacket and a small hat trimmed with brilliants, no brighter than her eyes.

"Wholeheartedly."

"I've got to face a couple of dozen hardened journalists out there—people who've seen it all."

"But think of the publicity, sweetheart. From rags to riches in five short years. From Julia Carey to Julia Carey (Design) Limited, with a bank balance that is running a temperature and a full commission book."

"Thanks to your unfailing efforts on my behalf."

Julia reached up on tiptoe to brush his cheek.

"I never lose sight of my own twenty percent for one minute—even when you happen to knock my eyes out." He had his hands on her shoulders. "You're good, kid. I mean really good."

"You sound surprised."

"You continue to surprise me on a daily basis. This hotel has got them scribbling fast and furiously; all the top-notch monthlies have sent a photographer, so you should find yourself decorating several inside pages and maybe—maybe—even a cover. I also did a little transatlantic telephoning and got a couple of European correspondents from American glossies. Your designs have got them talking; now you go out there and do the same. No more hiding your light under a bushel. You've served your apprenticeship. No more small, penny-ante jobs. This hotel is the first of the really big commissions that are going to come your way. Julia Carey (Design) Limited is headed for the big time—about which more later. For now, go and give your first press conference and knock 'em dead, baby."

IN BED, NEXT MORNING—it was Saturday so no work—Julia found herself in all the papers. There was concerted praise for the hotel—a brand-new one built in Knightsbridge with the object of catering to wealthy Arabs and decorated with them in mind—and not a little for Julia, whose career was commented on, as well as her partnership with Marcus Levin. Only the tabloids made mention of her brief marriage to a Proper Bostonian, and one of them had managed to find a photograph—an early one—of Brad, mentioning his present marriage to the former Caroline Norton of Philadelphia. Heavy play was made of her good looks and elegance as well as the fact that she had built up her business into a highly successful one-woman show which had carried out some very prestigious commissions of late. Marcus got his share, but the lion's share went to Julia, and before she had time to read all the papers properly, her telephone started ringing.

THAT NIGHT, she and Marcus had a celebration dinner, and Julia was both pleased and proud to be recognized as she entered the dining room of the Connaught. It was the first time she had been there since the morning of her wedding to Brad, but the headwaiter greeted her by name and several people said her name and smiled as she passed. Publicity is everything, she thought, conscious that she was again looking her best in deep sea-green faille, her red hair flaming. For five years she had made first a good, then, gradually, a luxurious living designing small restaurants, hairdressing salons, several "special" hotel suites and a good many houses, but it had taken a large, sumptuously luxurious West End hotel to make her famous. She found she liked it. Already, the day's calls had produced a dozen inquiries re lucrative commissions: she had at least two years fully booked up, and by people who could do her nothing but good, one of them an international sex symbol who wanted Julia to redo her house in the Boltons. Now, as she reached Marcus, still, in black tie, ever the hippie, he was ablaze with news he could not wait to give her.

"Baby, have I got news for you!"

"Likewise," Julia sparkled.

"Not like mine. *The* commission. The crowning glory of your career."

"Where? What? Who?"

"Another hotel—but this time it's going to be a real blockbuster. An Arab consortium with enough dough to buy and sell the one you've just been working for. They want a Byzantine extravaganza and have chosen you to design it."

Julia glowed.

"They flipped over the Sirocco but they want something even more—"

"Arabian Nights?"

"Exactly."

"Where?"

"Los Angeles."

Julia went out like a light.

"Now what?" Marcus glowered.

"I told you at the very beginning. No commissions in the United States. That country is a jinx to me."

"That was then! This is now. You are firmly established, famous and very successful. Time to spread your wings and fly. Besides, there is a mint of money here. Where's the sense of turning down a couple of million dollars just because it happens to be located in the land of the freeze?"

"Hester Bradford," Julia said.

"Oh, now, come on. She's five years ago."

"Fifty would make no difference to her once she made up her mind."

"What the hell can she do to you now?"

"Jenny," Julia answered.

Marcus stared. "Jenny! For God's sake, Julia. They took the Lindbergh kid almost fifty years ago and kidnaping is a federal offense. Even she would balk at that."

"She would balk at nothing to get me," Julia said, "but that was not what I was thinking of. What I had in mind was her getting the goods on me to prove me an unfit mother." She paused. "You know Brad's marriage is childless."

[214]

Marcus bellowed with scornful laughter, making heads turn. "Jesus, your fame has gone to your head, honey."

"It was her opinion of herself I was thinking of."

"But she hates your guts, so why would she want your child?"

"Because she is also Brad's child."

"Ah . . . now we come to it. That's the name that rings the bell. It's not her at all. It's him."

"Don't be ridiculous."

"Come off it, sweetheart. This is Marcus. I know you. That ex-husband of yours is the real reason you've frozen me out these past five years."

"I also told you at the beginning: no personal involvement."

"With me or any man! Your trouble is that you are stuck on the St. Julia the Martyr bit. You have demonstrated—endlessly as I am here to testify—your capacity to do without men. What I still can't decide is if it is sado or maso. What I do know is that it has to do with that vaunting pride of yours and the fact that you are an emotional coward—and all because of that spineless son of a bitch!"

"I don't need you to read me the list of my own shortcomings."

"Maybe not, but you owe me an explanation as to why you've never tried to stretch them!"

"I learned a short, sharp lesson and I never make the same mistake three times," Julia said icily. "I was honest with you from the start. Business only—and I've done damned well by you."

"Financially, yes. Done for me everywhere else."

"I haven't noticed you going short," Julia said nastily.

"I don't have your capacity for doing without, besides which I don't see why I should. But I didn't believe you then and I don't believe you now. I'll be damned if I'll let you turn down a couple of million dollars just to show how self-sufficient you are. When you told me the slate had been wiped clean you forgot to mention it had been written on in invisible ink!"

Julia's face was flushed. Marcus never minced words. He served them up as they came, however unpalatable.

"This is not just you, baby. It's me and my twenty percent. I'll be damned if I'll let you keep me down just because you are scared shitless of some old bat who probably hasn't thought of you in years or some ex-husband you have never, in my opinion, been able to wash out of your system." Marcus's voice was vitriolic. "That slate was no more wiped clean than your face right now."

"I am not obliged to explain myself to you."

Julia's voice was low but furious. People were turning to stare.

"You can't even explain yourself to yourself, in my opinion. Five years ago you stood back and let her louse up your life without so much as a word of protest, then took the veil. Get up off your knees, Julia, before they lock."

"Now you are being offensive."

"I am being truthful—and aren't you the lady who thrives on that? This Hester Bradford crap won't wash. You are an exemplary mother, there is not so much as a whiff of scandal in your life. You live alone, sleep alone; is that why you've always been so scrupulously careful to have me out of your flat by midnight at the latest? But you are paranoid where Hester Bradford is concerned, except she's the beard. It's not her you are really scared of. It's her precious son."

Julia's rapid breathing was the only sign of her inner perturbation; that and the look in her eyes.

"California is some three thousand miles from Boston, and what you do in Massachusetts you cannot necessarily do there, in spite of its reputation as the Kingdom of Kooks. California has more powerful and wealthy people than Boston and the entire state of Massachusetts can muster, while you yourself are no longer the nobody he took home to Mother. You have a name, a reputation and wield your own clout. She'd think twice about taking you on now."

"My only concern is to see that she is not given the opportunity."

"Liar!" Marcus was so brutal it was as if he had struck her across the face. "It's that bastard ex of yours. He has been between you and me from the start, with an armlock on your emotions."

"I am not going back to the United States and that is all there is to it," Julia said, iron in her determination.

"The hell it is! I am not letting this go on your say-so. I've worked too long and too hard to arrive at this deal and I'm damned if I'll let you throw it because you are yellow." In a voice as hard as her own: "You have a week to rethink everything, as only you can—into the bloody ground if need be. But in one week I want an honest—I repeat honest—answer."

JULIA THOUGHT OF NOTHING ELSE, yet each time she approached that locked and barred section of her life she averted her eyes. Too much pain and suffering lay there. She had bundled the remains of her second marriage into a bloody parcel, thrust it out of sight and then thrown away the key. The very thought of sending for a locksmith terrified her.

[216]

"I can't explain it to myself," she told Chris desperately, "and it is not for want of trying, but the very thought of setting foot in America terrifies me."

"Because *he* lives there."

"But how can that be? After what he did . . . what he is?"

"That makes no mind. He still has the power to undo you and deep down you know it. That is what you are afraid of—that he has the power to do for you again. He's your Achilles' heel, except that where he gets you is right between the legs. He is the only man who ever did." Chris shook her head. "He changed you, Julia; really made you into a woman and all that means, not just the person you thought you wanted to be. In spite of all the shouting the libbers do about self-fulfillment and consciousness-raising, for a woman to be truly fulfilled there has to be a man. They can laud masturbation as the key to real liberation but it never fitted *my* lock." Trenchantly: "Nor yours, either."

Julia's face was stunned.

"What I think is that you are frightened of what he turns you into: a woman you neither know nor understand. Worse, one you can't control. On the surface you've got it all together—everything running on oiled wheels, no problems—especially emotional ones, which, as you said yourself, you can't handle. Brad Bradford is the one person in the world who can send you right off the rails and what you are really afraid of is that you might meet him again and not be able to stop him doing it."

Holding Julia's stricken eyes. "He's the reason you've kept Marcus at several arms' length and never allowed any other man to pass through the barrier. He's got you split down the middle. Wanting but dead scared to take. Loving and yet hating at the same time, like that poor bastard Catullus. Remember that book you brought me back—that American translation? He was hooked on that whore—Lesbia—and hated her at the same time. *Odio et amo*—a perfect description of you, love." Nodding sadly: "I speak from experience and knowledge, kiddo. I've worked my way through a hundred men or more, but you had it all in your one. I wish to God I'd ever had a Brad Bradford." Flatly: "You blew it, Julia. You always wanted more than he could give you—that perfection of yours. Only the superbest is good enough for Julia Carey; that hundred and one percent at least. Didn't you ever stop to think that perfection is perfectly boring? Your trouble is you can't stand the warts. And if you feel this way now, after five years, why the hell didn't you fight for him at the time? I'd have dragged him by the scruff of his neck to where I could tell him and his mother a few home truths! But not you. Oh, no. You preferred to keep your dignity. Not for you to soil your hands or stoop to human behavior. You prefer the view from that pedestal of yours! And it's not as though you can't fight like the best when you have to. I've seen you—but only where business is concerned. You run like hell from anything else."

"I can't explain it either," Julia said in a stifled voice, "and it is not for want of trying."

"There are some things you can *never* explain. Everybody is a mixture of good and bad, hot and cold, fears and certainties. My theory is that it is because you grew up outside the normal rules. Mother, father, children. You lost your parents when you were too young to know what having them meant, and your formative influence was a domineering old woman every bit as arrogant as your ex-ma-in-law. She's the one taught you to regard love as a weakness of character; to be avoided as the ultimate in stupidity. No wonder, when it went wrong for you, you told yourself it was because you had not followed her particular line of truth. Except you also forgot she never had the monopoly on that! It comes in varying forms and sizes. Marcus is right: you are cutting off your nose to spite your face. Go on then—then see how you look in the mirror!"

Julia had never seen Chris so angry. It gave her cause for alarm. Pedestals? she thought. I'm not like that, am I? She got up, went across to the mirror, where she stared at her face. At that, she thought, I would look most peculiar without a nose.

WHEN SHE TOLD MARCUS to accept the Los Angeles offer, all he said was: "I knew you would see the sense of it."

She forbore to tell him that was the one thing she could not see.

HESTER BRADFORD reached out a hand to the ringing telephone. "Hester Bradford here—Ah . . . I've been waiting to hear from you." She leaned back in her chair, grimacing as she did so. Over the years, her arthritic hip had grown steadily worse; now she could not walk without a supporting arm or her stick. She listened to her caller, doodling the while on her scratch pad covered with figures. But it was a J she drew, convoluted and etched deep into the paper.

"You are quite sure . . . no last-minute doubts? Good, good. I do not need to remind you that your continued—well-being—even your security—depend on my being aware of everything at all times. No—no surmises, if you please! Facts; accurate and unshakable facts. You know I never leave anything to chance. Very well. And this time I want absolute and incontrovertible proof. You have been far too long about it as it is, and time is now of the essence." She listened again, her pencil enclosing the J in a maze of barbed wire. "Then try another tack. I have given you a great deal of latitude; you now have the perfect opportunity. Act on it." She listened again. "Very well. Keep me informed." She hung up.

Cradling the phone she sat with her hand on it, deep in thought. Then she became aware of what she had absentmindedly drawn. With a sweep of the hand she tore the sheet from its binding, crumpled it and dropped it into the wastepaper basket. Then she resumed her work.

"HERE?" JULIA ASKED, on a rising note. "*This* is our house?"

"Why not? In California you have to live as you would like people to really believe you live! And aren't you in the big time now?"

It overhung the side of a canyon, high in Bel Air; all fieldstone and vast expanses of glass.

"Is it a castle, Mummy?" Jenny asked, wide-eyed.

"You hit the nail on the head, Jenny-Wren," Marcus said, hoisting her to his shoulder. "You see, I've always wanted to see your mother let down her hair."

Julia shaded her eyes to examine the house, somewhat taken aback not only by its size but by its seclusion. She had seen no other houses on the way up the hill. Suddenly the front door opened and a Japanese stood there, hands on knees, bowing. "Welcome," he hissed, all smiles and teeth. "My name Ito; you come in now?"

Once through the front door Julia gulped and gasped. The luxury was overpowering, overdone, probably hideously overpriced. It was like the inside of a harem: flamboyant materials in riotous colors, lots of crystal and gilt, ebony and jade, gold and mother-of-pearl, and if it could be fringed, it was.

"Arabs like color," Marcus explained.

"All the comforts of home," Julia winced.

"It's for free! You don't think I'd let you pay rent on a place like this."

"Free!"

"Comes with the deal. Some Saudi prince used it as a place to throw parties."

"Orgies, you mean," muttered Julia.

"Terrific view. And there's a swimming pool." Marcus walked her over to the wall of windows: a vast garden, sloping down the canyon, a swimming pool curved in the shape of a belly dancer's body. Julia shuddered.

"Okay, so it's not to your taste but it's for free. Upstairs is better, come and see."

The bedrooms were of a sybaritic opulence which smothered. Carpets like waving grass, brocades, chandeliers like waterfalls, mirrored ceilings, sunken baths. One of them had an alabaster swan with its neck curving backward as though in the act of preening; its golden beak was a tap.

Julia chose one that was the most bearable; all palest pink and whitest white.

"It still smacks of the harem—and the house is awfully isolated," she said doubtfully. "Surely there are neighbors."

"Of course there are—just not too near, is all. In this neck of the woods you pay for the privilege of not having people looking down your neck, but if you'll come to the window"—lifting back the sheer voile curtain—"that blue through the trees? That's your neighbor's pool."

"Still a long way off." Julia was thinking that Bel Air was where one of her clients, the actress Sheila de Lisle, was robbed; three masked men had kicked their way into her house, beaten her Filipino butler and ransacked the place, leaving Sheila in a state of terror. "Is Ito the only servant?" she asked now.

"The only one who lives in. A cleaning service does the rest." Marcus made one of his instant decisions. "Tell you what. Since you obviously have doubts about being here unprotected, why don't I take one of the bedrooms? God knows there are enough of them. That way, you'll have a man about the house." A quick grin. "Make you feel safer."

"I would feel safer," Barbara, Jenny's young nanny, said quickly, but Julia was not so quick to agree. Having Marcus sleep in her house would make it look as though they were living together, and she was now within easy reach of Hester Bradford's long spoon . . . But this was kidnap country, and if anything should happen to Jenny . . . "All right," she agreed, resolving to give him the bedroom farthest away from hers—right on the other side of the house, in fact.

"Right," Marcus said, that matter settled. "Now, why don't you get yourselves settled while I go downtown and start balls rolling. Then we'll go out and celebrate. First night in L.A. and all that . . . I'll show you the town. Pick you up at"—a quick glance at his watch—"eight o'clock?"

"Fine."

"Can I come too?" Jenny asked.

"Not this time, sweetheart, but come Sunday I'm taking you to the most perfect paradise for little girls—little boys too, come to that." Significant pause. "Disneyland!"

Jenny's face exploded. "Ooohhh, Uncle Marcus—Disneyland! Can I see Donald Duck and the Enchanted Castle and sail on the big boat and—"

"Everything." Marcus promised. "We'll have the whole day there, okay?"

Jenny threw her arms around his neck, kissed him a smacker. "Oh, yes, please, Uncle Marcus!"

Julia regarded them smilingly. Jenny adored Marcus, who treated her as if she were the princess.

"That's my girl," he said, putting her down onto the floor. "Now run along with Barbara." When she had trotted off, "Best bib and tucker," Marcus said to Julia. "I want you should knock out the eyes of certain people. Wear that black dress—the one with the gold embroidery."

"Yes, O Master," salaamed Julia.

She was in the act of donning it, chiffon embroidered with gold thread in the shape of leaves; cut straight across her collarbones and slit to a deep V at the back, the waist defined by a wide sash of leather as supple as silk, when he called.

"I'm running late," he said. "Can you meet me instead? Grab a cab to the Century Plaza, it's not far away. I'll meet you in the lobby court there, eight-fifteen, okay?"

"Fine," said Julia.

She went to say good night to Jenny, sitting up in bed expectantly.

"Ooh, Mummy, you look like a fairy!"

"That is a lovely dress, Miss Carey," Barbara, who had come to them from the famous Norland Training College for nannies and had stayed ever since, told Julia admiringly. "You look stunning."

"That," said Julia gaily, "is the intended effect." She bent to hug and kiss her daughter. "Good night, darling. See you in the morning."

Ito was waiting outside Jenny's door. "Taxi here," he said, then: "Missus look good."

"Thank you, Ito!" Julia swept downstairs on a cloud of Chloé and out to the waiting taxi.

"Where to, lady?"

"Century Plaza, please."

"Comin' right up . . ."

EVEN AS HER TAXI turned out of the drive, Brad Bradford was leaving Los Angeles airport in his. He should have been on a plane for Boston, but a call had caught him just as he was about to leave San Francisco.

"Brad?"

No mistaking the throaty voice, laden with sex and vibrant with promise.

"Tricia!"

"A pleasant surprise?"

"Fantastic—one I'm in need of. Where are you?"

"Beverly Hills—the Century Plaza. Want to come and play for a while?"

"Do I! How come you knew I was in San Francisco?"

"I always know where you are, darling."

Just as he knew where she was at. Where he wanted to be right now.

"I'll grab the first plane," he said. "Don't start the party without me."

Tricia Tremayne was the current Hollywood sex goddess. Her body had men slack-jawed at the sight of it when she displayed it, usually half naked, on the silver screen. She also had a voracious sexual appetite and a sensuality which, always smoldering, ignited into napalm when she was in bed. Brad had met her at a premiere, which they had left to go back to his hotel and bed; the affair had gone on ever since, whenever and wherever they could meet.

Just what he needed right now. His mood lifted at once. He had been dreading going home. Always did, these days. Nothing to go home to. Except his drunk of a wife. It had not worked out, Caroline and he; they no longer had anything to say to each other, and her clinging petulance had come to irritate him beyond endurance. Added to which she was rapidly losing what looks she'd had under the bloat of alcohol. "Because I'm bored!" she flung at him. "Bored, bored, *bored!*"

And his mother would go on again about Caroline's seeming inability to conceive.

"It's not my fault," he had told her. "I've been checked and double-checked. So has she. There is no physical reason; it's that she is too damned desperate! She's been told she is defeating her own ends."

He dreaded sex with his wife; always ended up feeling he had been raped. Her frantic insistence that he impregnate her invariably defeated its own end. Her doctors had told her to let nature take its course; to enjoy sex for its own sake and not solely as procreation. But she would exhaust herself—and him—in a feverish bout, then wait, marking off her calendar toward the date circled with a red O. When, as always happened, she had to cross that out too, she would turn from the calendar and head for the bottle; get drunk then yell and curse and throw things.

"Is it any wonder I don't conceive when you've spent yourself in the beds of countless other women? You've fucked yourself dry by the time you get around to me!" she would shriek hysterically. "What are you trying to do—work your way through the entire female population? I can smell them on you, you faithless bastard!"

"You knew what kind of a marriage this was from the start. Don't blame me if you feel you've been shortchanged—and it's not my fault you don't get pregnant; it's yours!"

And so on, and so on.

"One mistake is enough," his mother had told him coldly. "I will not countenance a second one. You must make her ease up, Brad. She must have a child; you must have a son."

But after five years of marriage Caroline had not once missed a period. She was as regular as clockwork. So were her drunken spells.

God! he thought bitterly as his taxi drove off. All the women I've had and I wind up with two from the bottom of the deck! Thank God for Tricia. She would sweeten the current sourness of his days; give him something to look back on even if he had nothing to look forward to. As the cab turned onto the freeway he thought: By God, this had better be worth flying all this way for.

When he arrived at the Century Plaza he strode confidently up to the desk.

"Miss Tricia Tremayne, please. I'm expected. My name is Bradford."

As the desk clerk lifted the phone, Brad turned to survey the crowded and glittering lobby court, filled with people having drinks or meeting other people or waiting to be met. As always, his interest was in the women; assessing, surmising, grading or dismissing, until his roving gaze halted, became riveted, on one oh so familiar face. That of his first wife, stupendously beautiful in black and gold, sitting in one of the deep couches leafing through a magazine. His heart gave such a violent lurch he stepped backward, right onto the toes of the man next to him.

He apologized mechanically before moving away to a nearby rack of postcards, behind which he hid, staring obsessively. One of the elevators disgorged a crowd of people, obscuring his view. Impatiently, even frantically, he moved and then recognized another face. He opened his mouth to call the name which went with it, until he saw where the man was going. Right up to his first wife, unhesitatingly and jauntily. She looked up and he saw her face break into a radiant smile. The man bent down, drew her to her feet, kissed her mouth. They stood talking for a moment, then the man drew her arm through his and turned her toward the sliding glass doors of the entrance. Edging forward, Brad watched as they waited for a car to be brought up by a parking attendant, watched the man hand Julia into it solicitously before getting in himself. The big black Lincoln paused, taillights winking, before turning off in the direction of Los Angeles.

Brad stared after it for a long time. Then he turned and moved slowly, like a man sleepwalking, in the direction of the couch; sat himself down in the seat Julia had not long before vacated. It was still warm from her body; he could smell perfume, sensuous, feminine. As if in defense he closed his eyes tightly. "Oh, Julia . . . Julia . . . ," he found himself repeating.

He had not thought of her in a long time; had erased her from his life, he had thought. Now, it was as though someone had held that life over a flame, and through the agony, the months he had spent with her appeared slowly but ever more clearly, until they stood out black and strong, leaping out at him, knocking him down, especially that last, terrible confrontation. Which had started with that call from his sister Bitsy; hysterical, crying, wild with panic and distraught with terror. "Brad, thank God . . . I've called everywhere . . . It's Mother, she's had a heart attack and it's all Julia's fault . . . She caused it . . . She said such terrible things . . . Brad, you've got to come home—now! Come home . . . Mother is calling for you . . . I think she is going to die, Brad. Please . . . please come home . . ."

Stunned and shocked, he had gotten hold of Abby, who had confirmed Bitsy's story.

"Mother's in Massachusetts General—a coronary. I gather Julia hurled all sorts of filthy abuse at her, so bad it brought on her asthma, and that was so bad it brought on the coronary. She's in intensive care, but I would get here as fast as you can."

But not before he had confronted Julia. Her face rose up to haunt him; stark white, red blood trickling, the livid imprint of his open palm red across her cheeks. Opening his eyes he snapped his fingers at a passing waiter. "Bourbon—a double, on the rocks—Jack Daniel's—and quick."

He had not known it was possible to be so shocked, so disbelieving, so shattered. He had been mentally disoriented. The flight home was still a blur. He drank his way across the Atlantic, was still terrifyingly sober when at last he found his mother, all tubes and needles and bleeping monitors, paper-white face, thready voice, tranquilized to a zombie. He had fallen on his knees, babbled God knows what at her, pleading with her not to die. And she had opened her eyes, looked at him unrecognizingly for a minute until he saw the beautiful eyes glow; fill and spill. "My son . . ." He had barely heard the whisper. "I knew you would come when I needed you . . . Stay with me, Brad, don't leave me . . . please . . ."

He had been horrified; *his mother*—his impregnable, unshakable, unbeatable mother—reduced to this terrifyingly vulnerable, pathetic, frightened woman. If he had had Julia there he would have killed her; smashed that beautiful face in, broken every last chiseled bone.

He had refused to leave his mother until they pronounced her out of danger, which, once he was back with her, was surprisingly quick.

"You are better than any medicine," the doctors had told him. "She was fibrillating like a broken shutter in the wind not long before you arrived. Now her heart's steady as a new pump. Once she had you back she obviously put her mind to it. Didn't seem to care before."

Afterward, when they brought her back home, she was so sad about it all, blamed herself. "I'd been worried for weeks, darling, ever since you went to Paris, in fact. I was hearing such things. I was so worried about you, what she was doing to you."

"Why didn't you *tell* me?"

With sad reproach: "Would you have believed me? She had you blinded, dearest. You were not capable of seeing anything but her."

"What she showed me, you mean."

"I can be truthful now. I had my doubts about her from the very beginning. So cool and inhumanly controlled. Not natural at all. I always thought she was like a beautiful white stalagmite; so cold and hard." The beautiful eyes had welled. "I could not believe the names she called me, the abuse she hurled at me—"

"Hush. You must not upset yourself."

"Dearest boy . . . I knew you would come when I needed you. Haven't I always said you are my life?" Then, fretfully: "Why did she lie about those chairs? It was so foolish. I already had them in my possession. Why should I send her to Versailles when the marquise was not there?"

"That was her cover story. She wanted to be with that smarmy Swiss bastard."

"My poor, poor boy. How she has hurt you. I shall never forgive her for hurting you, never!"

"She won't get the chance to do it again. It's finished. Over and done with. I told her so."

With deep sadness: "I am so sorry, dearest boy. Forgive me."

"Forgive *you!*"

"I feel I have been the cause of all this—"

"Never! She used you, that's all! Never again. She won't get the chance. I want out—and the sooner the better."

"You shall have your freedom, dearest boy."

But Julia had gotten in first. He had known from his mother's face one morning that something was wrong as she read a letter. "Now what?"

"She is suing you for divorce." His mother's face had been stunned. "In such vicious terms . . . No, I will not have you distressed. Leave it to me, dearest. She will not do this to you." She had crushed the letter in her hand. "She will not blacken your name."

"What are you talking about?"

"Some woman and the night of the Embassy reception."

He had forgotten that. Nothing more than spit in the wind anyway.

"Not that I blame you. A man must find comfort somewhere. And with a wife like that . . . Do not fret, dearest boy. She will not find it easy. I am determined we will fight her—*I* will fight her! To accuse you —*you*—of such violence!"

"You must not upset yourself."

"I shall be upset if you do not let me deal with this—this adventuress! She will find me no mean opponent! Will you let me—deal—with her on your behalf? I cannot bear to see you upset."

"Do whatever you want," he had told her relievedly. "I know I can trust you to do what is right. You always do . . ."

And she had. He had not given a damn. He had signed what he was told to sign and brushed aside details. All he wanted was to be rid of the whole thing. And, true to her word, his mother arranged things so that there was not one breath of scandal. When he received his final papers he had asked only: "How?"

His mother had shrugged. "What else?"

So he had had to buy her off! Christ, what a bloody bitch! He writhed when he thought of it. He, Brad Bradford, the screwer, ending up being screwed—and into the ground. Especially when she threatened to sue for a fee for the hotel. That was all she had ever wanted— money! The taker had been taken—for a sucker.

For a while he had plunged into a blind, wild sexual rampage, wreaking revenge that proved totally unsatisfying. After that he fell into a pit of bottomless apathy. Never had he felt so defeated, so crushed. Never before had he been abandoned and rejected. That was when Caroline had been so kind, so patient, bearing with his moods, respecting his silences. Far more kind and understanding than he'd had a right to expect. If that was not proof of love . . . Except he had never been able to love her. Not in the way he had loved Julia. Not in any way, in fact.

His mother had been proved right there too. "Now are you sure Caroline is what you want, darling? It is not just because I think she is right for you?"

"I made my own choice before and look how wrong that was."

"Well, Caroline is no career woman. All she wants is you; with her you will always come first. She will not compete with you, darling, or betray you. She loves you far too much."

And expected too much, and demanded too much. More than he was able to give. He had tried, he really had, but it was just not there. Not as it had been with Julia. Surfacing from the depths of him into a desperate need that never lessened.

He visualized her as he had just now seen her. She had looked— successful; confident; happy. Her smile had been genuine; *felt*. She had looked expensive, too. She had always dressed well; even when she had supported herself she had obviously had more taste than money. To-night she had had the glitter of money about her; that dress had reeked of it. A model. And the whole woman: sleek, polished, glittering. Obviously she had done well; used the money she'd screwed out of him to good effect. Yes, she would have money all right. Why else would Marcus Levin be in on the act? That crooked son of a bitch could smell it buried fifty feet deep. Well, she had a different proposition there, he thought spitefully. He'd steal your eyes and come back for the sockets.

But what was she doing with him? Her lover, probably. He came out of his deep abstraction to hear his name being paged. "Here," he called.

"Mr. Bradford? Miss Tremayne is asking for you."

Damn! He had forgotten all about her, no longer had any desire to see her. He wanted to be alone to think.

"You didn't find me," he told the boy decisively. "Say I left a message I'd been called away—urgent business. And find out something for me." He felt in his pocket for a dollar bill. "I want to know if there is a Julia Carey staying here—oh, and a Marcus Levin. Come straight back and tell me."

He did. Neither was registered.

So be it. But they were somewhere. And he found himself bent and determined to find out where—and why, and whatever else he could dig up. He did not know why. Only knew it was something he had to do for his own peace of mind.

"YOU DID WELL, DARLING," his mother said to him back in Boston. "I knew you would."

"Your information was right on the button, as always. They are in financial difficulties and Switzerland turned them down. I was able to offer sixty cents on the dollar and it just fell into my lap. Fielding wasn't too happy but it was us or nothing, and at least he's kept his job."

"Only until we can ease him out. That he should have let things get so far is an indication that he is past his best. As soon as we can I'll replace him. So," she went on comfortably, "I thought you were going to Palm Springs for the weekend."

"Changed my mind. Thought I'd come straight home and tell you the good news."

"Dear boy . . . *so* thoughtful . . ."

But not for her. He had gone to the office first, called the firm of investigators Bradford & Sons employed when they wanted information on a competitor or a prospective deal. Briefly, Brad explained he wanted them to investigate a woman named Julia Carey, at present in Los Angeles, the Beverly Hills area. He gave a brief rundown on her history, said he wanted an exhaustive probe into her past five years: her job, her life, her financial standing, her friends for the usual fee and expenses; but thorough—nothing overlooked, even her personal life, you understand?

"And will do."

"How long?"

"Depends how deep we have to dig; three, four—maybe five days."

"Dig to the bottom—nothing left unturned. And send your report under plain cover to me, but not here. I'll give you the address."

He then called a friend in New York, asked her to call him when the envelope arrived, hold it until he could come and collect it personally.

She called him four days later. When he had spoken to her he made another call. "Marty? Brad. Listen, I want a bona fide reason to come to New York at once; can you come up with one?"

"What do I get for it?"

"Dodie Lawrence's telephone number?"

"You're on. Where do I call you?"

"The office—and like in the next half hour, by which time I'll be there."

"Will do."

"They've run into a snag on that Swedish deal," he was able to tell his mother with a show of annoyance later. "I've got to hop the shuttle . . ."

The contract was a big one, worth a lot of money, and he knew his mother would not want to jeopardize that. Besides, he was the company troubleshooter.

"Then you must go," his mother agreed at once. "But keep me informed."

"Naturally."

"WHAT IS IT?" his friend, asked as she handed it over. "Dirty pictures?" It was labeled STRICTLY PRIVATE AND CONFIDENTIAL.

"I'm hoping there will be a picture or two. Thanks a heap." He dropped her a hasty kiss. "I'll call you."

He left the apartment building, walked as far as the nearest bar and went in, selecting an empty booth. He was still sitting there, a whole hour and several doubles later, staring, face on knuckles, at the picture of a five-year-old girl with red-gold hair and his own face and eyes. Jennifer Carey. Born six and a bit months after he had left Julia. He was a father, and had never known. All that trying with Caroline and this child—*his daughter*—had been in existence. With not so much as a hint from Julia. Who had done extremely well for herself. He knew now all about Marcus Levin, Julia Carey (Design) Limited, the reputation she had acquired, the money she had made, the prestigious commissions she had undertaken, culminating in her present one in Los Angeles.

He ordered yet another drink in an attempt to quench the fire of resentment he was burning. The sly, deceitful bitch! She has no right! It's not fair! She *has* no right! Jennifer is my child too! How dare she? he thought self-pityingly. What right has she? Why should she have it all—while I have nothing . . . *nothing*.

That word flitted around in his brain like a mocking echo, refusing to be caught and ejected, eluding his grasp. I'm not leaving, it told him. It took me long enough to get here. He picked up his fresh drink, tossed it off; the word stared at him from the bottom of the glass. He ordered another.

He felt bewildered, upset, deeply hurt. Instead of feeling, as he should, that he had—and rightfully—swept Julia out of his life, he had

[229]

the feeling she had dispensed with him. She had come out best. It was just not fair.

Well, Mother will know how to deal with this, he thought. That's it. I've got to tell her . . . She'll know what to do.

He fumbled in his pocket for bills, found his hands were trembling so badly he dropped them on the floor, and when he bent down to pick them up his head filled with a rush of bourbon and everything blurred and whirled alarmingly. Staggering upright, he called to the bartender: "Get me a cab, will you."

"Ten cents," the bartender said.

The cold air made him reel across the sidewalk when it came.

"I ain't carryin' no drunks in my cab," the driver said truculently.

"I'm not drunk. I'm sick."

"You look like you been on the sauce to me—and this is a bar, ain't it?"

"I'll double the fare, please . . ."

He fell into the dirty, stale-smelling cab. From behind the mesh grill which separated front from back the driver said belligerently: "You throw up and it's triple, you hear! Where do you wanna go?"

His friend gasped when she saw him leaning against her door, pale and sick and trembling. "My God, Brad! What is it? You look awful."

"Black coffee," he croaked as she helped him inside. "And keep it coming."

"You had better lie down." She steered him to the big velvet couch. He fell into it, lay with his eyes closed, clutching the envelope she had given him, and when she came back with a cupful of black coffee she went to take it from him but he hugged it tight to him. "No . . . that's mine! Mine!" She saw his eyes spurt hot, bitter tears. "Mine," he said, before turning over onto his stomach. She saw his shoulders shaking, heard his sobs.

"Oh, Brad . . . Brad!" He sounded as if he were bleeding from the soul. She put a tentative hand on his shoulder and he turned, threw his arms about her and buried his face in her stomach. He cried for a long time, somehow sobering himself up.

Red-eyed, quenched, he gulped the coffee, holding it with one hand while he held tight to the envelope with the other.

His emotional state had to do with whatever was in there, she thought. A medical report? Dear God, he was not terminally ill!

Awkwardly: "If there is anything I can do."

"No, but thanks. You've done enough already."

"Well, I have to go to work soon." She was a showgirl with a sugar

[230]

daddy on the side; marvelous materially, lousy sexually. Brad had propositioned her one night after the show and they had conducted an intermittent affair ever since, he calling her whenever he was in New York. He had always been glitteringly confident, devastatingly attractive, fantastic in the sack. This desperate, defeated man was no one she knew. He frightened her, embarrassed her.

"It's okay, I'm going. He ran his hands through disheveled hair. "If I could just use your bathroom . . . ." He took the envelope with him.

When he came out he had freshened up, only his pale face and red eyes indicating the crying jag. She could not meet them.

"Thanks," he said abruptly, awkwardly for him.

At the door she reached up to kiss his cheek tentatively. "I'm sorry . . . whatever it is," she whispered hurriedly, then shut the door on him quickly. She hoped he would not call her again.

When he got back to Boston it was to find his mother had left for the farm.

"It being your mother's birthday, sir," Thomas said with some surprise.

Christ! He had forgotten. But he had her present all ready: the largest flask of Floris Red Rose to go with the flower he had had Van Cleef & Arpels make up in rubies and emeralds, with dewdrops of small diamonds. He went up to get it and then drove to the farm.

All the family was there, down to Patricia van Schuyler, to whom Bradford, Bitsy's eldest twin, had recently become engaged. They were waiting for him to go in to dinner so he had to go upstairs and change quickly, conscious of his wife's brooding gaze, and thus had no opportunity to talk to his mother alone.

"Are you all right, darling?" she queried on a frown as they all went in, she leaning on his arm.

"Fine. One of those liquid lunches, you know . . . ."

"But you got everything squared away?"

"Sure, no problem." Not there, he thought. Everything else was all to hell.

"Do keep an eye on Caroline," his mother murmured as he drew out her chair. "She had three double martinis before dinner. We must talk, darling. This cannot go on."

"I do want to talk to you," he said in a low voice.

She squeezed his hand. "After dinner."

But it was during dinner that Bitsy let the cat out of the bag.

"Guess who is alive and well and living in California," she asked, bright eyes sparkling.

"Who isn't?" Abby boomed.

"Well, by rights this one shouldn't."

"Which one?"

Bitsy's eyes went to her brother, morosely silent throughout dinner. "Julia Carey!"

The silence held its breath.

"Indeed," Lady Hester was forbiddingly displeased.

"Buffy Peyton saw her—in Disneyland, of all places, last weekend. And guess what? She had a child with her. A redheaded little girl. Buffy didn't get a good look at her but she said the child must be Julia's." A dramatic pause. "Better still, guess who Julia was with—Marcus Levin!"

Lady Hester glanced at her son. He was staring down at his barely touched plate, face expressionless.

"I thought he was in jail," Drexel Adams observed.

"But Mother didn't prosecute, did you, Mother?" Bitsy asked innocently.

"I did have a—fondness—for Marcus," her mother admitted imperturbably. "But I have not seen him since he left my employ." She paused, then said negligently: "It so happens, however, that I learned from another source that Julia Carey had returned to this country." A dismissive shrug. "People do so love to rake over old ashes."

"And obviously living with Marcus Levin?" sparkled Bitsy.

"You mean it is his child?" Abby asked, startled.

Lady Hester's face expressed thin-lipped distaste. "No. I have been reliably informed that the child is the result of that woman's liaison with Pierre Chambrun." She glanced tenderly at her son's impassive face. "I did not tell you so as to spare you, dearest."

Bitsy's laugh was triumphant. "Once a cold-faced bitch, always a bitch!"

"Who told you it was Pierre Chambrun's child?" Brad asked.

"Darling, I have my sources, you know that. Added to which—well, I deemed it proper to keep an eye on that one. She was such a dissembler. I had no intention of her foisting the child onto you. Fortunately, I believe the child is the image of her father."

She is, thought Brad. I've seen her. She is the image of me.

"How old is she?" Bitsy asked with greedy curiosity.

"I am told she will be six next birthday."

Abby sighed. "That fits."

Lady Hester dismissed the subject with a gesture. "Julia Carey and her bastard are of no concern to us. As far as I am concerned, she and

Marcus Levin are welcome to each other. Like will always unto like. Now then, shall we have coffee while I open my presents?"

Brad automatically helped his mother from her chair, his mind churning. His mother had lied when she had said Jenny was Pierre Chambrun's child. Not for one moment did he believe she had had the child "described" to her. His mother would make it her business to know all and everything, as was her invariable custom. If she had kept an eye on Julia, it would be an eagle one. Which meant she would know exactly what Jenny looked like. Which meant she had lied.

His mother a liar? Why? *Why?* You only had to look at Jenny to know she was a Bradford, and in view of Caroline's failure to produce an heir . . .

Something was wrong, somewhere. Somewhere? he thought. Everywhere. Had been ever since he saw Julia again. Seeing her had prised loose his carefully screwed-down life, except screwed up was what it actually was. And if his mother was lying to him . . . He stared at her, exclaiming delightedly over her presents. If she had lied to him about this, could it be—was it possible—she had also lied about other things?

As he handed his wife her coffee, she whispered in a voice only he could hear: "Thank you—*Daddy!*" He had to stop his hand from jerking, spilling hot coffee over her lap. He forced himself to hold her eyes, concealing his shock. How the hell . . . ? Why should Caroline say that? His inner tumult increased; he had a sense of everything falling apart, and as he saw Caroline down his mother's best Armagnac with a gulp and hold out her glass for a refill he knew things were rapidly going from bad to worse.

But she was the perfect excuse when, later, his mother said: "Now then, darling, what was it you wanted to talk about?"

"It will have to wait for now. I'd better get Caroline up to bed before she has to be carried up."

He saw his mother's nostrils flare with distaste. "Something will have to be done," she said decidedly. "Her appalling drunken habits are becoming the subject of gossip."

"That's what I wanted to talk about," he lied quickly. "But later, when I've got her safely out of the way."

"Of course, darling boy. You take her away, the sooner the better." His mother waved a contemptuous hand.

He had to hold Caroline up as they mounted the stairs, her feet stumbling, her body swaying. She had put away a bottle of claret at dinner on top of her three double martinis and God knows how many Armagnacs. But she was not so drunk that she could not whirl on him, as soon as their bedroom door was closed, to snarl belligerently: "That child is no more Pierre Chambrun's than I am!"

"How do you know?"

"What interests me is what you know! Or has your mother kept it from you the way she has everything else?"

"What do you mean?"

"I mean she has kept tabs on your ex-wife ever since she had her kicked out of the family, that's what! And she was far too quick to shove Julia Carey under the carpet tonight. If that brat really was that bitch's bastard your mother would have relished the fact with far more savagery than she did!"

Caroline's drunken logic made sense, but: "How do you know she has kept tabs on Julia?" Brad asked.

"She keeps tabs on everyone, you fool! You, me, your sisters, your sisters' husbands . . . She knows everything about everybody at all times."

"Me!"

"*Especially* you! And then never tells you anything but what she thinks you ought to know."

"That's a lie!"

"The hell it is! It's truth-telling time, folks, and boy am I ready and willing to tell it!"

Caroline weaved her way to the decanter and glasses on the nearby credenza, poured herself a glassful and gulped greedily. "You've always run like hell from that particular thing up till now; you wouldn't recognize it if it came up to you in the street and introduced itself! How could you, when your mother has been feeding you lies all your life?"

"That's *your* lie!"

"Oh no it's not! Tonight you will hear the real truth, by God! It's about time." Caroline was spoiling for a fight. The news that Julia Carey had a child was the last straw and it had broken her back. That bitch had it all. Especially the child she, Caroline Bradford, had been trying so desperately for all this time.

"That brat is your child! If it wasn't, your mother would have told you the minute it was born! She'd have shoved Julia Carey's face in the shit and trodden on it, she hates her so much! It's because it is *your* child she has not said a word—*your* child, you faithless bastard—*yours!*"

"For God's sake lower your voice! Do you want the whole house to hear?"

"I don't give a damn who hears; it's about time they all knew anyway." Caroline staggered to the door, yanked it open and bawled: "Is everybody listening?"

Brad lunged after her, slammed it shut, shoving his wife away so hard she staggered and almost fell, clutching the credenza to save herself.

"You won't shut me up; not anymore you won't. I've kept silent long enough—and what the hell for? You've proved your virility, haven't you, so our lack in that respect has to be my fault—as usual! I'm sick and tired of you and your bloody mother! I'm sick and tired of you fucking everything in skirts and leaving me alone for weeks on end. I'm sick and tired of you turning to your mother when you should be turning to me, your wife—your *wife*, do you hear?" Caroline's voice was a shriek, penetrating walls with ease. "You and your Little Boy Blue act, always running to your mother when something comes apart in your hands. How are you going to fix me, that's what I'd like to know. Between you, you've broken *me!* None of you gives a damn about me, only your own selfish selves—and you are that way because your mother made you, you poor sucker!"

Brad's hand met her cheek with a crack, sending her staggering once more. "That's right! Go on, beat me up like you did her. That was all because of an unbearable truth too!"

Brad seized her by the shoulders, shook her like a dog. "What truth! Tell me, what truth?"

"The truth that your mother has you brainwashed; she could tell you the moon was made of green cheese and you'd believe it because it came from her! She's got you tied so tightly to her you'd strangle if you tried to break away! She has made you think you are God's gift, and when you don't get the same treatment from everybody you run whining to complain. She knows what you will do in any given situation because she programmed you from the day you were born; the one time you stepped out of line she got rid of the interference!" Caroline laughed with delight at the expression on her husband's face. "You didn't know that, did you! That Paris blow-up was manufactured; a beautiful frame, which your mother then put you up to selling! She told me to bide my time, that in six months you'd be free and I could have you if I still wanted you—and I did, God help me, I did . . ." Caroline began to cry, her tears making her mascara run, turning her face into a clown's mask. "I was so crazy about you I didn't care what the hell she did so long as she let me have you! She was the one who pointed you in my direction—and at all those other women too! Don't you realize, you poor sucker, that your mother doesn't give a damn how many women you take to bed so long as all you want from them is sex? It was one, special woman you would actually *love* she was terrified of. She was jealous of Julia Carey! She was so jealous she couldn't see straight because *she* wanted you. Your own mother is in love with you!"

She fell backward as Brad's hand hit her face again. "Liar!" He was white, sweating. "Liar!"

"That's right, hit and run, like you always do! Just like your mother. She was the one who married me to you because she knew you didn't love me. Just as she knew how much I loved you; was prepared to give anything, do anything, to have you—only I never actually did have you. Isn't that the absolute end?" Caroline's laughter was hysterical. "The only thing I got from you was a piece of paper making it legal; you got me and your mother got all that lovely money from my father. My dowry! Your mother sold you, you poor sucker! How does it feel to be a piece of merchandise?"

Brad was staring at her queerly, a white line around his mouth.

"Lies, all lies," he said, utterly without conviction. "You are so drunk you don't know what you are babbling."

"Wrong! Drunk enough to tell you the truth for once! And do you know why? Because I don't care anymore—not for you, not for her, not for the whole bloody Bradford clan!"

"Then say it to her," Brad snarled suddenly. "Go on, I dare you to!"

"With pleasure! I've been dying to do it for years!" Her lips drew back from her teeth, baring them like fangs, as she made for the door, where she turned, hand on the knob. "Come on then! Let's see what she has to say after I've said my piece."

But Brad did not move.

"Can't do it, can you? Too scared, aren't you? Haven't the nerve to look at those feet of clay? She's *all* clay, you stupid bastard! So are you! She *made* you, shaped you with her own hands. Look at yourself!" Caroline darted forward to seize his arm, drag him to the mirror over the credenza. "Go on—take a look at yourself. That's not your reflection, it's your mother's. She owns your soul; what are you going to do when she finally gets around to demanding your body too?"

With a cry Brad swung round violently, his hands going for her throat. "Shut up! Shut up, you evil bitch!"

Tearing at his tightening hands: "Go on!" Caroline rasped from a rapidly reddening face. "Squeeze me to death as you are being squeezed to death. And thank your mother for that too!"

He let her go so suddenly that she fell to the floor. The next minute he was gone. She heard his feet taking the stairs two at a time. Then the front door slammed.

She was crawling across the floor on her hands and knees toward the credenza and the decanter when the door opened with a crash and her mother-in-law stood there, leaning heavily on her stick, her face livid, her eyes like Medusa's.

"You drunken slut! How dare you behave in such a manner in my house? Are you aware your hideous bawling can be heard all over it?"

" 'S'bout time," Caroline slurred. "Time somebody tol' truth 'round here . . ." She fell back on the floor, out cold.

Her mother-in-law lifted her stick, brought it down hard on the almost exposed breasts revealed by the pull of Caroline's dress caught around her knees. She was lifting it again when she felt her arm held, heard her elder daughter's voice say in shocked tones: "For God's sake, Mother!"

"Where is my son?" Lady Hester demanded. "Was that he who went out just now?"

"I think so."

"Then go and find him—go on! Find him, I say!"

Abby did not move. "No, Mother."

"Did you hear what I said?"

"Loud and clear and I'm still not going. I heard it all too. Brad needs to be left alone for a while. He'll come back when he's good and ready."

Lady Hester's face was unbelievable. "How dare you?" she hissed, face thrust toward her daughter. "You will do as you are told!"

"I will not," Abby returned immovably. "It's too late, Mother. Those are your skeletons all over the floor. You'll have to clear up the mess."

She brushed past her mother, bent down and with her considerable strength heaved Caroline up from the floor, dropped her onto the bed, covered her with the quilt.

"I want that slut out of my house!" her mother raved. "Now, this instant! She is forbidden it and any other house of mine in future! She is forbidden this family! Stupid, barren, drunken nobody!"

"Mother, the horse is gone," Abby told her firmly, taking her arm, trying to draw her from the doorway. Lady Hester shook it off.

"Unhand me! You are no daughter of mine! Now, when I need your help, you have refused it! I will not forget this, Abigail!"

Abby's face convulsed for an instant, then she said in a colorless voice: "I have my own memories, Mother. Now come along and I'll see you to bed. Where is Rose?"

"Do not touch me! I am not going to bed. I shall go downstairs and wait for my son!"

"Mother, you can't get down the stairs by yourself."

"I will get down them if I have to crawl down them backwards!"

Limping heavily, grimly clutching her stick, Lady Hester began a slow progress toward the stairs. With a sigh Abby followed her: "Here. Lean on me."

From their open bedroom doors, eyes popping, in various stages of undress, the other members of the family watched in silence. Then just as silently they retreated to the safety of their bedrooms.

"Now you've done it!" Drexel Adams said to his wife sibilantly.

Bitsy's face was alight with unholy glee. "Serve him right!" she said with hatred. "I hope he is going through the fires of hell!"

But her hand was trembling as she began to smear her face with makeup remover.

BRAD RAN. When he ran out of breath he found himself down by the pond. Gasping, a stitch in his side, he collapsed onto a bench and put his head in his hands, his ears resounding with Caroline's taunting, jeering words.

It could not be! It was just not possible! His mother's—creature? Lied to, manipulated, brainwashed into unquestioning obedience? No, it was all lies, lies! His mother loved him! Had she not demonstrated that time after time after time? Told him too? "Nobody will ever love you as I love you—nobody in this world. Between mother and son there is the unbreakable bond of flesh and blood; my flesh, my blood. I made you; created you inside my own body! Nourished and sustained your life with my own! Nobody can come between mother and son, nobody!"

He had adored her because he knew that whatever she did was because of the love she bore him. Love? he thought, recoiling. *Love?*

Had his mother set Julia up? Had that phone call been what Julia had told him it was? In his mind's eye, Julia's face appeared; bone white except for the red imprint of his hand, blood oozing from the cut corner of that luscious mouth; the gray eyes stunned and filled with pain. "Oh, Christ!" It burst from him like a bullet, and he took his head between his hands and squeezed, as though trying to extrude unbearable thoughts like toothpaste. "Your mother set me up." He heard Julia's voice.

Had she? Did the smiling, loving, radiantly limpid face conceal the blackest of hearts? No, no! It could not be! He would have known, seen, felt . . . His mother was truth itself! She *loved* him! Caroline was drunk, so drunk she had not known what she was saying. Yes, that was it. It was all a drunken fairy tale. It had to be. He could not live with it otherwise.

His own mother in love with him? Jesus Christ! His mind skittered away from that like water on a griddle, even as her voice echoed inside his head. "Nobody will ever love you as I love you, my son. Between mother and son there is a bond that can never be broken. You are a part of me. I created you, gave you your very life. We are flesh of the same flesh, blood of the same blood. We are a life, my darling. One heart, one mind, one life . . . I am yours and you are mine. Nobody can come between us, nobody, ever!"

Jesus Christ! No! *No!* He bellowed the word. It echoed across the silence of the pond, disturbing ducks that quacked and fluttered.

Lowering his head into his hands he sat there for a long time, awash with pain and shock, forcing himself to reach deep within himself, to bring up things long shut away and hopefully forgotten. He made himself examine them. He got up restlessly, paced back and forth, back and forth. He chained-smoked endlessly. He sat down, only to get up again, unable to sit still for the churning violence of his thoughts, moaning aloud, thrusting riving hands into his hair, biting his knuckles, standing still for long stretches of time, staring sightlessly.

The ground was littered with cigarette stubs, the sky paling at the edges with the first light of dawn, when finally he got up from the bench. He moved slowly, like an old man, his shoulders hunched, his head bowed, as he walked, like a man to the gallows, slowly back to the house.

HER MIND ABSORBED in matching colors, Julia reached out a hand to the phone and answered it automatically. "Julia Carey."

"Hello, Julia. It's Abby."

Julia jerked upright.

"I know," Abby followed into the ticking silence. "Surprise, surprise."

"Nothing the Bradfords do has the power to surprise me anymore," Julia answered, engaging her automatic pilot.

"Want to bet? I'm in California, Julia. To see you. Will you see me?"

"Why should I?"

"Because I need your help."

"In what way?"

"Brad."

This time the silence went on so long that Abby asked urgently: "Julia? You still there?"

"Why should I?" Julia asked.

"Because he's in deep trouble." When Julia did not answer: "To do with you," Abby went on.

"That is not possible anymore."

"If I tell you that the silver cord has snapped you will understand that it is."

"You are six years too late."

"Please, Julia. Don't brush me off. I've thrown up over almost three thousand miles. If I can overcome my fear of flying for him, can't you overcome your prejudices?"

"He gave them to me." Clearly and distinctly: "I want absolutely nothing to do with your mother, Abby—now, or ever."

"You won't have to. This is *because* of her, Julia. Brad has run away."

Julia quelled a hysterical laugh. "Abby, he's a grown man—"

"Now, he is."

There was another silence, which Abby broke by saying: "He's in pieces, Julia."

"I know the feeling."

Abby's sigh came down the phone like a gust of wind. "You have every right, of course."

Julia's ears pricked. "How would you know?"

"We all do—at long last. By that I mean it's all out in the open. Trouble is, Brad is drowning in it. There was a family row the other night—Mother's birthday dinner. Caroline—that's Brad's wife—lit the fuse and everything went up."

"Which still does not give him the right to come to me, of all people."

"That's why I'm here. To plead his case."

"You always did."

"He's my baby brother."

"Yes—baby!"

"Not anymore. Right now he's undergoing the hardest, cruelest maturing any man ever went through."

"Better late than never!" Julia countered angrily, her insides at a roiling boil, her hands, lips, everything—shaking.

"Please, Julia, if you would just see me, let me explain."

"You are six years too late."

Now Abby was silent. Her voice was heavy when she said: "Well, at least I tried."

[240]

Oh, God, Julia thought. "It's—that bad?" she asked.

"As bad as can be."

I knew it! I knew it! Julia was thinking, even as she said: "All right. When and where?"

"Oh, Julia—thank God! Your place and the sooner the better—like tonight?"

"All right. I usually get home about six-thirty. I live—"

"I know where you live," Abby interrupted. "Thanks, Julia. Thanks a heap. Six-thirty. See you then." She hung up.

Julia's own receiver was wet. Her whole body was soaked in perspiration. She got up, went into her private washroom, ran cold water on her wrists, splashed her face. Her face was chalk-white, her eyes enormous. Why did you come back? she asked her reflection. Why *will* you allow people to persuade you their way? You knew it would mean trouble. Brad at outs with his mother? Never! That was not possible! There must indeed have been an earthquake. No wonder the floor under her feet was heaving.

She was fit for nothing for the rest of the afternoon; finally wrote it off and left the office at five. She was tense, nervous, in anticipatory dread. This was what she had feared; that in spite of her being three thousand miles away, the web Lady Hester Bradford spun would spread even to California to trap her once more in its sticky strands.

SHE HAD NOT LONG entered the house before the phone rang. It was Marcus. "Hey, what's this, playing hookie?"

"Something came up."

"Like what?"

"Something personal."

"Can I help?"

"No."

"You all right? You sound—uptight."

"I'm fine."

"Dinner tonight?"

"No. I—I can't."

"The something personal?"

"Yes."

"Okay, so don't tell me. I'll see you later on, okay?"

"Yes."

She realized her hand was trembling as she replaced the receiver. Jenny, she thought. I'll spend more time with Jenny.

She was playing a game of tiddledywinks, Jenny already bathed and in her nightie and Bugs Bunny dressing gown when Ito came to announce: "Lady here say she come see you. Missus Amolly."

Jenny giggled. She loved Ito's inability to pronounce the letter *r*.

"I'll be right down," Julia said.

"But we haven't finished the game," protested Jenny.

"You have supper, then I'll come back and we'll finish it."

"Promise—cross your heart and hope to die?"

Julia did so.

Jenny relaxed. She knew her mother never broke a promise once given.

Abby was standing in the living room, an expression of horror mixed with disbelief on her face, turned when she heard Julia coming. "Scheherezade, I presume?" she asked, poker-faced. Julia burst out laughing and the two women went toward each other, embraced. "Good to see you, Julia," Abby said, eyes suspiciously bright. "At that, you look the same. How *do* you do it? Never so much as an eyelash out of place!"

Her own linen shirtwaist was badly creased, and she had a run in one nylon, but as she absentmindedly shoved her hair behind her ears in the old way Julia felt a sudden rush of affection. She had always liked Abby.

"It's been a long time," Abby said on a sigh. "Far too long . . ." Then, in her old direct way: "Friends?"

"Friends."

"Would you like a drink?" Julia asked.

"Would I!"

As Julia went to the ornate cabinet that served as a bar: "I can see you are doing well," Abby said politely.

"It is a bit Richard Burton," Julia laughed. "But I only rent it—and if I had my way, that's what I'd do with it—a large one from top to bottom!"

Abby giggled. "Oh, Julia, it is *so* good to see you! You haven't changed a bit."

"I'm six years older."

"Aren't we all." Abby took her glass. "You remembered!" she said, touched, of her Tom Collins.

"My brief time with the Bradfords is etched on my memory in acid."

"Ouch!"

Julia sat down on the Arabian Nights–style divan, turning to face her visitor.

"You said you had things to tell me," she prompted.

[242]

Abby took a refreshing pull at her glass. "Well, as I said, it was Mother's birthday dinner, and my dear sister Bitsy had brought along her long spoon . . ."

Julia listened in rapidly increasing but silent dismay as Abby recounted the horrors of the celebration that had turned into a wake.

"It was ghastly," Abby shuddered. "Caroline could be heard all over the house. Brad too. It left him in ribbons."

To her horror, Julia saw Abby's eyes fill with tears, watched her grope for a handkerchief—a man's and grubby—in her shirtwaist pocket. "Oh, Abby . . . Abby . . ." she exclaimed in distress.

"If you had seen him, Julia. He came to me afterward—hours afterward—as I knew he would; he always did come to me, you see, if he was in Dutch with Mother. Big sister Abby." She wiped her eyes. "But this time—this time"—Abby sobbed—"he looked like a man who'd been through every anteroom in hell looking for the devil, then finally found him by looking into a mirror."

Julia closed her eyes.

"It had to come someday, but not this way; not so violently or cruelly. It has smashed him, Julia." Abby's sobs were gouts of grief. "I know he's had the longest childhood in history, but what a way to have to grow up."

"What is it you want of me?" Julia asked.

"Would you see him—talk to him—tell him your side of things? He's trying to put the pieces together again so as to confront Mother but to do that he has to be in possession of the truth and nothing but, you understand? I know Caroline told him and he's talked to me, but"—again Abby wiped her eyes, blew her nose soundly—"this is Mother, and you know how he adored her. To find out that the one person you believe is one hundred percent perfect is a mass of flaws—and hideous ones at that—is hard to take. He *hates* himself—hates her—and yet at the same time still has that enormous reservoir of love. He's terrified to confirm what he suspects as truth but he knows he must before he can do anything about it all. Honestly, Julia, he is on the rack."

"Where is he?" Julia interrupted, unable to take much more of this.

"I don't know. After he talked to me he left the farm but he wouldn't tell me where he was going; that way I could tell Mother the truth when I said I didn't know . . . because if she thought I did she'd create merry hell till I told her. He's in touch by phone and it was when he called me night before last that he asked me to contact you."

"Why me?"

"Because of Paris. That phone call; what he did to you. That's

[243]

tearing him apart too. He needs to know the truth of that particular event."

"I did tell him the truth."

"But that was when Mother's was the only one he believed."

Julia twisted her glass around and around. "It would be like kicking him when he's down," she said reluctantly.

"He feels he needs to be punished." Abby's voice was acrid. "He knows he has to go through the fire because it is the only way out."

"He *has* changed," Julia said.

"I told you; you wouldn't recognize him!"

Julia sought support in her drink. "How did Brad know I was in California before Bitsy told him?"

"He saw you," Abby answered bluntly. "In the lobby court of the Century Plaza one night about ten days ago."

Julia's eyes were wide with shock.

"He had you investigated," Abby went on, hewing to truth. "That's how he found out about Jenny."

Julia's face turned to stone. "We will leave Jenny out of this," she said.

"But—Mother *knows!*" Abby said.

"And lied. I warn you, Abby: if she so much as looks in Jenny's direction I'll have her! I'm not the nobody I was before. I have money and power and my own sphere of influence. If she wants skeletons by God I can show her such a heap of bones—"

"As God is my witness she knows nothing about me being here—or where Brad is or anything. She's going crazy, driving us all up the wall with her ranting and raving. Brad has vanished and she can't stand that!"

"How do you know she hasn't got a tail on *you?*" Julia asked brutally.

"Brad warned me about that so I was careful. She thinks I'm in Wyoming looking at a horse. As it was I took the roundabout way here. Flew to Casper and then on to Chicago and then here. I kid you not, Julia; it took a handful of Librium and two double scotches to get me on those planes."

Julia pressed Abby's hands.

"Tell him the truth, Julia—what really happened in Paris. As a matter of fact, what did really happen?"

Julia considered her unseeingly for a moment and then repeated—verbatim because those particular conversations *were* etched in acid—what she had been instructed to do about the twelve fauteuils; the subsequent conversation following her acquisition of them.

[244]

"It was like those conversations you see in plays and films; you know, you hear only what the actor is saying; what he is supposed to be hearing you have to imagine. That was the way it was. Nothing I said came back at me with any sense. I thought it was a bad line."

"No," Abby said slowly. "It *was* a scene from a play. Mother even had the perfect audience: Bitsy." Her sigh was heavy. "You were set up, all right. Caroline was telling the truth."

"But how would she *know?*"

A shrug. "She and Mother were in cahoots, weren't they? She knew Mother had gotten rid of you." She sighed again, shook her head. "It's a mess."

"And none of *my* so-called making this time. Your mother can go through my life with bloodhounds, she'll still find nothing she can use against me."

Abby stared into her empty glass. "You are not living with Marcus Levin, then?"

Julia set down her own glass with a crack that made Abby flinch. "I told you—"

"Brad had you investigated . . ." Red-faced: "Seeing you again set off some sort of chain reaction. He asked me to find out the truth from you—"

"He has the use of a bedroom, no more—and not mine! This is an isolated house, and California being what it is, he offered himself as resident man about the house and it seemed like a good idea. That is all —and I mean all!"

"How did you meet him?" Abby asked, vastly relieved but still curious.

Julia explained.

"It is due in no small measure to him that I've made it this far. He's dedicated to the pursuit of the dollar and what I earn he gets his share of."

"Yes," Abby said on a smile. "Marcus always did like money."

Something in the quality of the silence brought her back to the present with a guilty start. One look at Julia's face and she made one of her own. "Oh, shit!"

"You *know* Marcus?"

Uneasily: "He used to work for Mother—ten, twelve years ago."

"What?" Julia rose, even as her voice did.

"Now, Julia—"

"Used to, you said."

"She fired him. He got caught with his hand in the till."

"Marcus!"

"His is an expensive habit. He's a high roller, as they say."

"Marcus gambles!"

"Oh, now you must know he'd bet on the time of day!"

"I know he likes the horses and cards—but—" Julia's agitation had her pacing the room. "Oh, my God!" she said in a voice that bled.

"Now wait a minute—" Abby rose, put out a restraining hand.

"If he's a gambler—and a loser—where, then, did he get the money to back me? It cost thousands to set me up. I'll tell you where he got that money. From your bloody mother."

"You are jumping to conclusions—"

"Did he go to jail for stealing?"

"Nooo . . . Mother wouldn't prosecute. She liked him; he was the only one who would stand up to her—"

"You see!" Julia's voice was a wound. "She set me up again! Every now and then Marcus disappears for a few days; business, he says, but it is always in America." She fixed Abby with eyes that burned. "He comes back to report to your mother. Every last thing I've done, said; who I've seen. He's your mother's spy." Julia fell onto a couch. "That's why he goes back to America at regular intervals. To report to her!" Julia's sense of betrayal was making her feel actual nausea. "He's a fink —a dirty, double-crossing, lying, cheating fink! Of all the people in the world I would have trusted—I did trust!—Marcus Levin!" She closed her eyes prayerfully. *"Thank God* I didn't ever let him get me to bed!"

"Now hold on there." Abby labored gallantly to stanch the wound in Julia's amour propre. "You are supposing to hell and gone. Where is your proof?"

"I don't need proof! I can spot your mother's fine Italian hand a mile away. She set me up with Marcus because of Jenny; to get the goods on me as an unfit mother. That's why she denied her paternity to Brad; it did not suit her that he should know then—not until she could prise Jenny away from me and hand her to him, all nice and shining. 'Look, darling, what a lovely surprise Mother has for you!' " Julia's voice was savage.

"Then you have to tell Brad," Abby said decidedly. "This is the sort of thing he needs to know—every rotten thing Mother has done or was prepared to do in pursuit of her own ends—not his."

"Once I've told Marcus I'll be happy to tell Brad anything he wants to know!"

"No!" Abby's forcible command stopped Julia in full tirade. "Tell him and he will know his cover is blown, which will be reported back to

Mother at once! No; Marcus must not suspect anything. We have to be careful, Julia; not make two and two add up to anything except four."

"But it all fits! Don't you see? It's all a piece! He came to me only a few months after Paris! Dear God, why didn't I *twig*? She played me for a dumb fool again!"

"Mother thinks everybody but her is a fool," Abby said unemotionally. "Just don't fool Brad is all I am asking."

"Give me the chance and I'll blow his ears off!" Julia promised recklessly.

"Where and when?"

Julia was taken aback; she had not expected such a prompt response.

"He told me to tell you he would meet you any place, anytime you care to mention."

Julia cursed her too-ready tongue, but, "I have to be in San Francisco next Thursday," she said reluctantly. "If he could meet me—"

"He will."

"I shall be staying overnight at the Hyatt Regency. If he'd like to meet me there—"

"Anywhere."

"Tell him in the lobby—by that big pool. Six o'clock Friday night."

"Right." Abby repeated it. "Six o'clock in the lobby of the Hyatt Regency on Friday night." Her smile penetrated Julia's red mist of rage, wrung her heart.

"Thank you," she said.

"Mummy!" An aggrieved voice made them both look up at the balcony above the stairs. Jenny stood there. "I waited and waited and Barbara says it will be bedtime soon."

"Sorry, darling. I'm coming now."

But Jenny was looking at Abby. "Hello," she said in her frank, Bradford way. "Who are you?"

"An old friend of your mummy's. Come and say hello," Abby smiled. With alacrity, Jenny was down the stairs, trotting up to Abby with total lack of shyness and stunning self-possession. "How do you do," she said politely, holding out a hand as she had been taught.

"Much better for seeing you," Abby returned promptly. "My, but you are a big girl for what—five, is it?"

"I shall be six next May," Jenny corrected kindly. Her smile made Abby catch her breath; she had seen it on her brother's face so many times. "I'm big for my age." Her calm aplomb was pure Hester Bradford.

Abby's face was a study, especially when Jenny went on candidly: "You are big too, aren't you?"

"Jenny!" Julia warned, but on a bitten lip.

"Always was," Abby answered cheerfully.

Barbara appeared at the top of the stairs.

"Run along, darling. I'll be up in five minutes—promise."

"You said that before," Jenny answered, unimpressed.

"We got to talking," Abby apologized humbly. "You know how it is with old friends."

Jenny considered her. "Yes, you are old, aren't you?" she said.

Abby put up a hand, coughed into it.

When she could control her voice, "Up you go, darling. But say good night to Mrs. Amory first," Julia said.

"Ito calls you Mrs. Amolly," Jenny said in a giggle.

"I've been called worse," Abby told her serenely, "Do I get a good-bye kiss?"

Jenny looked at her mother, who said: "That would be nice."

Jenny went forward as Abby bent down from her considerable height and kissed the proffered cheek.

"You know," Abby said, reaching for her handbag, "when I was a little girl and I used to go to England to visit relatives, I had an uncle who always gave me a crisp new five-pound note. Well, I don't have one of them but I do have a nice crisp ten-dollar bill. That's about five pounds. Would you mind if I gave it to you?" Once again Jenny looked at her mother, who nodded slightly.

"Oh, thank you," she said in awe, holding it in both hands. Then turning she ran up the stairs to Barbara, waving it. "Look, Barbara, the lady has given me ten dollars—and it's worth five pounds. Isn't she a kind lady?"

They heard her voice disappearing along the corridor, detailing how she intended to spend it.

"Bradford, through and through," pronounced Abby proudly. "And not only to look at, either." On a headshake: "Thank God Bitsy's bosom bow only got to glimpse her." She turned to Julia, embraced her again. "You've turned up trumps again, Julia. Already you've shed a lot of light in dark corners. I'm sure Brad will be able to see his way once he has talked to you. If he can't make Friday I'll call you; if you don't hear it's on, okay?"

Julia nodded.

"And don't fret yourself to a frazzle meanwhile. You know better

[248]

than to voice your suspicions." Placing a finger to her lips: "Mum's the word, as you English say."

Julia's face trembled, then broke, and at the same instant, realizing what she had said, Abby exploded into laughter. They held on to each other while they laughed, on the edge of hysteria. Wiping her eyes with her already wet handkerchief: "Thank God we can laugh," Abby said feelingly. "It's a hell of a sight better than crying." With a last quick hug she turned and set sail for the door.

Julia tossed and turned all night. She felt riven, not only by what had happened to Brad but by the brutal shock of Marcus's perfidy. That he should have been lying to her from the word go left her shattered. She had liked him, trusted him, regarded him as her friend. Thank God she had not given him the tumble he had never ceased to try for. Under orders, of course. Bastard! she thought vehemently. Then: Bitch! She felt bruised, battered, her pride in ruins. Truth to tell, she was hard put to decide which troubled her more: Brad or Marcus. At least, she thought justifyingly, Brad never deliberately lied to me; just didn't tell me the truth, that's all. Which brought her slam bang up against how he must be feeling right now, having to cope with his mother's treachery, even as she was having to cope with that of Marcus. And for the first time, through her own anguish and pain, she began to perceive that of another.

Sleep was out of the question. She got up, put on a robe and went down to the kitchen to make coffee, sat there until the sun came up, thinking.

Marcus called next morning to say he would be tied up for the next couple of days. "A movie deal with my singer. Worth umpteen zeroes on a contract."

"And don't you just love those!"

"I haven't heard you complaining about the ones on your contracts."

"I'm not." Careful, thought Julia.

"Call you in a couple of days."

"Do that," Julia agreed, thinking of the names she would call him— eventually.

But he called her on Thursday morning to say he had to fly back East.

"Something up?" Julia asked casually, every muscle tensed.

"Nothing I can't handle but I've got to be there to do it."

"Trouble?" I hope, Julia thought.

"Oh, money hassles, you know."

Which means you are being called to account, Julia thought.

"You don't have any problems, do you?" Marcus went on.

"Like you, none I can't handle," Julia answered, vowing silently to do so, and in as painful a manner as possible.

"Call you when I get back, okay?"

"I shall count the hours."

He had gone to hear His Master's Voice; every instinct quivered with certainty. Brad's disappearance must have driven Lady Hester to extreme measures. Last-minute instructions, perhaps? Julia had these feelings from time to time. She did not know where they came from but she knew that they were invariably right. So she always obeyed them. Now, before leaving for San Francisco, she gave Barbara strict instructions as to Jenny.

Friday was hopeless. Brad and their forthcoming confrontation simmered below consciousness all day while she visited furniture galleries, comparing and struggling to decide. Usually she loved browsing; now she could not stop fidgeting, checking her watch, her nervousness increasing with the day. At four-thirty she could take no more; went back to the Hyatt to prepare herself. She made herself take a long, leisurely bath, hoping it would relax her, liberally scenting it with oil (she would wear the matching perfume later).

For some (probably perverse) reason she had decided to wear black. Tit for tat and Drexel Adams's snide remark the night she had first met Lady Hester, but once it was on she felt doubt creep in. Would Brad think she was in mourning? For him? For their marriage? But black had always suited her; made her skin pearly, her hair flame. And Brad had always liked her in black . . . I'm damned if I do and damned if I don't, she thought frustratedly. Oh, the hell with it! She kept it on. And was glad when she surveyed her finished reflection. The dress was a Hana Morae: black silk crepe. A shoestring strapped slip under a blouson of sheer silk chiffon, tying at the waist with a rouleau of black satin. With it, she wore ten-denier nylons with seams—also black because Brad had always liked her to wear black stockings with suspenders—and stilt-heeled strappy sandals which tied at the ankles in bows. A small clutch bag, pearls in her ears, face made up to the nth degree, hair upswept but for fronds at nape and brow, a final subtle spraying of "Y" and she was ready. She was aware, on a deeper level, that there was an element of punishment in her presentation of herself as of a gift: but not for him. He would be able to look only. And maybe realize what he had thrown away? But she still called room service and ordered a double whiskey sour.

6

game. animal or bird that is hunted; quarry, fair g. that which can be legitimately hunted or attacked

BRAD HAD STATIONED HIMSELF at one corner of the enormous pool, where the water had the appearance of cellophane, falling soundlessly over the rounded edges into the profusion of greenery below. From where he stood he had a clear view of the elevators, glass baubles which slid, like the marker on a slide rule, up and down the sheer walls of the atrium. As always, the huge area was ababble with noise, though he heard none of it: two orchestras vying with each other, the clatter of crockery and cutlery from the two restaurants, the clink of glass and ice from the bars, the chatter of voices, a woman's laughter. Everything in him was concentrated on watching and waiting.

He saw her the moment she stepped from the elevator, the men standing aside to watch her as she did. She came toward him with that long-legged, head-up, shoulders-back walk he knew so well; the one that meant she was oblivious to the stares, the smiles, the come-ons. She was wearing what he now thought of as her "public face"; the one which precluded any chance of an opening: aloof, remote, as well chilled as a good martini.

When he stepped out of the overhanging greenery to confront her she stopped dead in her tracks and although she made no sound he saw her eyes, as large and as smokily gray as ever, widen, the black pupils dilate. For a moment they stared deep into one another and then he heard himself say: "Hello, Julia. It's been a long time." She nodded, and he saw her swallow. She was as nervous as he was, he realized. And it made him feel better.

"It was good of you to come," he went on.

She nodded.

"Thank you."

Still she said nothing, stood while he let his eyes rove over her lingeringly; as always, they felt like fingers. She was as tight as a clenched fist.

"You haven't changed," he said at last, and wonderingly.

You have! thought Julia, dismayed. He was thirty-six now, looked forty-five. The lines of wit and impudence were now grooves; there was a delta of others around the chiseled mouth, now tight with strain, and the sea-change eyes were dull, as if they needed cleaning.

And his diffidence was new when he said: "I thought—a drink before dinner?"

"A drink, yes. I can't make dinner, I'm afraid. I have an eight-thirty plane to catch."

"Oh." He looked disappointed, sounded it too, so much so that Julia found herself saying:

"Why don't we go up to the revolving restaurant up top? I love the view of the city from there."

"Fine."

He did not take her arm as they walked back to the elevators, and kept well away from her. This time around he made no effort to imprint himself on her consciousness; was careful not to crowd her space.

In the dim, crowded lobby of the restaurant foyer a man inquired whether it was cocktails or dinner, and on being told it was cocktails summoned a waitress who led them to a table by the wall which, as they seated themselves, one on either side, was sliding by slowly.

"Isn't it a fantastic view?" Julia exclaimed. "I always come here whenever I'm in San Francisco. I only wish I were based here instead of Los Angeles." She made a face. "Forty suburbs in search of a city."

She was aware she was chattering almost wildly, making frantic conversation, thoroughly overset by this totally strange yet oh so familiar man.

"Everybody leaves their heart in San Francisco," Brad said dryly. "You are no exception—in that respect, anyway."

Julia rushed to plug that gap. "You know it well?"

"Well enough. I have a lot of friends here."

She quelled the impulse to ask if this was where he was staying—hiding from his mother—but she felt oddly shy, found it hard to meet directly those somehow muddy eyes which once had shone like the sun on the sea. She knew him better than she had ever known any man, and yet this man she did not know at all. He had indeed changed, and not only in looks. He was so much older. Yes, that was it. That Brad had been a boy; this one was a man. As Abby said, he had just undergone the most painful maturing anyone could undergo. It showed. Once again she felt the recrudescence of the pain she had felt sitting at the kitchen table the other night: her own sense of betrayal and loss but intensified at least one thousand times. Marcus had been a friend only; Brad had been betrayed by his own mother.

The silence lengthened, moved from hesitancy into awkwardness. The waitress saved it. Brad ordered a Jack Daniel's and Julia a Mai'tai. "The best I've tasted," she told him.

"You never were much of a drinker."

"I still don't—but I've become hooked on Mai'tais."

Brad got out his cigarettes. "And I still don't smoke," Julia said, noticing that when he lit his, his fingers were yellow with nicotine. She also noticed his slight tremor.

He noticed her noticing.

"It isn't easy, is it?"

"No." Glad to be honest, Julia felt her uptightness oozing away.

"I feel we are talking across the Grand Canyon instead of a small table."

"Six years would stretch that far, I suppose."

"So would my nerves."

That was better; that was the Brad she remembered.

"It has taken all I have to face you again after what I did." The tremor was in his voice now; that tiny vibrato which she knew of old indicated some inner uncertainty. And he was playing with his lighter, tossing it up and down, turning it around and around. With a stab, Julia realized she had been so intent on her own feelings she had not really given any time to his. The very thought had the effect of bringing him closer, as though under a giant zoom lens: she saw him writ plain:

anxiety, fear, guilt and all. Yes, he had grown up. Peter Pan had finally left never-never land and was having a hard time of it in the real world.

"Abby told you about—everything?" he asked finally.

"Yes."

There was another pause while he stared out of the window, but with a gaze that saw inward rather than the view.

"I had it coming, of course. And for a long time. I was the one who shoved it under the carpet after all. God knows how I didn't trip over the pile it made before now." He drew fiercely on his cigarette. "It's probably too late now, to do any good, but for what it is worth, I am sorry, Julia. Will you believe that? It's not much of a word but it's the way I feel right now; desperately sorry. You probably think I deserve all that's come to me—and I do—but"—a deep breath—"I need a helping hand right now and yours always was a strong one."

He was speaking words with the care of one who was afraid they would break in his mouth, but it was his honesty which impelled Julia to say gently and—she realized with astonishment—truthfully: "I didn't come here to pass judgment on you, Brad. I came because Abby said you needed my help."

He drew back to allow the waitress to serve the drinks. When she had gone: "Even so, after all I did to you it was kind of you to agree to do so." Pause. "I have no right to expect consideration of my feelings from you."

Julia moved her shoulders awkwardly. "You had—reasons."

"True, but it is not the Sins of the Mothers that are at issue here; it is the Sins of the Perennial Child." Julia swallowed hard as he went on: "You never did go a bundle on forgiveness, as I recall; one chance was all you gave, but if you can find it in your heart—"

"What exactly is it you want from me?" Julia interrupted, not able to take much more of this.

"Your side of things—to check it against my own."

"For what—flaws?"

His flush made Julia kick herself mentally, resolve to bridle her ready tongue.

"Yes, but not yours."

"All right. Where shall I begin?"

"Where it all ended. Paris. Would you tell me what Mother actually said to you; from that first phone call."

Once again Julia told her story. He listened silently, but she saw his hands, as he stubbed out his cigarette, were grinding it to shreds.

"Thank you," he said colorlessly, when she had finished. Then he raised his eyes to hers. They made her clench her hands. "Forgive me, Julia. I bought what happened to me; I never meant to buy enough for two."

Once again, the painful honesty in those eyes drove Julia to say: "It wasn't all your fault. I was warned about your mother from the start."

"I should have listened to you. Sally Armbruster, wasn't it?"

"Yes. That Sunday she asked us round for drinks. She told me your mother would do for any woman who threatened to take you from her. I thought she was just showing jealousy; she was still in love with you, that was obvious. Yet she also hated you for not loving her. Anyway, I told myself it was pure spite. But afterwards . . ." Sad with lost chances: "If only you had told me."

"What? That I was in emotional hock to my mother so deep I was drowning?" He downed his drink in a gulp. "You are forgetting. I was brought up in the Faith."

"Which you have now lost?"

"Along with everything else—not that I am looking for a replacement; don't think that. How can you believe in anything if you first of all don't believe in yourself? What I would like to explain to you, though, if you will let me, is how I came to acquire it."

Hesitantly: "I think I already know—now."

Reading her eyes, her voice, with his new understanding: "Jenny?"

"Yes." Another hesitation, "About Jenny—"

"You had every right to keep her hidden. With a mother like mine . . . But tell me how she caused you to understand."

"Being a mother. I had never had one, and thus had no experience by which to judge, compare—most of all measure. My aunt shouldered a responsibility in me, no more. I was well fed, well dressed, reasonably well educated. What she never gave me was love. I had to have Jenny to understand what I had missed."

"Then you will understand when I say that from the day I was born my mother had me in thrall; always a shining light to me. Mother Incarnate. Perfect in every way. She was my life, my world . . . Wherever I turned she was there. Loving me, protecting me, helping me. She was willing to risk her life for mine, had made it clear she would do it again—and willingly. Told me again and again there was nothing she would not do for me." Brad paused, a look on his face which made Julia avert her eyes from its unbearable emotion.

"That kind of love is—insidious." Staring blindly into his glass. "To discover that it was also—twisted, thwarted, perverted—even sick—is all but impossible to accept. Yet I have to accept that it was because of

[255]

that love she did the most terrible things—and in its name." Voice, eyes were stone. Julia turned her own eyes to the window: they stung, hotly.

"I have to accept that my mother, whom I thought beyond fear, was so terrified of losing me that she would go to any lengths, commit any act, to keep me." This time he lifted his glass and looked around for the waitress. "But what is worst of all is that deep down, where I would not have to face it, I knew it; used that same love for my own ends." This time the silence went on so long that Julia had to turn her head to look at him, blinking to disperse tears, swallowing hard to rid herself of the lump in her throat. "You had me pegged right from the start: little boy lost running wild and spoiled rotten, confident that his mother would pay for any breakages." Acrid with bitter regret: "I even used you. You, in whom I thought I had found the knife that would cut me free. It was the truth I told you when I said I needed you. My mistake was in not telling you why."

Julia bent her head to her straw; the bleak bitterness, the raw pain of realization were too much for her.

"I know I said truth between us, but what I meant was your truth; I was used to dealing only in self-deceiving lies. You, on the other hand, were painfully honest. I should have known—*known*—that you were telling me the truth when you said Chambrun was not your lover; but I was not thinking straight, not thinking at all, only feeling."

"You always were the one who felt," Julia acknowledged. "I was the one who thought. Far too much and to obsession. Always rationalizing and analyzing, even my love for you."

"I know. I used to see you watching me sometimes, with such a strange expression on your face. As though you were thinking: What am I *doing* here?"

"You see," Julia said, bleak herself now. "I told you it was not all your fault."

"But you didn't know about love, did you?"

"No. I'd never had any."

"Which is probably why you couldn't handle mine."

Julia opened her mouth, closed it again.

"There were times," Brad went on, "when I had the feeling you wished yourself anywhere but with me; regretted marrying me, regarded it as an aberration; a mistake made in the heat of the moment." Pause. "And we did create some heat, didn't we?"

Throat constricted, Julia could only nod.

"Is that how you felt?" He knew but he wanted her confirmation.

[256]

"Yes. Dead set on finding a rational explanation for something wholly irrational. I wouldn't accept that there was not a reason; tore myself to shreds trying to find one." She looked straight into his eyes. "That's why I relegated you. I felt safe in my work, whereas, with you— around you—I became someone I didn't know; did things I believed were out of character. They weren't, of course; only parts of a character I refused to acknowledge."

Still holding her eyes: "You have learned from your mistakes, then, if you know enough to recognize them."

"I hope so."

With an effort she tore her eyes from his, bent her head to her straw again.

"Abby tells me you have your own business now," Brad said, changing the subject. That brought Julia's head up. "I know you had me investigated," she said flatly.

His unwontedly pale skin flushed.

"So you will know I am now Julia Carey (Design) Limited, with a full commission book and just started on my biggest job yet."

"You deserve to do well. I always knew you had the capability." Now he paused. "And Marcus Levin? Where does he fit in?"

"Not in my bed!"

Red ran under his skin like flame. "I didn't mean—"

"Then don't assume."

"I wasn't," he said quietly. "It's just that I know him."

"Did Abby tell you anything about him?"

"Only that you and he had a business relationship."

"He backed me," Julia said. "With your mother's money."

She saw the dulled eyes flicker, as though pain had stabbed. "Tell me."

She did. "You have no actual proof of all this?" he asked, as he lit another cigarette, and this time the tremor was pronounced.

"I don't need proof. I *know*."

"Have you said anything to him?"

"No. Abby said I should tell you."

"I'm glad you did." Once again eyes met, held. "I'm sorry."

She knew what he meant. "I thought he was my friend. He came along at a time when—I know now—I needed one. He somehow—gave me back to myself as a worker. I trusted him—" In spite of herself her voice broke.

"He is not a trustworthy man. This time *I* know."

"So do I. A Judas."

"Which makes me what—the Prodigal Son?"

"I've told you; I have my own blame to bear. If I had heeded the warning I was given—"

"Sally had good reasons. I did her wrong too. She did want to marry me, but I didn't want to marry her. She was crowding me . . . so I went to Mother. Armbrusters make electronic components for us; we are seventy percent of their business. Mother told Roger Armbruster that either he pulled Sally off or she would cancel their contract." His eyes were dark. "You see the sort of thing I could never tell you."

"I still wish you had tried. Then maybe I could have been honest about myself. Like admitting I was a fake. What you thought I was and what I really was, was a case of never the twain. I was terrified to commit myself, to—give myself wholly. Being alone was no hardship; it was security. Nobody could get at me then. Except you did, in a way which terrified me, because you turned me into a woman I did not know, could not deal with—worse, could not control. That is why I kept searching for a rational explanation. I was always very good at the practicalities of life; useless when it came to emotions. They frightened me. Like the relationship you had with your mother. I knew it was—not right, but I was scared to probe too deeply. Afraid of what I would find out. I told myself that it was best left alone—which shows I had no confidence that anything I did would still leave our marriage unshaken. And it relieved me of the responsibility of being the one . . . What I was," Julia finished, staring unflinchingly at Chris's unflattering but deadly accurate portrait, "was an emotional coward."

Just as unflinchingly she made her own penance. "You are not the only one to have to say I'm sorry."

As they stared deep into each other's eyes, Julia knew that he knew, even as she did, that the war was over, even though battle was still to be joined. "Your mother knew what I was; had she not she would not have been able to do what she did. Yes, she knew me, all right, better than I did myself."

"You've been in the wilderness too," Brad said.

Julia looked back over the past six successful, brightly burnished, Jenny-filled years yet could still answer truthfully: "Yes."

"You *have* changed," Brad said.

"I hope so."

Sensitive now, in his own pain, he gently steered her to safer ground. "Tell me about Jenny. What's she like?"

"You."

"Me!"

"Not just to look at. I see you in her—oh, in so many ways. She is quicksilver, as you used to be; up one minute, down the next, restless, gay, moody, enchanting, infuriating—but I wouldn't change her for the world; she *is* my world."

"Perhaps, someday—you'd let me see her."

"Would Sunday be all right?"

Brad stared.

"We are going to Disneyland. Jenny firmly believes it is where little girls go when they die. If you could just happen to be there about eleven A.M.—"

"Where?"

"Well, when you go through the turnstiles you come to a railway arch by the station; that brings you to the top of Main Street, U.S.A.—my favorite part of the place; about halfway down is a marvelous reproduction of a general store, circa 1910; on the corner outside is a flower stand where all the Disney animals congregate to have their photographs taken."

"I'll be there."

As Julia bent her head to her drink, shaken by the impact of the emotion in his eyes, he said: "That must be slush by now; let me order you a fresh one." When the waitress had gone: "That was as unexpected as it was welcome," Brad said. "Thank you."

"She is your daughter too," Julia said steadily. "I'd be a poor sort of a mother if I deprived her father of the pleasure of her company."

"I wouldn't have blamed you if you did, but be reassured: I won't let *my* mother harm a hair of her head."

"Just so long as you remember she not only knows about Jenny but I am sure she has her eye on her; that was the whole reason for Marcus. If she could prove me an unfit mother—living with a man who'd been fired for theft—"

"She won't," Brad said flatly. "From now on, my mother is out of it. I mean *out*, Julia."

"That's all very well; you may be painting her out of your picture but you know she never paints any but her own."

"You have every right to be suspicious, but things are different now. *I* am different." Once again, as though aware of the thin ice, "Tell me what I can expect come Sunday," he asked.

"Sore feet."

His laugh was a first.

"I mean it; she's tireless. Jenny could solve the world's energy problems."

"How do you cope, then?"

"A firm hand; two firm hands, mine and Barbara's."

"You always did believe in discipline; especially self-discipline."

"Look around you; undisciplined children grow up into undisciplined adults. Jenny has *not* been brought up according to Dr. Spock!"

"Mummy spank?" Brad asked with a crooked smile.

"When and if necessary. She's got a strong will; if I let her she'd take over, and while I don't go along one hundred percent with my aunt's dictum of children not being seen or heard, I don't think they should be pandered to or given free rein. I use a loose one, but I never let it out of *my* hands."

"Abby told me she is already a character."

Yes, your mother's, Julia thought, deciding that was something he would be better finding out for himself.

There was another silence while the fresh drinks were served. Feeling thirsty now, Julia drank deeply, only to almost choke when Brad asked: "You never married again. Why?"

"After a double fault?"

"Not all yours, surely."

"Even so." Her tone was dismissive, warned him off. She changed the subject. "What do you intend to do now?"

"Face Mother—once I've got my act together."

"I wish I could be in *that* audience."

His face hardened. "No. This will be a private performance."

"I'd love to show her what I can do, even if she did turn me down at my audition."

There was another laugh, and a genuine lightening of the opaque eyes. "I have to do it myself, Julia, so that I know I have done it—and alone."

"A sort of 'look, Ma—no hands'?"

This time his laugh was open and free. "Oh, Julia, it is so good to talk to you again." The laugh faded as eyes met, held, clung . . .

"Forgive me for hurting you so," Brad begged with a humility that undermined. "For believing my mother's lies when deep down I knew you were truth itself."

"Yes, you hurt me," Julia answered steadily. "So much so I thought I could never do more than hate you—but that was before I knew about Jenny and thus came to understand. Yes, I will forgive you, Brad, if you will forgive me."

[260]

"I would rather you forgave yourself; that is what comes hardest, I now know."

Julia was silenced. When she could: "You have indeed changed," she marveled.

"I indeed hope so."

Once again, as their eyes met, Julia thought that in his she could detect the light at the end of a long, dark tunnel.

"Julia . . ." Brad's voice was taut with emotion. "This has meant so much to me. How can I begin to tell you—"

"Brad? Brad Bradford?" The voice smashed the fragile web as Brad looked up and Julia followed. A glittering West Coast couple stood by their table, the man dressed in a young fashion that did not go with the old face: pale blue jacket, white striped trousers, silk shirt and knotted scarf, a lot of chains in between, gold bracelet, heavy rings. His wife was in tight black velvet trousers, a white silk chiffon frilled blouse through which it was obvious she was not wearing a bra. Her heavy breasts swung as she moved, bending to kiss Brad full on the mouth in a way that betrayed a knowing intimacy. "Jack and I thought we'd lost touch for ever!"

"Jack—Denise . . ." Brad's face broke into a flash of clamped-down anger; then he was smiling, but politely, quite without warmth.

"We thought it was you. Just had to come and make sure," said the man, Jack. He turned his eyes to Julia, assessing her with a connoisseur's eye, frankly sexual and openly lustful. "I see you can still pick 'em."

Julia murmured a greeting, somewhat embarrassed by their openly sexual dress, the laden-with-meaning appreciation of them both; the man to Julia, the woman to Brad.

"It's been an age," Denise was gushing. "Not since that open weekend in Palm Springs. Will I ever forget *that!*" Her eyes sparkled at Brad with the knowing complicity which gave Julia a deepening sense of unease.

"I'd rather you did," Brad said, in a way that erased the woman's smile.

She glanced swiftly at Julia and then said: "Oh-oh . . . Sorry, I guess we assumed you were still on the swing."

"Not anymore," Brad said.

"Pity," Jack said, obviously a tryer. "We came down to meet a couple we swung with in Malibu earlier this year but the wife's gone and got jaundice . . . left us at something of a loose end. Sure we can't interest you in a little party?"

"No, thanks," Brad said. His tone was cool, dismissive. "We were just leaving. A plane to catch."

Both expressed open disappointment. "We heard you'd sort of tapered off," Jack said disbelievingly. "Vibes bad? You have to be very careful, as *we* know."

Brad did not answer, only rose to his feet, peeling off bills which he tossed onto the table.

"Must you go?" Denise asked, laying a hand on his arm, pressing her breasts against it.

"Yes, we must." He reached down to take Julia's elbow, draw her purposefully to her feet. "Sorry," he finished, obviously not in the least so. "Neither of us is interested." He bore Julia away at the double.

"Sorry about that," he said as they waited for the elevator. "People —and things—I now look back on and cringe."

Julia said nothing, though she knew what had been talked about. Marcus had told her about swinging. He did it. "I think the nearest you get to it is what you call wife-swapping. Back home that is not so much as mentioned. The only thing that matters is that the vibes are right and the body matches up."

Now, Julia found she was conscious of the same distaste; felt the gulf yawning again. It was part of his past and obviously something he regretted, and she could not think why she felt so shocked; she of all women should know about Brad's compulsive sexuality. Yes, *then,* she reminded. This is now and he has changed—thank God. She found herself looking at the rapidly fading image of the old Brad with some- thing like relief. Looking at the new one, lines, strain, hesitation, un- certainty and all, she knew she preferred it one thousand percent to the old one. Swinging would have been part of his attempt to escape from his mother. So what if he had slept with Denise—who was so obviously very eager to repeat the experience. That was then. The old Brad would probably have accepted, expected maybe that Julia would go along . . . She pinched off the thought before it could kill the tender young shoots of her new understanding. What he was is over and done with, she told herself. It is what he can become, that matters. But she was also aware, on a deeper level, that she was also more than mildly jealous. Denise had been very luscious . . .

Brad accompanied Julia to her room, waited while she got her bag, which was all ready and packed. As he took it from her: "Julia, I really am sorry about those two sex junkies back there. They are not—never were—friends of mine; just people I met at certain parties. Part of a life I don't intend to live anymore. I want you to know that."

"I do."

His eyes searched hers. "Do you? It was a sick world I lived in. *I* was sick—spiritually, anyway."

"I know."

"I don't want that now, I don't need it. I thought it was total freedom; all it was, was rattling my chains."

Julia laid a hand on his arm. "I know what you are trying to tell me and I do understand; honestly, I do."

"I guess what I'm trying to say is—you've changed. Me, I'm still trying. But I intend to. I don't have any choice. If I don't—can't—I'm done for."

Julia met the desperate eyes. "I am in your corner, Brad."

His deep breath expelled his rigidity. "That's all I wanted to know."

The moment which had been shattered was magically restored. Once again Julia felt him slide inside her, but there was no sense of panic this time; only a sense of coming home; of being restored to something she had once lost and never thought to find again. And was able to accept for what it was, once and for all.

He did not drive the same way, either. All of him seemed to have slowed down, changed gear into first. They chatted easily, without strain, mostly of things other than themselves. That had been gone over, ordered to bed rest. But it would be allowed visitors later.

He accompanied her as far as he could. As he handed over her small bag, he retained her hand in his. "It has been a pleasure, Julia. I mean that. And I've more to look forward to. Once again, thank you."

He bent to graze her cheek with his lips, stepped back and away. "Till Sunday."

"Sunday," Julia echoed, then fled.

It was on the plane that her mood changed, dismayedly regretted her impulsiveness. Why had she done it? she thought. She had not meant to; she had been as surprised as he was when the words slid from her tongue. As always, she reflected hopelessly, around him she became another woman; someone who obeyed none of the usual strictures, slyly slipped the guard on her tongue, ignored the prominently displayed warnings. Even now, after all he had done, all she had suffered at his hands, he still had the power to undo her every knot, turn her into something all loose and pliable, responding instinctively to his every look and gesture. Chris had been right, as usual. He was the reason she had avoided coming back to America all these years; because she was afraid of him; realized—*knew*—deep down, that he still held power over her, always would. Even now, showing signs of actual wear and tear, worried, chain-smoking, shocked and despairing, he was still possessed, for her anyway, of some potent attraction which was irresistible. He had aged; she had actually seen gray hairs among the thick sheaf of blond ones; his dazzle was dimmed and his buoyancy leaking badly, yet she could still feel him; his effect on her, *in* her. She found she was trembling, dry-mouthed, scattered like a dropped basketful of shopping. And she had meant to be so calm, so composed, so —unforgiving. One look and she had melted, let him have his way with her, even invited him to spend the day with her and Jenny on Sunday. I must be mad, she thought, as she huddled in her window seat. I have to be to go anywhere near his mother, and yet—and yet . . . He needs me, she thought. He needs anybody who can help. And in this particular instance, if it is against *her* he needs all the help he can get.

Unaccountably her mood swung again. I will help him, she thought defiantly. I would be a queer sort of human being if I didn't help anybody to escape from Lady Hester Bradford. Besides, I owe her for what she did to me. And that debt has been a long time in the paying . . .

FROM HIS POSITION by the flowers, he saw them coming. Julia's flaming hair was eye-catching enough, but it was matched by the corona of red-gold floss around the head of the small girl straining at the leash, tugging her mother along like a recalcitrant puppy. From where he stood he could almost feel the blaze of excitement which made her glow like a coal fire. She was very brown, in denim shorts and a T-shirt, Mickey Mouse's wide grin decorating its front. Her legs were bare, her feet in English-style brown-leather sandals. She was tall for her age, but slender. As they reached the corner, he saw Jenny wriggle her hand free from that of her mother and fling herself into the fray, elbowing aside a little boy who was just inserting his hand into that of Donald Duck, fastening her own instead, with a triumphant grip, administering a well-placed kick to a bigger boy who tried to muscle in. Only then did she turn to her mother with an imperious: "Quick, Mummy! Have you got your camera ready?"

An English voice, naturally; tones he recognized. It might have been his mother. Involuntarily he looked at Julia, but she was focusing her camera. Quickly he remembered his own—he had gone out and bought a movie camera—and set it in motion so as to catch Jenny as, with his mother's implacable but indifferent determination, she inserted herself by each and every one of the Disney animals; smiling confidently up at Pluto, throwing her arms about Mickey Mouse, kissing Winnie the Pooh. It was only when she had accomplished her objective that he realized she was advancing on him. He lowered his camera. She bent on him a haughty look before demanding: "Why are you taking my picture?"

"Jenny . . . ," warned Julia.

"But you said I was not to have anything to do with strange men."

"This is not a stranger, darling. This is—an old friend of mine."

Brad squatted down, held out a hand. "Hi," he said. "Your mother invited me along today. My name is Brad."

Jenny unbent. "How do you do," she said grandly, as her small, sinewy hand vanished inside his own, giving him the oddest feeling. "Is that the kind of camera that takes moving pictures?"

"Yes."

"Will you let me see them?"

"Anytime."

She flashed him another smile; the one his mother used when she had won. "Shall we go then? There is a lot to see, you know." She sounded like his mother showing the Historical Society around the Mount Vernon Street house. "We will go to Wonderland first." A hop, skip and jump. "That's my very favorite place. What's yours?" she asked, unconsciously taking his hand.

"I've never been to Disneyland before," Brad apologized, in a voice that had Julia eyeing him.

"Oh . . . then I'll show you round, shall I? Would you like that?"

Brad swallowed. "Very much."

"I've been here two times already!" Jenny told him importantly. "Once with Mummy and Uncle Marcus and once with Barbara. Barbara's my nanny," she explained kindly. "She didn't come today; she's gone to Santa Barbara to a beach party."

"Is that so," Brad said, struggling manfully.

"Come along, then. We've lots to see."

Brad turned dazed eyes on Julia as his daughter led him away.

Dancing between them, Jenny led the way down Main Street to the central plaza, off which opened the various Lands; beyond the entrance to Wonderland could be seen the towers of the Enchanted Castle. As they went around the enormous flower bed in the center of the plaza, Brad felt Jenny dragging on his hand, looked down to see her gazing fixedly at the popcorn stand.

"Oh, thank you!" she said, sounding oh-so-surprised, as he placed the box into her hand. And she offered him the box first, without having to be prompted. As they passed the vendor selling frozen bananas: "We'll have one of them later," she consoled.

Watching his face, Julia decided the best thing to do was stand back and let Jenny have her way.

So Brad rode in one of the teacups on the Alice in Wonderland carousel; boarded the Dumbo train; mounted a pink elephant; went willingly and happily wherever she directed. He had bought three sets of tickets and Julia had two, so they had enough and to spare so as to ride every single attraction. They would come off one only to make instantly for the next.

Having exhausted Wonderland they went into Adventureland, where they went on Jungle Safari, took the raft to Tom Sawyer's island, where they shot guns in the fort. In the shop there, Brad bought Jenny a miniature Indian warbonnet and matching deerskin moccasins, which she at once put on. He drank root beer and ate cotton candy, entered into the spirit of things with such enthusiasm that Jenny confided happily to Julia as he was buying them all hot dogs: "He's nice, Mummy. I like him."

When they went inside the caves of the Pirates of the Caribbean, it was Brad who got soaked when the boat, dipping down a chute, nosed into water which cascaded. Jenny, who had also received a drenching, fell about with laughter. "I knew that would happen," she giggled. "That's why I took the front seat." But she made amends by drying him off with his handkerchief.

On entering Tomorrowland, she was bitterly disappointed to find she was still too young for Space Mountain. Brad consoled her by taking her on Magic Mountain instead. "She's got iron filings in her stomach," he marveled afterward, but Jenny was tugging at his hand. "Now for the submarines."

He was glad to sit at a table in the New Orleans café and drink a cup of coffee while Jenny demolished a banana split the size of which he just had to get on film. "So people will believe me."

He roared with laughter at the Puppet Show, delightedly donned turn-of-the-century clothes with them to have a picture taken, obediently sat for a silhouette. By this time, Julia had two carriers and Brad one, so it was his hand she held, absolutely trustingly, her acceptance of him whole and happy.

She was a marvel, Brad thought emotionally. An incredibly composed yet uninhibited five-and-a-half-year-old. Childish in her joy, unaffected in her delight, her absolute belief in the truth of all she saw, yet astonishingly adult in her vocabulary. You could *talk* to her, hold a real conversation. But then, with Julia for a mother . . . She could display all her mother's aloofness, yet be totally heedless of self when enthralled. But what caught at Brad, more and more as he saw his daughter's personality revealed, was her unmistakable resemblance to his mother, who kept surfacing at the most unexpected times. As when Jenny, following a three-hundred-pound lady in sky-blue shorts, wrinkled her nose and said: "Ugh!" or when, her frozen banana having melted, insisted on more than a wipe with a handkerchief, and being taken to wash her hands. Or the way she bent an eagle eye on a dozen pairs of Minnie Mouse sunglasses before finally deciding, and trying on endless Mickey Mouse hats before making her choice.

"Brad, you are indulging her shamelessly," Julia chided, but deeply pleased.

"I have five years to make up. Let me, please?" The smile was the old Brad: laden with irresistible charm.

Jenny sat on his shoulders to watch the midday procession of all the animals prancing behind the band; sat beside him upstairs on the horse-drawn tram, ditto the bus, clambered about the Swiss Family Robinson's tree house and clutched at him in the Haunted House.

He had dropped his careworn air like a cloak, and even if it was only for that one day, was the Brad Julia remembered. Lighthearted, gay, sunny, and the best possible company, relishing everything with unaffected delight: just like his daughter.

"This is the bestest day ever at Disneyland," Jenny pronounced, just before she bit into another hot dog laden with relish, pickle *and* mustard.

"Best, darling," Julia corrected, then: "But I agree with you."

"So do I!" Brad affirmed. They smiled at each other.

By four o'clock, Julia was ready for a sit-down, so when Jenny suggested they go and play the machines in the arcade, Julia demurred. "My feet are killing me, you two go. I'll just sit here on this bench and get my breath back." She dropped her laden carrier bags with relief and toed off her sandals.

"You sure?" Brad asked hopefully, eager to have Jenny to himself.

"Positive. Keep an eye on Jenny and those machines, though, or she'll bankrupt you."

She watched them go off hand in hand, Brad adjusting his stride to Jenny's trot, she talking his ear off, then leaned back, closed her eyes and sighed. With contentment. It had been a marvelous day, even if they had walked miles. Right around every single one of the five Lands —in which they must have sampled each and every attraction. Apart from brief sit-downs to eat or drink something, they had been on their feet since 11 A.M. Brad had gallantly overcome his dismay at finding that Disneyland offered nothing more alcoholic than root beer, but had said the coffee was good. Everything had been good, Julia thought. They had been a family: father, mother, child. She found she liked the feeling. Brad obviously found it highly satisfactory, notwithstanding the fact that Jenny had led him around not so much by the hand as by the nose.

"She's a marvel, Julia," he had said, never taking his eyes off her as she went swooping by on a swing. "I never knew kids could be so much fun."

"She is not all sweetness and light," Julia warned.

"I hope not! She's got character. Haven't you noticed"—he broke off as Jenny waved to him and waved back, but Julia thought she knew how he was going to finish—"how like Mother she is?"

JENNY WAS DISPLAYING HER ANCESTRY more and more as she got older, and her imperiousness, her lofty disregard for the claims of others, her determination when she wanted something, her preening self-congrat- ulation when she got it—all these were her grandmother's traits. Which was why Julia and Barbara wielded a firm hand. Jenny already knew that wanting did not automatically mean receiving. Yet now, here was her father giving in to her every whim. Well, *one* day. But if Jenny was going to see more of him that would have to be nipped in the bud.

She yawned; she felt pleasantly worn out, closed her eyes. The sun was no longer burning; merely hot. She turned her face up to it, drifted into a gentle doze.

A small boy firing a cap pistol right by her ear awoke her with a start. Checking the nearby clock she saw it was four-thirty. They should be back soon. She yawned, sat up, felt for her sandals. She felt thirsty, ready for a glass of that deliciously chill, freshly squeezed orange juice. Rummaging in one of the carriers she found her sunglasses, checked that she had all the various bits and pieces, then looked up to see Brad coming toward her at a fast clip. Alone.

Before she could speak: "I'd gone to get some more change while she played one of the machines. Honestly, I wasn't gone more than a minute or so, but when I got back she'd vanished. I swear to you, Julia; she was standing there, feeding nickels!"

Calm, Julia thought, as she rose to her feet. Don't panic. Brad's white face was bad enough. "It's that quicksilver mind of hers. If something takes her fancy . . . She would follow the gypsies if they came by.

Come on, we'll look for her. I expect she's playing a different machine."

"I looked around them all; she's not there."

"Somewhere else, then. Let's check every shop. You do one side of the street, I'll do the other. Meet you at the top by the railway station."

Brad's eyes begged forgiveness. She touched his arm. "She'll be somewhere. I know my daughter. She's a butterfly—flower to flower. Come on, the sooner we look the sooner we'll find her."

But they didn't. When Julia finally reached the station, after checking every shop, every arcade, asking assistants if they had seen a small redheaded girl wearing an Indian warbonnet, it was to find Brad waiting for her. Alone. Her heart sank. Disneyland was enormous. There were thousands of children and this was one small girl . . . "Lost Children," she said with false confidence. "Come on."

"She'll be somewhere, ma'am," the young man—his name, Randy, pinned to his lapel as with all Disneyland employees, said. "We get hundreds of children through here every day. If she is brought in we'll hold her for you and meanwhile we'll circulate her description; have our people keep an eye out. She'll be somewhere, don't you worry. Kids turn up in the darnedest places."

He made it sound such a normal, everyday occurrence that Julia relievedly berated herself for jumping to panicky conclusions.

"Could she have wanted to watch the second parade?" Brad asked suddenly. "You said there was another at five o'clock."

"Of course!" Julia all but laughed with the relief of it. "I'll bet that's what she's done. Probably sitting right in the front of the crowd."

But she wasn't. Again they each took a side of the street. No Jenny. And when they went back to check with Randy she was not there either. By this time it was six o'clock, and Julia was jumpy.

"She knows she is not to wander off," she muttered tightly. "I'll kill her when I find her. I've told her and *told* her. She has this Pied Piper mentality."

"She is only five," Brad said gently.

"Sorry . . ."

He took her hand, tucked it in his—as in the old days. "We'll find her," he said.

They roamed all five sections, eyes searching for the brightly feathered warbonnet, which Jenny had refused to take off. At least, Julia thought thankfully, it would make her easy to spot.

But by seven o'clock she had not been spotted anywhere. Once more

[269]

they returned to Lost Children. Randy, by now not quite so jaunty, admitted there was no sign of her.

"Oh, God." Julia gulped. "There's the lake with the steamboat . . ." They had ridden on it earlier, and Julia had had to insert her fingers in Jenny's waistband as she leaned out over the rail. She had Brad's recklessness.

"No, ma'am," Randy corrected firmly. "There's no way any child can fall into our lake. We are too careful for that. And you can't get onto the landing stage without a ticket. Besides, if a child on its own tried, our people would spot it at once and know something was wrong. Disneyland prides itself on its safety record, ma'am."

"I know . . . I know."

"And if she hasn't got a ticket she can't ride anything."

"Let's go have a last look," Brad suggested calmly.

"We've got people looking for her," Randy said confidently. "If she's in Disneyland we'll find her."

But the enormous complex was closing, people streaming wearily for the exits. Brad and Julia each stationed themselves to one side so as to scan the homegoing crowds. By the time the last tired child had gone through the exit, Jenny had not been one of them.

"I've *told* her not to go off on her own. She wouldn't, I know that. She's been warned too many times. I even told her again just before we left the house—"

"What is it? What have you thought of?" Brad asked quickly, as Julia's voice faded.

"A phone. Where's the nearest phone?"

"A phone! What—"

"The nearest telephone. *Please!*"

No, Ito told her, Mr. Levin had not come by but he had called, asked where Julia was. "I tell him Disneyland for day."

"Levin!" Brad looked baffled. "Why Levin?"

"He's your mother's hatchet man, isn't he? She knows about Jenny and he *knows* Jenny. And you have gone awol . . ."

Brad stared at her.

"Jenny is not in Disneyland because she has been taken away. We have looked everywhere. She knows she is not to wander off alone. She wouldn't, I'm positive. If she has gone it is because someone has taken her—and somebody she knows. She would scream her lungs out otherwise. The only other person she knows apart from me, Barbara and Ito is Marcus, and she would go with him unquestioningly. She trusts him." Julia's voice clogged.

[270]

"But how the hell would he come across her in a place the size of this?"

"We've been here all day, haven't we? He could have been waiting his chance."

"You are letting your imagination run away with you."

"Wrong! It is Marcus who has run off with Jenny!"

"Why in God's name would my mother want to snatch Jenny?"

"Because she knows you have seen me. I'm to be punished for daring to allow that!" Julia's voice had risen. "Jenny is not lost, I tell you! If she was, she knows enough to go up to somebody and tell them so. She knows the drill, Brad! I've taught it to her. I once got lost myself; I remember so well the sheer terror—" Julia's voice was ragged, her nerves strained. "The one hope is that if it is Marcus then Jenny won't be upset. She wouldn't have gone willingly with a stranger, *she wouldn't*. You saw how she was with you earlier."

Brad bit his lip.

"Why won't you believe me?" Julia seethed, her voice echoing in the now empty silence. "Oh, God, why did I come back? I didn't want to in the first place. I knew it would be a disaster. Why did I ignore my instincts? This bloody country has never been anything else than trouble for me. It's jinxed as far as I am concerned."

Her voice was rising, her composure falling away in shreds.

"Julia!" Brad took her shoulders, shook her. "As God is my witness, if my mother has done this I'll—"

"You'll what—do something? Since when have you ever done anything against her say-so except marry me, and look what happened to that! We are wasting time," she flung at him. "Marcus has got her, is probably taking her to your mother right now!"

"We have no proof!"

"Jenny is missing; what more proof do you want? By now Marcus probably knows he's been blown. So does your bloody mother! I'll kill her. So help me I'll *kill* her!" Brad slapped her across the face. She put a hand to her cheek, her eyes wide, then she burst into tears.

"Julia . . . Julia . . ." Brad took her in his arms, his face on the bright hair. "I know how you feel but don't do this to yourself, please. The first thing to do is check Mother's whereabouts. Let me call Abby. Find out what I can."

Lady Hester was at the farm; had been since Friday night.

No one had seen Marcus Levin.

"He would hardly be stupid enough to take her right to your

mother!" Julia withered him. "But she will know where he *has* taken her."

"Then we must ask her," Brad said, frighteningly calm. "But before we do that we ask the police."

By the time they boarded the plane Brad had chartered, there had been no news of Jenny. The police had been alerted, done their own search of Disneyland, dogs to help them. She was not there. They had even dragged the lake. Nor had there been any anonymous phone call demanding ransom money; no note—nothing. Jenny had vanished.

Julia boarded the Learjet in a state of inner terror; screaming silently, holding herself together by sheer force of will. She kept telling herself that of course Lady Hester would not harm Jenny. She was Brad's child. Yes, and mine, she thought. She did not dare imagine how Jenny might be feeling; told herself firmly that if she was with Marcus, whom she loved and trusted, then she would be all right. She was positive Marcus would not hurt her daughter; was sure his feelings for *her* were genuine. Please, God, let her be all right, she prayed, please, God. I'll do anything you want, be anything you want. Only let Jenny be all right, please, God, please.

Brad was so angry he had a blinding headache. If his mother—his terrible, mad-with-jealousy mother—had planned this hideous thing, then *he* would kill her. He would put his hands around her throat and squeeze. Which was how his head felt, as if an iron band were being tightened remorselessly around his temples.

He had a sense of being punished; every sin he had ever committed had been called to account and his punishment was to surrender his peace of mind, his pride as a man, his life—his very self.

He knew his mother had no love for children; her grandchildren she tolerated, no more. The only time she had ever looked at anyone with love was when she had looked at him. Love? he thought with revulsion. That's not love, that's psychosis. My mother is mad; probably always has been: clever with the brilliance of the truly insane.

The more he thought about it, as the plane droned on, the more certain he became that Julia was right. His mother had ordered Marcus Levin to abduct Jenny as punishment for his abandoning of her; as a punishment of Julia for daring to insert herself in her son's life once more. It had always been herself she had thought of first, he realized now. Always. What *she* wanted; how *she* felt. People were things to her. To be ordered about, used as she thought fit, discarded when used up. The way she had taught him.

He put his hands to his head. It felt on the verge of explosion.

[272]

"Are you all right?" he heard Julia ask. He could not see her clearly; she seemed to divide, and divide again.

When he came to he was stretched out on one of the seats, a white-faced Julia leaning over him. "Oh, thank God . . ."

"What happened?"

"You went out like a light. No, lie still. Here, drink this."

It was tea; hot and sweet and soothing. He gulped gratefully, felt the band easing slightly.

"I'm not surprised," Julia said angrily. "You've probably been living on your nerves ever since it happened. I know what that's like. I've done it. Please, don't drive yourself over the edge. I need you, Brad. I'm scared and I'm—" He saw her swallow convulsively. "I've never felt like this before; so—so terrified."

He felt for her hand, entwined it in his. "You're right. It all came together suddenly, rolled right over me. But I'm okay now."

"Perhaps if we tried to sleep," Julia said. "Move over. If we hold each other . . . There is room for two."

He put her at the back, against the window, both seats tilted as far as they would go, his arms around her under two blankets. She was shivering, but his body warmth, always greater than hers, seemed to calm her. She had her arms around him, laid her head on his shoulder. He felt again the old womanly warmth, the roundness and solidity.

"What time is it?"

He lifted his arm, peered at his watch in the dim cabin light. "Just gone after two A.M. Another three hours."

"I keep praying," Julia said.

"So do I." They held tight to each other for comfort.

"We'll find her," he said. "I promise you that, Julia . . . on my own life . . . we'll find her."

They dozed, off and on, but as they came in to Logan, the stewardess came to wake them. "Will you fasten your safety belts? We have clearance to land."

It was still dark and just after 5 A.M. And raining. As the cabin door was opened a cold wind made them shiver. Both were in the clothes they had worn to Disneyland: Brad in jeans and a shirt, Julia in a cotton dress.

"There should be a car waiting." Brad peered into the lights under the driving rain. "Yes, there it is. Bring it right up," he shouted.

Inside it were Abby and Seth.

"Just as well I thought to bring something warmer to wear," Abby said practically to Julia after they had embraced. "Here . . . put this

[273]

on." It was a mink coat; torn under the arm and the hem dragging, but blessedly warm. To Brad she handed a sweater and a jacket, as well as a topcoat.

"You always come up trumps," Brad said gratefully.

Abby was pouring hot coffee from a thermos. "Now," she said when they both had it inside them. "What's all this about Marcus Levin abducting Jenny?"

"I've made inquiries," Seth said from the driving seat. "Marcus Levin has not been seen around Boston."

"Have you seen Mother?" Brad asked.

"No. We're excommunicated," Abby said expressionlessly. "Right now, Bitsy is the only one Mother has time for—and only to bully worse than ever. I've never seen her like this; she's out of her mind."

Brad and Julia looked at each other.

"But then, to do a thing like this she has to be," Abby went on flatly. "Of all the half-assed ideas—"

"Does she know I'm coming?" Brad asked.

"*I* haven't told her."

Abby turned to pat Julia's cold hand. "We'll find your little girl. Don't you worry." She turned to Brad. "But be careful. Her fuse is very short."

"So is mine."

As soon as they entered the house, Annie, always an early riser, came through the swinging doors of the kitchen at the rear of the hall, bringing with her the smell of freshly made coffee. Her face lit when she saw who it was. "Mr. Brad! Thank God! Your ma has been like to lose her mind—" She broke off in consternation as she saw Julia appear from behind him, Abby's tentlike fur coat hanging over her shoulders and down to her calves, the sleeves reaching to her finger tips.

"Mrs. Brad! I mean—Miss Julia . . ." She flushed and wiped her hands on her apron, all of a rabidly curious fluster.

"Hello, Annie."

"Is my mother awake?" Brad asked.

"I just now took her tea."

Brad turned to Julia. "Why don't you go with Annie? Have a cup of coffee, something to eat. I won't be long."

Julia did not move. Seeing her expression, Abby pushed Seth in front of her and, jerking her head at Annie, disappeared into the kitchen.

[274]

"Jenny is *my* daughter," Julia began.

"And mine."

Julia's tired paleness took on color but she held her ground as Brad went on: "And it is *my* mother who has had her abducted." The pink deepened to rose.

"Back in Disneyland you accused me of not being able to do anything without her; now that I am about to you don't trust me to do it without you."

Julia stared at the ground, but stubbornly.

"After five hours on that plane, surely you realize *I* have to do this," Brad went on reasonably: "I'm more than ready for her."

Julia's face burned. Her propensity to take over wherever she saw what she thought of as muddle or mess had overridden all other considerations; as usual, she was understanding intellectually rather than emotionally, in spite of her wholly emotional fears for Jenny.

"You said I had changed—as you had. Are you now telling me you've changed your mind?"

Julia shook her head.

"Trust me," Brad said.

"It's not you I don't trust."

"You think she'll retie me, is that it?"

"She'll try."

"Of course she will. But I won't let her. Trust me," he repeated.

She raised her eyes to his face. "You will be—careful."

"I know how to handle my mother—better than anyone. I'll get it out of her, Julia."

"But—but this is Jenny!"

"I know. My daughter."

Again Julia rosied up.

"You forget, I know Jenny now. I've been with her, enjoyed her, delighted in her. I want her back for my own sake as well as yours."

What had happened to him? she wondered. On the plane he had looked so awful, sounded worse. When he'd blacked out she had been terrified. Not that it was to be wondered at considering the emotional stress he had been under for days. What she was feeling now he had suffered for those days, not hours. Oh, God, she thought despairingly. I've gone and done it again.

"I'm sorry." Ruefully: "I wasn't feeling, only thinking."

His smile was brief but understanding. "I know . . ." He put an arm around her shoulders, walked her toward the kitchen. "Go on, join the others. Eat something if you can. It's more than twelve hours since you last did."

"I couldn't."

"Then have some of Annie's good coffee. I'll come to you as soon as I know."

She searched his eyes, managed a tremulous smile and then went into the kitchen. But as he turned and walked away, she pushed the doors open again, watched him go up the stairs, around the corner, in the direction of his mother's bedroom. His step was resolute, his head up. Help him, God, she prayed. What he has to do is the most terrible thing. She tried to put herself in Lady Hester's place; imagined it was Jenny coming up the stairs to some terrible confrontation with her. Oh, God, help him.

7

game. the g. is up—everything has failed

AS HE KNEW HE WOULD, Brad found his mother sitting up in bed, leaning against her padded back-and-armrest, her early-morning tea tray—Lapsang souchong, no milk or sugar, and one digestive biscuit— over her knees, the day-late copy of the London *Times* held before her face. This was lowered as she heard the door open, went flying as she flung her arms wide. "Brad! Oh, thank God! Dearest boy, where have you *been?* I have been so worried!"

Brad turned, slipped the lock on the old door, then, instead of rushing into his mother's arms, turned to face her.

His mother's arms dropped. "Brad?"

"Where is Jenny, Mother? What have you done with her?"

She stared. All bewilderment. "Jenny? Who is Jenny? What are you talking about?"

It was then, sick at heart, he knew it was all true. If his mother knew *of* Julia's daughter she would know *everything.* God help us both, he thought. But it had to be done.

"Jenny, as you well know, is Julia's daughter—my daughter. The child you had Marcus Levin spirit away from Disneyland yesterday afternoon."

"Disneyland! Dearest boy, what *are* you on about?"

"You know."

"I only wish I did. As it is, I have not the slightest idea."

"Oh, it was all your idea. I don't doubt it for a moment. Nobody else would dream up anything like this!"

There was a distinct cooling of her warmth. This was not what she expected. Her eyes held his; that relentless gaze, intended to bring him to his knees. When he remained standing where he was she swiftly changed roles. "Oh, Grandmama, what great big eyes you've got!"

"All the better to see you with—at last."

The teasing smile vanished; once more she changed roles. "Oh, my poor darling. You are upset, aren't you?" She opened her arms again. "All you had to do was come to me and ask me to explain after the horrible things Caroline accused me of—"

"It is too late for explanations, it's Jenny I want. Where is she, Mother? What have you done with her?"

"Done with whom, darling?" Her tone said she was trying to understand, but really . . .

"Jenny—*my* child, not Pierre Chambrun's. I've seen her, Mother, I know—as do you. Why else did you have her snatched?"

His mother's face took on a pained expression at his use of what she termed the vulgar vernacular. "I do not know in which context you are using the word, but I can assure you, I have snatched nothing and no one."

"No; but Marcus Levin did."

"I have not seen Marcus Levin for years."

"Why not? Does he do his reporting by phone?"

"Ah . . ." It was a soft breath of comprehension. "Now I see. You are still under the influence of your wife's drunken ravings."

"Caroline told me the truth. That's why I went away. To think about it. About you—about me. Most of all about us."

"I have done nothing but think of you," returned his mother simply. Her smile blessed him; this time it was indulgent. Silly boy, it said. This is your mother! Your mother who adores you and would never do anything to hurt her dearest son.

"It's too late, Mother. I *know*. You set Julia up again, didn't you? Wanted the goods on her as an unfit mother so as to be able to take

Jenny when you were good and ready, only when I took off you couldn't wait—and you just had to punish Julia, didn't you?"

An impatient gesture: "Really, Brad!" The use of his name was the first warning. "I have never heard such a farrago of nonsense in all my life!"

"Oh, it's stupid, all right. You've made a mistake this time. Jenny is not the kind of child to go off with just anyone; you forgot who is her mother."

"I neither know nor care," his mother cut in impatiently. "My only concern is you. Why did you run off like that? Why did you not come to me?"

"After what Caroline told me that was the last thing on my mind."

"Are you telling me you believed her load of drunken calumny?" Deep hurt vied with disbelief.

"Caroline did me the kindness of telling me the truth; of showing me what I was turning into—all but had, in fact: your windup toy!"

"I will not deny I have built my life around you."

"Wrong—you built my life around you!"

"Ah—" The break in her voice was faultlessly placed. "Now I see; it is all to be my fault. For doing nothing more than loving you."

"Love! More a killing by kindness!"

His mother shrank back against her pillows. "How can you say such a thing to me?"

"Because—at long last—I am finally able to."

"I have denied you nothing—nothing!" was the passionately proclaimed rebuttal. Then a soft moan: "Who has done this to you? Who has poisoned your mind against me? Filled you with monstrously wicked lies?"

"It is the truth which is monstrous!"

"I have been out of my mind with worry. Nobody would tell me where you were, even my own daughters conspired against me. I have been betrayed by my own children!"

"And you know all about betrayal, don't you?"

This time the moan was anguished. "How can you say such things?"

"Because it is time I did."

"I have always loved you, always, and that is the only thing I have ever done to you!"

"Loved to possess, you mean! Loving is not taking, the way you take and take and take. It is giving, wanting the one you love to be happy. With you, it was always what you wanted which came first—and last and always! What I wanted—needed—never came into it!"

"Lies . . . lies . . ." It was piteous, distraught. "I have denied you nothing!"

"Except the right to be my own man! When I was born you took that cord and you tied it around my neck and it's been strangling me ever since!"

His mother's face convulsed. "Do not dare say such a thing to me! No one—not even you—has the right to such slanderous abuse! And I refuse to justify myself to you—yes, even you!"

"It wouldn't be any use anyway. All I am interested in is Jenny. Where is she and what have you done with her?"

"I have done nothing to anyone!"

"You will tell me in the end, one way or another."

"I will tell you nothing! How dare you speak to me in such a manner? I am not some betweenmaid to be ordered around in my own house! Remember who you are—and remember who *I* am!"

"As if I could forget!"

She changed tactics without missing a beat. "Ah . . ." This time her hand went to her heart. "Do not say such things to me . . ." Her eyes were wet, beseeching. "We are saying things we will regret, things we do not mean. We never quarrel, you and I—and not just because you know how dangerous it is for me."

"No emotional blackmail, if you please! Only tell me where Jenny is and I will trouble you no longer."

"Will you stop insisting that I know!" Her voice rose.

"No, I won't, because you do know. I know you have got Jenny hidden away somewhere—"

"You know nothing, nothing!" Again she drew back, dropped her face into her hands. "What have I done to deserve this?" she pleaded brokenly.

"Every rotten thing in the book—and all in the name of your precious love! The hell it was! You have never loved me, only yourself!"

Weeping brokenly she drooped in her supporting bed chair, her hands over her face. "My son, my son . . . What are you doing to me? I cannot believe that you would take your wife's drunken ravings as truth, though I am well aware she has been trying to turn you against me for years." She lifted her wet face. "Darling boy"—a supplicating hand—"come and sit down and we will talk this whole thing out . . . There is nothing that cannot be put right. Don't I always put you right?"

"Right in it, you mean—and always where you want me!"

Her droop became a ramrod spine. "Do not be insolent, sir! You

[280]

begin to weary me with your crude language and baseless accusations. I tell you again, do not speak to me with such insolence! I would not accept it from your wife and I will not accept it from you!"

"I don't give a damn what you will or will not accept. Let's stop wasting time. I repeat: where is Jenny?"

"I will not listen to this!" Her hands were over her ears. "I will not be hounded like this! Nobody demands of me, not even you! I have made endless allowances where you are concerned but there is a limit even to my patience!"

"Then it is as well I have acquired some of my own."

"You seem to have acquired a great deal in the last week—all of it highly unpleasant! I can see you have not given any thought to *me!*"

"I assure you, Mother, I have thought of little else."

"And all under the influence of that tawdry, barren wife of yours!"

"I have not seen Caroline since the last time I saw you."

"That you should believe that—that common little nobody before me, your own mother! How could you! My own beloved son. How *could* you!"

"It wasn't easy."

"And I? Do you think I have had an easy time of it? You flounce off without so much as a word, you leave me desperate for news of you, then, when you do decide to return, you accuse me of the wildest, most impossible things! I would not have thought this of you, not *my* son!"

"That's because I am not *your* son anymore."

That brought her head up again, to regard him from horror-stricken eyes. "Ah . . . no . . ." Again the imploring hand, the beseeching face. "You cannot mean that—"

"I have sat five hours in a plane during the worst night of my life and mean every word. You still don't care, do you? All I have said—all that I am, now—none of it means a thing to you. All you care about is keeping your hold on me . . . bending me to your angle. No more, Mother. Do you hear me? No more!"

The violence of his voice, the look in his eyes, struck her silent. Once more her face disappeared behind her hands while her mind worked furiously. "You are not yourself. I do not recognize you. What has happened to *my* son?"

"He's finally grown up, that's what. Take a good look, Mother; I'm not your little boy anymore."

She did look up, and the flash of her eyes leaped the room like lightning, seeking to destroy. But it only came back at her. In desperation she fell back into the pose of the Mater Dolorosa. "Dearest boy, what is happening to us? You are hurting me so deeply . . ." Her eyes welled, ran. "If I have done wrong then I apologize for whatever it is you think I have done. For loving you too much, caring too deeply. It is not like you to be so callous of my feelings."

"You never gave any thought to mine."

Her moans were piteous, her shoulders heaving, but she was watching him through the cracks in her fingers.

"You will tell me if I have to stay here all day. *Where is Jenny?* Do you know what you are doing to Julia? Do you care?"

"Do you care what you are doing to me?" she screamed. Her eyes burned. "Now I see who has put you up to this. Whose baleful influence has been at work—that woman! And after all she did to you."

"What you did, you mean!"

He saw the telltale flush of color stain her throat, always the first sign of rising temper, but he was not afraid this time. "I know it all, Mother. I've seen Julia; she told me the truth of it. And you say you are my loving mother! A cat's a better mother than you are! No one with even the minimum of love in them could do what you have done—and to another mother! You, who have endlessly proclaimed all that being a mother means! What you didn't realize was that I know what it means to be a father. I want my daughter! Do you understand? *My* daughter!"

A high whine exploded from his mother's throat. "Your daughter! Your daughter! It is your mother you should be concerned about!"

"You have enough of that for yourself—and to spare!"

He saw the cup coming and dodged. It smashed against the door and shattered. It was followed by the teapot; tea—still hot—drenched him. He lunged from the door, and before she could raise her own his hands were around her throat. "God damn you!" he shouted. "You are no mother, you are a fiend! Why won't you tell me where Jenny is? Do you want me to squeeze it from you?" His own voice was strangled with rage and pain; inside he could not believe what he was doing; could not stop himself. Pain seemed to be rising through every nerve in his body to concentrate at the top of his skull, as it had last night. "Tell me what you have done with my daughter!" A violent shake. "Tell me!"

But her eyes only glared at him with the light of the fanatic. "Go on —kill me! End my life! Have I not told you all along that you would be the death of me?"

He flung her from him with an oath, some inner warning still obtaining a measure of control, and it was then he became conscious that the pounding in his head was not his own blood but against the locked door.

[282]

"Brad, let me in! Brad, please—it's Julia. Let me in—"

"It's all right, Julia." He forced calm into his voice, though the rest of him was trembling violently.

"But I know where Jenny is. Marcus did take her; Thomas saw her in his car—"

The door was opened so violently that Julia, Abby right behind her, all but fell in.

"You!" Lady Hester's voice was the hiss of the cobra. "I might have known." She began to rise in her bed, preparing to strike.

"What did Thomas see?" Brad demanded urgently. It was Abby who answered.

"Marcus called at Mount Vernon Street to collect the keys to the old warehouses in the North End; Mother told Thomas to hand them over. It was as he was closing the front door that he saw there was a little girl in the back of Marcus's car; he said she had red hair—"

"Look out!" It was Abby who thrust Julia out of the way so roughly that she fell.

Lady Hester, who had managed to lever herself from her bed, was in the act of lifting her stick so as to lay it across Julia's shoulders. But it was Brad who caught the weight of it across one arm as his other rose to grasp it and wrench it away.

"It is your fault!" Lady Hester screamed at Julia. "I should have done for you totally as I did that other redheaded bitch. She also thought she could take what belonged to me."

Teeth bared, she lunged at Julia, fingers ready to rend and claw, but once again Brad interposed himself, while Seth came from behind Abby to pinion his mother-in-law's arms, she struggling violently all the while. "Go on—take Julia and go find Jenny," he urged. "We'll cope—go on; your presence only makes her worse."

But Brad was staring at his mother, whose face was bedlam. Julia put a hand on his arm: it was rigid, and the look on his face as he stared wide-eyed at his mother was that of a man looking into hell.

"Brad . . ." He turned his eyes to her and she felt his pain like her own. "Jenny," she said.

"Jenny," he repeated, and she saw him draw a deep, jolting breath. "Yes—Jenny . . ." With a violent movement he grabbed her by the arm and all but dragged her from the room and down the stairs at a great rate. Lady Hester's body struggled to be free as he disappeared, but when she heard the slam of the front door her head went back and from her throat came a howl that raised gooseflesh. "Brad! B-r-a-d!

B-R-A-D!" Cords stood out in her throat. "My son . . . my son! I have lost my son!"

For a moment Abby, Seth and Annie, with Jonas behind her, were all rooted in horror, which allowed the demented woman to wrench herself free and bend to seize her stick, which Brad had let fall. In an instant she was whirling like a dervish, the stick in front of her, hitting anything and everything that got in its way. Like a demented spinning top she began to reel around the room, slashing, sweeping, smashing. Pictures went flying; crystal, porcelain, anything the stick met was sent crashing as she went on an orgy of destructive rage. Dodging the flailing stick both Seth and Abby tried to get to grips with her, suffering painful blows in the process. And then Abby became conscious that the name her mother was screaming had changed. She was no longer calling for her son. It was: "Papa! Papa! Come back to me, Papa! Why have you left me? Come back to me, Papa!"

It was Annie, with stoic New England common sense, who stuck out a leg over which the whirling figure went sprawling, the stick flying from her hand. Jonas snatched it up while Seth and Abby bent to pick up the fallen woman, who by now was screaming the most foul obscenities. Abby was thinking desperately about straitjackets when suddenly she felt her mother's body buck and arch. Her voice was cut off as if by a hand on her throat, and her mouth only opened and shut soundlessly, while her face congested to an alarming shade of red which slowly began to turn purple.

"Her asthma! Oh, my God! The inhaler—quick—for God's sake—in the top drawer of the chest—hurry!"

Jonas yanked the drawer open so violently it came clean out of the chest, cascading its contents. Quickly he bent to scrabble among them before coming up with the inhaler, which he thrust into Abby's hand; she in turn thrust it into her mother's mouth, avoiding the fingers which clawed so desperately, while Annie held on grimly. Suddenly, both women felt the struggling body surge upward before arching like a bow. From the mouth came a half snort, half grunt, and Abby felt something warm trickle onto her fingers. There was a sudden foul smell and as Abby watched in horror her mother's face faded to a doughy gray as she sagged, like a sackful of meal, the blood from her nose staining the already befouled and torn nightgown.

"Mother!" screamed Abby in terror. "Oh, my God! Mother!"

BRAD DROVE in a manner that was as demented as his mother's; hurling the car across intersections, barreling across the Longfellow Bridge and into the North End, a part of Boston Julia did not know. The rain had made surfaces greasy, and the car kept sliding, once turning a complete circle, Brad skillfully going with it until he could put his foot down again. Julia, her own feet pressed to the floor, hung on to the door handle, but said not a word. She had heard, via the raised voices, enough to keep her silent. Soon they were in a part of the city that was run-down, decaying, the faces on the early-morning streets a mixture of ethnic minorities. In this part of Boston the tall, narrow-fronted houses of the Hill had degenerated into crowded tenements housing a dozen families, and the narrow, twisting streets, typical as Julia remembered from her brief stay in the city, were grimy with litter. When Brad turned into a dark, narrow alleyway, its walls green with damp and hung with rusty fire escapes, she moaned inwardly. Oh, Jenny . . . Jenny . . .

It was a cul-de-sac, the blocked end a huge pair of wooden gates, a smaller door inset.

With an urgent "Come on!" Brad was out of the car and thrusting the door open, holding it for Julia to hop through. A large, cobbled yard, piles of rusting machinery, a rackety old building on stilts, half wood, half corrugated sheet metal, a sagging flight of wooden steps. Following Brad as he made for it at a run, Julia's eyes scanned dirty and broken windows, and at one of them she saw her daughter's dirty face appear—still wearing its red Indian warbonnet. "Jenny! Oh, darling . . ." As she burst in through the door she saw Brad in the act of launching himself at Marcus, who was sitting at a battered table, a pile of comic books littering its top.

"Mummy! Where have you been? I've waited such a long time!"

"Jenny, darling!" Julia went down on one knee, enfolded the small body which hurtled into her arms. In between kissing her with enthusiastic abandon, Jenny asked aggrievedly: "I waited and waited and I'm hungry! Marcus promised me a Big Mac but I haven't had it yet—" This ended in a wail as the table went over. "Why is Uncle Brad hitting Marcus?"

Picking her up, Julia retreated to the rear of the room, away from the thrashing bodies, the grunts, the sound of bone on flesh.

"Because he is very angry with Marcus, who took you away without telling us. Oh, Jenny darling, why did you go with Marcus? I've been so worried."

"But Marcus said—" Jenny cowered against her mother with a squeal as Brad picked up a wooden chair and smashed it over Marcus's head. One look at his face had Julia screaming: "Brad! Brad, for God's sake. You'll kill him!" She had never seen such demonic anger and though she knew he was working off his grief and pain in the one way he could, she still tried to reach him. Marcus was bigger but Brad had the strength of the temporarily insane. Now he had Marcus on the floor and his hands were around his throat, squeezing, squeezing. "Brad!" Thrusting Jenny aside Julia ran forward. Brad's eyes were wide and fixed, his lips drawn back from his teeth in a snarl as his hands squeezed and Marcus's face empurpled and he scrabbled ineffectually with his own hands at the iron grip around his throat. "Brad!" Julia drew her arm back and with all her strength hit Brad across the face. "Stop it! Stop it!" she screamed at him. "He is not worth killing!" Jenny wailed and Julia screamed at him: "You are frightening Jenny!"

That name penetrated Brad's red mist and Julia saw the hands slacken, prised them loose from Marcus's neck with her own. He coughed, lay with his eyes closed, gulping air. Brad was bleeding from the nose, his face was red where Marcus's punches had landed, and his shirtsleeve was torn. Breathing hard he spat: "I should kill the lying bastard."

"You almost did."

"Is Jenny all right?"

"Yes, but you frightened her."

"Sorry," Brad said, not sorry at all. "He had it coming."

Jenny ran across to her mother now that it was safe to. "I don't like this place," she wailed. "And I'm hungry."

Brad laughed. Suddenly his mood had done a complete volte-face. "I might have known." He squatted down beside her and with a serious expression and in a stern voice he asked: "Why didn't you come and tell me you were going off with Marcus?"

"Because he told me not to," Jenny answered indignantly. "He said it was a surprise. We came on an aeroplane and I had Coke and ice cream and—"

"I thought you were not supposed to go off with anybody unless your mother said so."

"But it was Marcus," Jenny explained patiently.

"Even so. You don't do it again, understand?"

Jenny looked at her mother who was regarding her gravely. "Not even Marcus?" Jenny asked in a small voice.

"Not with *anyone*—even me. You understand?"

Jenny nodded.

"Your mummy was very unhappy. Do you know how worried she was, looking for you, wondering where you were."

A large tear rolled out of Jenny's left eye. "But Marcus said—"

"I don't care what Marcus said. You are never to go off with anyone —repeat, *anyone*—ever again unless your mother says you can. Is that understood?"

Jenny nodded. And at last Julia also understood—what she had found hard to believe when she had been married to Brad: that he could be hard, a man to watch for and one better not to cross. She had never seen him at work so she had never known that Brad. She had only seen the good-time, hard-playing, hard-laying man of the good looks and charm, or the reined-in terrorized man being emotionally blackmailed by his mother. This one, the man laying down the law to Jenny in such a way that she was instantly and obediently submissive, was the one that Seth—Abby too—had said was there, if you looked beneath the surface. Which, she thought acrid with bitterness, I never did. Him or his mother. Just because he never showed that strength to me—what need had he?—I never believed he had it. Oh, God forgive me, she thought. I made my own hash of things.

"I'm sorry," Jenny was saying in a small voice.

"That's my girl." Brad picked her up, kissed her, and she threw her arms around his neck and kissed him back. "I'm starving," she said hopefully. "Marcus promised me a Big Mac but I haven't had it."

"Then you shall have it. It so happens there's a McDonald's down the block."

"And can I have fries and a milk shake and—"

"Whatever," Brad agreed.

Seizing her chance: "Why don't you and Brad go along and order for the three of us," Julia said cheerfully. "I'll come and join you as soon as I've had a word with Marcus."

Brad turned, but before he could say anything, "This one is mine," Julia said quietly. Again their eyes met in a long look and then Brad nodded, satisfied.

"Come on, then," Brad said to his daughter. "There's a tap in the yard. Let's go and clean up; otherwise they might not serve us."

"Shall we order for you, Mummy?" Jenny asked as they reached the door.

"Yes. Some coffee—and a Big Mac. But lots of hot coffee."

Her face broke into an almost tearful smile as she looked at them. Jenny's once white T-shirt was now battleship gray; there were traces of dried tomato sauce at the corners of her mouth, and though her face, arms and legs were filthy, her Indian warbonnet was still firmly in place. Brad had sundry scrapes and bruises, a cut lip and the beginnings of a shiner.

"Go on," Julia said softly. "I won't be long." Again, she and Brad exchanged a long look, then the door flapped behind them. Julia turned to Marcus. He had dragged himself up onto the other chair and was sitting mopping at the cut over his eye with his pocket handkerchief. "And as for you . . . ," she said with loathing.

"Not now, Julia," Marcus winced as he spoke because a tooth was loose. "I'm in no shape."

"How *could* you, Marcus? I thought we were friends."

"It was easy. Always is when you have no choice. The old bat had me by the short hairs."

"But to abduct Jenny! I thought you loved her."

"I do. But I love my freedom more."

"What in God's name was her reason? She must have known I'd twig."

"She was beyond reason because she'd lost her own. I told her it was a half-assed idea but she wouldn't listen. I told her you'd trained Jenny not to go off with strangers but it was a waste of time. She was so mad she couldn't see straight."

"I know how she feels. You conned me; from the time you first came to the cottage you conned me. Pretending to be surprised at my pregnancy. It was because I was that she sent you, wasn't it? *Wasn't it?*"

"So she had you under surveillance. What else is new?"

"The fact that I have discovered you to be a liar, a cheat and a thief—as well as a kidnaper. It was her money you used to back me, wasn't it?"

"Well, *I* didn't have any."

"And the twenty percent—she got that too?"

"Fifteen; she was kind enough to allow me a measly five!"

He sounded aggrieved. Typical Marcus. Not sorry for what he had done; only sorry he had been caught.

"And to think I trusted you," Julia said.

"Look, if it hadn't been for me stalling the old bag you'd have been done to death long before this. Once I got to know you I was on your side."

"But not far enough to warn me. You played both sides, didn't you? Right in the middle of the seesaw."

"I did what I had to," Marcus said tiredly. "When you've done what I've done and been where I've been you soon learn enough to know that."

"I thought you weren't sent to jail," Julia said cruelly.

[288]

"Not that time," Marcus agreed, with a flash of his old humor.

Julia's laugh was incredulous. "And all that trying to get me into bed —her idea?"

"But my own inclination," Marcus said gallantly. He looked up at her then and she knew it was true. Not that it made any difference.

"Words fail me," she said at last.

"It will be the first time."

"It is also the last as far as you and I are concerned. You can take your twenty percent and shove it. Right where it hurts."

He probed his loose tooth. "It does."

"More than being blackmailed? You were, weren't you? It was either jail or—"

"I was doing her dirty work long before I got fired. That was what I went to Bradford & Sons to do. I was the one bought and sold; made the payoffs, arranged the bribes, organized the spying, the industrial espionage, as they call it nowadays. That was why she didn't prosecute. I knew too much. It was a standoff—well, more or less. And by that time she had her precious son under training." Marcus's voice curled as he said the last words.

"You hate Brad, don't you?"

"What's to like in the first place? Too cocky. The Golden Boy at Harvard. Foreign sports cars, the cream of the Radcliffe girls, careless tabs at coffeehouses, dinner *upstairs* at the Ritz. Why should any human being have so much? All I ever had were my wits. I didn't even have a real name. Nobody could pronounce my grandfather's name when he shuffled through Ellis Island so they made it plain Levin. He didn't even manage to bring his own name out of Russia!"

Too late Julia perceived, beneath the deliberately cultivated air of a man who cared for nothing but a fast buck, the old jealousies, the rancor, the envy—on all of which she had no doubt Hester Bradford had played.

"I took from the Bradfords because they could well afford it. It was my own fault I was careless that last time. She had me in the vise ever since."

"You must have died laughing sometimes," Julia said bitterly.

"Listen, working for Hester Bradford is no laughing matter."

"When you report back to her—and God help you when you do—"

"I'm not about to report back, forward, sideways or any way," Marcus said, still dabbing blood. "And if she has a mind to come after me tell her I have copies of certain documents which would put *her* in jail."

He laughed. "Bradford & Sons would become Bradford & Suborns—the last thing she wants."

Julia's hand cracked across his face with such force that he all but fell off the chair.

"That is the last thing I have to do where you are concerned."

The door flapped on its hinges behind her.

SHE WAS STILL AT WHITE HEAT when she entered the warmth of McDonald's, but as her eyes searched for then found her ex-husband and her daughter, again she had the urge to laugh. Jenny was chomping on a Big Mac while Brad, chin on hand, watched her with loving absorption. The smell of hot coffee made her mouth water, and as she joined them at the table a sudden lethargy hit her, and it was all she could do not to put her head down on the tabletop and close her eyes. Brad pushed a capped plastic beaker toward her. She took off the top, inhaled the smell, then sipped, sighed. "Oh, that's good."

"This is yours too, Mummy," Jenny pushed forward the plastic box containing her Big Mac. "Be quick or it will be cold."

Julia smiled but made no attempt to open the box.

"Aren't you hungry?" Jenny asked, puzzled. "Uncle Brad wasn't either so I ate his."

Julia burst out laughing. "You ate *two* Big Macs?"

"I was hungry," Jenny said.

Brad grinned. "She eats like a hungry tiger," he said. Then: "How'd it go?"

"All I thought was right. He was her spy. Had been for years. He also said that if there was any idea of going after him he has certain information which would result in Bradford & Sons changing its name to Bradford & Suborns."

Brad frowned. "Is that so . . ."

Julia turned her coffee cup. "He said—he said he did what you started doing when you went into the firm." She lifted her head, stared straight into his eyes. "The Department of Dirty Tricks," she said.

Brad met her eyes steadily. "That's right," he said. "That's where I served my apprenticeship. But I changed things somewhat once I had the power to do so. Mother did not need to do half the things she did; it was because she liked doing them."

Julia nodded. She was saddened but glad that Brad had told her the truth. This time, she thought, maybe it really can be truth between us . . .

"What now?" she asked.

[290]

"I go back to the farm. But first I take you back to Mount Vernon Street. I don't want you around Mother."

"If you can get us on a plane we'll go back to California."

"I think you should get some sleep first. Maybe tomorrow?"

She sensed he did not want her to rush off so she said merely: "All right." Then: "There is nothing I can do?"

"No. I don't want you involved in this."

"Too late. I am involved because of Jenny."

"Maybe, but you've got her back, thank God. It's my job to get to grips with the rest of it."

Knowing he was thinking of the screams that had reached them even through closed windows, Julia said encouragingly: "Abby will have coped."

"That's what I mean. She shouldn't have to. This is my ball of wax."

She could feel his tension now that the combination of euphoria and adrenaline had cooled. As it was, the close warmth of the restaurant coming on top of her own release of tension was producing a lethargy and sudden heavy tiredness which had her struggling to keep her eyes open. Jenny, too, was beginning to droop, unable to make it all the way with her second hamburger. As she put it down she yawned. "I'm tired, Mummy."

Brad made to rise with such alacrity that Julia realized he was impatient to be gone. Of course, she thought. No matter what, she is still his mother.

Jenny went to sleep on her mother's lap, the combination of a full stomach and reaffirmed security proving too much for her. Julia herself wanted nothing more than to crawl into bed. But Thomas, as he opened the door to them, looked unaccustomedly strained and flustered. "Mr. Brad, thank God you are back!"

Brad frowned. "What's the matter?"

"It's your mother, sir. She had a stroke early this morning. Mrs. Amory called not long ago to tell you that she has been taken to Massachusetts General. I explained you were not here but she said to tell you when you arrived."

Brad was glued to the floor. *"A stroke!"*

"Yes, sir. Mrs. Adams is also at the hospital and I have informed the rest of family."

Julia made a decision. "Can I put Jenny in a bed somewhere? She is so tired I am sure she won't wake, but if you will, have someone keep an eye on her."

Thomas's face changed as he registered who it was standing with the child in her arms. "Mrs.—Miss Julia! Of course . . . of course . . . I am sorry. The shock, you understand."

"Wait," Julia commanded Brad. "I'll go with you."

He did not answer.

Julia hurriedly put Jenny into the bed of the first bedroom Thomas showed her; she did not wake, just curled into a ball and put her thumb in her mouth.

"I will have one of the servants sit with her," Thomas said.

"Thank you, Thomas. If she should wake—though I doubt it—call me at the hospital."

"Very good, Miss Julia."

Brad was standing exactly as she had left him. She touched his arm. "Come along. I'll drive you to the hospital."

THOMAS HAD TOLD THEM Lady Hester was in intensive care, and as they entered the waiting area, Julia saw that the entire Bradford clan, down to second and third cousins, was gathered.

Abby sat with Seth, who was holding her hands. On her other side sat Charley, much changed: thirty pounds lighter and fashionably chic. Behind them stood their two boys—except they were now men. Under the window sat Bitsy, a son on either side of her, her husband staring out until he turned to look at Julia.

Everybody else merely stared.

Abby rose at once. "Brad! Thank God. You got Jenny?"

"Yes. What happened?"

"She went on the rampage after you left—lost that temper of hers. That led to her asthma—bad—which led to a cerebral hemorrhage. She suffered what the doctors called 'a massive insult to the brain.' She's in a coma; on a life-support machine."

"Can I see her?"

"I'll take you."

As they disappeared through swing doors with portholes, Julia turned to look for somewhere to sit, and as her eyes ranged the room and found nowhere, they met those of Bitsy, fixed on her like holes burning paper. "Go on, take a good look!" was hissed at her venomously. "All this is your fault! You only have to appear on the scene for this family to turn into a disaster area!"

"Bitsy!" Seth snapped out the word as he rose to his feet.

"Don't you Bitsy me! I'm only saying what is true. If she hadn't come back none of this would have happened. It's because of her Mother and

Brad rowed, isn't it? Just as it is because of her my mother is dying now!"

Seth reached Julia, pressed her arm. "Julia is here because your mother abducted her child!"

"Because she was Brad's, you fool! I've yet to see the day when she gave so much as a thought to *my* children!"

"You forget yourself! In all fairness—"

"Fairness! Since when did fair have anything to do with Brad and Mother? Her dice were always loaded in favor of her only, precious son!" Bitsy rose to her feet, advanced toward Julia like an animal about to spring. "Why did you ever come into this family? You brought nothing but trouble! I didn't like you then and I don't like you now, you insufferably superior bitch! Who the hell did you ever think you were, anyway? You were about as natural as a spray of white gladioli!"

"Bitsy!" Seth was thunderous. "Julia has done nothing to deserve such abuse from you."

"It's because she never has done anything—not a goddamn thing—that she did for me—for Mother—for Brad! She just stood by and let Mother have her way, didn't she? If she loved Brad, why didn't she fight for him? But not her, oh no! She would not stoop so low! She might get the hem of her skirts dirty—and she always so careful to draw them aside! She never gave a damn about anybody but her own selfish self!"

"You are demonstrating some pretty obvious selfishness of your own right now!"

"I am demonstrating how I feel—which is more than she ever did at any time!"

"What Mother did to Julia was indefensible!"

"I only wish to God she had cared enough about me and my children to do the same! But it was always Brad, only and ever Brad. Brad . . . B-R-A-D!" Spittle sprayed Julia's face as Bitsy howled her anguish before, as her husband came up to her, she collapsed into his arms, weeping hysterically. His glance at Julia was cold, bitterly accusing. Everybody else stared with fascination at the floor, obviously wondering when it was going to open up.

Julia felt a hand on her arm, looked up blankly to see Seth regarding her worriedly. "That was unforgivable of Bitsy. I can only ask for your understanding. The shock . . . She is in a highly emotional state."

Why aren't I? thought Julia. Instead, she felt numb, found she could not move her legs.

Bitsy's deadly accurate fire seemed to have landed right in her control center. She was only expressing an opinion, Julia told herself numbly. Yes, but the fact that you don't recognize her portrait of you does not mean it is still not a valid likeness. A white gladiolus? So stiff, so white, so lifeless . . . She shuddered.

"My dear." Seth was concerned. "Please, do not distress yourself. Surely you know by now that every picture Bitsy paints is warped by her jealousy of her brother."

Warped? Julia thought. How come it has made me see straight, then?

"You have had a traumatic twenty-four hours," Seth went on consolingly. "I think you should go back to your daughter and rest. There is nothing you can do here." A sigh. "This is a terminal vigil, I am afraid. Her brain is irreparably destroyed. Go back to your daughter. I will explain to Brad."

Moving her along like an automaton, Seth accompanied her all the way to her car, bent to peer through the window with a last "You are sure you are all right, now? Perhaps I had better drive you back."

"No. You stay with Abby. She needs you. I'll be all right. Really I will." It was just that she did not know when.

He watched her until she was out of sight, and as soon as she was she stopped the car, put her head down on the wheel and shook. Never in her life had anyone spoken to her with such brutal frankness. It had the effect of smashing her self-image to smithereens. What she had always thought she was and what other people saw were obviously no relation whatsoever. Disdainful? Insufferably calm and collected? Was that how her deliberate striving for cool control had seemed to others? Had the image she had been at such pains to perfect been taken for reality? Well, had not appearances always been of paramount importance? Her aunt had told her (and *told* her): "People take you at your own value, Julia. Never let them see you as anything less than perfect."

Chris had told her she worshiped perfection. And a lot of other things. Which she had brushed aside. Pride, she thought now. Rampant, arrogant pride. Hester Bradford must have spotted it at once. No wonder she was able to manipulate me every which way. She saw, all right. And capitalized. Had she not known how I would react she would never have been able to succeed.

Another no-no, Julia thought, as she forced herself to grope among the broken glass for the bleeding remnants of her self-esteem. First Chris, now Bitsy. It must be true. I am like that. To other people, anyway. I had no idea—no idea at all. She had deceived herself for so long. Like telling herself that not making waves was what Brad wanted when what he had needed—and desperately—was someone to do exactly that, even if he had not known it himself. Drexel Adams had said she was strong. Was rescue. She had known—yes, *known*—Brad was afraid of his mother and yet let her own terrors dominate her actions. She had drawn her skirts aside; she had—had always had—a shuddering distaste of emotional brangles. She had not even wondered *why* Bitsy was jealous; merely accepted that she was.

For some reason the words of the General Confession, half remembered, sifted into her brain. How did it go? ". . . left undone those things which we ought to have done; And we have done those things which we ought not to have done and there is no health in us." And she had thought Hester Bradford was sick! Oh, God, she thought. What have I done? What have I not done? Brad had confessed to the sins of the perennial child; she had confessed to what she had thought were her sins of the emotional adolescent. She had not seen for one moment that she was totally ignoring the sin of pride. One of the seven deadly ones . . . She remembered what Brad had said, the first time they met, about waste being the eighth. She was guilty of that too. She had wasted time, her marriage, everything.

Shaken and trembling she stared at "The Portrait of Julia Carey" in all its hideousness. A white gladiolus. Stiff, white, unbending. Bitsy's accuracy stripped away her pride in shreds. She *had* been rigid, *had* been unbending. Had never for one moment understood *emotionally;* only intellectually. It was only now, in her own pain and suffering, that she felt, with a twisting, inner agony, what Brad must be feeling right now.

A sob exploded from her; tears, hot and blinding, spurted from her eyes as jolting sounds erupted from her body. Dear God, forgive me. The accumulated tension of the previous twenty-four hours went off in an explosion which shattered her. She was not conscious of anything but her feelings and for the first time in her life gave way to them; let them take her over, spew out her incarcerated emotional life. She wept until all she had left was the dry heaves, and even then sat on, her head on the steering wheel, shuddering at the memory of an anguish not to be borne, yet feeling as if she had gone through the fire. But Brad was still being roasted on his.

She sat up, pushed her hair out of her eyes, felt for a tissue, dried her face, glanced at it in the driving mirror and looked quickly away. Should she go back? Wait with the others? Show them she was not one to crawl away with her tail between her legs? Pride! she warned herself. What the hell does it matter what they think? It is Brad who matters; what he is going through, what he is suffering. Go back to Jenny, wait for him. He is going to need you more than ever. Be there. Do it right this time, Julia. You have to. It's your last chance. You failed him before. For God's sake—for his sake and for your own—don't do it again.

As she started the car again, she felt she had been filtered through a strainer; that the residue was a Julia shorn of every superfluity. She felt light-headed; only hoped that what was left was enough to see her through whatever was to come. Well, she thought. All I can do is try.

CAROLINE BECAME AWARE that someone was shaking her, shouting at her.

"Will you for God's sake wake up! Caroline, do you hear me? *Caroline!*"

"Go away . . . leave me alone . . ."

"I've left you alone and look what's happened! You are so stoned you are unrecognizable. *Will you wake up?*"

"Nothin' to wake up for."

"But there is, that's what I want you to see!"

Forcing open sticky eyes, Caroline saw her mother's face hovering above her, alight with blazing triumph. She blinked, tried to focus and saw that her mother was clutching handfuls of the dailies. "Such news! Hester Bradford is dead! It's the truth! She had a stroke yesterday morning and died late last night. Look, it's on all the front pages."

Heaving herself up, Caroline knuckled her gummy eyes. "Here . . . drink this." Her mother shoved a glass of ice-cold orange juice into her hand. Its stinging chill helped clear Caroline's befogged mind.

"Go on. See for yourself. The old bitch is dead, all right! I never thought I'd live to see the day!" Eloise was beside herself with delight.

Rubbing her eyes again, Caroline peered blearily at the papers her mother thrust at her. A picture of her mother-in-law, a banner headline: "BOSTON'S ULTIMATE GRANDE DAME DIES." It was a Boston paper; Eloise Norton took them all; carefully cut out any reference to her daughter as Mrs. J. Winthrop Bradford for her scrapbooks. "It's true." Caroline said stupidly.

"Of course it's true! Now come on. There's no time to lose. You've got to get back to Boston—but not before you've had the works first. *Look* at you! Talk about going to seed!" Her mother could have wept. "It's Arden's and the works for you, my girl. I'll call the lawyers too. Stop the divorce. No need for that now with the old hag out of the way. Come on, then! Don't you realize what this means?"

Hester Bradford actually dead! Caroline's alcohol-drugged brain could not take it in. People like her didn't die. They went on forever; spoiling chances, suborning hopes, clinging tightly to sons.

Her mother bustled back from the bathroom. "Will you come *on!*"

She dragged Caroline from the rumpled bed, dislodging an empty bottle as she did so. "And no more of that either!" Eloise dropped it in the wastebasket. "From now on you are on the wagon, hear? God, what a mess you are!" Her disgust made her wrinkle her nose at the puffy face, the black-rooted hair, the stale smell of booze. She shoved Caroline into the shower, nightdress and all, and turned the tap on to full. Caroline yelled but her mother refused to turn off the cold water. "One way or another you are going to be stone cold sober when you get to Boston this afternoon."

And it was a very different Caroline whom Thomas let into the house. The magicians behind Miss Elizabeth Arden's red door had worked wonders. Her face was exquisitely made up, her hair newly blonded to a bright, guinea gold, her Oscar de la Renta suit of black velvet set off by a chic hat with a fine mist of veiling which helped conceal eyes still somewhat bloodshot.

"Mrs. Bradford!"

"Where is everybody, Thomas?"

"At the farm, madam."

"The farm!"

"Yes, madam. They all returned there after—when Lady Hester died."

Damn! She should have thought. It was always the farm for births, marriages and deaths. The Bradfords had this thing about going back to their roots. And she dressed for Proper Boston.

"I'll just go upstairs and change." Sailing past him: "Have the Mercedes sports brought around, will you? I'll drive to the farm myself."

Quickly she rummaged in closets still crammed with her clothes. There should be that black wool dress . . . Ah, yes, that would do nicely. Just right for the country. She exchanged her high-heeled pumps for low-heeled walkers, took down her Russian sable coat. She was still Brad's wife, after all.

She was confident she could get him back. At a time like this. He would be leaning badly; a twentieth-century Tower of Pisa. She knew just how to handle him.

But when she saw the cars packing the drive and lawns she knew it was not going to be so easy. Damn and damn! The whole goddamn state was paying condolences.

[297]

"Well!" Abby confronted Caroline four-square. "You are the last person we expected to see!"

"Why not? Everybody else is here!" The enormous living room was packed with people, all with a drink in their hands, talking in low, death-in-the-family voices. "I *am* Brad's wife, you know!"

"But not for much longer, surely. You went back to Philadelphia screaming divorce at the top of your lungs."

"That was then. Things are different now."

"And how!" Abby retorted grimly.

"You heard the way your mother spoke to me, the names she called me. She was the one who ordered me from the house!"

"Exactly. All this goes straight back to you. You've got some nerve showing your face around here!"

"I have a right to be here with my husband. Where is he?"

"Busy. We are not exactly alone, you know."

"I can see *that!*"

"Leave him alone, Caroline. He has enough on his plate right now."

Caroline would choke him, Abby thought angrily. The last thing Brad needed. And with Julia here. But Brad had been adamant. "Julia stays—Jenny too." Bitsy had been livid but Abby was glad. Her glance fell on Caroline's overnight bag. "You haven't come to stay!"

"Of course I have! As Brad's wife—"

"Oh, for God's sake, don't keep rubbing it in! And don't bother him right now. Make yourself useful, instead. Take some of these people off our hands."

Caroline found herself pushed toward a group of people, had no choice but to shake hands, accept condolences. Well, she consoled herself, it would only serve to consolidate her position in the family.

Her eyes searched the room for Brad; finally found him at the far end, in the middle of a large group—mostly women. As she circulated, moving ever nearer, she watched him covertly. He looked awful! she thought gloatingly. Positively haggard! And so much older. About time he grew up. Everybody else had to. This tired, strained, suffering man was not the Golden Boy she had married. And no wonder, she thought vengefully. He's got to stand on his own two feet from now on and he doesn't know how. Nobody to hold him by the hand anymore. This Brad would not give her any trouble, she gloated. This Brad she could take and mold to *her* design. And by the time I'm through with him, *nobody* will recognize him.

But when she finally did manage to get to him there was no welcome in his eyes; there was nothing in his eyes. They were dead. And when he kissed her cheek, shook her hand, it was as he would greet a well-meaning stranger. "Caro, thank you for coming."

"What do you mean? I'm your wife, for God's sake!"

Just then, old Mrs. Peabody, who never left her house in Louisburg Square except for visits of condolence, came across on her youngest grandson's arm. Caroline watched her husband give her the same politeness she had received. I'm not having this! she thought. He's got a nerve, treating me like I was just another visitor. Fuming, she watched him escort Mrs. Peabody to the door, and then saw his younger sister bearing down on her. Deliberately she turned her back, walked away. That one needn't think she was going to take her mother's place. She made for Charley, pale and red-eyed. "What's going on here!" she demanded. "What's happened to Brad?"

Charley's mouth thinned with distaste. "His mother has just died."

"I know that! I mean the change in him."

"Wouldn't you be if it was your mother?"

No, I wouldn't, thought Caroline, who lied quickly: "Of course, I know how awful it must be but— Oh, come on, Charley. You know how it was."

"All that matters to Brad right now is how it is," Charley said quietly.

"It will never be the same," Caroline agreed, thinking: Thank God!

Charley shuddered. "No. It was awful— Mother said—" But she remembered to whom she was talking and forbore to say that before murmuring something and making a hasty escape.

Awful? thought Caroline, sixth sense twitching. Had there been some kind of trouble? Something to cause the old bitch's death? Why else should Brad look so—so poleaxed? From what she had managed to pick up, via condolences, it was obvious that the death had been unexpectedly sudden, but then, strokes always were, weren't they? I wonder, thought Caroline. Did something send her over the edge and bring it on? She never had a day's sickness that I ever knew of and she was always monitored by her doctor. Something must have caused it. And then it hit her. Brad? Oh, no, she thought gleefully. He caused it? No wonder he looks like he's under his own sentence of death. She had not seen him since he had fled the house that night, and on her own return to Philadelphia, after the old bat had ordered her from the house and told her never to show her face again, she had taken refuge in the bottle. Damn! What have I missed? Had Brad confronted his mother after all? Had he finally seen the light? That would make the old bat blow her top all right. I have to find out, she thought. This is important. If he's got guilt shoved up to here I have to know exactly why and how . . . She cast about the crowded room for her husband, only to see Abby come out of the study with a look on her face that told Caroline instantly that something was going on in there. Waiting until Abby was swallowed up in a group, she made quickly for the study only to find it empty. But the French windows at the far end were open and through them she heard the high, excited laughter of a child. "Higher, Uncle Brad . . . higher . . ."

In a couple of strides, Caroline was through the windows and onto the flagged terrace overlooking the lawns beyond, only to stop short with a grunted "Oh," much as a man will utter when hit by a bullet. So, she thought. That was it. Her. And the brat. I might have known.

On the swing tied to the big elm, a little girl was laughing delightedly as she went soaring upward, only to be pushed forward again when she swung back. Pushing her was Brad, and standing nearby, watching, was Julia Carey.

Julia saw her coming. "Brad . . ." He turned.

"Well!" Simmering with grievance: "This is why you've been avoiding me, your wife!"

"Come along, darling." Julia stopped the swing, lifted Jenny down. "Let's go see the horses."

"You stay right where you are," snapped Caroline, "where I can see what you are up to!"

"Take Jenny to see the horses," Brad said quietly. Jenny looked from him to her mother, who said: "We'll come back to the swing later."

As they walked off, "What's she doing here?" Caroline demanded belligerently.

"I asked her to come."

Caroline's jaw dropped. "Not while your mother was here, I'll bet!" she rallied.

"No."

"Of course not! You wouldn't expose *her* to your mother's spite, would you? But you left me to it, didn't you, running off like the coward you are! I had to stand the brunt of that vicious tongue of hers. I won't sully mine with the names she called me! I wouldn't speak to a dog the way she spoke to me!"

"I'm sorry, Caroline." He sounded it. "In fact," he went on in the same quiet voice, "I have to ask you to forgive me for many things. Like marrying you. It was wrong, I see that now. It was never what either of us wanted; only what my mother decided."

"That's not true! I did want you—from the moment I first set eyes on you I wanted you!"

[300]

"You mean you wanted to be Mrs. J. Winthrop Bradford."

"Because I loved you—love you."

"Do you, Caro? I wonder . . ."

"It's true. I've always loved you!"

"Me—or what I represented?"

"How can you say such a cruel thing?"

"Because I can, now. Don't you see, Caro—"

"You are the one who doesn't see! Never has seen anything but what your mother put in front of you! You never saw, for instance, the misery she made of my life! Always sneering at me, looking down at me, despising me. Always hinting I wasn't a real woman because I couldn't produce a child—oh, yes, you never heard her because she never did it while you were around—and a lot you cared anyway. All you ever cared about was fucking everything in sight!"

Brad's voice was smothered when he said: "Forgive me for that too, if you can."

Caroline stopped in mid-tirade. "What's happened to you?" she demanded querulously. "I don't know you anymore."

"Thank God for that."

"What's been going on around here? What has happened to make you like this? And why is that woman here—and that brat!"

"My daughter," Brad corrected.

"I see. I'm to be dumped, am I, because I could never give you one!"

"No, it is not like that. It never worked in the past and it won't work in the future. There is nothing *there*, Caro; you know that as well as I do." The quiet but resolute firmness in his voice drove her wild.

"If you think you can bury me with your mother you've got another think coming! After all the years I served? No way! I haven't spent five years in hell to let some other bitch enter my paradise!"

"It's no use, Caro. I can't make you happy; you can't make me happy, either. I did you a great wrong by marrying you, and I ask you again to forgive me if you can. But I am not going to try and revive something that died a long time ago. Take your freedom, Caro, and go look for someone else."

"I don't want anybody else. I want you, I've got you and by God, I'll keep you!" Her face had flooded with bright scarlet blood and her voice risen along with it. "My father bought you for me; you are mine, mine, do you hear? I'll be damned if I'll let you dump me for that redheaded bitch!"

"Watch what you are saying," Brad said, in a voice which changed

[301]

the red to white. "It's over, Caro. A lot of things have come to an end. Our marriage is one of them."

"Not if I have anything to say! Who the hell do you think you are, you suddenly sanctimonious son of a bitch! You are the last person in the world to have suddenly got religion! It won't last, either! I know you too well! You won't dump me, Mr. High-and-Mighty-Boston-Bradford! I'll raise such a stink nobody will be able to stand downwind of you!"

But he only repeated, this time with sad finality: "I'm sorry, Caro," before turning to walk away.

"Don't you dare turn your back on me!"

But he did, walking steadily away.

"Bastard!" she screamed after him. "Rotten, stinking, cheating, bastard!"

"Why is that lady shouting at Uncle Brad?" Jenny asked, frowning like her grandmother.

"Because she is very angry." Poor bitch, thought Julia. Mangled, like everyone else within shouting distance of Hester Bradford, only Caroline was bent and determined not to suffer alone. Which, Julia thought heavily, was exactly what Brad was doing right now.

He had woken her on his return from the hospital to tell her his mother was dead. "I told them they could pull the plug," he said, voice, eyes, empty of everything but defeat. "There was no hope, they said. No hope at all. Her brain was all but destroyed."

Julia slid out of the big bed, careful not to wake Jenny, and put her arms around him, holding his cold, stiff body against the heat of her own, bed warmth. "It is for the best," she said—knowing it was so in all ways as well as the physical. "She would not really have been alive on that machine. Just—a living-dead thing."

"She looked so small," Brad said, sounding puzzled. "There was nothing of her, yet she had always loomed so large. How was it she looked so small?"

She had seen the glitter of tears, bright as shards, and she felt them slice her flesh. For she knew now she loved this broken, bitter, pain-filled man as she had never loved the dazzling Golden Boy who had bowled her over and left her crippled—emotionally, that was. For this unhappy, stricken man she felt a tenderness that welled unstoppably; as had her love for Jenny, when first she had held her in her arms. This man needed her as the other never had; this man had nothing to offer her but years of accumulated pain and grief, along with the remnants of a persona he was struggling valiantly to hold together, yet she found she wanted him—warts and all, she thought gladly—as she had never wanted the old one. And with her heart, not her body. That was the difference, she realized. This was not sexual at all; sex did not come into it. This was wholly emotional.

"Oh, my poor love," she said, cradling him as she would a hurt child.

"I killed her," he said, in the same, empty voice. "I knew damned well it was fatal for her to lose that terrible temper but I goaded her to it by abandoning her. She couldn't take it. I was her life; she told me, time and time again that I would one day be the death of her—"

"No!" Julia's vehemence made him jerk. "You must not think that! Your mother did for herself! If she had learned to control that temper, learned to understand that she must let you go, she would not have killed herself. But she did. Because she could not let you go; could not accept that you had to. Yes, it was her temper that did for her. Because she could not have what *she* wanted. You must not blame yourself for something that is not your fault!"

As she pressed her face against his she felt the wetness of his tears. "I loved her so much—and hated her so deeply. I wanted desperately to be free of her but I was terrified of something like this; that is why I could never do it . . . She was right, though. I was the death of her."

"You were not!" Julia's voice was impassioned. "She was the death of herself! Even she could not gainsay that!"

She put him away to look at him, but his eyes were closed. His face was gray with fatigue. No wonder, she thought, awash with compassion. How long is it since he had any sleep? Forty-eight hours at least. He was a dead weight in her arms; sandbagged by the accumulation of exhaustion and his own torment.

"You are tired," she murmured tenderly. "You need sleep . . ."

"Tired," he mumbled. "So tired . . ."

Carefully she lowered him to the bed, where he fell back, already unconscious. She took off only his shoes before lifting his legs under the covers. Then she got in beside him. Mumbling something he moved close, buried his head in the hollow of her shoulder in the old, familiar way, his arms instinctively finding their way about her. He sighed once, and deeply, then was fathoms deep in sleep.

My poor love, Julia thought achingly, contented as she had no right to be; glad to be able to hold him, give him comfort, warmth, whatever he needed. Just so long as she was able to. He had needed her before, in that tyrannical way of his; this was different. It was not forced, this time; he was not running from, he was turning to. And there was, she discovered, such an enormous difference. It was strange, she marveled. There was nothing sexual about it at all; always, when they had held each other like this it had been either a prelude to or the afterglow of sex. Not this time. As she held him, he blissfully unconscious, she was equally blissful, because, for the first time ever, she felt that now, he really belonged to her. And not just because his mother was dead. Not just because he was caught by her face and desired her body; but because he needed *her*, Julia Carey: the *person* she was, not just the woman. It had been her he had come to for comfort, for reassurance, for tenderness. And oh, how marvelous it was to be able to give it.

She smoothed the hair back from his forehead, noticing how deeply the lines were there engraved. She traced them with her lips, also the golden stubble on his cheeks. He murmured something, shifted his body even closer. Beyond him, Jenny turned over and snuggled herself into his back. He was lovingly sandwiched in between two people who loved him. And that is what he needs, Julia resolved. Not smothering, possessively greedy love, but simple acceptance of all that he was—and was not. Which, she also realized, was what, at last, she had finally managed to achieve. All he was, all he was not, just so long as he was. It had taken her a long time, but she had finally arrived at the truth of things: that only through another human being was real fulfillment to be found; mutual acceptance and affirmation of what it meant to be what she had been so afraid to be: human.

Sighing, she fitted her body against his, legs entwined, arms about each other, his breath warm on her throat, one arm over his body so that it could rest lightly on their daughter. Then she closed her own eyes and joined them in sleep.

CAROLINE STORMED BACK to the house blind with rage, headed straight for the bottle, not caring who saw, though the last of the visitors were getting into their cars. She was desperate for a drink; poured herself a hefty slug of scotch, which she downed before refilling her glass. Thoughtfully taking the decanter with her, she retreated to the windows, where she curled up in the corner, hidden by the curtains, burning grievance at a fast rate. She felt she had been badly used; thrown out in the general clearance that always followed upon a death: old clothes disposed of, old marriages too. The hell he would! She conveniently forgot she had stormed out of this very house only a week earlier threatening the messiest of divorces. After all, there had been no point in hanging on, then. Not after that row to end all rows she had had with the old bat. Now, she had been gotten rid of. Everything was different now. I'll never let him go, she vowed, never! He won't get rid of me without a fight! By God, I'll show him a list of names that will stop him dead in his tracks! Just let him try and dump me! I knew I was right to keep score! Gulping more whiskey she once more refilled her empty glass. The rake reformed! Like hell! Just let him begin to feel the draft from the hole his mother had left in his life and he'd soon revert to type. Then we'll see, she thought with gleeful spite. If he thought she would allow him to supplant her with that redheaded bitch he had another think coming! Let him see what it was like to be desperate, to want and never be able to have. Oh, yes, that would serve him damned well right! He could want that English bitch as much as he liked—and that ginger-haired brat of theirs; he would get neither! Not if she had anything to say about it! She was here and here she would stay.

"I DON'T CARE what you say," Bitsy said aggrievedly as she followed Abby into the living room. "She was my mother too, and I have as much right as Brad has."

"Oh, turn the record over!" Abby seethed long-sufferingly. "What the hell can you do anyway? Mother's will is absolutely explicit. All Brad has to do is follow her instructions."

"Even so, I have the right."

"Oh, go with him then. Haggle over the kind of coffin if you want to. I only hope it makes you feel better!"

"Nobody knows how I feel!"

"It's not for lack of trying!"

"I have to do *something*. I can't just sit and think! It's driving me up the wall!"

"Did you ever stop to think Brad might be climbing it!"

But at that, Abby thought, they were all milling about in confusion; with the linchpin gone the pieces were falling all over the place. Thank God Mother's will was so absolutely explicit.

She was to be buried at Arun, beside her father. She was to be embalmed, as he had, but the use of cosmetics was forbidden. She was to be buried in a dress they found put away in a drawer in her bedroom; carefully wrapped in a plastic bag which was airproof. It was a white dress, style circa 1930, and there were white satin T-strap shoes as well as a pair of pure silk stockings. It was the dress her father had bought her for her twenty-first-birthday dance. The coffin was to be of English oak, not a casket, and it was to be sealed at once. There would be no viewing the body. The funeral would be private, family only, but she had left detailed instructions for two memorial services: one in Boston, one at Arun. She had drawn up an order of service for all three: the prayers to be used, the lessons read, the hymns to be sung. There was to be no eulogy.

Her will was equally explicit. Her Bradford A shares went to her son, along with the bulk of her personal fortune, the amount of which staggered them all. He also got all her property holdings and her extensive stock portfolio. Her jewelry she distributed among her daughters and granddaughter, which made Bitsy even more rancorous because instead of the emeralds, which she coveted, she got the rubies she hated. Abby got the emeralds, and Charley the diamond parure. There were bequests to long-standing servants such as Thomas, Annie and Jonas, as well as to the charities on whose committees she had served. Mount Vernon Street already belonged to Brad; he also got the farm. Nothing was left to chance or any one else's whim. She had even left typed drafts of the death notices to be inserted in the London *Times* and the Boston papers. Even in death, she was still issuing orders.

Abby looked up as Brad came in, shrugging into his topcoat. "You are coming then?" he asked Bitsy, who was wrapped in what had been her mother's sables, which she had appropriated before anybody else had even thought of them.

"Of course I am!"

"Suit yourself. Won't be too long," he said to Abby. "I hope."

"Are you sure you are up to it? I mean—"

"Don't fuss, Abby," was all he said.

Just then, Julia came downstairs. She had a piece of paper in her hand. "If you are going into Boston, I wonder, could you bring me back a few things? We brought absolutely nothing with us."

"Anything you want, Julia," Brad answered readily. "Just say."

Bitsy stalked off in high dudgeon. The front door slamming behind her.

Which was what woke Caroline. For a minute she did not know where she was. Her head was splitting and when she tried to stand up her legs would not hold her. She could hear voices, but from a long way off. She sat for a few moments, then heaved herself up to open the window. Raw, rain-wet air made her shiver but she gulped it greedily. As she did so, she heard her husband's voice say: "Go and wait in the car out of the cold. I'll wait for Julia to finish her list."

"It's about time she went back to wherever she came from," Caroline heard Bitsy say viciously. "How you can stand to have her around after what she did—"

"A hell of a sight easier than I can stand some other people," Brad answered curtly. "Leave off the mauling, Bitsy. It's not Julia's fault and you know it. If you can't say anything nice then don't say anything at all. Julia is staying and that's that!" Caroline saw Bitsy stalk past the window on her way to the car.

After what Julia did? Caroline wondered. I had better have a little talk with sister Bitsy. She froze as she heard Julia say: "I think this is all."

"Anything you want," Brad assured her. "Anything at all, Julia."

"It's mostly stuff for Jenny. Charley has been kind enough to lend me a few things. She's about my size."

"About is right. And they don't suit you. I remember your size. I'll see what I can bring back."

"Caroline!" Abby's voice was so thunderous that Caroline clutched at the curtains. "I thought you had gone— Oh, for God's sake, not drunk again!"

"I am most certainly not!" Caroline refuted with drunken dignity.

"Then I'd hate to see you sober! The best thing you can do is sleep it off. Come on, up those stairs before I kick you up! God, do you *ever* think of anyone but yourself!"

"Why shouldn't I! Nobody else ever does! I might as well be just a piece of furniture around here for all the notice taken of me!"

"That's your trouble: unless you are the center of attention you raise hell. Go on, get yourself up those stairs one way or another!"

Shoving Caroline in front of her, Abby prodded and poked her upstairs, where she thrust her into the first bedroom they came to, with such force that Caroline landed on the bed in a heap, clutching at the covers to keep from falling.

"And don't come down until you are fit to be seen!" Abby slammed the door on her. Crawling into the bed, Caroline flopped down on her stomach. She did feel tired. A little sleep would do her good. *Then* she would tackle Brad about that English bitch.

As SHE WENT BACK into the living room Abby encountered Julia. "Stoned!" she snorted disgustedly. "I'm not having Brad put up with that as well as everything else."

"Too late." Julia told her about the scene down by the tree.

Abby heaved a hopeless sigh. "If it's not one thing it's another, mostly my dear sister. I haven't had a minute to say so, but I'm sorry about the going-over she gave you."

Julia made a dismissive gesture. It had been a salutary experience in more ways than one, and in spite of everything she found she was more grateful than grieved. Bitsy's onslaught had shaken loose a whole basket of rotten apples, and it took only one to spoil all the rest.

"She went for Brad too, you know. Accused him of killing his own mother."

"Oh, Abby, no!"

"Oh, yes. She's always lacked a top skin where he was concerned and that's been eaten away by her jealousy. Now she'll never get to first base with Mother." Abby raised her hands helplessly. "You see how we are? Punch-drunk, all of us. Just remember that under the hard icing is a bitterly unhappy and frustrated woman."

"I know." Now, thought Julia.

"Mother's scythe was an indiscriminate one except where Brad was concerned, and the funny thing is I don't think Bitsy would have minded the cuts if Mother had minded her." Another sigh. "I was lucky. I had Seth; since I was seventeen I had Seth. Bitsy never really had Drex, if you know what I mean. That was one of Mother's little mergers."

"How did you manage to escape?"

"I eloped. Oh, yes; as soon as I was eighteen Seth and I ran off to Maryland. By the time Mother caught up with us I was carrying Seth, Jr. And in spite of looking like a mournful hound, my Seth has teeth *and* a bark. Maybe if Bitsy had had my luck . . . But she never had anyone. Drex didn't marry her for love. She never has been loved. That's her trouble."

Abby sighed again. "Anyway, what concerns me right now is that Brad feels he is among friends. And he adores Jenny. She's good for him. Around her he shows some sort of life. That's why I want to say how grateful I am to you for agreeing to stay on. After what this family did to you, you had every right to tell us to get lost."

"Right now, it is Brad's being lost that worries me."

"Me too. And I've got the feeling that we are in the eye of the hurricane. God only knows what lies ahead . . ."

CAROLINE AWOKE TO DARKNESS. Her head was banging, until she realized it was a window, rattling in the wind. Heaving herself up, she went to shut it. It had been raining again; the lights from the porch revealed pools on the gravel of the drive, the glitter of drops on the leaves; everything was wet and shiny. She leaned her muzzy head against the coolness of the glass, only to jerk upright again as she saw her husband and his first wife, warmly wrapped up against the damp cold, descend the steps of the porch and walk off, hand in hand, into the darkness.

Rage prodded her with its goad. In a flash she was across to the door and leaning over the banister rail. Silence. Her stocking feet were soundless as she ran lightly down the stairs, across the hall and out of the front door. She did not feel the wetness soaking her to the ankles, or the bite of the gravel as she made for the red Mercedes parked under the trees. She did not feel the raw cold, either; her anger was at boiling point.

She was beyond conscious thought as she switched on the engine, put the car into first gear, but some coolly working part of her fevered mind kept her from switching on her lights. Carefully, she let the car inch forward, crunching gravel momentarily before rolling forward silently on the thick, wet grass. Where were they . . . ? Yes, there they were, directly in front and about fifty yards ahead, just about to leave the radius of the lights that edged the drive. As soon as she was directly behind them she switched on her lights even as she pushed the accelerator to the floor. The car leaped forward as she rammed it into top gear, roaring like some killer cat. She saw the two figures stop, turn, squint into the glare from behind raised hands.

"I'll show you, you bastards!" she shrieked gleefully. "You won't get together to plot to get rid of me!"

As she roared on to them she saw Brad place both hands on Julia's shoulders and push her hard; she went flying backward. But his own leap to one side was not fast enough; the hood of the car caught him in midair; threw him into blackness. Caroline laughed her triumph even as she turned the car to do the same to Julia. But Julia was on her feet, running. Caroline gunned the engine, the fleeing figure caught in her headlights. As, suddenly, was the enormous trunk of the gnarled old oak looming up directly in her path. Frantically she wrenched the wheel, but the grass was slick with rain; the tires would not bite. The car half turned sideways and then, as Julia frantically threw herself beyond and to one side of the tree, it slid inexorably toward the massively ancient trunk.

Even as Julia threw herself to the ground the Mercedes hit the tree at full speed; there was the sound of crunching metal, breaking glass and then, reaching out to sear her as she cowered, hands over her head, the huge, blossoming flower of bursting flame.

8

game. to give the game away . . . disclose a secret

IT WAS GOING TO BE a white Christmas. The Sussex countryside was bleak and bare, the lowering sky heavy with impending snow, but they were almost there, and Jenny, who had slept most of the way from London, now woke to ask eagerly, after a prodigious yawn: "Are we nearly to Auntie Chris's, Mummy?"

"Another five minutes, darling."

Julia found her own eagerness growing apace. She had seized on Chris's invitation as a lifeline. To get away, to go home, to see her oldest and closest friend and the stable comfort of a happy family life, that was what she needed right now, after the cataclysmic events of the past weeks. She longed to put her foot down, but the Sussex lanes this deep in the Downs were narrow, a series of bends with high hedgerows. Julia found herself smiling. Chris, of all people, the big-city girl, ending up some four years ago as a farmer's wife, spending her life deep in the country and her time in rubberboots, giving birth to twins within a year after marrying and even now happily pregnant with her third. Yes, happy. Her letters testified to that. Happy in a way Julia envied; no dramas, no traumas, no complicated relationships; just a husband who adored her and children to complete the magic circle. Chris had been the one with the men, the endless affairs, the—almost frantic toward the end—searching for some anchor to her life. Now, there was no doubt she had found it. It was Julia, with her scrupulous avoidance of those same affairs, who had still managed to land herself in the boiling water, and she was still carrying the scars of her burns.

They turned the last bend and there was the sign: Appletree Farm. Even the name was a cliché. Julia turned into the newly graveled lane and the tires scrunched as the car slowed to travel the last hundred yards between the trees that gave the farm its name. And there was the farmhouse: old, thatched, smoke coming from the chimney, lights already on as it was a dark afternoon and just about teatime. To one side hens scratched and strutted, while somewhere a horse whinnied and through the car door, as Julia opened it, came the unmistakable smell of a farmyard and the distant drone of a tractor. And even as she lifted Jenny out, the front door opened and a small, rotund figure was standing there, arms outstretched.

"Welcome, strangers."

"Chris, oh, Chris!" Julia hurled herself into the open arms, Jenny following to clutch at the figure's knees. Then Julia burst into tears.

"Don't look at me," were Chris's next words, once she and Julia had wept into each other's shoulder. Her eyes were bright with happy tears. "All those fruit pies and dumplings."

"You look like one yourself." Julia's throat was thick with emotion and the sense of coming home.

"Tactful." Chris threw her arms about Julia and once again the two women hugged each other hard. "God, but it's good to see you again. It seems like an age."

"I know, but it is only months. Oh, Chris, it is so good to be home again. I can't begin to tell you—"

"But you will, I hope! And Jenny!" Chris bent as well as she could over the bulge she was carrying to hug and kiss the child. "How you've grown."

"Can I see the twins, Auntie Chris?"

"That you can. I heard stirrings just before I heard you coming. Go on upstairs; you know where they are."

Jenny made for the wooden stairs.

Julia looked around the warm, comfortable room and sighed happily. It was decorated for the season: paper streamers, holly, a big tree in one corner festooned with shiny balls, silver stars and gaily wrapped parcels. A huge log fire blazed in the brick fireplace, and there was the smell of fresh baking. Chris was wrapped in a bright print apron and had flour smears on her pink cheeks. The two women gripped hands and smiled at each other. "I'm so glad you could come to us for Christmas," Chris said.

"Christmas in California with a temperature in the seventies? No way."

"Well, this deep in the Downs, when the snow comes it will be like Alaska."

"Lovely. Then I will know I'm home."

From upstairs came squeals and giggles.

"Let 'em play," Chris said comfortably. "Then we can have a nice cozy prose."

"Over a drink," Julia agreed, turning for the door once more. "I've a bottle of Jack Daniel's in my flight bag."

Once the bags were brought in and dumped to one side—"Bill can take them up later when he comes in. He's out in the field on his beloved tractor"—the two women bestowed themselves in the two shabby but comfortable armchairs which stood one on either side of the fireplace.

"Angel!" Chris exulted, as Julia produced the Jack Daniel's. "I've been hooked on this since that first time with Brad, a propos of which I am dying to hear all—and I mean all. But let's get one down us first."

She poured liberal libations. "Ah . . ." She licked her lips. "It reaches every corner." And when Julia produced a carton of Kent Golden Lights: "All the goodies! I've given it up, really—better for Junior, here"—she patted her bulge—"but this is an occasion so one won't do any harm; but don't tell Bill, for God's sake!"

"How is he?"

"The light of my life, as always. All those years searching for Mr. Universe and I end up with Mr. Universal. My Bill is as square as they come but he has rounded off my life to perfection." Impulsively: "I wish I could say the same for you, love." Her glance was troubled. "You didn't say much but I read between the lines. It sounded like Armageddon."

"All part of our Apocalypse."

"Tell me all. You know what they say about a trouble shared."

But a cry prevented the carve-up. "Here we go." Chris heaved herself up. "Battle stations, everybody!"

Her twins, a boy and a girl, were three-year-old terrors, born with their mother's bubbling personality and their father's stolid build and brown eyes and hair. They went to anybody, offering beaming smiles, patting touching, kissing. "When's the next due?" Julia managed to ask, as they attempted to smother her.

"Spring; can't come soon enough for me. I think it's a bendy toy." She made for the kitchen. "Let's get them fed first—marmite soldiers all right?"

"Perfect. I took a couple of large jars with me to California."

Julia sat happily, dividing her attention between the twins and Jenny and Chris, efficiently and briskly setting the table with mugs and plates and a pile of toast cut into fingers and dripping with marmite butter. All three children took a chair and sat happily munching away, also disposing of large mugs of milk.

"Oh, Chris"—her voice was thick again—"it is so *good* to be back."

"It was bad?"

"Horrendous."

"I read about it in the *Times* before I got your letter. A lengthy obit. You realize we are only ten miles from Arun as the crow flies. How about that as a turnup for the books, me ending up where all your troubles began? We went along to the memorial service, you know. The marquis is our landlord. It was quite a turnout."

"All Lady Hester's own work."

"How's Brad?" Chris asked next.

"Changed. Oh, so changed, Chris."

"Better or worse?"

"Oh, better. Much, much better."

"Is he out of hospital yet?"

"Yes. That's why the funeral was postponed. He had concussion as well as the broken arm and collarbone—and the cracked ribs, of course."

"Poor sod." Chris sounded subdued. "Talk about cups running over. His is running into his shoes." She got up from her chair again to rummage under the cushion. "Here, I kept this for you."

It was a copy of the Arun *Argus,* a special edition covering the funeral of Lady Hester Bradford, though the press had been barred from the actual service.

There were a lot of pictures of the family walking to and from the private chapel. Brad looked blank-faced, remote. Abby was hidden behind a veil, but Bitsy's face was uncovered and Julia gasped. She was the image of her mother, staring straight ahead with an expression

Julia had seen her mother-in-law wear so often. One of indifferent arrogance.

The article was lengthy, devoted mostly to local memories of Lady Hester, who had been, as the reporter gushingly put it: "a transplanted English flower who clung fiercely to her roots." She was called— tactfully, no doubt—"a towering, unforgettable figure in local memory," which, Chris said when she came back with a tray of tea, was putting it mildly.

"I think everybody turned up out of curiosity. They wanted to be sure she actually was dead! Honestly, the things I heard about her from local people! No, really, Julia, she was regarded as something between Queen Victoria and Messalina! Bill employs an old man every harvest —casual labor, you know—born on the estate and about the same age as Motherdear; well, he said—and I quote: 'Saw 'er near take the 'ide off a poacher once . . . proper flayed 'im, she did . . . reg'lar Tartar that one . . . temper like a fiend out of hell.' "

"That's what killed her," Julia said.

"Some people said they went out of their way to avoid her; evidently there was a local vicar who used to turn tail. And the present incumbent—such a nice man, by the way—he himself told me she scared him out of his wits. 'And my father,' he said, 'went in fear and trembling.' " Chris spooned sugar. "Which is no doubt why she was able to suborn somebody as streetwise as Marcus Levin. Honestly, when you wrote me about what he had done . . ." Chris shook her head. "Judas, just like you said. I mean, he seemed so trustworthy!"

"Yes, seemed."

"Have you heard or seen from him since?"

"No. He's gone to ground—not that anybody had time to spare for him anyway what with everything else."

"It must have been awful."

"I can't begin to tell you."

"Oh, but do! Your letters had me hooked! Far better than any best seller."

Chris sat wide-eyed and disbelieving as Julia told her what had happened, from the moment Brad had seen her to Caroline driving the car at them, amplifying her own experience with what she had learned from the others.

"She'd been drinking, of course, but it was quite deliberate. She wanted to kill us. I caught a glimpse of her face just before Brad pushed me. It was right out of Bedlam. The car was a torch . . . and she—she was unrecognizable when they got her out."

Chris shivered.

"I'm only thankful that Brad was out of it all in hospital. Because Caroline's mother made the most terrible scene. Screaming and shouting and threatening retribution. She accused me of egging Brad on, called his mother everything under the sun, reviled the Bradford name —you name it and she tore it to shreds. Then she went back to Philadelphia and spilled the beans on television." Julia's voice and face were dark. "We were more or less prisoners . . . the press everywhere, TV cameras. A Very Proper Bostonian family shown to be hiding a positive graveyard of skeletons. Then there was the inquest when Brad came out of hospital . . . and Caroline's funeral, from which Mrs. Norton barred Brad. She even sent his flowers back; when he opened the box they were ripped to shreds."

"Jesus!" muttered Chris.

"I told you, Apocalypse."

"Poor sod."

"He has suffered, Chris, if only you knew . . ."

As SHE DID, NOW. At long last, the truth had finally been told.

While Brad was in the hospital she had not visited him, long though she might. Instead, she flew back to California to see her clients, explain the situation, not in the least that she would have to return east for the inquest on Caroline Bradford. Strangely enough, they seemed to be more impressed by the fact that she had once been married to a Bradford than anything else; it seemed they knew of Lady Hester; were both shocked and awed by her, a woman, running such a vast business empire. They assured Julia they were quite prepared to allow her a leave of absence for as long as it took.

When she got back, Brad had been released from the hospital, walking with a limp and his arm still in a sling, but able to give evidence at the inquest.

It was held in the meetinghouse in Bradford village, and the press and TV outnumbered the population, though people had come from far and wide for the spectacle because Eloise Norton had hired a famous lawyer, who subjected Brad to the most vicious and sensation-seeking cross-questioning as to the state of his marriage, his relations with his first wife, the heavy drinking of his second, the role his mother had played in his life, and the violent quarrel which had, according to Eloise Norton, driven her daughter from the farm in terror.

He did his best to make Brad admit that it was his affair with his ex-wife which had been the cause of the desperate actions on the part of his present one; that her alcoholism was the result of deep and unbearable unhappiness. The latter Brad admitted while flatly denying the first. The Norton lawyer then tried to bring Jenny in, but the Bradford lawyer's objection was sustained by the judge, to Julia's relief.

She was aware of the behind-hands whispers, the surmising stares, the pointing fingers, and when, on taking the stand, the Norton lawyer painted her as the Scarlet Woman in the case, it was not just because of the color of her hair. Taking her cue from Brad she answered forthrightly and honestly, head up, voice firm and clear, refusing to rise to his baited questions, aware that Brad's eyes never left her, though she never once looked at him.

The final verdict was accidental death, the major contributory factor being the ingestion of more than a pint of alcohol.

It was as they were leaving the meetinghouse that Eloise Norton launched herself at Brad, fingers curled into talons, spitting, hurling abuse. "Murderer!" she screamed at him. "Between you, you and your harpy mother destroyed my poor daughter! I'll get you for this, see if I don't! You and all the rest of your wax-veined, ancestor-worshiping clan! You are a murderer, do you hear! You and your whore!" And she spat in Julia's face.

As they had hustled her away, Brad had turned to Julia, spoken to her for the first time in days. "I would have given my life to spare you this." Julia did not dare touch him, could only answer him with her eyes.

They drove home in separate cars; he with Abby and Bitsy. Julia went with Seth, who had been a tower of strength where she was concerned. He had taken her hand, pressed it warmly. "Thank you, Julia. From all of us." That was all he had said, but to Julia it was more than enough.

On the afternoon before the family was due to leave for England, where, finally, Lady Hester's funeral would take place, Brad had approached Julia diffidently and asked her if she would care to go for a drive.

"I'd love to!" At last! she thought gratefully. She had begun to think they would never get back to where they had been when Caroline had driven at them. Since coming out of the hospital he had undergone a further internal implosion. He spoke only when spoken to and then it was all surface and no depth. He ate little, slept not at all. Abby reported that his light was on all night. He looked awful, sounded worse, and such was his remote "Keep out—this means you!" attitude that no one had dared approach him.

Longing to do just that but afraid and shy, as the song said, Julia carefully remained behind the line he had drawn, though she worried herself into the ground as to what it was that had him on the edge of fragmentation.

Take your choice, she thought bitterly. God knows there's a fantastic selection. His mother's death? Her life—which was even worse? The effect it had on his own? His wife's death? The fact that she had tried to cause his own? Shut your eyes, pick, and it is still low card. Considering what he had gone through—was obviously still going through—it was a wonder he was functioning at all. She took it as a good sign that he was when he asked her to go somewhere with him. The new emotional closeness which she felt was sprouting shoots she had earlier thought dead under the icy blast of his detachment and remoteness, but obviously he had been nursing it, even as she had.

He did not talk as he drove her into Boston, nor did he take the familiar turn which would end at Mount Vernon Street. He drove instead to the Bradford Building. It came to her suddenly. Marcus! Those deadly papers he had told her he would use if necessary. Was that what had been discovered? Evidence of dealings so devious, so illegal, that Brad, as the new chairman of the board of Bradford & Sons, could face a jail sentence? She repressed a shiver as she followed him into the building. But he did not take the express elevator, which would take them to the top floor, where Lady Hester had had her office. The elevator stopped, instead, at the eighteenth floor, where he led her down a corridor to a plain door marked J. H. LOOMIS, M.D.

Julia glanced at him in horror. Was that why he looked so ill? Because he was? Had his injuries brought to light some other, fatal disease? Panic rose like bile. Oh, God, she thought. Not that. Don't let *him* be under sentence of death.

As they entered a reception area, a pretty girl looked up from her desk and smiled. "Mr. Bradford. Dr. Loomis is all ready for you."

She pressed a switch on an intercom. "Mr. Bradford is here, Doctor."

"Send him right in."

A door on the other side of the room clicked, and Brad ushered Julia into a comfortable room furnished like a sitting room. Pictures on walls, deep easy chairs, flowers and plants in pots. A man got up from a table—it was not a desk—and came around it to meet them. He was almost as tall as Seth Amory, but as bald as a billiard ball and wearing heavy horn-rims. He was very elegant in a smart three-piece suit of superfine gray worsted, a gold chain draped across his middle.

[317]

"Brad," he said, in a dark-chocolate voice, before turning to Julia. "Miss Carey. Nice to meet you at last."

At last? Julia thought. Her puzzlement and dismay deepened. What was going on here? She looked from one man to the other. Brad was looking at the doctor, who said easily: "I've got no other appointments scheduled this afternoon so we have plenty of time."

For what? Julia thought, stomach churning. Why would Brad not look at her? His eyes were hanging on to the doctor like fingers on a ledge with a ten-thousand-foot drop below. He *is* ill, she thought. And he can't bring himself to tell me. That's what the doctor is going to do.

She was unaware that her face was all eyes; that she was clutching her handbag to her breast in an attitude of protection and that she was even paler than Brad, who was already colorless. A parade of terminal illnesses flashed across her mind. Cancer? Some fatal heart disease? A bone disease? Multiple sclerosis? Parkinson's disease? But he's only thirty-six, her mind screamed. She stared at Brad as though trying to see through his skin, but he had not removed his eyes from the doctor, who nodded, communicating silent support, before turning to Julia to say disarmingly: "All will be explained, I promise you."

Julia's increasing fright made her abrasive. "I hope so!"

Turning back to Brad: "Come back in about thirty minutes, okay?"

Still careful not to—or unable to—look at Julia, Brad nodded before quickly leaving the room.

As the door closed on him: "Would you please tell me what is going on here?" Julia demanded.

"Brad has not told you."

"Nobody has told me anything! He asked me to go for a drive but brought me here. All this mystery is driving *me* mad!"

"Brad is not mad," the doctor said quietly, as though the word had been a clue to her feelings. "But he has been under a great deal of stress."

Julia found herself flushing.

"That is why he has been coming to see me. I am an analyst."

Julia stared. An analyst! Whatever she had dreaded, she had not given his mental state so much as a thought, but of course it made sense. What Brad had undergone in the last month or so would be enough to shatter many a much stronger man.

"Why don't you sit down," the doctor suggested, again reading her expression. When she had done so: "Mind if I smoke?" he asked, indicating a pipe.

"No."

As he filled his pipe with shreds of aromatic tobacco: "I was called in on this case by the hospital. When he was a patient it was his mental state which disturbed them most. He was having trouble sleeping—mostly because he was afraid to, because it gave rise to the most dreadful nightmares. It was obvious he was on the edge of a nervous breakdown so they sent for me." He struck a match, sucked deeply. "I was able to talk to him, and in the end, to get him to talk to me."

"He needed to talk to somebody. I'm glad it was—a professional."

The doctor blew out the match but sat puffing at his pipe, regarding Julia with his spaniel eyes in a way that had her feeling she was being radar-scanned.

"You wish to help him, then?"

"I've been trying to."

"Good." The doctor puffed fragrant smoke Julia's way before asking: "How much do you know of his relationship with his mother?"

"That is was intensely close; claustrophobic would not put too fine a point on it. It allowed of no other person; was so—intimate—as to exclude even me, when I was his wife."

"Exactly. You have chosen the right word. Intimate is exactly what it was. As in sexual."

Julia stared back at him. When he was satisfied that she was not going to do anything else but sit there, he went on: "How well did you know her?"

"Well enough to fear her." It was automatic; the rest of her was struggling with the controls.

"Did you ever hear her talk about her father?"

"Constantly."

"In what way?"

Julia thought as best she could from a whirling mind. "She believed in him the way other people believe in God."

"And Brad is made in his image?"

"Yes."

"Exactly," the doctor said again, nodding in satisfaction. "And as she worshiped her father, so she adored her son. It is my belief, based on what I have learned from Brad, that his mother's relationship with her father was also sexual."

Julia said nothing. She was frozen-faced.

"In his case, it was defined by his paralysis, with Lady Hester as the dominant partner, which she always had to be. By that, I mean that she fellated him."

Julia hung on.

"The act of fellatio is one which puts a man wholly in a woman's power; she controls his sexuality, his body—his very self. That, in my considered opinion, was the kind of sexual relationship which Hester Bradford preferred. What she wanted—needed—was total possession and control."

Once again the doctor puffed silently. Julia waited, numb with shock.

"Brad has described to me, with total recall, how his mother used to bathe him when he was a child. It was a nightly ritual she refused to yield to his nanny. She used to work up a rich foamy lather and then spread it over his body; caressing, stroking, manipulating. When she dried him, she followed the towel with her mouth. His memories of this are very vivid, as our initiation into our own sexuality always is. He has told me not only what she used to do but what she used to say. And it always concerned her father. How she had done exactly the same thing for him; the only other male she had ever loved. She also told him her reason. That same love. Brad, of course, was too young to understand what she was doing to him. He only knew he liked it, looked forward to it, came to crave the feelings she aroused."

Julia was biting hard on her lower lip; forcing back a bubble of nausea which swelled and threatened to burst.

"By the time he was old enough to understand, the damage had been done. Many adults are unable to handle the physical and emotional intensities of sex." Julia felt that jar. "A child is wholly vulnerable, which is why we have laws to protect them while they are too young to understand the grave perils of such acts. In Brad's case there is only one conclusion. His mother corrupted him."

Julia stared at her hands. Her knuckles were showing.

"What we must not lose sight of, in all this, is the fact that she was obviously in the grip of her own deeply rooted neurosis, which had taken her over to the extent that it dictated every action. There is also the question of her own emotional and sexual deprivation. A lonely, widowed mother, an adored son. It is so easy to slip over the very fine line between a mother's affection and a woman's needs. Except that in the case of Hester Bradford her need was for power; the kind that came from unassailable control." Julia felt another jar jolt through her at his last word. One with which she was only too familiar. She found her first wild impulse to laugh had gone, leaving her strangely detached, as if sealed off in a glass bubble from which she could see and hear, but not feel.

"The guilt which follows such a relationship is appallingly destructive, the more so when it involves the seduction of an innocent. And

[320]

what is more purely innocent than a child? Such relationships, of forbidden consanguinity, taboos which strike at the heart of the structure of our society, are always furtive, always secret, inevitably guilty. In Brad's case, his mother told him that it was because of the boundless, selfless love she had for him. Never for a moment did she cease to emphasize that no one would ever love him as she did. Had she not created him? Carried him inside her own body? Given him his very life? He *was* her; they were two halves of a whole and, as such, truly indivisible. Between mother and son, she insisted, time after time, was a bond so strong it could never be broken, except by death; they were flesh of the same flesh, blood of the same blood, life of the same life. It scarred him forever, of course, bound him to her as she intended it would, for she was, I believe, desperately, even insanely, jealous of him, even then. From what Brad has told me, I think his mother got rid of any woman who threatened to come between her and her father." The doctor puffed again. "Later on, of course, she was to do exactly the same thing with her son." Julia closed her eyes. Only when she felt them drop on her hands did she realize she was shedding tears.

"His guilt, of course, only served to tighten his bonds. He became afraid, not only for her but of her; of that terrifying love which, as she was careful to tell him, had the power to be the death of her, thus creating further guilt at being responsible for such love, for being possessed of the terrible power to deprive her of her life should he reject her."

"Oh, my God . . ." Julia bit hard on her lower lip.

"She was a supreme exponent of emotional blackmail. Because of hers, Brad developed a terror of both loving and being loved."

"The women—"

"Yes; they had a twofold purpose. To escape his mother and release the sexuality she had created—but never her way. Full, sexual congress was what he needed; to be the dominant partner in any sexual relationship; to be the *male;* the doer, not the done to. And by losing himself in sex he also avoided the danger of love. It was thus a cathartic cleansing. Totally apart from anything done to him by his mother and therefore totally free of guilt."

Julia had the strange feeling that the stunning blows she had felt she was being dealt had realigned her eyes. She was seeing now, with brilliant clarity, what before had been hidden by the smog of obfuscation.

"All this is what he has been slowly revealing to me during our sessions over the past weeks. Things long buried deep, and never

[321]

revealed to a living soul. Things that have festered and poisoned until they had him all but emotionally crippled. That he has managed to preserve some hold on his own identity shows me that there is, fortunately, some inner strength which needs bringing out, developing, building up, as a man will develop his muscles. His mother was, of course, quite mad. Her jealousy and possessiveness were abnormal, but at the same time she was incredibly clever, as the mad often are. That heart attack you were supposed to have caused, for instance. I have gone through her medical records. She had a heart like a lion. It was her brain which killed her. In my opinion the heart attack was psychosomatic—her brain again. Brought on by a deliberate desire to increase her hold on her son. You had all but destroyed her but the fault was really his because he had married you."

Julia could sit still no longer. She got up from her chair to walk, stiff-backed, to the window, where she stood looking out, but seeing nothing.

"It is, of course, a terrible tragedy. There is not an area of his life wherein he has not been manipulated by his mother." Another pause. "Which he now knows."

Julia turned. Her face was stark. "But could not bring himself to tell me?"

"Yes, even while wanting you to know. It is important to him that you do, as you are important to him."

"He is important to me."

"Is he?"

"Yes."

"You do not—recoil—from the knowledge I have just given you."

"No."

"How do you feel?"

"Sad. Terribly—sad."

"It is sad. Like I said, a tragedy."

"I always knew there was something—not quite *right*—but I never for once thought it could be this."

"One never does. There are still some taboos left, even in our free and easy society. Incest is perhaps the most terrible."

Julia shuddered, as feeling started to come back.

"It has all but torn him apart, of course. The mental strain has been intense. Hence his nightmares." The doctor puffed thoughtfully at his pipe. "The mother-and-son relationship is a very delicate one; quite unlike that of father and daughter. The mother creates all life; nurtures it within her own body. Which is why so many religions worship goddesses. Men were long afraid of the fertility of women and the power it held over them. And Brad had no father; no male influence to counteract that of his mother. His knowledge of his father he has gained from his sisters, who remember him. His mother never mentioned him, or the part he played in his son's creation."

Julia remembered her thought the night of her first family dinner. "Parthogenesis."

"Exactly," the doctor said again. "An extremely and dangerously clever woman."

Julia opened her handbag, took out a tissue, wiped her eyes and blew her nose. "What can I do?" she asked. "Tell me. What can I do?"

"Accept. Understand."

"I can, because I do, now. Understand, I mean."

"Then tell him so. That is what he needs, and quite desperately. He feels he has betrayed you monstrously; that you married a fake—"

"That cuts both ways," Julia said. "I was one too."

With clinical clarity she told him of her own painful voyage to self-discovery, culminating in Bitsy's disemboweling revelations. "It was not her picture which was warped. It was my own. Egotistical pride had me bent right out of true. My mother-in-law may have needed to control other people; my need was always to be in control of myself. That is why I had reservations about Brad. Because he was the one man who did for that control and it terrified me. His mother may have *been* inhuman but I *tried* to be. Bitsy had me dead to rights. I was afraid to unbend, to open myself up. That is why I did not fight for him as I should have. And she knew it." Julia stared into the past. "That's why she was able to get rid of me; because she knew I was not one hundred percent sure either of myself or of my feelings for her son. I had doubts and she capitalized on them."

"We all have them. I would not be in business else."

"Even so. I let mine corrode everything else. I had this thing about perfection—"

"Had?"

"It is our flaws which make us human. I would rather have Brad as he is, flawed and cracked and willing to take me on, flawed and cracked as I am, than achieve the nirvana of perfection and have nothing but myself. I have had myself and I know. It is not enough."

"That is one of the things he is afraid of. That he will not be enough for you."

Julia's smile was simple. "He will always be more than enough."

"Then tell him that also. Tell him everything."

The doctor took his pipe out his mouth, regarded it for a moment, then said: "There is, however, one last thing I have to tell you. He is also impotent."

He was watching Julia steadily, and when she said: "That doesn't matter," he knew she meant it.

"Then you do *love* him."

"If he never laid a finger on me again I would still love him."

"I don't think there is any fear of that. It is a temporary malfunction only."

"'. . . a temporary malfunction. I'll soon fix that.'" Brad's voice, in all its brass-bound confidence that night they first met, rang like a clarion call in Julia's memory; the old Brad: glittering with self-confidence, wits-befuddling in his handsomeness, deeply unsettling in his sensuality. Oh, my poor Brad, she thought achingly.

"His mother was his sexual drive; now that she is gone, so has it. He has no need to escape her now, in sex or anything else. Once he has found himself, his own identity as a man, he will find his *own* sexuality; the norm of a normal male. But he wanted me to tell you everything."

"Warts and all . . . ," Julia said, on a trembling smile. "It's all very complicated, isn't it?" she added.

"Human beings are."

"I was always so sure I knew myself. In reality, I did not know myself at all."

"That again is why people come to me; the very thing I am now trying to do with Brad. Help him find himself; the self he really is."

"How long?"

"Months certainly, years perhaps. There are decades of repression and suppression to straighten out. What will be of great help to him will be your support. I believe in having an aim; something to work toward. Right now he feels he has only the hope without the confirmation. That is why I agreed that you be put in the picture. What unnerves him most is the feeling—for the first time in his life—of being totally alone."

"He never did like that."

"Another hangup created by his mother. Her way of punishing him, when he was young, was to withdraw herself from him."

"God, but she was a bitch!" Julia said from clenched teeth. "A fiend right out of hell!"

"Which is what he is having to come to terms with."

Julia felt that too. And if it hurt her, how must he be feeling?

[324]

Impatient, obviously, because just then the doctor's intercom buzzed and the receptionist announced that Mr. Bradford was back.

"Ask him to wait. I'll be right out." The doctor laid his pipe aside before rising to his feet. "I will send him in to you. Tell him—show him —that you understand and accept. And without judging."

"I do."

"Good."

The doctor smiled, then went out. Julia rose to her feet. Her feelings had her wholly in their control, and when at last the door opened again and Brad stood there, they took her across to him, to put her arms about him, say his name.

He was stiff under her hands, tensed for the worst, but as he felt her warmth, her concern, she felt his tension snap, change to an uncontrollable tremble. His arms went around her as though around life itself. She felt him struggle to speak, held him even closer.

"Forgive me what I am," he managed to say at last.

She drew back so as to be able to look at him, laid her fingers over the tight-with-strain mouth. "Was, my darling," she said simply, all she felt in her eyes and voice. "Was."

CHRIS HAD TO LOOK AWAY from her friend's luminous face, so expressive was it of all she was feeling. She had never seen Julia look like that before. So open, so unguarded.

"You wrestled with your devils, then?" she asked finally.

"And won. We talked it all out, Chris. I mean really talked. No masks, no games. Everything. And nothing but the truth."

"Sort of True Confessions?"

"Something like that." But Julia's smile said it was something else.

"Are you in touch with him?"

"All the time."

"He writes, then?"

"Yes. And such letters, Chris. Oh, such letters . . ."

"You are waiting for him, aren't you?"

"Yes."

"And sure he will come."

Another smile. "Quite sure." The confidence of the secure.

"It took a long time," Chris said, "but it was worth it."

The clock struck the hour.

"Want to toss for the bathroom?" Chris asked.

"I'm sure we can get them all in together. Let me do it. You take the opportunity to put your feet up."

"I won't give you an argument on that."

"I don't argue anymore," Julia said. "Not even with myself."

"I told you you were always your own worst enemy."

"So I have discovered."

"You do look," Chris observed, "as though you are expecting to win the Nobel Prize for something."

"I've already been told about that," Julia smiled. "All I am waiting for is to be told the date of the presentation."

As she tucked her daughter into her bunk bed: "Did you write your letter to Father Christmas?" Julia asked.

"Yes . . . here it is . . ." Jenny produced a grubby, much-erased piece of paper. Julia read it. The last item, printed in painstaking block capitals, after the doll and the pram and the house with furniture, was the name BRAD.

"Do you think Father Christmas will send him?" Jenny asked hopefully.

"If you wish hard enough."

"Shall we wish together? You want him to come, don't you, Mummy?"

"Very much."

"Let's wish together, then."

Jenny squeezed her eyes tight shut, concentrating so hard her face went crimson. On a splurt of breath: "There! I wished hard as hard."

"So did I."

Maybe, Julia thought, as she went downstairs, wishing *would* make it so. She longed for him, dreamed of him, ached for him. In her letters she encouraged, supported, exhorted, laid bare her feelings without restraint, received letters back which she read and reread.

His last one, just two days before, had said: "Soon, Julia, soon. I feel I have almost reached the brow of the hill, and the eagerness I feel to see the view is something I can't explain, because I know you are on the other side, waiting for me. I climb toward that, Julia, with Abby and Seth pushing from behind. Even Bitsy has taken to removing obstacles from my path. Keep on writing; your letters are my direct line to the future. Meanwhile, know that I love you, not as my salvation, but as my reason for living, my purpose in life. You and Jenny and all that you mean to me. I long to see you, touch you, talk to you, hold you . . . and I will, my lovely Julia, I will, and soon, soon . . . ."

Julia must have expressed her thoughts out loud, because Chris, in the act of dragging a large cardboard box from the hall cupboard, looked up and carried on: " 'So keep on wishing, and cares will go . . .' "

Julia went to give her a hand, and as Chris straightened, hands to her aching back: "I can guess what you are wishing for," she said on a grin, "and if it is any help, *I* always believed in fairies."

Even as the words left her mouth there was a loud, confident, eager knock on the front door.